FORK IN THE ROAD

FORK IN THE ROAD

Marie Menna Pagliaro

FORK IN THE ROAD

iUniverse books may be ordered through booksellers or by contacting:

iUniverse
1663 Liberty Drive
Bloomington, IN 47403
www.iuniverse.com
1-800-Authors (1-800-288-4677)

ISBN: 978-1-5320-0549-7 (sc)
ISBN: 978-1-5320-0548-0 (e)

Library of Congress Control Number: 2016914134

Print information available on the last page.

iUniverse rev. date: 08/30/2016

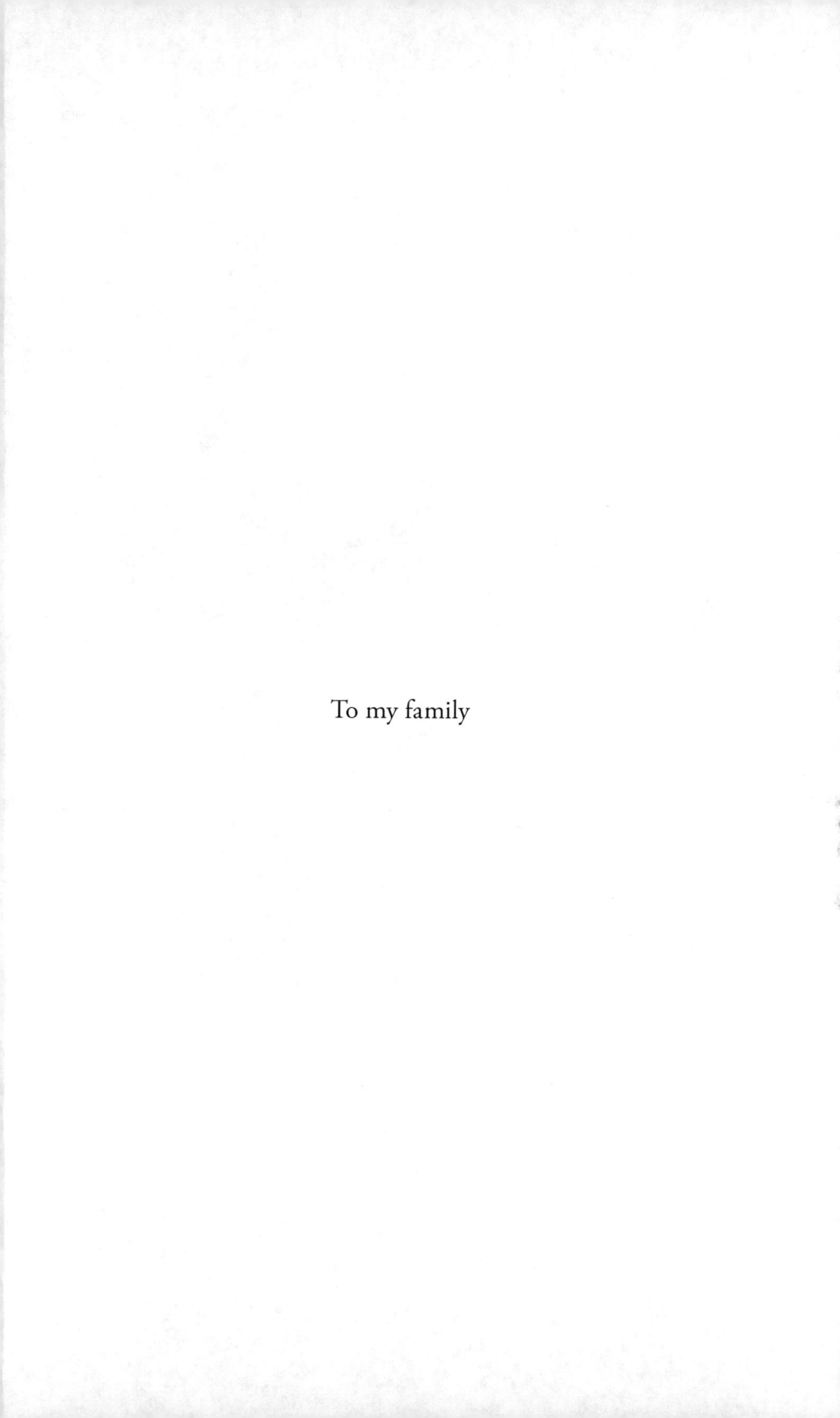

To my family

ACKNOWLEDGMENTS

The author wishes to acknowledge the transformative works of Dr. Richard Paul and Dr. Linda Elder on the subject of critical thinking, that made a significant contribution to Chapter 13.

CHAPTER 1

PAUL BARONE HAD already closed his office door but held onto the doorknob anyway, gripping it for several seconds. When he finally released the knob, he straightened out his fingers and felt warmth flow through them again.

He turned around to reluctantly confront his desk, propping up unopened newspapers and a mound of routine papers awaiting signing and rerouting. Might as well get them out of the way, bury himself in work, even if it was busy work.

He sat at his desk, picked up some papers, shuffled them, his eyes straight ahead, then threw them back on the pile next to the unopened newspapers. Most of the papers found their way to the floor. He left them there, stood up and stretched.

No good.

Maybe swiveling in his chair might reduce some stress. He plopped down, placed his right foot on the floor and pushed hard against it. The chair began to spin. He let his foot drag on the floor, the third spin slowing, the fourth finally stopping, landing him in front of the wall behind his desk where he faced diplomas from prestigious universities, a photograph of himself with Senator Chambers at the previous year's commencement, and a laminated article from the *New York Times* announcing his appointment as academic dean.

He swiveled back to his desk to encounter a picture taken with his wife and two bright healthy sons. Everyone constantly reminded him how lucky he was, that he had everything—a prestigious job, a wonderful family.

Yet, he didn't have what he wanted most.

With a little more than three months before the fall semester, his load would be somewhat lighter. A few meetings, just two interviews so far with prospective faculty, some routine clerical work, and reports, reports, and more reports. Who ever read all these things? And if past was prologue, summer session would be a breeze.

His appointment calendar was open to May 14, 1979. Condensed versions of April and June crammed the upper left and right corners. He flipped the pages to reach August. There, for the first time, he could see in the upper right corner, a miniature version of September. He longed for September, when the faculty would return, and kept staring at the month as if staring at it long enough would allow the intervening months to disappear.

His stare moved to the opposite wall where he caught the black and white photograph of Maestro Toscanini, baton high in the air, a finger crossing his lips. Was he trying to lower the volume of the orchestra, or hush up the secret behind those passionate eyes?

Then Paul gazed at his favorite painting, A Girl Reading a Letter at an Open Window. Vermeer's fascination with light gave her a jewel-like glow. Some day he would take a trip to Dresden to see the original canvas. The girl was blonde with soft creamy skin, pink cheeks. As his eyes became more fixated on her, the girl's hair turned auburn. Only her profile was visible, so he wasn't sure if her eyes were green.

Did the open window represent her desire to leave her routine life or show that she wanted to ignore the outside world to focus on the letter? The tilted dented metal bowl, spilling its fruit onto a table in the front of the painting, set the girl apart. The fruit, a symbol of Venus. And the apple, a sign of infidelity. Were these clues revealing that the letter was a love letter fostering an illicit relationship?

The Fragonard. Its frame had to be straightened. As he got up to adjust it, his eyes wandered to the glass-covered prints surrounding Maestro Toscanini. He moved closer to the prints and examined his reflection carefully. He had to admire the classic design of his nose, his haunting blue eyes. And for a man approaching forty, there were no signs of losing that full crop of curly brown hair.

Yet, he stood slightly hunched, drawn, and noted that even his three-piece suit was not able to hide a potential paunch.

He sighed.

If he were to feel any better at all, he would need some fresh air.

He drifted toward the window, stepping over the papers he still hadn't picked up. The weather report had predicted sun, but heavy clouds hung over the campus. Would the sun continue to hide behind them, or eventually become more virile and burn them up?

Leaves and tendrils from the aggressive vine he could never remember the name of, its runners running amok, were intruding on his window, worming, twining their way over the sill, displacing its thick layer of soot in the attempt to twist a route to the floor. He had to have a talk with the maintenance and cleaning personnel. And while his mind was on cleaning, he'd get a dust cloth and Pledge, the one with the lemon scent, from the bottom right desk drawer for the wooden frames of the Monet and Renoir reproductions, as well as those from other artists, mostly Romantic.

The air conditioner, sitting on the other window, was grinding away, seemingly on its death bed. He turned off the switch. Didn't need air conditioning today anyway with the cloud coverage taking care of the temperature.

He opened the window and noticed Alex Vitale's car in the parking lot.

Ah, yes. Alex Vitale. He straightened his hunched shoulders. What was she still doing here?

His eyes settled on the grass the guests and folding chairs had trampled on and dug into at yesterday's graduation. A few blades were already managing to spruce up.

The buzzer was ringing. He hated the droning sound, but today the buzzing made him perk up. He picked up the phone to hear the expected, the voice of his secretary, Mrs. Knowlton.

"Dr. Vitale is here and would like to speak with you." Then she whispered, "I could say you have someone with you."

"No, no, send her in."

Why was Alex back? They had just completed a meeting of department chairs, shaken hands, and wished each other pleasant summers. He bent down to collect the papers which had fallen behind his desk, and when he stood up, Alex was handing him those which had fallen in front. He laid his pile on top of hers, and placed the papers back on the desk.

Her top blouse button, closed at their earlier meeting, was open. Her wavy auburn tresses, usually pinned to the top of her head, were unleashed and flowing over her shoulders. The air was suddenly saturated with Chanel or some other expensive perfume his wife never wore.

He went instinctively to close the door but just as he grabbed the knob, he recalled his predecessor's resounding advice. "When you are alone in your office with a member of the opposite sex, always keep the door ajar." So he made sure to leave it open a crack.

"Alex, did you forget something?"

"No, I was just debating with myself whether or not to come back. There was something I wanted to tell you, something important."

She didn't say another word, just continued looking at him, her soft skin pinker than usual, the green eyes exploding excitement.

"Well, what's so important?"

"I…I couldn't leave campus today without telling my academic dean some good news." Alex approached him to whisper in his ear. "Paul...Paul, my novel's going to be published."

He could feel his jaw drop. "My God, Alex, that's wonderful. Why didn't you tell me before the meeting, I would've announced the good news to everybody?"

"That's just what I wanted to avoid. Didn't want to sound as if I was showing off, and you know how much professional jealousy there is around here."

With that he had to agree, but he felt none of it himself. Instead he was so elated for her, as though her success in being published had happened to him. "There's going to be even more envy now because it was you who wrote a novel. That's supposed to come from the

English department, not the science department, especially not from its chairman. Oh, excuse me", he said, lowering his head, "chair*woman*."

"I still can't believe it, and it's my first attempt at fiction."

A published writer, a damn good teacher. Two achievements which usually didn't go together. "Did you go directly to a publisher or get an agent?" With his open hand, he offered her a seat opposite his desk. As soon as she took his offer, he settled comfortably in his chair waiting for her response.

"Actually, for a while I was caught in the vicious cycle. A publisher wouldn't even read my material unless I had an agent, and an agent wouldn't take me on unless I had already been published. I kept pushing and finally got an agent. But men and women agents had different advice about the same text."

"How so?"

"The women wanted the scenes longer and more drawn out, and the men wanted me to get right to the point, get it over with more quickly."

He smiled. "So what else is new?"

Alex caught his smile, then blushed. "There was one thing they all agreed on. They're in the entertainment business, more so than trying to find the novel which'll win a Pulitzer. They're somewhat keen on what's currently in vogue, but what it all boils down to is while they want the writing to be good, it's what sells that they were most interested in. And the funny thing is that editors don't really know what will sell."

"No surprise, what's your novel about?"

"What most of them are about, men and women, what keeps them together, what keeps them apart."

"Tell me, though," he hesitated, scratched his head, "I've read that most first novels are largely autobiographical."

Her eyes skirted his. "Probably true, there's a lot of me in it. You learn a lot about yourself when you write a novel."

He leaned toward her, his eyes flickering. "What did you learn?"

Alex paused, blinked several times before saying, "You don't expect me to tell you, do you? Why don't you read it yourself and tell me what you think you learned about me? I left a copy of the manuscript in the library."

"The library. Interesting. I might just do that. What'll you do this summer now that the novel's finished?"

"Write another one."

He thrust his chair back, and as he stood up, opened his hand in a truce gesture. "Now wait a minute, that's what I'm supposed to do. After all, literature is my field, and I always wanted to write a novel."

"Then why don't you?"

"I…I'm too busy. Uh...no, I couldn't do it."

She stood up, too, so quickly that her chair tipped over but she managed to catch it before it fell. "Sit down, Paul, and listen to me."

Her voice was so firm that he found himself following her directive.

"I received so many rejections before my novel was accepted for publication that it's my turn to give them, and I reject your rejection."

"But I never took a course in creative writing, and, and I don't have the time, especially now that I'm in administration. Work year-round, no longer one of those college professors who works thirty weeks a year, twelve hours a week."

"A course in creative writing." She shook her head slowly, smacked her lips. "Huh, some excuse. I never took one of those courses and you don't need one. I know people who spend more time going to writers' conferences, talking about and studying writing that they never get to actually write. Just delay tactics. You've done enough reading to know what you need to know about writing. All you have to do is write. I don't have the time either but I've always heard if you want something done, ask a busy person to do it."

His eyes checked out the ceiling. "I never heard that before, but it's probably true. I'm making excuses."

"So stop making excuses. You should be annoyed with yourself for not trying."

"Maybe I need a push."

"A push? I'll give you one. Suppose that we write one together, collaborate on some ideas."

He remained silent but his silence didn't stop Alex. "You know," she said, "there are certain criteria for two people collaborating successfully."

"Which are?"

She moved her chair next to his. "First of all, do they have mutual respect for one another, get along?"

He didn't need to wait to say, "We're okay on that one, what else?"

"Can they compensate for each other's weaknesses? I think we have a lot going for us there. You could do the proofreading, and I'll keep you to a schedule."

His knit brows relaxed. "You still don't need me. You've done very well on your own. And write about what? I don't even know where to start."

"You're right, I don't need you. It's just that since I'm going to be published, I have the obligation to sponsor new writers. There's a novel in everyone, Paul, maybe more than one. And as far as ideas, you should write what you feel passionate about."

He scratched his chin. How could he possibly reveal what he felt passionate about?

"There must be something in that category," she said with a hint of impatience, "and though it's not routine, there's precedent for two people writing a novel. And even if there wasn't, who's to say we couldn't do it anyway? Besides, the conventional wisdom says you should write about what you know."

"I've been an academic all my life, all I know is academia."

"That's a good start, and a subject I feel comfortable with. Now," she swirled her eyes coyly, "what do you feel passionate about in academia?"

He turned away, taking some time before he answered. When he did, he did so without looking at her. "Perhaps the most compelling is the effect of the Sixties and this decade on our students, on our country. But that's nothing new."

"A good ax to grind, you know that's my concern, too. Declining standards, academic and moral, the future of the family. The future of our country in the Eighties, Nineties, and into the next millennium. We've always been on the same side of the fence with those issues. And as far as nothing new, you're right, there's very little in that category. What you have to do is give something old a new twist."

He tapped his fingers on the desk. "First we'd have to write an outline."

"Boy, you are an academic, do everything by the book. Outlines work for most people, but not for me. I began just writing one scene, one that was vivid for me. Then I wrote some more, finally put them together and filled in the gaps. Getting started is the hardest part. You need a challenge and you need discipline. I challenge you to write a chapter."

"I really don't know if I can do it, I mean write any fiction at all."

"Trust me when I tell you once you get into it, it'll be such a narcotic you won't be able to stop. Now, now," Alex pounded on his desk like a judge calling for order, "will it take someone from science to shame you into it?"

"I can't. I___"

"We'd probably make a good team, because while you have the reading background, we scientists work in teams and've been trained to be good observers. Which reminds me, keep a tape recorder, or a pad with you all the time and jot down things you notice. At the end of each day, think about what happened and jot that down too. You never know when you're going to be able to use it." She looked aside. "Though perhaps the best advice I can give you is just...just. . .pay attention to life."

"When you come up for air, Dr. Vitale, is there any other advice the science professor would like to give the literature professor besides paying attention to life?"

"Am I reading into that question you want to do it?"

"No, just a knee-jerk reaction, Freudian free association."

"Those are most sincere." Alex moved her chair closer to him, put her hand firmly on his arm. "Now, Paul, listen to me. Carefully. You're going to write." Her eyes were open so wide he wasn't sure they'd remain lodged in their sockets. She was on the brink of, no, actually badgering him. "I'm ordering you. You can do it. You *will* do it."

What was causing this 180 degree personality shift from her casual, aloof self? Why was she so insistent, buttering him up with all these positive comments? He was searching his mind for some answers when a carpenter bee flew into the room, humming and weaving figure-eights in the air.

Maybe the Chanel invited it in. Both he and Alex sprinted out of their seats. He searched for something to swat the formidable creature with as they ducked on several occasions before the bee zoomed out the window.

"You see, Paul, it's an omen. You're ducking your destiny, your responsibility, but only living up to it will make you free."

His eyes narrowed, then brightened. He began pacing around the room, still holding the unread newspaper he had twisted into a bee-swatter. "What do I have to lose, won't I be working with a published novelist? Now," his eyes narrowed again, "how should we begin?"

"Let's start by naming our characters."

"Are you sure we shouldn't start with the plot?"

"With the characters, Paul. Name them, that should make them come alive. And for the sake of convenience, make their names short. Save on syllables so you don't waste time typing too many letters. And since readers'll bring their own perceptions to your names, avoid those which have become associated with generally negative connotations such as going to the John, or Richard, which along the way, will inevitably turn into Dick. And," she held up her index finger in a way that warned him he'd better heed what was to follow. "Be careful in developing your characters, they need a past. Put yourself in their place and ask yourself what it is in them that's like you. They'll drive the plot. Can you think of anything, some context in your past you could start with?"

"The only thing which immediately comes to mind, I mean my first recollection is of all things, Catholic school, but if there's anything I know about writing, it's that you have to hook the readers immediately, and they'd probably find Catholic school boring."

"Are you serious, Paul, I went there, too, and readers who went would be able to relate to it, and those who didn't would find reading about what went on there such a trip." She covered her mouth in an attempt to stifle the laughter just about to erupt.

"Did you use it in your novel?"

"No."

"Then going to Catholic school couldn't have made much of an impression on you."

She looked aside. "I never realized how much it did. Everybody hated it while we were there, but it's only now that I look back, that I appreciate it." Alex glanced at the window. "You know, Paul, it may not be a bad idea for you, for both of us to begin there."

He went back to his swivel chair and began spinning it, this time by pushing a forceful hand against the desk. "The wheels are turning. I'm getting ideas already."

"Great, now that you have as the saying goes, the inspiration, the rest of it is perspiration. I'm going to give you a deadline, next week for the first section, the development of the major characters."

"Next week! I need more time."

"No you don't, I'll also write about my characters, then we can meet."

"Don't you think there's something else I should know?"

"Sure, lots, though it makes more sense to talk about other things you should know if you have something written already, something concrete to work with first, but if it'll make you feel more secure," she handed him a book she had placed on the floor, under her purse, "look this over. It's a handbook on novel-writing, you probably already have one and I'm sure you already know what's in it but it's a good review. I found it helpful."

He took the book from her and kept it in his hand.

The bee was back in the room, flying with great speed, its built-in sonar allowing it to repeatedly swoop in opposite directions to avoid smashing into the walls. This time he and Alex didn't duck.

"What, what about revising?" he said.

"While it's true that most of writing is rewriting, you're jumping the gun. Before we look over each other's work, we first have to have something to revise, so just get something on paper and see if we can speak with one voice. We'll revise later. However," she raised her warning finger again, "keep it simple, I repeat, simple. Literary pretentiousness is for hacks."

"At my stage of literary development that's probably what I am."

"With your background I doubt it, but it may be also in your background to tend to write like a Victorian novelist, go on forever, ten pages of narrative, five paragraphs describing a road, a room, a flower. That's how they entertained people in those days, but today we need a different type of entertainment. It has to move fast.

"And you know, it's an occupational hazard that we both have to explain and re-explain everything. We want to make sure our students get it. So be careful of over-explaining." She tilted her head. "Personally, I find a lot of what's written overwriting, contrived, straining for effect. It's like acting, if you know the actor's acting, it's not good, and if you know the writer's writing, that's not good, either."

Too much explaining. Overacting. Overwriting. Fast. Of course he knew it. He considered not asking any more questions, but finally said, "How do you think this story should end?"

"We don't even know how it's going to begin yet. I heard that the writers on the set of *Casablanca* didn't write the ending until the film was almost finished. Besides, I'm sure you know, I mean it's well known in literary circles, that Hemingway wrote the last chapter of *A Farewell to Arms* thirty-seven times. So stop worrying about the last chapter, just write and see what comes of it."

"The conventional wisdom has always been that the last chapter should be written first. Everything that comes before it should propel itself and the reader to the end."

"The hell with conventional wisdom." She dug into her purse, pulled out her appointment book, and tossed it unopened on his desk. "How about next Monday at one?"

"So soon?"

"Your deadline, I have to make sure I throw you off equilibrium, give you just enough frustration to get you going. And remember, it'll be easier if you keep your first attempt short."

He buzzed Mrs. Knowlton. "What do I have scheduled for next Monday?"

"You're tied up in meetings all morning, won't be free until twelve. Now you make sure you take a full hour for lunch so you can relax. I insist on that."

"Do you anticipate anything else that may come up?" He waited for mother hen's feedback, then glanced at Alex. "I'm free at one."

"One's good for me, too."

How could she be sure of it unless she checked her book?

A ray of promised sun had finally found its way into the room. Paul's eyes met his calendar once again. It appeared as though a magnifying glass had highlighted the space next to one o'clock which he filled with the name, Alex.

This time he hoped September would never come.

Before removing the tip of his pen from the calendar he said, "Suppose I find I don't have an ax to grind."

"Believe me, everybody does. And when you start writing you'll find out which one it is, if you don't already know, and you'll probably find several."

"I know we've already said goodbye at our meeting this morning, Alex, but maybe now it's more appropriate to say 'au revoir'".

"Au revoir, Paul, I'm glad you made the," she spelled, "W-R-I-T-E decision. It'll be good therapy, you can unload and won't have to spend time you could be writing with a psychiatrist." She winked. "Pardon the misplaced phrase, English professor."

Alex began gathering her belongings. Then she looked straight at him. Making deliberate exaggerations with her lips and tongue, she mimed, pay...attention...to...life. She picked up her appointment book, still closed on the desk, just about to pack it. Instead, she opened it, turned a few pages, and with an impish smile, faced a page toward him.

It had already been marked 'Paul' in red in the Monday, one o'clock slot.

CHAPTER 2

PAUL WENT HOME early to begin his unexpected assignment. But before he could begin to think about writing, he had to first stop at the library. Then, after a few days of procrastinating, the pressure of his deadline began to gnaw at him. Would she think less of him if he didn't measure up to her expectations, couldn't perform for her?

Why did he agree to do this project anyway?

Did he really have to ask?

Alex had said to pay attention to life. When he wanted to know if her novel was autobiographical, she said there was a lot of her in it. Suppose he would reveal too much of himself, his life?

What else did she say? Just get started, and the rest would take care of itself. He opened the novel-writing reference book she had given him, and read out loud some of the statements he was very familiar with but had underlined anyway. Show, don't tell; imply, don't state. Avoid the passive, use your experience, imagination. Be honest. Take risks. Though he knew it all thoroughly, there was a big difference between knowing about it and actually implementing it.

He'd think about it later. Right now, his lawn needed weeding, mowing, and fertilizing. The maple tree had to be pruned before its roots overtook the house.

Nevertheless, he found the typewriter beckoning him and meandered toward it. He plopped down in front of it. Had to remember not to take on too much in his first attempt.

Keep it short. And simple.

Simple.

What was it that would make someone take the stands on issues the college and the society had been struggling with?

Just sitting in front of the typewriter stimulated him. He wrote, read, re-wrote, read again, and contrary to what Alex had advised him, revised, knowing full well they'd have to do it over and over again.

* * *

Charles Pastore stumbled into the wooden box. A faded blue velvet curtain folded behind him, the edge sticking to the back of his pants. He brushed the curtain off. The box had a musty stink, like the bungalow Uncle Mike rented every summer in the Rockaways.

Dark.

Spooky.

All he could see in front of him, a little larger than his head, was a rectangle. He knelt down, slowly placed his hand over it, tracing its dusty edge with his finger. Then he moved his ear closer to the rectangle.

Mumbling, not yelling.

Good sign.

So much sweat coated his forehead that his hair stuck to it. He was itchy all over, didn't know where to scratch first. And what a time for cramps! Should've gone to the bathroom when he had the urge. He also had to pee. Still kneeling, he managed to move one thigh over the other and squeeze.

Too late to run away?

Before he could think any more about escaping, some light came through the rectangle. A fuzzy man appeared. He looked like the pictures Charles made when he was younger, the ones where he connected the dots.

He froze.

"Yes, my child," the shadow of a man whispered.

Charles didn't answer for a while. He was still thinking about running out of the box. His throat was dry, and the lump in his chest had crawled into his stomach. But the outline's voice was soft and gentle. Encouraging.

He finally began. "B...bless me Father for I have sinned. Th... this is my f...first confession." He had memorized the opening lines well, the result of Sister Bernadette's lessons. But he was so quick to get the words out that he forgot to make the Sign of the Cross while saying them.

He started the confession again, this time crossing himself. "Bless me Father for I have sinned. This is my first confession."

There. He did it right.

"Yes? Go on my child."

He pressed his teeth together to keep them from clicking and spoke through them. "I told thirty-seven lies."

A long wait. He had to double-check the number on his fingers.

"I said twelve curse words. And I took my friend's pencil. Twice."

After some silence the priest said, "Is that all?"

"N-no, I hit my brother. Four, five times. Or maybe it was six. I'm not really sure. And. And..."

"Yes?"

"And I watched my cousin Lena take a bath...through the keyhole."

A pause.

"How old is Lena?"

"Fifteen."

The priest cleared his throat. "I see."

"And I didn't help my mother when she asked me. Seven and a half times. That's it."

Father Dunn felt the relief emanating from the other side of the confessional. He couldn't help chuckling. Seven and a half times. Twenty years a priest and never heard the fraction, any fraction before. The boy might've started some task he didn't finish. With children anything was possible. "Is there anything else you have to tell me?"

"No, that's all."

He weighed the confession. The boy's first experience with the sacrament of Penance had to be memorable, provide inspiration that would last a lifetime. "Why did you take your friend's pencil?"

"I forgot mine. And, and his was a better color."

"I'm sure that Sister keeps extra pencils on her desk, it shouldn't be necessary to take your friend's. One of the ten commandments is, `Thou shalt not steal'. And a pencil writes no matter what color it is."

"If it has a point."

"Well, whether it does or doesn't, remember what Saint Matthew tells us in his gospel. If your hand is what causes you to sin, cut it off. If it's your eye that causes you trouble, remove it. Think of that if you ever want to take something again that doesn't belong to you. Now whom did you say you hit?"

"My brother."

"Oh yes, the same thing goes for that, your hand was the troublemaker. And why did you watch your cousin take a bath?"

The boy hesitated. "I...I wanted to…to look at those two bumps on her chest."

Father Dunn puttered a cough. Obsession with those two bumps seemed to be occurring earlier and earlier. "You shouldn't think impure thoughts. When you get impure thoughts you should force yourself to think of something else. Put something in your head right now that you will use to stamp out impure thoughts. What is it?"

No answer.

"Are you thinking?"

Eventually the boy said, "Two cars crashing, or…trains."

"Good. When impure thoughts come to you, think of two trains crashing. That should give you such a headache it will shove the bad ideas out of your head. Now I already told you and I shouldn't have to repeat that if your eye causes you to sin, cut it out."

Charles got chills. Cutting his hand off. Removing his eye. Ouch! How it would hurt to take them out! And what would he look like without them? He'd be a Halloween freak.

"Why didn't you help your mother?" the priest said.

"I wanted to go out and play with my friends."

"Don't you love your mother?"

"Sure I do."

"Well, many times we have to do things because they're our responsibilities. We'd rather do other things but our responsibilities come first," the priest said slowly and firmly. "You have to learn to give up what you want to do for what's the right thing to do.

"Now your mother loves you and has given up a lot for you. Saint John in his gospel reminds us that there's no greater love that one person has for another than to give up his life for that person. So if you really care for your mother, you'll at least give up some of the time you'd like to be playing with your friends to help her. Do you think you can do that? Remember that Jesus loved us so much that He gave His life so that ours would last forever in the next world."

He thought about it for a while. Give up his life for somebody. Give up his eye, his hand. Maybe yes. Maybe no. "I'll try."

"God asks only that we do our best. He's always there to help us, all we have to do is ask. And remember, my child, there is nothing we could ever do that God couldn't forgive. Nothing. Do you understand?"

"Yes, Father. Nothing."

"Now tell me in your own words what I've said."

Thank God he was paying attention. He ran through the scary part. His hand. His eyes. Then he said, "Give up what we want to do for what we have to do."

"What else?"

"Uh…uh…there is nothing we could do that God wouldn't forgive us for."

"Very good. So now, for your penance, say five Our Fathers and five Hail Marys. Please make your act of contrition."

For a moment he couldn't remember how to begin. He should've brought the card with the prayer printed on it. But then it was so dark in there, he couldn't've read it anyway.

The priest said, "O my God..."

Charles recited in a sing-song way, "O my God I am heartily sorry for having defended Thee."

"Offended."

"O my God I am heartily sorry for having...de-...offended Thee, and I detest all my sins because I dread the loss of heaven and the pain of hell. But most of all, because they defend...offend Thee, my God who art all good and deserving of all my love. I firmly dissolve..."

"Resolve."

"I firmly resolve, with the help of Thy grace, to confess my sins, to do penance and to cement...affend...no that's not it." He snapped his fingers. "Amend my life. Amen."

Charles pushed aside the blue velvet curtain and darted out of the box. He was in a hurry to rush down to the basement when the next boy on line, Buddy Moran, grabbed him. "What happened, Charles? How was it?"

"Not bad, I was lucky. It was Father Dunn, I recognized his voice. Good thing it wasn't Considine. You could hear his voice all over the church, and I saw him throw a kid out of the confessional once."

Buddy twisted his shoulders as if he was doing the jitterbug. "What did you get for a penance?"

Charles pressed his thighs together before starting to walk backwards, with difficulty, toward the basement steps. "Five Our Fathers and five Hail Marys."

"Ain't bad at all, should take only a few minutes to say them." Then Buddy entered the wooden box.

Charles turned around to continue his run for the basement. As soon as he saw "Men" on the door, he already felt relief. All the stalls seemed empty. He got on his hands and knees to check for feet. He spent a few minutes on the toilet. When he was finished, he considered not washing his hands even though his mother always told him he should. But if he didn't, the Holy Ghost, flying over the ceiling might swing down and nip at his hands. Charles made sure to scrub them. He began just shaking the water off his hands onto the floor, then with the

Holy Ghost watching him, pulled a paper towel from the roll, blotted and rubbed his hands until they were thoroughly dry. He made sure to throw the towel into the wastepaper basket.

He went back up the steps to head for the main altar. On other days he would've skipped down the aisle, but today he tiptoed. He knelt at the altar rail for a while. Before reciting his prayers, he turned his head very slowly, keeping his chin against his chest.

The statues he'd seen many times before, but today they were alive, frightening.

Saint Sebastian with arrows stuck all over his bleeding body. What kind of sin was he trying to avoid?

The Sacred Heart with thorns piercing His exposed heart, the heart pumping, pumping. Getting larger, then smaller. Charles grabbed his chest. His heart was pumping the same way.

Hanging upside down on the cross was Saint Peter, his hands and ankles tied to it with rope instead of nails. Charles felt blood rush to his head, so much it was throbbing. Sister Bernadette had already told his class that Saint Peter did not consider himself worthy enough to die in the same position as Jesus.

Charles covered his eyes after he looked at Saint Lucy, holding her own eyes in a plate. Maybe she wanted to watch her cousin take a bath so she could look at his wang.

He was getting the willies when he thought of what he would look like with no eyes or hands. And dying for someone else? Really nuts.

With his eyes tightly closed he recited the five Hail Marys and five Our Fathers.

A hand touched his shoulder. He jumped.

Charles turned to Buddy Moran's screwed up face.

"I got ten Our Fathers and ten Hail Marys," Buddy said. "I must've been double as bad as you." He chewed on his lips. "But it could've been worse, I could've got a hundred. I'm just glad it's over."

"Me, too.

CHAPTER 3

ALEX VITALE HAD to follow her own advice. But somehow, now that she had convinced Paul to write this novel with her, one which by her own recommendation, if not order, lacked any direction, she regretted dragging him into it.

Sure, she was going to be published, but that's because she did it on her own. How would this project work out with him? Why did she set this up in the first place or what if she couldn't write as well as she had before? Did composers, artists worry about subsequent works once they had one success, and she had no idea whether or not her novel would be a success.

Worse yet, what if he would write better than she? That might happen, considering his background and experience. Still, she'd be totally humiliated.

What experiences define who and what the main characters are, she had told him to consider. She lay in bed, thinking and thinking. She was willing to do the perspiration, but there was still no inspiration.

She gulped down a tall glass of water and shortly afterwards fell asleep.

At two-thirty in the morning, she had to go to the bathroom. Afterwards, she went back to bed but kept tossing around, straightening out the pillow, placing it behind her back, then under her head again, yanking off the sheet. She didn't want to awaken her husband. Maybe she'd watch TV.

She held on to the banister going down the steps in the dark to the den, and was about to turn on the TV, but her eyes caught the word processor. She walked up to it, tinkered with the keys, then switched it on. It produced its usual sizzle followed by a bright light, and a surging hum which dwindled to a soft steady one. She rolled a chair in front of the word processor and sat down.

* * *

Sister Mary Theresa closed the lid to the cigar box then held it high above her head She began shaking the contents, forty-three slips of paper each containing the name of one of the girls in the class. The students followed her gyrations with their heads.

Sister shuffled the box up, left and right, down, then up again. The oversized rosary beads, carefully wrapped around her waist, vibrated with her.

When she finally stopped the shuffling, the crucifix hanging from the rosary crashed against her thigh.

The students held their breath.

Sister Mary Theresa surveyed the room twice before settling her eyes on a petite blond girl who was sitting up straight with folded hands. Her face yearned to be called on. "Susan, come up, dear, and select one of the slips."

Susan unclasped her hands, slid out of her desk, and walked to the front of the room.

While keeping the box above her head, Sister opened the lid. Susan moved a chair close, then climbed on it, and turned her back to the box. She lifted her arm straight up before arching it into the box. Sister noted that it still smelled of cigars. Whether they were expensive or not, she didn't know.

Susan thumped her fingers around the box, scratched around it, and shuffled the papers until she finally pulled one out and handed it to her.

Without further hesitation Sister announced the name, "Steve Arcuri." Sighs of disappointment came from the other forty-two girls.

Steve Arcuri was so shocked, she couldn't move. Could it be? She had prayed so hard for this. Was she the one who would crown the Blessed Virgin Mary?

"Steve shouldn't've had her name on the paper," Isabel Burke yelled out, "she doesn't even look like a girl."

"Now Isabel," Sister said, "Steve has every right to be given a chance like everyone else, she's very much a girl but just hasn't discovered it yet."

"Maybe she should crown a boy statue like St. Joseph instead," Isabel said.

The class laughed.

Steve stood up so quickly her loosely screwed-in desk shook the floor. She was about to run for Isabel, smack her face, grab her throat, scratch her eyes out. But Sister stepped between them.

Steve tightened her lips and paced around the room. "Men saints don't get crowns, at least crowns made of flowers."

"And Steve isn't even Irish," Isabel said.

Steve was heading for the set of encyclopedias now. A good time to throw one of the volumes at Isabel. "If you were so smart, you'd know that St. Joseph or Mary weren't Irish either, and neither was Jesus, and that Saint Patrick was Scotch, and the Pope's Italian, and he lives in Rome not Dublin. And if being Irish means being like you, I'm glad I'm only half-Irish, so there, smarty pants."

"Now stop this nonsense, girls," Sister said, "your behavior is not making the Blessed Mother very happy."

Steve didn't care whether the Blessed Mother was happy at that moment. She was just happy that Isabel Burke's slip wasn't picked. She hated her. Always the first to stand, sit, kneel, or say "Amen" in church, always speaking louder than everyone else during Mass so she could show off how well she knew her prayers. Such a goody-goody-two-shoes.

It meant less to her that she won than that Isabel lost.

At dismissal time Steve dashed between the spaces left by dozens of students leisurely walking home, her shoulder school bag flapping in the wind. Her house was the only detached one on the block, and the only one with a lantern in front. She ran up the steps across the porch with its cement flower pots supporting red geraniums, to the front door and rattled the knob.

The door was locked.

While ringing the bell every second with her right finger, she pounded on the door with her left hand.

She tapped her heel and scratched the lock with her fingernail. Then she rang the bell again, this time keeping her finger on the button.

Finally, her mother opened the door. "Steve, what's the matter?" She felt her forehead. "Your face is all flush and you're in a sweat. I hope you don't have a fever."

"Mommy, Mommy, guess what. I'm going to crown the Blessed Virgin. Susan Auletta picked my name from the cigar box."

Her mother's face lit up. "Saints be praised. Daria and Megan were never picked when they were in your grade. This is a wonderful honor the Holy Mother has bestowed on our family." Mommy kept hugging her. "We'll have to tell Daddy as soon as he comes home. I'll bet now he'll be so happy he had a third daughter."

A third daughter.

Her lungs lost their air.

She lowered her head and pouted. "Do we have to wait till Daddy comes home? Can't we call him now at the office?"

"No, baby, he may be examining a patient, doesn't like to be interrupted. It's not too much to ask, not too much of a sacrifice for you to wait till he comes home."

"But suppose he has to go to the hospital tonight and doesn't come home until after I go to bed?"

"In that event I promise I'll wake you up and you can tell him yourself. Your sisters'll be home shortly, and in the meantime you can tell them."

Steve darted up the steps and into her bedroom. As she started to remove her uniform, she pressed her nose up against the window pane. She had removed only one arm from her jumper when she spotted

Megan. She tapped at the window, but Megan didn't seem to hear it, just kept walking toward the house.

"Megan, Megan," she ran out of the room screaming her name, then jumped down the steps two at a time before reaching the landing. She rushed to open the door.

Megan pushed her wavy chestnut brown hair away from her face, then twisted her mouth. "Do you always greet people half in your uniform and half in your underwear?" With her whole arm she shooed her inside. "Get in, don't let the neighbors see you."

Steve wouldn't budge from the hallway. "Megan, Megan, don't tell Daddy if you're awake and I'm sleeping because I want to tell him myself. I'm…I'm going to crown the Blessed Virgin Mary."

"Who, you?" Megan tilted her head. "How did that happen?"

"Out of all the girls in the class my name was picked."

Megan put her hand on Steve's head and ruffled her hair. "I only hope the day of the ceremony you won't look like such a tomboy, Steve. We've got to make sure you look the part. Need a dress and something to put over your head instead of a baseball cap. Your communion dress doesn't even fit you any more."

"I'll tell Daddy. He'll get me something, you'll see."

"He'd better. We don't want to embarrass the family."

Most of her excitement left her. "You won't be abarrassed."

"Embarrassed."

"Em-barrassed."

The class had rehearsed every move, every hymn for the coronation scheduled for after the twelve o'clock Mass, the first Sunday in May. On that day all the girls dressed in white, as they did for their first Holy Communion. Each carried a basket of fresh petals. Sister Mary Theresa led the procession walking backwards down the center aisle, the young ladies following her along the pews. Her lips were moving as she counted under her breath. Every tenth step she pressed her clicker, and the girls curtsied while dropping some petals in the aisle. Sister Mary

Theresa had warned the flower strewers not to use too many petals in the beginning so there'd be enough to last to the main altar.

Following the girls, four boys carried the canopy, one pole each. Under the canopy two other boys rolled a dolly on which sat the pedestal carrying the statue of the Blessed Virgin.

Steve was the last to proceed down the aisle, the only girl assigned to wear a long white dress, one her mother had a dressmaker create to cover her neck and arms just as the Virgin was covered. An eyelet bodice topped the tulle skirt. Covering her head was a matching white eyelet mantilla with a pearl hatpin holding it in place.

She carried the crown, woven from lilies-of-the-valley and orange blossoms, on a silver tray. It seemed as though every candle in the world had been collected and lit, throwing off so much flickering light that all she could see were people and flowers blending into each other. The parishioners were standing while singing "Immaculate Mary" along with the organ and choir.

Steve noticed tears flowing down her parents' cheeks as she passed their pew.

Finally, the main altar. Thought she'd never get there.

She climbed the three steps, then walked to the right, where in front of the side altar the statue of Mary was waiting.

Mary, always on the side, never in the center.

One of the boys moved a small wooden table and four-step ladder in front of the pedestal. Steve placed the silver tray on the table. With trembling hands, she lifted the crown from the tray and began climbing the ladder.

She had never rehearsed with the long dress. The hem got caught in her shoe, and she tripped.

The congregation gasped.

Steve balanced herself and the crown just in time so she didn't drop it. She kept the crown firmly in both hands. More cautiously this time, she climbed to the top, kicking her skirt out of the way with each step.

The Virgin's blue eyes stared up at her. For a moment she didn't move but stared back at the Virgin. Then slowly, slowly, she lowered the crown over the statue's head. Chills fluttered through her body. She knew goose-bumps were safely hidden under the long sleeves.

She bent her head toward the statue and prayed silently, "Holy Mary, Mother of God, forgive me for tripping a little when I just went to crown you, and thank you for not letting me fall in front of everybody. Sister told us if we pray to you, you'll help us be pure like you. I pray that you'll keep me pure, keep my balance, and help me not trip in my life."

She stepped down the ladder backwards, careful to lift her skirt until she was steady on each wrung, and her feet were firmly back on the marble.

The organist shifted down a few keys and played the introduction to, "O Mary, We Crown Thee with Blossoms Today." The parishioners soon joined in.

The boys brought the canopy into the sanctuary.

Father O'Connell reminded everyone to use Mary as a model, then led the congregation in one decade of the rosary.

Time now for Steve to lead the recessional. The organist played the first line, then the participants sang,

> Hail holy queen enthroned above, O Maria.
> Hail mother of mercy and of love, O Maria.
> Triumph all ye cherubim. Sing with us ye seraphim.
> Heaven and earth resound the hymn. Salve. Salve. Salve, Regina.

Today was the only day in her life Steve was pleased she wasn't a boy.

CHAPTER 4

PAUL MOVED HIS gaze from the slightly open door to Alex, trying to read her reaction while she read his chapter. Her face remained blank. How long would it take her to say something? He followed her eyes down the pages.

When she reached the end, she removed her glasses, looked up and gazed at him. "Catholic school was really something, I could identify with much of your story. In fact, I could write a book, maybe two about my experiences in Catholic school. But what's really remarkable is that I really expected you to use a lot of flowery language, figures of speech, metaphors, similes all over the place. Instead our style is so similar, we both seem to be speaking with one voice."

He took a deep breath, exhaling with a grunt before rubbing his forehead with the outer part of his hand. "Since we're going to be partners in this venture, I have to be up front with you."

"Up front?"

"Yes." He glanced at her, then looked away with the guilt of a boy getting caught with the answers that might be on a test inked into his palm. "I cheated."

"I...I can't imagine you ever doing that."

"I went to the library, took out your novel. Wanted to get a sense of how you wrote so I could do it the same way. I couldn't get over how easy it was for me to write like that, as though we're both on the same wave length."

"Well?" She lowered the pages she was holding. "What did you think of the novel? Give me some critique, beat me up. Nobody ever improves without criticism."

"While I wouldn't put you in the same class as Dickens or Steinbeck, I wouldn't want to compare you with them anyway. You can pick up a lot of technique from different writers, but it would be wrong for you to copy someone else. You should write the way you feel comfortable, just being yourself. And as far as I'm concerned, I really enjoyed your novel, read it twice. Could relate to a lot of it."

"Well, Dr. Barone, if you found yourself writing the same way I did, then you're no Dickens or Steinbeck either, but coming from someone who's done as much reading as you, I'll consider the fact that you enjoyed my novel a compliment. Now since I want to keep on track, we'll talk about my novel some other time."

"Getting back to my writing, how did I do for a beginner?"

"For a first try, extremely well. You're a natural, and I see you took the advice in the manual about not writing all the time in complete sentences. Remember how we were taught to diagram sentences? Subject, predicate, direct object, prepositional phrase." She drew the corresponding lines in the air, chuckled, before becoming serious again. "But you have the momentum so don't stop to make any changes yet. Let's keep the flow, we'll revise later. That's going to be tough, especially when you have to cut. After putting so much effort into it, you'll want to keep every syllable. Every syllable's your baby. But enough of that. What did you think of my section?"

"Reminded me of my sister. She always wanted to crown the Blessed Virgin but never got to do it. But where did you get that name, Steve, for the girl?"

"You'll have to read the next chapter to find out."

"What do you think the next section should cover?"

"Since we both started with two children, let's see how they grow up."

"How they grow up. That should challenge my imagination."

"Next week, same time, same place?"

Paul didn't enter anything into his appointment book. "I've already arranged to keep all the Mondays open for the next several weeks."

"I'm pleased to see you're really getting into it."

"Actually, I didn't know until I got started how much I'd enjoy it. Do you think we'll finish by the end of the summer?"

"We should, or be close, as long as we're disciplined and keep to the schedule. And with the two of us reinforcing each other, we should make it. But Paul, you should really look into getting a word processor. Once you use one, you'll never go back to a typewriter."

He didn't answer for a few moments. Then he said, "I'll look into it."

Alex stood up, gathered her papers. "See you next week when your boy, Charles, grows up."

"I'll look forward to hearing about your boy, or is it girl, Steve."

A word processor. Even the college didn't have one yet.

He was lucky to have an electric typewriter. Did Alex think he was rich like her husband?

Paul confronted the typewriter once again. His fingers were still.

What was important about Charles's growing up?

* * *

Charles marched into the classroom with the rest of the children, hung up his coat and took his seat. All of it was predictable. Lesson titles for the day, each in different colored chalk, already surrounded the top of the blackboard, separated by lines he had always seen Sister Stella draw with a yardstick. Reducing Fractions to Lowest Terms was in red. Spelling -ie and -ei Words followed in green, Avoiding the Double Negative in purple, and Peru in all three. Under the titles across the blackboard were five lines drawn with that gadget with the five pieces of chalk Sister Stella used to draw the music staff. A timeline titled, "The Civil War" surrounded the room interrupted by a short break for the doorframe. A green Ft. Sumter and a red Appomattox headed the beginning and end of the timeline with a lot of space in between.

As soon as the bell rang, everyone stood up to recite the Pledge of Allegiance followed by a short prayer. Then Sister Stella called the roll. Every day when she read Kevin Pascucci, she shook her head and sighed. Once after calling the name, Charles heard her say, "The way the country's going."

After calling the roll, Sister filled in the small rectangle in the upper left hand corner of the blackboard, meticulously set apart with double white chalk lines also traced with the yardstick. Number of Boys topped Number of Boys Present, with a space underneath for the difference. Sister quickly filled it in. The week's attendance monitor copied the information on a 3x5 card, then card in hand, left the room.

Next came the religion lesson. Today was the third lesson on the Ten Commandments. Time to recite them in unison, first with their Baltimore Catechisms open, then closed.

"I am the Lord thy God, thou shalt not put strange gods before me." Why the first God had a capital letter and the second did not, they had already learned.

"Thou shalt not take the name of the Lord thy God in vain." Okay. They shouldn't curse or use God's name disrespectfully.

"Remember thou keep holy the Sabbath day." Never miss Mass on Sunday under pain of mortal sin.

By the time they got to, "Thou shalt not commit adultery," Sister's explanations got kind of fuzzy. But he had learned to break up words to find other words in them. Adult was in adultery. He'd worry about it when he became an adult. Was it dult or dolt that meant a stupid person? He'd check the dictionary.

"Thou shalt not covet thy neighbor's wife," brought a sharp sting on Charles's shoulder. He turned around to see Ronnie Fontana's sneering grin. With a toss of the head, Ronnie signaled Charles to pick up the paper airplane he had just stung him with.

Charles un-crumpled the plane. It read, "What does covet mean?"

The boy sitting next to him read the note after pulling it from his hand. "I think Sister made a mistake," he whispered, "she means cover."

Charles wrinkled his face. "Why would you want to cover your neighbor's wife anyway?" It didn't add up.

Sister Stella adjusted her glasses, then folded her arms. "Boys, if you don't stop fooling around you'll have to write these commandments ten times each, and we should all know what ten times ten means. Now pay attention, you're going to have a test on them soon."

She seemed as though she was getting ready to scold them further when Father Reardon entered the room. Everyone jumped out of his seat and stood up straight.

"Good morning, boys," Father Reardon said.

"Good morning, Father," they answered in clear loud voices trained to address the clergy.

"You may be seated."

"We were just having our religion lesson, Father," Sister Stella said.

"What is the class studying?"

"The Ten Commandments, do you want them to recite them for you?"

"No, Sister." He pulled out his chin to adjust his collar. "I'm sure your instruction is fine."

She beamed. "Next week we'll begin the Beatitudes."

"Is that in the curriculum?"

"I don't know, but I like them."

Charles's eyes followed Father Reardon's head saturated with silky gray hair as he moved about the room looking along the wall at the student-created maps of the Western Hemisphere. Coffee beans pasted over Brazil, tin over Chile, nothing yet over Peru. Cotton over Mississippi, and paper boats sailing the main blue waterways. Tacked to a large bulletin board were the five best Palmer penmanship compositions entitled, "Tin Mining", each with a large gold star.

The surface of the next bulletin board was covered with the results of the students' art instruction, Thanksgiving turkeys formed from construction paper, all the same size and shape except for the colors of the feathers. Silent drums assembled from Quaker Oats containers decorated with Indian designs rested on a side table.

"Very impressive for fourth graders," Father said.

"I'm so proud of them." Sister Stella focused her eyes directly on Ronnie and him. "At least, most of them."

Father Reardon found his way to the front of the room, and straightened out his collar again, this time just with his finger. "I'm here to speak to you boys about a very important subject."

Ronnie whispered to Charles, "He probably wants to give us all chance books for a car or a basket of cheer or something."

"As you know," Father Reardon continued in a very serious tone, "last year we recruited altar boys. Many volunteered but more than usual didn't last very long. So this year I need to come back to your class to ask for more volunteers, we need a larger pool. Is there anyone who'd like to volunteer?"

Father Reardon looked around the room. The boys turned around to check, also. No one's hand was up. Who could be crazy enough to get up so early to serve at the six o'clock Mass?

Father Reardon shook his head. His sagging cheeks vibrated. "I'm surprised there's no one who'll give of himself to help the parish celebrate Holy Mass, especially after what this parish has done for all of you." He looked more disappointed than annoyed. "I'll be back in a few minutes, give you more time to think about it."

All the boys jumped out of their seats again when Father Reardon headed for the door.

After he left, they sat down to recite the Ten Commandments until most could parrot them without referring to the text. During the recitation, several spitballs flew across the room.

Time to copy into their notebooks today's spelling words five times and write a sentence using each word. While he was copying 'receive', Sister Stella said, "Charles, please move up to this desk."

Why did Sister ask him to move, especially now that he was ignoring Ronnie and the rest of the boys, and working on his spelling, i before e except after c? She should've picked on the troublemakers instead of him. But he didn't feel like arguing, so he collected his books and pencils and moved to the assigned desk closer to hers.

No sooner did he sit in his new seat when onto the desk he'd just left came crashing the huge glass globe which covered the light bulb, carrying with it the heavy chain that attached it to the ceiling. The class was startled, shaken, everyone gaping at the empty desk, glass strewn all over it, and on the floor around it. Their eyes moved to Charles who sat staring at his former desk thinking that if he had disobeyed Sister or waited a few seconds longer, he could've been killed by the lamp. A messy miracle it was, but nevertheless, a miracle.

Sister dropped on her knees and made the Sign of the Cross. The class followed her lead.

This had to be a sign from heaven. God wanted him to become an altar boy. That's why He inspired Sister to change his desk, spare him a tragic fate.

Better to get up early than be dead.

Charles watched the janitor sweep up the shattered glass. Later that morning when Father Reardon returned, Charles volunteered to serve at Mass for the rest of the year.

Immediately after lunch Sister read the first sentence under the purple grammar heading. "Mark did not give his brother nothing. Now think about what this sentence, as written, means." She read it again, this time emphasizing nothing.

Several hands went up.

Sister called on John Keenan, in the front of the room.

"If Mark did *not* give his brother *nothing*," John said, "then he gave him *something*."

"Good thinking, did you all hear that? There are two negatives in that sentence. What are they, John?"

"Not and nothing."

Sister made sure she underlined both negatives in purple chalk. Then she turned around. "Tell me how the sentence should read so it actually says what it's supposed to mean."

"Mark didn't give his brother anything."

Without turning his head, Charles knew it was Francis O'Rourke's voice.

"Correct," Sister said, "because two negatives make a positive, and it works even if you use the contraction. Can someone say it another way?"

It took a longer time for hands to go up.

Charles raised his hand and Sister called on him.

"Mark gave his brother nothing."

"How many negatives are in that sentence?"

"Only one".

"What is it?"

"Nothing."

"You're all doing so well today that I'm *not* going to give you *no* homework." Sister smiled while she waited for the students' reaction.

One by one everybody snickered.

"Why are you smiling?" Sister said.

"Jee, Sister," Jimmy Carlino said, "you're trying to trick us. Two negatives make a positive and what you meant was if you were not going to give us no homework, you would really give us some homework."

"Excellent," Sister said, her face beaming. "The way I said it you're right, now copy the rest of the sentences. Underline the double negatives in the first five sentences and rewrite them any way you like to make them correct. If you get them all right, this time I won't give you *any* homework."

Charles wrote his sentences quickly, and feeling confident, was first to bring them to Sister. Before checking his work, she cleaned her glasses with the sleeve of her habit. "You know, Charles, I've been meaning to tell you that you have an extraordinary vocabulary for someone your age. I hope your grammar will be as good." She took his paper and read it. "Excellent, you really understand not to use the double negative, see that you avoid it in speaking as well as in writing. You know that in Romance languages like Italian, Charles, the one you're familiar with, the double negative is correct but not in English. Now since you did so well on this assignment you won't have any homework tonight."

He returned to his seat with an A on his paper. Several other students who had just completed their sentences also brought them to Sister.

When most of the students were finished, Sister handed Charles purple chalk and asked him to underline the double negatives in each of the remaining sentences on the board. After he did so, he blew away the purple dust that had collected on his hand.

Charles skipped home from school, his books tied with a strap slung over his back. He was in a hurry, had to finish *Moby Dick* before next week, when it was due back at the library. And he'd do it, even if he had to stay up late every night. After all, only kids in the eighth grade were assigned that book. But the first thing he would do when he got home was look up the word, covet.

Today the sun shone on the brick tenements turning them red-orange, the rust from the pitted wrought iron railings blending in. As Charles walked on the pavement, he was careful not to step in the cracks. Didn't want to break his mother's back. At least that's what the girls always said when they strolled along the sidewalks. But there were so many cracks on the pavement that only flying would make him avoid them. He was going to step in the cracks if his mother ever insisted he wear knickers to church on Sunday again.

With a full block to go before reaching his apartment, Charles knew his father was home much earlier than usual. His opera records blasted all over the neighborhood. Many people lifted their windows, most proudly displaying banners with navy blue stars, a few, gold, to hear the recordings. Even those who sat on the stoop looked up toward the Pastore apartment listening, their faces radiating passion. Some became the tenors and sopranos themselves, singing and playing out their roles in the street.

Charles loved the music, too, but it was hard concentrating on reading when the volume was always so loud. He would have to ask Papa to lower it.

Charles knew the opera. He had listened to it many times. *Tosca.* He stood in the lobby before climbing the steps. The church chorus was singing the "Te Deum." His father sang along with the baritone, *Tosca, mi fai dimenticare Iddio* (Tosca, you make me forget God). He wasn't quite sure how Tosca made the man with that deep powerful voice forget God, but it must've been bad, because the chords which followed were strong and scary, sending a cold chill from his toes to his scalp.

On Sunday, Charles, his sister Anna, brother Frank, and his mother went to Mass. As usual, his father stayed home. Mass, according to Papa, was for women and children. Only weak men went to Mass.

Charles studied every move the altar boys made. He had to remember when to ring the bells, bring the water and wine to the priest, what answers to give in Latin. When he sat at the main altar facing the parishioners, would he fall asleep during the sermons, the way he frequently felt like doing, but now with everyone watching him? He said a special prayer of thanksgiving to God for sparing his life. He'd be a good altar boy. He promised.

After Mass they followed the aroma of freshly baked Italian bread to it source, Fava's Bakery. His mother purchased a long seeded loaf. Mr. Fava wrapped it in white paper tied with a thin white string. Charles always volunteered to carry the bread so he could sneak his fingers into the white paper to break off the end of the bread, the coolie they called it, and the crunchiest, and munch on it all the way home.

This Sunday was going to be special. He hadn't seen his mother so excited for a long time. Today she was wearing makeup, pink rouge over her already pink cheeks, mascara, and penciled brows which framed her soft brown eyes. She had eaten her breakfast wearing curlers, probably after sleeping on them all night. If the curlers caused her pain, she was well rewarded by the puffy, silky brown pompadour and pageboy.

When they returned to the apartment, she breathed a sigh of relief. "I'm glad I spent most of yesterday preparing all these different dishes. Now all I have left to do is cook the pasta."

She immediately opened the top breakfront drawer, removing from it a starched, white linen pinafore-type apron.

"Do you want me to help you with something?" Charles said.

"There's nothing left to do. Anna already set the table and'll help with the dishes. Franco's in charge of clearing the table, and putting the garbage in the dumbwaiter when the super rings." She touched her finger to her forehead. "Oh, it's Sunday, he won't ring today. But Franco can put the garbage in there anyway. And you, Carlo, all I want you to do is play with Joey."

"Mama, you were born in this country. When are you going to stop calling Frank, Franco, and me, Carlo?"

"Never. Papa was born in the old country and that's what he wants, and we all have to listen to him."

"Not even when I'm twenty-one?"

"Not even then, if I'm still alive."

"Stop talking like that."

She shook her finger at him. "Then stop asking me to change your name."

"I won't play with Joey unless you call me Charles. And how come you don't call Joey, Giuseppe?"

"Stop it, you should be ashamed of yourself. Joey just lost his father and doesn't have time to think about names. He's going to have to help support his mother when he's older. You make sure you're good to him, and to Zia Palma. How'd you like to be in their shoes, no husband, no father? Now you promise me, Carlo."

"Okay," he said, his head drooping, "I'll be nice to them. Uncle Mike would've wanted that. But I was always nice to them."

Mama first pointed her finger at him, then poked her finger into his chest. "You make sure that today, the first time they come here since he died, you make sure you're especially nice. You know how Uncle Mike always let us stay with them in the Rockaways in the summer for free." Tears were beginning to smudge her mascara. "Poor Zia Palma," she sniffled, "no more husband."

"Do I have to call her Zia Palma, why not Aunt Palma?"

His mother put her finger over her lips then waved her hand for him to leave.

As soon as Charles went into his room, he tripped over Frank's helmet and canteen. He kicked Frank's utility belt under the bed, sat in a corner and read *Moby Dick* until the smell of Captain Ahab's salty ocean wind became overpowered by the pork and beef of simmering gravy. He inhaled deeply, just as the bell was ringing.

Not until they were all in the living room did his father come in to greet them.

Zia Palma was draped in black, from the hat with the slanted feather down to her stockings and buckled shoes. Joey's hair was slicked back with Vitalis he must have poured on himself after he put on his black suit, white shirt, and black tie because his jacket had smears of grease on the shoulders and lapels. Even Zia Palma didn't let Joey wear knickers.

They all hugged and kissed each other. His mother served everyone a glass of red wine.

Charles pulled Joey by the elbow into his room. "Joey, want to look at some magazines, read some books?"

Joey's eyes scanned the room. "You got more books here than the library."

"See any you like?"

"Nah, I hate reading, let's play a game. Cards, Chinese checkers."

"How about chess?"

"I don't like that game, can never remember which piece is which. Let's play cards."

Charles didn't want to play cards but he had promised his mother to be good to his guests. "How about five hundred rummy?"

"Okay, you keep score. And don't cheat."

He took out a deck of cards from his drawer, then a pencil. He ripped a sheet of paper out of his loose leaf book. Before drawing a line down the middle of the page, he wrote a J at the top left, and a C at the top right. Both he and Joey sat on the floor. Charles shuffled the deck several times and dealt the cards. Just as he placed the last card on the floor right in front of him, his mother called out that dinner was ready. "Hungry, Joey?"

Joey rotated his open hand over his stomach. "I'm not hungry, I'm starving."

Anna had set the table with a long table cloth, long enough to cover a table that opened for twelve. Since it was just the seven of them eating dinner, Anna had added only one leaf, allowing the table cloth to hang down at the head and the foot.

After each course, Joey and Charles continued their card game in his room until his mother called them back. Every time Frank tried to enter the room, Charles and Joey threw him out. Little brothers could be a big pain-in-the-ass.

By the time they were ready for dessert, Charles had already accumulated four hundred eighty points to Joey's two hundred sixty-two. Charles considered whether as a good host he should've made Joey win because the kid seemed bored.

Joey wiggled then stretched. "I don't want to play rummy no more, let's play hide-and-go-seek."

Didn't want to play rummy no more. The jackass didn't know anything about double negatives. And hide-and-go-seek. A game for younger kids, or for dummies. Perfect for Joey. "That's not fair to you, it's my apartment and I know the hiding places better than you."

"Let's play it anyway, right after dessert. First let's go eat some cannoli."

"My favorite."

He and Joey joined the dining room table once again, each taking a whole cannoli and shoving it into their mouths.

"What's the matter with you two?" his mother said. "You're going to choke, chew your food."

No sooner did she stop speaking when his father stood up. His blue eyes went right through Charles's, and Papa's curly brown hair shifted from side to side as he violently shook his head. "Carlo, the next time you eat without chewing I going to slap you head and knock the food right out of you mouth. You understand?"

"Yes, Papa." Why was Papa scolding him with such nasty language, especially in front of guests?

His father sat down again.

"Let's go," Joey said. "You hide and I'll try to find you."

"Okay. Go to my room and wait for me to hide. When you come out start counting to a hundred. Slowly. Say Mississippi very, very slowly between each number, and make sure you start with zero, remember Joey, zero. If you don't find me by one hundred, you lose."

Joey went back to Charles's room and closed the door.

A little later he heard Joey begin, "One, Mississippi, two Mississippi..." Did the jerk ever listen? Even more important, where was he was going to hide?

The bathroom. He walked toward it but that was probably the first place Joey'd look.

Maybe the kitchen. In the sink, plates stacked upon plates. He opened the broom closet, peered in. Nah, not a good hiding place. Didn't fit into it anymore, not without squashing himself to death, or ripping his Sunday pants rubbing against the nails and hooks.

Charles sneaked along the hall and peeked into the dining room. His brother, sister, and all the adults were eating pastries, chatting, and sipping espresso from multi-colored floral demi-tasse cups. A bottle of anisette was the only tall item left on the table.

Hm. The table. The cloth long enough to reach the floor, so it had to be long enough to cover him. Joey would look everywhere but under there.

Charles slipped down on the floor. On his belly he wormed his way under the table to the center, careful not to shake the table and rattle the anisette bottle, or have anyone see him to give him away. He straightened out the edge of the tablecloth he had dragged in with him so it wouldn't look disturbed, then sat down Indian-style, his head just about touching the table top. For a while he remained still, careful not to breathe.

A cramp in his leg. Had to move it.

He rotated to get more room, stretch his legs.

Then...

The black buckled shoes!

A feeling went through him as though he was standing on a fault during an earthquake. He felt like throwing up the cannoli which seemed to be blocking his windpipe even though it had already passed through his esophagus.

His eyes traced the shoes to the ankle, then up the leg.

Papa's hand.

On Zia Palma's thigh.

The garter near the inside of her thigh was unhooked, letting the top of the black stocking on that side fall just above her knee. Her hand moved over his father's, and she was pushing it up and down, up and down over her thigh.

The word, covet, from his catechism lesson popped into his head. He had looked it up. Want somebody else's property, yearn to have, desire. He couldn't move, not believing what he was seeing. It seemed to be something they were both used to, and it was wrong.

Very wrong.

"Eighty-three Mississippi...caught you," Joey blasted, crawling under the table, peering at him, the edge of the table cloth draping his cousin's shoulder.

No, caught them. Caught them, all right.

The sting of Joey's words far outweighed the sting of Charles's leg cramp. He slid on his butt back out from under the table and stood up.

Joey followed him, then jumped up and down. "I won, I won."

Charles turned around. In an urge he couldn't control he began punching Joey and didn't stop until blood came pouring from his nose, adding more red stains to his white shirt already spattered with gravy spots.

The adults quickly jumped out of their seats and separated them.

Papa's arms felt particularly muscular as he held him back. "Is that the way you treat you cousin, just because he won? You say you sorry, right now."

Charles wrestled his way out of his father's arms with a force he never knew he had in him. "I'm not apologizing to anybody. I hate him, I hate him."

Zia Palma kept wiping the blood off Joey with a linen table napkin. "Is there any ice in the ice box, or some cold water?"

"Go to you room, Carlo," his father said, "I take care of you later."

Charles stood as erect as he could, his nose high in the air. He marched back into his room so enraged that his tears remained clogged in their ducts.

A little later his father opened the door. "You aunt and you cousin go home now. Come out and say goodbye to them."

Charles lay prostrate on his bed. He lifted his head and mustered up the most defiant look he was capable of. "I'm not saying goodbye to them, I don't ever want them to come here again, I hate them both."

"Oh, really." Papa removed his belt. He dragged him off the bed by the arm, and whipped his behind.

Charles remained still.

"No enough for you? Here some more."

The pain was unbearable but Charles said, "You can beat me until I'm dead, but I'm not saying goodbye to them now or ever." Papa stepped back when Charles made a deliberate effort to convey hate through his eyes.

His father left the room, breathing heavily, mumbling, snorting, dragging his belt, the metal buckle making a scratching sound on the linoleum.

Through the door Charles heard him say, "I apologize for my son, Palma. I never seen him like this. Maybe he have too much wine. He seem to have went mad."

"Boys can get that way sometimes," Zia Palma said. "Thank you for inviting us. The meal was delicious and we had a good time."

Charles bet she had a good time. How many times did she have a good time with his father, maybe even in Rockaway, when Uncle Mike was alive? She wasn't a widow dressed in black, she was a black widow, spinning her evil web, and his father was already trapped in it. Though it didn't seem he was having much trouble being trapped. Charles would never look at her or her son again.

He put his ear to the door.

Quiet. They must've left.

But then he heard footsteps. Headed in his direction.

Charles got down on the floor, avoiding pressure on his rear by lying on his side to read.

His father pushed open the door. Charles wouldn't so much as lift his head, burying his nose deeper into *Moby Dick*.

"Is that the way you treat guests in our house?" Papa said. "You show no respect for you aunt. Now you stand up and tell me why you do that."

Charles wouldn't budge.

His father removed his belt again, this time thrashing it over his head. Before today he couldn't remember the last time Papa had laid a hand on him.

Charles's face accumulated disgust. "You seem to treat guests in our house very well. Very, very well," he said, exaggerating his speech. "I won't talk to you till you tell me you hate her, too."

"Hate who?"

"Aunt Palma."

"You call her *Zia* Palma."

"This is America. I'll call her Aunt Palma."

"She a good woman, she never did nothing to you."

He was about to answer his father back when instead he paused to plant a smirk on his face. "You said it right, Papa, when you said it in the double negative. She *never* did *nothing* to me and she *never* did *nothing* to you." He sensed his eyes turn the same color as the purple chalk, and could still feel its dust all over his fingers.

"Double negative, what you talking about? Goddam kids. Send them to school in this country, they use big fancy words and they lose all respect." He stomped out of the room.

For a while it was quiet in the apartment. Too quiet. Papa must've gone back into the living room. Charles could hear the opera recording again. *Tosca*. His father humming along. The chorus in the church singing the "Te Deum". The man with the deep voice sang the part just before the scary chords. Charles braced himself, clenched his fists. But then his father blasted his voice above the music, *Palma, mi fai dimenticare Iddio* (Palma, you make me forget God.)

Charles unclenched his fists and punched his hands over the wall. Thou shalt not covet thy neighbor's wife was still jammed in his head.

His father.

The son-of-a-bitch!

This time the chords which followed made Charles more angry than frightened. He rushed for his dresser, lifted the picture which framed the smiling faces of him and his father, and hurled it against the door. The frame came apart at each corner and the glass cover smashed into hundreds of pieces.

Splattered glass again. This time, not a miracle.

The intense pain on his buttocks, the welt on his head, the sense of betrayal. They hurt badly enough.

But only the aching he felt for his mother finally unleashed the tears.

"You fourteen years old now, Carlo," his father said, "got to go to work. You make sure you in my shop every day when you come home from school."

It could've been worse. Papa might've made him quit school altogether.

"When you come in you can take care of the customers in the front and watch the cash register while I fix the shoes in the back. I start to get tired now, this way I no have to run back and forth so much."

The only advantage Charles could see was that while he was in the shop, his father couldn't receive any unwanted visitors, at least none that Charles wanted. "Can I do my homework in between customers?"

"Books, homework." His father shoved him by the shoulder twice. "Sometimes I think the more you study the more stupider you get."

"More stupid, Papa."

"What you are, wise guy? That's what I said."

Father O'Hara was analyzing word problems in his after school SAT review class. Motion problems, time problem, mixture problems. The alcohol had to be divided by the total amount of alcohol plus water. A lot of people forgot that. Charles was so absorbed in the explanations that he had forgotten the time.

He glanced at his watch.

Jesus Christ in holy heaven, he was going to be late for work. He gathered his pile of books so quickly he didn't bother putting them in size order, so when he ran out of the classroom, the books kept sliding out from one another onto the floor. It must've been a moment like this which made someone come up with the expression that haste makes waste.

He reached the store panting. Almost five o'clock. His father was going to kill him.

He entered the door which, when opened, sounded a bell attached to a string, expecting his father to come out yelling at him at any second. He waited for the attack, first the verbal followed by what he was sure today would be the inevitable fist.

Neither.

Creepy. But he was distracted when his eyes reached the wall. For the first time he really looked at it. Then he studied all the walls. Peeling paint. Black soot behind the radiator, looking like its shadow, whether or not there was any light in the room. Warped, dusty pigeon holes. He'd buy a paint scraper, some paint, lemon oil. During the summer he'd refresh the place by painting the walls himself, and polish the pigeon holes. A break between novels and adventure stories.

The bell again.

Mrs. Colavita trotted into the shop, the pleasant features of her southern Italian face blending into a smile. She immediately began digging into her pocketbook. Finally, she handed him her claim ticket.

They exchanged greetings. In the pigeon hole with her ticket number, Charles promptly located Mrs. Colavita's highly polished brown shoes with brand new heels. He delivered the shoes to the counter. Then he placed her dollar bill in the cash register and returned two quarters to the counter.

Within a few moments she was gone. She had been so busy examining and admiring her shoes that she had forgotten to pick up the change. Should he run after her, leave the store unattended? What if his father came in and didn't find him there? He'd have to risk being punished because he could never, never, keep what didn't belong to him.

He tried to catch up with Mrs. Colavita, but didn't see her on the street. He poked his head into the dry cleaner's next door, Fusco's, got a whiff of cleaning fluid, then continued into Vincenzo's butcher shop, kicked the sawdust off his feet, and finally found his way to the luncheonette, where though it was late in the afternoon, someone was cooking bacon and eggs. Mrs. Colavita, nowhere to be found. He asked if anyone had seen her. No one had.

Charles returned to the store, put the quarters into an envelope, marked it, "Mrs. Colavita," and placed it in the cash register. He debated with himself whether to also put a note in the pigeon hole from which he had removed her ticket to indicate where the change could be found, but decided against it. She was a regular customer, and the envelope would remind him or whoever was at the register the next time she came in to give her the change.

The sun had almost set. He was about to turn on the lights when he noticed light seeping in from the bottom of the folded curtain which separated the front and back rooms. While he was looking for Mrs. Colavita, his father must've come in. Might as well face the music, get it over with.

Charles pushed the curtain aside. Papa still wasn't there. He never left the shop unattended, especially with the lights on. Charles was about to go back to the front door to see if in his anxiety about being late, he had inadvertently failed to notice that his father had turned the hours sign over to closed. But then Mrs. Colavita wouldn't have come in, and if Papa had left for the day, he would've locked the door.

Charles was still trying to figure out where his father had gone when the telephone rang. Papa calling him evidently, checking up on him. He ran to the wall to pick up the phone.

There, behind the shop table.

He almost tripped over it.

His father's body.

For a moment Charles couldn't think. Then he ran for the phone that was ringing to death, and picked it up. "Call back later." He hung up, then picked up the phone again to get the dial tone, called the operator.

He lowered his hand, ever so reluctantly, on his father's face. Thank God it wasn't cold. It would've given him the creeps. He removed his hand but couldn't remove his eyes from the ashen face. A half-hour, maybe longer passed before the police and an ambulance were in front of the store, his father on a stretcher.

Goddam city.

Why did it always take them so long to do anything?

"Looks like a heart attack," one of the ambulance crew said, "but he's still breathing so let's hurry."

Charles hitched a ride with the ambulance crew to the hospital. They were cracking jokes with the radio blasting Frank Sinatra over them. No place to be sick.

When they arrived at the hospital, the crew rolled Papa into a room, and slammed the door shut. Charles immediately approached the nurses there. They told him to go home, that they didn't know anything yet, and if they did, only the doctor could speak to him. And no one would be allowed to see his father for forty-eight hours, the critical period.

Whatever it was, then, it was critical. The smell of antiseptics was catching up with him, making him queasy.

He tried to argue his way to his father's room, but the nurses were adamant. He sat in the waiting room for a while, thinking, and thinking. What he had to do now was go home and break the news to his mother. And knowing her temperament, reaching her was going to be difficult.

And he was right.

Her screams were so shrill that he was sure everyone in the apartment house could hear them. He moved behind her, put one hand over her mouth, shook her shoulder with the other hand and forced her into a chair. "Mom, you've got to calm down. Papa's going to need someone, you in particular, to be strong. You can't fall apart at a time like this."

"I've got to see him."

"You can't see him yet. He's not supposed to have visitors until he's better, and they're not sure yet it was a heart attack."

She stood up, pushed the chair aside and ran to the hall closet. "I'm going to the hospital."

"No, you're not." He grabbed her arm, yanked the coat she had ripped off the hanger. "If you're really thinking about Papa instead of yourself, you'll wait until they tell you it's okay." He led her to the kitchen table and guided her back into the chair.

For a moment his mother seemed resigned. She wiped her tears. "He's such a good man, Carlo. How could he get a heart attack, such a curse. He's only forty-three."

Such a good man. Hah. He gritted his teeth. "Don't jump to conclusions, they don't know what it is yet. Could be an ulcer, something wrong with his digestive system, so don't always think the worst. You get some rest. Anna and Frank'll need you. I'll go to the hospital and talk to the doctor. Then if it's early enough, I'll go to the library, take out some medical books. As soon as it's time that Papa can see us, I'll take you. Shouldn't be too long."

She put her hands over her face, then rested her head on the table. Through a twisted mouth Mama murmured, "Yes, you go. You're smart, know how to talk to the doctors."

On the way to the hospital Charles held an on-going conversation with himself. What would happen to them if something went wrong with his father? No, it couldn't be serious. A digestive problem, from all those hot peppers he ate. If Papa had a heart attack, he'd just have to take it easy for a while. And if it had been a serious one, he probably would have died already.

He found himself at the nurses' station again. "I was here before. Charles Pastore, Filippo Pastore's son. He was taken here earlier this evening, how is he, can I see him?"

The woman with Mary Quinn, R.N. on the tag over her pocket said, "He's in the second room down the hall, 304, on the right, all the even numbers are on the right. You have to speak to the doctor about his condition. We called Dr. Falcone, he's not here now but I'll give you his number. And your father's not allowed to have anyone visit him for at least forty-eight hours. That's routine in these situations."

"Routine in what situations?"

"You have to talk to the doctor." She paused. "304 did I say, let me check. Oh yes, that's the room someone went into who won't leave, ignored our orders."

"Someone? Who?"

"I don't know. She put up quite a fight, so much we thought it better to let her stay than have her antics upset the patient, not to mention the other patients on this floor."

Charles headed toward his father's room.

Mary Quinn called after him, "I just told you you can't go___"

His mother, such a thickhead. The minute he left she sneaked out of the house. Yet he couldn't blame her for acting like a concerned wife.

Charles pushed open the door to room 304. Two beds in the room. A man with thick gray hair and a beak nose, his mouth half-open, snored in one. And around the other bed, a curtain drawn just enough to reveal his father's head under an oxygen tent. The tent read NO SMOKING, and underneath NON FUMARE.

His mother, holding his father's hand.

She had made believe she wouldn't go to the hospital just to trick him, even though she tried to make him feel he was for a time the man of the house, in control.

Charles shoved the curtain aside. With his mouth open ready to scold his mother for putting Papa at risk, he instead found himself in a choking gasp.

He was staring down at Zia Palma.

How in hell did she find out about his father?

She jerked her lips off his father's hand.

Charles was shocked, paralyzed for a few seconds. Then rage overtook him. "Get out."

Zia Palma dropped his father's hand, gathered the few items she had brought with her, slouched down while scurrying out of the room without looking back.

His father spent three weeks in the hospital. According to the doctors, he made a miraculous recovery.

The first day his father was home, he had another heart attack.

From that one he did not recover.

CHAPTER 5

ALEX THUMBED THROUGH some papers on her desk. Notes about camp for the children, appointments to transfer to her calendar, phone numbers to add to the address book. She had written some ideas regarding what she wanted to include in this chapter, but had misplaced the pages.

Alex returned to the word processor. She would have to recall what she had jotted down, or risk wasting writing time trying to find the elusive papers.

* * *

"Is it okay if I invite Bob McMahon for dinner, Trish?" Dr. Arcuri knew his wife would agree but he wanted to ask her first.

"It is. Just give me enough notice."

"I'll ask him to come the day before the reunion. They'll be so many of our classmates there, if I don't see him before all the ceremonies, we won't have that much catch-up time together."

She lifted the sofa pillows one by one, then fluffed them before gently putting them back. "Do you want me to make an Irish dish or an Italian one?

"Bob's always been crazy about Italian food, and you make it better than my mother did."

"Thanks for the compliment. Keep'em coming and I'll keep cooking."

"My mother's main concern was that I'd overdose on corned beef and cabbage or die from a garlic deficiency. Even she had to admit that you're a good cook. I always had the feeling she was a little jealous of that, didn't want you to steal her thunder."

"My father could never understand how an Irish girl with my breeding, actually he'd never admit, a *lace curtain* Irish girl," she emphasized with sarcasm, "could ever marry a WOP, he used to mutter under his breath. How could you ever support me in the style to which I was accustomed? After all we were the Phelans of Park Avenue in the winter, and the Phelans of Southampton in the summer, and that brought dates with the sons of his colleagues on Wall Street."

He meandered to the curved living room window of their Victorian home to examine the ivory lace curtains, putting on his glasses to see them more clearly. "The only reason your father finally approved of our marriage, ever so reluctantly I might add, was that I was at least Catholic and my reddish brown hair made me look Irish enough so he could pass me off as one. Used to stumble over Arcuri or sneeze or cough when he said it so he could make it sound something like Archer whenever he introduced me to someone. But then Archer was too Brit-like. He could've done worse for a son-in-law. Now at least he has someone who could support him after all those dumb investments he made. I noticed that when the Phelans of Park Avenue and Southampton became the Phelans of the poorhouse, none of his snobby Irish friends came around to help him out."

"Nor his other children who've all disappeared." Trish punched one of the pillows she had just puffed up. "When I think of how I fought for Mom and Dad's approval, it was all worth it." She took his hand as soon as he returned from the window. "I wake up each morning loving you more and more, Rudy. I knew what I was doing even then. A woman couldn't ask for a better husband, even if," she winked, "he's Italian."

A smile took over her face. She chuckled, covered her mouth. "I have to laugh at my mother's directive. Do you remember when she ordered me to order you to tell all your relatives not to show up at the wedding with cash in envelopes but to mail checks ahead of time? She didn't want her daughter walking around the reception carrying a pouch."

"She did have a point. But the Italians at our wedding didn't have checkbooks, though at least those who came or were invited gave cash, generous amounts, not some cheap item like a dish towel or a spatula from your ritzy family. Getting back to your mother, Trish, I could never understand how a woman who perceived herself as so sophisticated and so religious could be so superstitious."

His wife's smile grew into a robust laugh. "She was superstitious. I still can't get over how she contacted all our female relatives and told them to hang rosary beads on the clothesline the night before our wedding so it wouldn't rain. Of course we didn't have to worry about clotheslines because we had a laundry room and several maids. But," she said, pointing an accusatory finger, "your mother was no slouch either when it came to superstition. Remember how she'd cross the street whenever she saw a nun because if she was on the same side that would give her bad luck all day. And she made sure we all had some straw from the crèche at Christmastime and told us to keep it in our wallets so they'd never be empty."

"Well, maybe if your father had taken some straw, he'd still be rich."

The laughter she started out with waned, and a scowl replaced her smile. "Now, Rudy, let's not get into any ethnic battles or I'll get my Irish up and bring up the only person in your family, besides you, of course, who owns a house. Uncle Angelo. And I'll not refer to the lions in the entrance or the donkey cart in his front yard. Besides," the smile returned, "I'm not in the mood to argue, I'm in the mood for a kiss."

"An Irish woman asking me for a kiss and rubbing my hand this way must've absorbed some Italian blood."

"My father always warned me the darker the skin, the hotter the blood."

"Well, Trish, if that were the case, you should be hotter than I am."

"It's not the blood, Rudy, it's the garlic." She kissed him with great passion.

She was still a beautiful woman with a great Irish wit. Her chestnut brown hair had a few strands of gray. The green eyes had the potential for being cold but they never were, even when she was angry. He had often heard other women say that Trish's nose was one they would kill for.

With their hands still interlocked, he pulled her closer, and kissed her again.

Steve waited for Uncle Bob behind the curved living room window, the lace curtains decorating her shoulders. Uncle Bob was already an hour late, and the plane was supposed to have landed on time. She kept turning around, clicking her head between the window and the clock so many times she felt like a metronome. Her mother had always said that a watched pot never boiled. Today it seemed that a watched clock never moved.

Finally, a taxi. A tall thin man, gray suit and hat. The driver handed him a matching suitcase.

She ran to open the front door. "Hi, Uncle Bob, we're so happy you're here."

He dropped his suitcase and lifted her high in the air. "Well, which one are you, and whichever one you are, you're getting pretty heavy for Uncle Bob." He kissed her cheek while letting her down.

"I'm Steve, the baby of the family."

"Some baby, how old are you now?"

"Eight."

"I can't believe I've never met you. Met your sisters but never you. He walked around her, studying her. Don't look like your sisters did. It's great being___"

Her parents entered the hallway.

"Trish, Rudy, so good to see you."

The three embraced each other.

"It's been too long," her mother said, "ten years."

"Some things haven't changed in ten years," Bob said. He closed his eyes, inhaled deeply. "I can smell that you're still a wonderful Italian cook."

"And let me ask if your favorite drink hasn't changed."

"You remember, Trish?"

She nodded.

"Then let's see if your memory serves you well. Bring me the usual."

Steve watched her mother go back into the kitchen while her father and Uncle Bob strolled into the living room, arms over each other's shoulders.

Should she help her mother with the food or go sit on Daddy's lap? She was just about to join her mother when she heard Uncle Bob say, "This is the first time I ever saw you with a mustache, Rudy. How long've you been sporting the brush?"

"Since after my second daughter, Megan, was born," he sighed. "It's an old Sicilian custom to grow a mustache until you have a son. I was sure Stefania would be a boy, and even though it's been eight years since she was born, it doesn't look like Trish will have another child, but I can still wish. Therefore, the mustache."

She arched her back into the wall just outside the living room, edging her ear near the doorframe.

"There's no justice," Uncle Bob said. "I have three sons and no daughters. Looks like the oldest is showing an interest in law."

"You're so lucky, I always wanted one of my children to follow in my footsteps, walk into my practice, help me out as I got older. But when you really think about it, that's kind of selfish. Kids should be what they want, not fulfill their parents' unexpressed or expressed desires. Still I would've liked it, loved it, if one of my children was a physician. Don't you feel that way about your kids?"

She didn't wait for Uncle Bob's answer. Instead of going into the kitchen, she dashed up to her room, slamming the door behind her. She had locked her dolls in the closet and hidden the key to make it easier to resist the urge of wanting to play with them.

A few remaining parts of her erector set sat on the floor, as well as the derrick she had finished putting together just after breakfast to give to Uncle Bob. Walking dinosaurs, a bicycle, even the same kind of parachute her family had taken a ride on the only time they went to Coney Island. She had constructed them all, and displayed them around her room. Wasn't that enough for Daddy? She kept blinking back tears with such force that an eyelash loosened and got stuck in her eye.

She had always cut her hair short, cut it herself every month, over her mother's objection. Kept sharp barber scissors in her top bureau drawer, a second pair, and a scissor sharpener. Even practiced keeping her pinky in the hook of the barber scissors while she kept cutting.

Steve yanked from the shelf the Ferris wheel, her pride and joy, her most complicated design, and shook it. It disassembled, the pieces scattering all over the floor. She stomped on them over and over again, and with her heel made sure any of them still uncrushed finally gave up the ghost.

She threw herself face down on the rug, kept kicking the floor so hard, stopping only when she felt she might have broken some toes. Only then did the pain send her a belated message that when Uncle Bob let his suitcase go to pick her up when she jumped on him, he could've stubbed, maybe even broken his toes. How selfish of her.

She wanted to be a nun. The statues would be her dolls. The Blessed Virgin, Saint Theresa, Saint Jude, baby Jesus. She wanted to be a teacher. A nun. A teacher. A nun-teacher.

Yet the choice was ever so clear.

Nothing, yes nothing would ever prevent her from becoming a physician.

Steve put her hands over her ears to mute the shrill whistle accompanying the train as it started pulling out of the station. She and her father had just climbed onto the steps of the sleeping car, and handed the conductor their luggage.

He checked their tickets while greeting them in a voice which seemed to have picked up the piercing sound of the whistle. "Welcome aboard, Dr. Arcuri, I was just about to sell your compartment to a passenger who wanted an upgrade." His wide smile revealed one gold tooth, off center, under his upper lip.

"Glad you didn't. I had to see a lot of patients today, and ran a little late. I've been rushing around too much. I really need privacy so I can get some rest."

"Well, you settle in now. I'll come back later, let you know when the dining car is ready to begin serving."

The train's chugging eventually became smooth and Steve noticed that her father seemed to have changed along with the rhythm. She wrapped her arms around him, dug her head into his chest. "Sorry, Daddy, that I put you through all this trouble."

"Don't be silly, you know how much I enjoy when we're together. We're so much alike, but don't tell your sisters I said that, I love them, too."

"Everybody thinks it's funny that Megan looks more Italian, and Daria more Irish."

"What's in a name? And besides I look more Irish than your mother. But what's important is that you look like me. Maybe that's why we're so close."

"I may look like you, but you're good looking and I'm not, and my sisters are prettier than I am."

"What are you talking about? You're only twelve. You'll see by the time you're fifteen or so, you won't even recognize yourself."

"That's not true, Daddy. There are girls in my class who are already pretty, and they're not fifteen."

"Well, I'll put my money on you."

She didn't believe it for a second, especially now that she was checking her reflection in the sleeping car's shiny aluminum wall, but she said. "Thanks, Daddy, you always make me feel good even if you tell fibs. Now don't you go tell Mom but I'm glad that she has a cold and you're coming with me instead. It's not that I don't love her, but I'm glad you're here."

"Even if she didn't have a cold I'd be with you anyway. Do you think I'd miss my daughter's representing the Bronx in the," he pushed out his chest, resting his open hand on it, and spoke as though he was issuing a proclamation, "Scripps-Howard National Spelling Bee? How many fathers could even have that opportunity? We could've gotten someone to stay with the girls, or for two days they could've missed school, too. It might've been fun for all of us to take a tour of Washington."

An aroma tug of war was coming from the dining car, the roast beef winning out over the chicken, making her hungry. But it was Friday, damn it, so she'd have to settle for fish, and if they didn't have any, a grilled cheese sandwich, or baked macaroni.

She kept her head down, pursed her lips. "Are you really proud of me Daddy?"

"Who wouldn't be? You're my scholar."

That she knew he really meant, and it made her tingle. If not his son, she would always be his scholar. "I overheard Sister telling one of the other nuns that she had spoken to you at Open School night."

"And?"

"And she said she told you that I was homelier than my sisters and to compensate for it I developed my personality and my intelligence."

Her father cleared his throat. "Not exactly, what she really said was that if you were absolutely gorgeous which we both know you aren't...yet, and neither are your sisters, you'd be concentrating on developing that beauty instead of your personality and intellect. Then you'd be putting your effort into developing something that passes instead of getting more substance and acquiring skills that will last a lifetime."

"Oh, it sounds much better the way you said it."

"Trust me, Steve, when you're older you'll have all three."

She looked past him. "But suppose I don't win tomorrow, will you still think I'm smart?"

"Only if you stop asking silly questions like that one. You know how you had to compete to get this far. If you don't win, I wouldn't worry too much about it. You don't win everything in life and if you learn only that lesson, you'll have learned a lot."

You don't win everything in life.

Comforting.

The pressure was off, but she still had to give it her all. "I may not win but I'm still going to do my best." She took out the worn faded blue dictionary that seemed to weigh almost as much as she did and continued studying it.

Her father stroked her cheek. "That's my girl."

She smiled, lifted her head for a moment, looked back at her reflection on the aluminum wall, an ugly duckling trying to imagine how her image would change if she were pretty. But she gave up and stuck her nose back into the dictionary.

Sister Mary Joachim's forehead showed premature signs of aging as she tapped her foot and wagged her finger with the same rhythm. "Dr. Arcuri, you're going to be responsible for that girl's losing her faith."

He was already losing his patience. "Steve's only going to Bronx High School of Science, not Moscow Prep."

"The public schools teach all kinds of crazy ideas, like evolution and family planning. And there are boys there, in the same class. They'll keep Steve distracted." Sister Mary Joachim plopped herself into her desk chair, picked up the attendance book and fanned herself with it, while still tapping her foot. The air was saturated with her disapproval.

"Stop worrying, Sister, she comes from a family of strong faith. We'll make sure she stays that way. And her older sisters, one is at Ursuline Academy, the other at Good Counsel College, they're good models for her."

Her forehead was still wrinkled, but she finally stopped tapping her foot. "Sometimes I think that a girl being smart is a double-edged sword. It's always better to be smarter than not, but who would want to go to a girl physician, it makes her less feminine. And she's already so," she screwed up the rest of her face and shook her head, "plain-looking."

"Why, Sister, how can you, a woman of the cloth, say that, that's not supposed to be important. Steve has the most gorgeous green eyes, auburn hair, and tremendous charm."

Sister Mary Joachim raised her eyes to the ceiling before closing them. "Only a father."

"Anyway, my mind's made up. She's going to Bronx High School of Science."

"Bunch of atheists, communists. I'll pray for her, for all of you." She clutched the crucifix of her rosary which hung a little below her hip, and made a spastic Sign of the Cross. "God knows you'll need all the prayers you can get."

He scurried out of the room without giving Sister so much as a handshake.

Eighth grade graduation. How exciting! A day that brought Steve a special dress, a pair of baby doll shoes, and a pink rosebud corsage. She had always heard that a corsage should be worn in the directions the flowers grow. So now after Megan pinned it on her upside down, Steve tried to adjust it. But it still remained lopsided.

Even though Sister Mary Joachim had ignored her recently, Steve knew she'd have to receive many prizes. That was old hat, didn't thrill her. But the invitation to her very first party. That really made her bubble up.

The first hour of the party the boys held up one side of the wall and the girls, the opposite one. The boys kept glancing over to the other side, and when caught, turned away and talked to one another. The girls peeked over at the boys, shifting eyes in another direction when they made contact.

They were living examples of Steve's dictionary definition of wallflower. They were all wallflowers.

When the food came out, all flowers detached themselves from the walls and gathered in the dining room around the cold cuts, rolls, coleslaw, pickles, potato and macaroni salads. Balloons, blue and white, the school colors, stuck to the ceiling. Alternating strips of twisted blue and white crepe paper draped the walls. Waiting at the end of the table was a large punch bowl, bubbling and brimming over with what smelled and looked like ginger ale, and well on its way to melting ice cubes while keeping afloat sliced strawberries and oranges. At the far end of the table a three-tiered cake read, "Congratulations Mary Lou," a silver cake knife resting close by.

The guests loaded their plates. When most were empty, Mary Lou put on, "I'm in the Mood for Love," and a few girls began to dance with each other. Little by little, a few boys, slouched, dragging their feet, cut in and danced with the girls, feet cemented to the floor, shifting their torsos back and forth.

Steve noticed that the crowd began to thin, but she didn't see anyone leave. She drifted around the first floor of the house. Some guests were going into the basement. A boy stood by the basement door, rotating his head back and forth. Then some of the guests were allowed to pass through the door.

Steve followed them. She reached the bottom of the steps. Boys and girls sitting on opposite sides of a circle. Henry Coulehan, on his knees in the middle, spinning an empty Hoffman's cream soda bottle. When it stopped, the narrow end pointed toward Lillian Regan, the blunt toward Sean O'Hanlon. Sean promptly went over to Lillian and kissed her.

On the lips!

Then Henry spun the bottle again. This time Loretta Ryan and Nick Conte lined up with it. They kissed, also on the lips.

Fascinating.

Steve sat in the girls' semi-circle and the next bottle faced her. In a split second Greg Ruisi was kissing her. The kiss was awkward, but it was her first. Henry spun the bottle and she and Greg were kissing again, this time much less awkwardly. By the time they played Flashlight, whenever the light shone on them, she and Greg weren't even coming up for air. At least, when the time came she wouldn't have to say she was sweet-sixteen and had never been kissed.

It must've been the boy guarding the basement door who flickered the lights. All the guests rushed up to a member of the opposite sex, started dancing even though it took many seconds for someone to get a record going. Mrs. Bucci came down and asked if they'd had enough to eat.

Steve was awakened to the fact that with boys in the same classes in her new high school, it was going to be more difficult to concentrate on her studies.

But down deep she knew, no matter how distracted she became, it would always be the mustache that would keep her in focus.

CHAPTER 6

ALEX REFLECTED AFTER reading Paul's text. "If a boy ever saw his father and aunt or any woman other than his wife in that kind of relationship, it would have to make a lasting impress___"

"Traumatic." With the outer part of his hand he massaged his forehead. Then he covered the top of his head with his hand. "Very influential on his decision-making."

Paul looked so distressed that Alex decided to change the subject. "So, am I looking at a walking miracle, or is the lamp-on-the-head scene far-fetched?"

"That actually happened to me, besides didn't you say to keep the readers entertained?"

"Entertained, but believably entertained. Though," she raised her hand in an apologetic gesture, "if you say it really happened, who am I to argue with the truth? Besides, isn't truth supposed to be stranger than fiction?

"At first I was wondering where you were going with that double negative. I thought for a while it was overkill, but as I continued to read, I realized what it was leading to so now I'm not so sure. Maybe we should stay with it. We'll see.

"Anyway, let's move on. But before we do so I'd like to mention that one of my editors told me that if a character has little or no role in the story, don't bother to use that person's name. You referred to 'the woman with Mary Quinn, R.N. on the tag over her pocket' when you could just say nurse. But we can discuss that later." She circled the section in red. "Steve and Charles are both off to an interesting start regarding what makes them who they are."

"Yes, but they have a lot more growing up to do, don't you think?"

"It seems as though they're headed for high school and college, so why don't we write the next section at least through that point."

"Probably will be a lot of information for that part, so suppose we try to write two chapters each for next week."

"Look who's pushing now! First I have to convince you to try to write, and remember I'm the one who brings keeping to a schedule to this collaborative effort, now you're pushing me to be more productive." She looked to the right, then to the left. "I guess I could write two chapters, though don't ask me where they're going."

"Good, two chapters it'll be. I always heard that writing was a full-time job."

"Indeed, it is."

"But I'd like to ask you something." Paul paused. "How did you get the name Alex?"

"Why do you ask?"

"Just curious."

She took her time before answering. "My name is Alessandra."

"Then why weren't you called Sandra, Sandy, or Alexis?"

"Because I don't like those names and Alessandra in English is Alexandria and I prefer Alex." She heard the impatience in her own voice.

"Sorry I asked."

When Paul got home, it was extremely hot, one of those early June nights which warned that the summer heat was a zooming force to be reckoned with. He considered not writing that evening. He should go out and buy an air-conditioner. Instead, he filled a glass with ice, removed from the shelf both a red and a green jar of instant coffee. Which should he mix, the regular or decaf? Regular was the victor.

* * *

The day after his father's funeral, Charles and his family huddled around the kitchen table, where over vast amounts of food, important decisions were always made.

"You can think better on a full stomach," his mother would always say.

His mother.

Charles noted how haggard she appeared, older than her forty-one years. She wept and spoke in an arrhythmic pattern, nothing that made much sense. In his sudden awesome role as man of the house, he would have to bring stability to his family, if not financial, at least emotional. Anna and Frank seemed to have tuned Mama out, and after her endless babbling, it was no wonder. They both leaned their bodies toward him.

He opened his hand and extended his arm. "People like us, we don't go on home relief. That's a *vergogna* (disgrace)."

His siblings and mother nodded in agreement.

"So let's start from scratch. Mama, did Papa have any insurance?"

"I think so, look in the drawer."

He pushed his chair backwards. Usually it would slide along the highly polished wooden floor, but today the chair scraped against it, making a gritting sound. He stood up and walked directly to the drawer that housed the family documents. He placed a collection of disheveled papers between his hands and carried the pile to the kitchen table. Charles pulled the chair back to the table. It made the same gritting sound. He slipped into the chair. "As long as I'm going through these papers, let me organize them for you, put them in categories."

Anna was quick to offer her assistance.

"Anna," he said, "you find the birth, marriage, baptismal certificates, things like that. They usually have an official seal bulging out, and a decoration around the edge. Anyway read through everything and feel for the seal. Ask me if you don't understand something."

He was about to hand Anna the papers when he realized that while enjoying his new status, he was making much ado about nothing. He started sorting the papers himself, the lot reminding him of his family's station by what they did *not* contain. No statements from brokerage accounts, no closing or tax statements for property owned, only a meager bank account.

He found a promissory note from a Raimondo Orsini for three hundred dollars with no documentation anywhere indicating how much, if anything, Orsini had paid back since the October, 1943 date. The note was now three years old and Charles didn't know who Orsini was, didn't remember ever hearing the name.

An expired passport and a certificate of citizenship produced the same two pictures of his father. Charles's eyes swayed back and forth between the two pictures, probing them, trying to see if he could learn more about his father. Just looking at them brought tears to his eyes.

Among the papers were several leases for the apartment, each lease with a two dollar a month increase. And tucked between the insurance policy and the lease for the store, a picture of Zia Palma, safe amidst the mess of papers his father undoubtedly knew his mother would avoid. And if his mother had come across the picture, she was so naive as to think how wonderful it was to have family remembrances, would even have smiled before checking the back of the picture for a date, or an occasion.

Charles immediately acted like a magician mixing the papers and shuffling them as though they were a deck of cards while he made the picture of Zia Palma disappear up his sleeve. The loss of his father wasn't so wrenching now.

The family members kept watching him as if they were trying to anticipate what conclusions he would inevitably come to after processing the documents. His next move, his first official act. As soon as he took care of another matter, he would give them their wish.

He shuffled a few more papers, then stopped suddenly. "First I have to go to the bathroom."

His mother, Anna, and Frank sat back in their chairs groaning.

Charles rushed into the bathroom and quickly closed the door. He removed the picture of Zia Palma from his sleeve. He tore the picture into as many pieces as he could and threw them down the toilet. He pulled the chain. None of the pieces still floated on top. Still, he waited for the tank to fill up, then yanked the chain once again, his eyes following the swirling water.

He felt purged.

He went back into the kitchen. "Okay, now here's what I think we should do."

His mother kept blinking as she let out a deep sigh. "Tell us what you think."

"Do you always get inspiration in the toilet?" Frank said.

Charles slanted his eyes toward Frank but decided not to answer him. "There's five thousand dollars in life insurance, that's more than I figured Papa would've bought. It should tide us over for a while. Before that even begins to run out, Mama, you're going to have to get a job. No big deal, a lot of women started going to work during the war. You were born in this country and went to school here, so you'll have to decide what kind of job you're suited for. I learned in my history class that since the end of the war the economy's booming so you should have no trouble finding work."

She shifted her eyes up and down as though she was considering his suggestion.

He stood up, shoved his chair under the table, and supported himself leaning on the back of the chair. "Any extra money should be a safety cushion so we'll be prepared for a situation like this, if it should happen again. Frank'll shine shoes after school and on Saturdays for now." Charles turned to his brother. "Set up a station near the social club. Those wise guys, at least most of them are big tippers, and even those who don't have their shoes shined'll put a quarter in your pocket anyway.

"But you remember," he pulled Frank by his tie, "if they ever come up with an offer for you, you say no. Because if you say yes and they don't eventually kill you, I will. *Capisce*? (Do you understand?) Holding Frank so close reminded him how much his brother looked like Papa. The scene under the dining room table jumped into his head. Charles pulled Frank's tie with his right hand, forcing the knot into his throat with his left. When Frank's eyes were on the verge of popping, Charles released the tie and returned to the business at hand, leaving his brother loosening the knot without looking at him.

"We'll sell the store to some immigrant and that'll be extra money for a while. It won't be much but at least it'll be something. Lots of them are being sent for by their families here and we can make an arrangement before they even come. I'll get a job after school, probably as a security guard, the night shift. It'll give me a chance to study, and on Saturdays I'll deliver groceries."

His mother covered her mouth with her handkerchief while muttering, "A security guard. You could get shot."

"And a piece of concrete could fall on my head. Don't you remember Pat Forlenza? In a few major battles, Anzio, or was it Salerno, saved one of his buddies, had a hero's parade for him, and he's home two weeks and gets killed crossing the street. A hit and run. So stop being silly and stay on the subject."

"Anna's sixteen now," his mother said, "knows how to type. She can quit school and get a job as a secretary."

"Anna's not quitting school. And," he prepared them for the rest of his statement by pausing long enough to make sure he had gained their full attention. "She's going to college."

He leaned his elbow on a dish at the edge of the table and the dish fell clattering onto the floor. Couldn't have timed or punctuated his decree more perfectly himself.

"College!" his mother and Frank called out simultaneously. Charles caught a quick smile on Anna's face.

"Yes, you heard me. Her average is 94, high enough to go to Hunter College in the Bronx, free tuition." He turned to Frank. "And you're going to college, too, so decide within the next few years what you want to study and where you want to go."

Charles took his mother's hand. "Anna's got to be more independent than you, has to prepare herself for the time she may become a widow."

Mama tugged her hand away to cover her face. "God forbid."

Charles stood up. "I have to go to the bathroom."

"What's the matter," his mother said. "You just went, two minutes ago, you have a bladder disease?"

"Maybe I do."

In the spring of 1949 Charles received good news. He was accepted at Holy Cross. He read the accompanying package of materials carefully. Didn't have to declare a major right away, just needed to begin by taking an array of liberal arts courses. But he already knew his major would be English. The acceptance letter was standard except for two additional paragraphs describing how the faculty who reviewed his application were impressed with the articles he had written for his high school newspaper, *The Informer*, in particular, with the piece where he analyzed the novel, *David Copperfield*. He was expected to work on the college newspaper and assist Dr. Francis Bacon in his English courses.

Francis Bacon.

What a coincidence.

His mother fell into her usual sobbing hysteria. "You're going to Massachusetts, Worcester, Worcester," she lifted her eyes, "it sounds like food, maybe then it's not so bad. When will we see you?"

"You'll see me all the time, so many times you'll be glad when I go back. You should be proud, Mama, first generation Italians, if they go to college at all, usually go to local colleges."

"Why can't you go to one, too? What difference does it make?"

"This one gave me a scholarship. And it's a Jesuit college."

"So's Fordham, and you can even walk there from here. Why can't you stay in the Bronx? You know what all the sign posts say, that the Bronx is the Borough of Universities."

"I've spent too much time in the Bronx already. A large part of your education is exposure to new places, experiences."

"Your sister's getting an education and she lives at home." She hesitated before shaking her open hand at him. "And it'd be nice for you to be home, too, to keep an eye on her and her dates."

He smiled while nodding. "Now I know why you're bothered so much that I'll be leaving. But don't worry, Anna knows how to take care of herself."

"Did you ever speak to her about, you know," she blurted a cough, "the birds and the bees?"

"You mean sex, Mama, sure I have, but it'd be better if you discussed it with her, too. It's probably too late now anyway. She's twenty years old, she knows what she needs to know."

"I can't talk to her about that thing. But you make sure if she comes to visit you this summer at your job, you keep an eye on her. Even though you're younger than her, you're like a father to her." Tears trickled down her cheek.

"You worry too much, Mama."

"With girls you've got to worry."

The Maple House was etched into a valley in the Italian Catskills about fifty miles northeast of the Borscht Belt. The summer resort had little of the glamour of the resorts to the southwest, but provided homey atmospheres and enough outdoor and evening activities to make thousands of Italian-Americans leave their hot city apartments to gather in the security of their own ethnicity. As other resorts outdid themselves in the celebrity of entertainers, lush lounges, plush lobbies, and dining rooms overwhelmed with crystal chandeliers and sconces, the Italian resorts competed with each other in the quality and quantity of food.

Charles was pleased to get a job as a waiter at The Maple House. One of his high school classmates, Jerry Acompora, recommended him to his uncle who owned the place. Jerry had assured his uncle that Charles was hard-working, reliable, and honest.

Just before the beginning of the season, Jerry's parents drove them to The Maple House in a '39 Ford, which after crossing the George Washington Bridge, rattled its way up 9W, and churned up dust for three and a half hours on the remaining roads.

The guests were scheduled to arrive the following day for the start of the season, the July Fourth weekend, so for now he and Jerry and several other waiters had the whole place to themselves. The green of the surrounding mountains made the whole place feel peaceful, but he guessed, not for long.

Before he and Jerry had a chance to place their luggage in the waiters' quarters, Jerry took him on a tour. First to the taxidermists' delight, the log cabin casino. Its recently polished juke box daring the attack of fingerprints. The fireplace, stoned up to the ceiling, the black vestiges of previous fires creeping their way up the stone. Someone had forgotten to sweep the cinders blanketing the floor, and thinking of his mother, Charles made sure not to step on them lest he'd leave black footprints. Next they visited the lake, already replete with tight-budded water lilies floating on their not quite heart-shaped green leaves, row boats with moss already growing over a quarter of the way up the sides.

An open gate to the swimming pool area invited their inspection. He was impressed by its size, which verified the number of guests expected, and the corresponding amount of potential tips. Jerry had assured him that since The Maple House provided lodging and meals for the help, and the waiters could persuade most of the girls to do their laundry, expenses would be minimal, and he could leave at the end of the summer with as much as two thousand dollars, all in cash. A hell of a lot more than Charles's buddies got in office jobs that paid thirty-five dollars a week, maybe, and they had to take the subway in the heat to get there.

After walking to the end of the diving board, he jumped on it to test its spring.

Ample.

A freshly painted marker on the concrete floor under the diving board read 9 ft. He visualized himself in his black and yellow trunks, standing on the bottom of the pool near the diving board with the water three feet above the top of his head.

Jerry led him up the hill to the wishing rock which beckoned lovers to sit and fantasize about their futures. Not to be missed were the paths under the pine trees where Jerry assured him girls could be taken for a lot of action.

How much was truth, and how much wishful thinking? He had often felt envious when his friends who went to coed public high schools bragged about the contacts they made there. Trysts on tar beach. Back seats of cars with front seats pushed up as close as they could get to the dashboard.

Would the pine-needled path Jerry pointed out give him his first sexual contact this summer?

Among the first guests assigned to Charles's table was Angela Gallo, a thirty-five-year-old widow with a reputation as a big tipper. Everyone said how lucky he was to be able to serve her. "Last year she gave her waiter thirty bucks for the week," he'd been told.

Wow!

Thirty bucks. And for just one person.

She strutted into the dining room with much fanfare, obviously wallowing in the attention everyone was giving her. Her vanity and cockiness were repulsive. He'd be polite, but not cater to her any more than he would to any other guest.

All through lunch Angela Gallo ogled him whenever he approached the table to deposit food or remove dishes. While scraping the dishes, he felt he also had to scrape her eyes off him.

She kept up the staring, demonstrating a sense of satisfaction when he dropped a spoon and rattled two plates onto his tray. The more he tried to ignore her, the more brazen her stares became.

Dinner brought more of the same.

When all of the other guests had left the dining room, Angela lingered over her coffee and watched him collect cups, saucers, and dessert plates which he transferred to a large round stainless steel tray.

"Chuckie," she finally said, "a good-looking guy like you must have a girlfriend."

None of her goddam business. He wanted to tell her to get lost, but it was his first full day on the job, and he had to remember the rule: Treat each guest with courtesy. "My name is Charles," he said going about his chores and avoiding looking at her.

"That's what I said, Chuckie."

"Charles is the name, and why do you ask?" He forced a smile. "Do you have a daughter or some young girl you think I'd be interested in?"

One up on her, and she asked for it. That should put her in her place.

She moved closer to him, put her hand on his shoulder, and began to trace circles down his arm with her long glossy fuchsia fingernail, continuing the circles especially when she reached his palm. "No, but I have a woman you'd most definitely be interested in, a real woman, an older woman with more, shall we say, experience." She shook her bracelet, rattling a hodgepodge of dangling gold charms.

He looked at her directly for the first time. She had a round face, pleasant, and was rather innocent-looking except for her eyes which seemed to be adept at spotting young virgin men.

She extended her arm. "Come here, I want to show you my charms."

Charles set down the tray he had picked up in his attempt to escape to the kitchen.

Angela lifted the first charm. A cupid with an arrow. "This, Chuckie, my late husband gave me on our first anniversary. He was a real love."

"It's really nice," he said in a deliberate monotone. "And the name is Charles." He gazed at the lighting fixtures.

"This one was for one of my birthdays, April, that's why the diamond's in the corner." She continued chattering about the charms while he deliberately yawned.

She rattled her bracelet again. The next charm was a penis and testicles. She opened her mouth and ran her tongue around her lips.

Angela held out the adjacent charm. An erected penis and testicles. She wrapped her hand around his arm, massaging it up and down, up and down. "This one I got because I'm an expert at knowing how to turn that charm into this one."

She deepened her voice to accompany her diabolical stare. "My cabin's number 412, Chuckie. I'll be expecting you. Remember four twelve. Four...one...two."

"My name's Charles, and I'm not coming. I wouldn't go near your cabin with a ten-foot pole."

"Right, Chuckie, you'll come all right, with your pole. See you later, alligator." Angela swiveled her hips all the way to the door, turning around when she reached it to send him a smile which bordered on a sneer.

Alligator.

Some dumb bitch she was! Bet she thought he was going to give her the in-a-while-crocodile routine. Crocodile. Bet she even shed crocodile tears. She was a viper, a real snake setting him up to eat the forbidden fruit. Who the hell did she think she was? He didn't answer her but picked up his loaded tray and marched into the kitchen.

Screw her stinking tip.

Immediately after he served dinner, Charles retired to the waiters' room, a barracks-type facility housing ten single beds with springs that had to have been the original models for the patent. He searched for some lubricating oil, any oil. Nowhere to be found.

Cigarette burns dotted the tan, newly waxed linoleum floor. In the screens were holes and square screen patches covering most of the holes. The place smelled like a Flit factory. There, on a cracked wooden table in the corner, a Flit cylinder. He picked it up, held it high in the air, ran around the room pumping and pumping the piston into the cylinder, in and out, until it spurted the last drop of liquid.

Angela flashed through his head.

When he went to lie down on his squeaky bed, he noted that the only wall decoration was a pine panel, with black-painted dart boards sectioned off by year, beginning in 1946. Printed names of waiters who had scored and those who at least had some action were dotted-lined to either the bull's eye or to one of the several concentric circles surrounding it. Waiters who achieved neither were listed in the periphery. The dart board for 1949 was already painted on the wall, no names on it yet. By the end of the summer, would his name be in the center, in any of the circles, or on the periphery?

Charles tossed around in his bed asking himself the question over and over again.

The night was steamy, the humidity close to a hundred percent. Moisture was collecting on the screens, and on the patches over the holes in the screens, with some dripping already starting.

He wished for a thunderstorm. Lightning. Torrential rain. Any kind of relief.

By ten-thirty he was in such a sweat, and tingling, gnawing in his groin, he was pleased none of the waiters had come into the room yet and turned on the lights. Hot enough without them.

Angela's fingernail making swirls on his arm.

Just lying still, the heat was unbearable.

The bitch could change that charm into this one.

Jesus Christ. He was getting a hard-on.

Down, down, damn cock. Holy shit, how could such a dumb thing come into his head? Why couldn't he be a normal kid? Maybe he should major in history, business, instead of English, read a little less Shakespeare.

Angela again, staring at him, massaging his arm, fingernailing circles in his palm.

He leaped out of bed and darted outside to run the shower nozzle hooked on the side of the outhouse in the back. Cold showers. The advice he'd received from the priests in his high school. Cold showers and sports took your mind off things you shouldn't be thinking about.

Not very effective he found out.

Angela's finger now swirling down his arm.

For a while he didn't dry himself, hoping the heat from his body would evaporate the water, cool him off. But he found himself fighting off the mosquitoes this sticky, sultry evening, and wished the crickets would shut the fuck up.

Fuck the crickets. Fuck The Maple House. And fuck Angela. No wonder her husband died. She probably fucked him to death.

He put on fresh clothes, couldn't find his comb so he finger-combed his hair.

He wandered around the grounds. Twice he found himself gravitating to Cabin 412 but kept turning around. The third time he passed in front of it. The cabin was more removed from the others and the only one with a light on, a beacon to guide stupid horny kids into the harbor. He tiptoed up to the cabin, tried to peek in the window.

Silence. No movement.

He was safe.

She probably wasn't even there, just left the light on so she wouldn't need a flashlight when she came back from the casino.

He approached the door, tapped it with his knuckles. No answer.

The silence made him feel secure enough to knock, then bang with his fist.

The little cock-teaser. He gave the door a swift kick with his foot.

He turned, took a few steps, then heard the door creak open.

He stopped. A wave of heat surged through him. Dare he turn around?

After a few seconds he couldn't stand it any longer. He spun around so quickly his legs almost got twisted with each other. Angela was standing in the doorway, wearing a smug look which said, 'I would've bet on it.' A shawl draped her body. He forced his eyes beyond her noting on the dresser a thin citronella candle just about spent.

She let the shawl slip to the floor.

Naked.

His eyes perused her body, and he couldn't believe the difference between his cousin Lena's breasts he had viewed from the keyhole years before, and Angela's.

Why had his brain suddenly left him for lower parts?

He dragged his feet across the path to the door. Angela yanked him out of the doorway.

Within the next half-hour he was assured of his place center stage in the 1949 bull's eye.

Later that night Charles returned drained to the waiters' quarters. His thoughts went back to his first confession. Boy, did he need another one now! What was it Father Dunn had said? If your hand causes you to sin, cut it off. When Charles recalled what Angela had done to him and what she made him do to her, his hands reflexively went to his mouth and crotch. And he should have shed his skin.

He shivered.

But as he had always been told, the spirit was willing, but the flesh, weak.

That week he visited Cabin 412 every night. Never slept more soundly afterwards in his life.

Angela was no angel. She had given him an initiation to manhood he could never forget. When she left The Maple House at the end of the week, she gave him a fifty-dollar tip, kissed him goodbye, and called him Chuckie.

He didn't bother to correct her.

The following summer Charles returned to The Maple House. He had made $2200. the year before and though the work was messy and hard, with no days off from the end of June through Labor Day, he felt the money worth the effort.

Anna hadn't had the opportunity to visit him the previous summer but she did come this year. Though he felt close to his sister and wanted to see her, the visit would put an additional strain on him. He'd have to spend every second he wasn't working making sure she wouldn't be reason any of the waiters achieved the bull's eye.

Anna took her meals at one of Charles's tables, helping him set up and clean up. "What were big sisters for?" she said.

"This isn't much of a break for you, working all week and working for me on your vacation."

"No, really, I'm having a great time. Met some nice people, the Perinis. Do you know them? They own the pastry shop on Washington Avenue."

"Since pastries are not in my budget, I never go there. Maybe Mama knows them."

"I'd like you to meet them, they know I'm here alone and've been great about making sure I'm not left out of any activities. They're sitting at one of Jerry's tables." She pointed them out but he didn't turn his head.

"Sure, I'll meet them. Did they bring any cannoli?"

Anna balled a napkin and threw it at him. "You and your cannoli, the way you used to eat them would drive Mama and Papa crazy."

"My table manners have improved since then. Most of my friends at Holy Cross are well-to-do, belong to country clubs. I can't help thinking what they would think if they ever saw Pop eating his fruit with the same knife he'd just peeled it with."

"Aren't you getting uppity. That's probably the worst thing he's ever done."

His brain retrieved Zia Palma's image, all dressed in black. "Believe me, there were worse."

"What do you mean?

"Nothing."

"Well, don't put Papa down. He didn't know any better about table manners, or not sitting in front of the window or on the fire escape in his undershirt. He didn't have your opportunities. Just make sure when the chips are down, you know better."

"Spoken like an older sister."

Anna attempted to lift the tray of dirty dishes.

Charles rushed toward her. "Don't try to pick___"

"Are you ready, Anna?" A young girl poked her head into the dining room.

"Oh, Claudia, come here, I'd like you to meet my brother."

The girl pushed both swinging doors to the dining room. She was wearing a female variation of a sailor's uniform, a white dress with navy blue polka dots, and a navy blue bow across the chest. She approached Charles's station, her eyes on Anna. "My father's waiting in the car to take us all to the movies. By the time the band gets here we should be back."

Then she faced him. "Hi, Charles, I'm Claudia Perini. Anna tells me you live around the corner from us."

He saluted, clicked his heels. "Hi, Captain Claudia, it's really funny that I never saw you before."

"Well, I saw you."

"When?"

"Picked up a pair of shoes for my mother in your father's shop but didn't know you also lived in the neighborhood."

"God, that must've been at least five years ago. How old were you then?"

She dug into her navy blue purse, pulled out a comb, and ran it through her silky brown hair. "Thirteen."

"Well, five years ago when I was fourteen," he said, "I only looked at older women."

Claudia's round brown eyes smiled. "Be careful of older women, they could get you into trouble."

Had she heard about Angela? Impossible. Just his guilt.

Claudia pulled Anna's arm. "Let's go."

Anna glanced at Charles, then at Claudia. "I don't want to leave my brother flat."

"So bring him, too. My father won't mind, he's always taking everyone with me and Gilda." She turned toward Charles. "That's my sister." Then she turned to Anna. "They don't call Pop the Pied Piper for nothing. Come on, I'll help you clean up."

"Did your father bring any cannoli?" Charles said.

"We have a load of them in the guest kitchen refrigerator. Miniatures, regular, vanilla with chocolate chips, even chocolate with chocolate chips on the ends."

"Then who am I to refuse an invitation?"

When Charles went home at the end of the summer, he stopped in Perini's Pastry Shop. He admired the red, white, and green flags that pierced the *pignoli* cookies. It took just a whiff of vanilla in the shop to make him feel lightheaded.

Claudia was not behind the counter but her sister was.

"Hi, Gilda, is Claudia around?"

"Sorry, just missed her, she's here full-time only on Saturdays, goes to college during the week. Going to be a teacher."

"Just tell her I said hello. And while you're at it, give me a half a dozen of those cannoli, not the miniature ones, the big ones. I have to get my fill before I go back to Worcester."

"Sure, half a dozen."

"For starters, and I'll take a lemon ice, too."

"I put extra cannoli in the box," Gilda said with a coy smile and a wink. "From Claudia."

"Be sure to thank her for me."

CHAPTER 7

DID HE REALLY have to write two chapters this week? He was completely drained after having written this one. Paul glared at his calendar. Already almost the middle of June. They weren't close to meeting that August first-draft deadline, and he still had no clue as to where it was all leading, if anywhere.

Discipline. That's what he needed. He dragged himself back to thc typewriter. Perhaps he might not finish the second chapter, but at least he'd begin.

* * *

Dr. Francis Bacon's office was lined with leather-bound copies of books chronologically arranged from Chaucer to Dylan Thomas. Charles observed Dr. Bacon adjusting his pinch nez, his nose approaching, then receding from the paper in his hand.

"This is excellent, Charles, couldn't've done a better job myself."

"Thank you, sir."

"You have a lot of talent, can't stop here, have to pursue graduate work."

"Never mind graduate work, I have to go to work."

"Think you should try for a fellowship of some sort, teach courses to freshmen while you get a doctorate."

"A doctorate?"

"Yes, you should teach on a university level. You have all the qualities. And I've recommended you for a Fulbright."

In the time it took for Charles to absorb the last sentence, his blood went from a smooth flow, to a perk, to a rolling boil. "I, I don't know what to say. That was most kind of you."

"Not at all, it's what I think you should do to prepare for your future, spend some time in England where all this literature took place. Give you a context, a feel for the place, be a great experience."

Charles had never thought of going to England, Europe, or anywhere, but after hearing Dr. Bacon mention it, images of Westminster, the moors, and Stonehenge zoomed through his head.

"And since we're discussing your future, there's a scholarship available for a doctorate in English literature at New York University. Sponsored by the alumni for a Holy Cross graduate who shows promise in this area. Don't have to get a master's first with this program but go straight for the Ph.D. Of course you'd have to meet N.Y.U.'s entrance requirements, but there's no doubt you already exceed them. You and Tim Doyle will be vying for the scholarship which is up to the alumni board. He's also an excellent candidate, but it's not for me to decide."

Dr. Bacon thumbed through some papers on his desk. "Here's the application. Fill it out and return it to me with the supporting documents. I'll forward it all to the board. If the scholarship doesn't work out for you, then we'll discuss the fellowship possibilities."

Charles suddenly saw himself wearing a vest, a bow-tie, and sucking on a pipe. No, not that. The smell was horrendous. "Thank you for your confidence and support, Sir."

"Just keep up the good work."

Charles returned to his room with the application. He read it over. It would take a long time to complete. He'd have to collect recommendations from other professors, articles he had written, documentation of his service to the college and to the community.

First he copied the application headings on a separate piece of paper, completing the items under the headings in pencil. What he didn't like, he erased and rewrote. When he was satisfied, he typed the information on the original application and prepared an envelope addressed to the alumni board.

He made a few phone calls. After the four professors he contacted agreed to write recommendations for him, he put their recommendation forms into unsealed stamped envelopes addressed to the alumni board. He had to remember always to be professional. Then he personally delivered the professors' envelopes to their campus mail boxes.

Within the next few days Charles gathered all relevant materials—a paper presented to the National Council of Teachers of English, articles he had published, research prepared as part of his English coursework, then categorized them with paper clips. He placed all the documentation into a large manila envelope and brought it to Dr. Bacon's office.

Dr. Bacon's door was open, but he wasn't there. While Charles was deciding whether or not to leave his materials on Dr. Bacon's desk or come back to deliver them personally, he noticed another manila envelope on the desk. The name in the upper left corner, Timothy Doyle.

Timothy Doyle, of all people.

His competitor and a great student.

Charles's blood started to circulate much faster.

The envelope was thick, thicker than his. And it was unsealed.

What if he peeked into the envelope, or just felt inside it?

What if he removed some supporting data from it?

Who would ever know?

No. That wouldn't be fair.

But there was a lot on campus that wasn't fair. And when would a Pastore in front of a Holy Cross alumni board, even with a thousand published articles, ever win over a Doyle?

His teeth were grinding with the temptation to open Tim's envelope. He even went so far as to put his hand just above it. But he remembered the cross he always passed at the end of the hallway, the symbol after which the college was named, and Father Dunn's ingrained admonition about what to do with his hand if it caused him to sin.

Charles left with his envelope, leaving Tim's untouched.

By the time the plane landed, it was already one o'clock in the afternoon, London time. Heathrow was a big disappointment. Charles had been glued to the window expecting to see the Thames, Big Ben and the Parliament building, perhaps even catch a glimpse of double decker red buses just the way they looked in the travel brochures. He even tried to guess where the imaginary longitude line that passes through Greenwich might be. He missed out on all counts.

Instead, he found himself a good half-hour away from London, in a hectic airport where he couldn't locate the two suitcases he had checked in at Idlewild. Just his luck they'd be on the way to Paris or Beirut or God knows where in Pan Am's maze of routes. The airline assured him his luggage would probably be on the next flight that would arrive the following day.

Some consolation.

The Pan Am representative arranged for him a free night at a hotel near the airport and provided him with a small navy blue leather bag they kept a supply of for circumstances such as this. Enough bags filled the special closet at the Pan Am terminal to let Charles know that mishandling luggage was a frequent occurrence. When he opened the bag, he pulled out a toothbrush, a small tube of toothpaste, a washcloth, and a bar of Camay, the soap of beautiful women, Charles recalled from the advertisement. Beggars couldn't be choosers.

The only positive thing he thought of was that with the twelve-hour flight and the five-hour time difference, he probably would've slept most of the day anyway, so the airport hotel was good enough. Besides, this was just one day out of almost a whole year he'd be spending here.

The next morning his luggage arrived. Charles couldn't wait to get on a bus to the London flat which for years had hosted American students who studied in England. What he wouldn't do for another hot shower, this time with a change of clothes.

As he rushed up the dark stairway with his two suitcases, one in each hand, he slammed the jagged metal corner of the one on the right into a young man who, rushing down the steps, hadn't had a chance to jump aside to avoid contact.

"Sorry, hope I didn't hurt you," Charles said. He rested one of the suitcases on the steps, freeing his hand to examine the ripped trousers on the side of the man's knee. Some blood oozed out. "Hold on a second, I have just what you need." He leaned his leg on the suitcase, placed the other suitcase on a lower step, sifted through the bag he was carrying over his shoulder, and pulled out a bottle of peroxide and a sterile cotton ball. "After I cure you, I'll pay you back for the pants."

Just his luck. On a tight budget, and on his first day in England, he had to literally and figuratively rip into a Brit.

"I'm afraid I'll live," the young man said. "But before you minister to me, let me introduce myself." He offered his hand. "I'm Mitchell Broderick. Mitch."

Charles placed the cotton and peroxide on the suitcase and shook Mitch's hand. "Charles Pastore."

"Looks like you're going to be here for a while. What part of the world do you come from?"

Charles looked askance. "Do I detect a Massachusetts accent?"

"Sure do. The caaah won't go faaah. Can spot it anywhere in the world."

"I went to college in Massachusetts, picked up a tad myself. What brings you to London?"

"I'm here on a Fulbright, to teach some courses and do research."

"No kidding, so am I, the research, not the teaching part. Hey, let's get out of this stairway, and go where we can talk. I'm still trying to find my room."

"Which number is it?"

"302."

"Come on, mine's 301, right across the hall. I've been here several weeks already so I know all the ropes, where to get meals cheap, clothes cheap, so it's no problem to replace these rags. And where to find broads, cheap ones."

"Broads, now we're talking."

Charles found his room, unlocked the door and dumped the luggage on the floor. He had envisioned his room to be something out of Dickens. Instead it had two chairs with straight legs, actually sticks, which looked wobbly. What was supposed to be a sofa was a board with pillows. Both the chairs and pseudo sofa were lined up against the wall. Sheer off-white window curtains had rips mended enough times to create a design, an irregular one. A light bulb was screwed into the ceiling. One thing was positive. The room was clean.

Charles looked for the light switch. "How do they expect us to study with such low wattage? It's bad enough we're so far north we're going to have shorter days in the winter, but it's always going to be twilight in here."

Mitch stood in the doorframe, and even with the dim light Charles could see his deep blue eyes, straight brown hair he wore back with no part, and regular features. He just about fit under the frame.

"You look disappointed," Mitch said. "But my room's worse, and wattage is the least of our problems. Wait till you see the kitchen, if you can call that closet a kitchen. You have to go into it sideways. You can't open the refrigerator door all the way because it'll slam into the sink. No problem for most people here because the food stinks and you couldn't gain enough weight so that you wouldn't fit. And I've already heard that the biggest challenge is trying to stay warm in the winter."

"My mother packed enough blankets to warm the student body of the British Empire." Charles opened one of the suitcases, pulled out an Afghan and a red and yellow plaid wool blanket. "Look, ugly as hell, but one for you, and one for me. Say, why don't you pull up a chair and sit down, I want to examine your wound."

Charles dragged the board-turned-sofa to the center of the room. He moved one of the chairs to face the sofa, but the chair was so unsteady he returned it to its previous position. "On second thought, we'd both better sit on the sofa, or is it a couch."

"Neither. A board is a board is a board."

He checked Mitch's leg. The gouge had stopped bleeding but had bled enough to have made a rivulet on the trousers.

He squeezed some more blood.

Mitch winced.

Charles wiped the wound with peroxide, took another sterile cotton ball and pressed it firmly against the wound, while digging into his bag with his other hand. "Besides the blankets, my mother packed all these toiletries and antiseptic junk for me, too. Laughed at her when she did it, but between being stuck near the airport for a day and tending to your cut, maybe she knows more than I give her credit for."

"She didn't give you a needle and thread, did she?"

"I have it somewhere but I really want to buy you another pair of pants, could use a pair myself."

"Well, let me change and we'll go find the pants shop, I mean trouser shop I discovered last week. A lot of stuff in the window and great prices."

"And on the way, find me a good place to eat. I'm Italian and I'm starving."

"I grew up in an Italian neighborhood and starving's in their genes. Need a constant food tube. But you're not going to get Boston's best Italian food in London. You're going to have to settle for a meat roast of some sort, potatoes, a boring vegetable with no flavor and those goddam scones. Not quite Italian pastry."

"Then by the time I go home, if nothing else, I'll probably go home slim. How long will you be here?"

"Till the middle or end of May and then I'm going to spend the summer traveling through Europe. Probably my only chance to see it. Going to have to go to work next September. My old man keeps reminding me I'm twenty-six years old and never worked a day in my life. Tells me I was born in December of 1927, two years before the crash. He lost his job soon after, couldn't find another one, and now that there are plenty of jobs, I don't have one. He's always talking about the Depression."

"Are you close to your father?"

"Wasn't so much in the beginning, but now that I'm older, I understand him more. How about you?"

"Pop died when I was fifteen. A heart attack." Charles's thoughts reverted to the scene under the dining room table, the same fury flowing through him. “Never could figure him out. What are you studying here?”

“Literature. I was a science major, biology. Got this Fulbright so I could take courses to make me more liberally educated.” Mitch flipped the tip of his nose up with his finger. “The current thinking is that science courses are not liberating…too pragmatic.”

“I was an English major, here to study more literature. So if you need help with any lit courses, which I’m sure you probably won’t since you were smart enough to get the Fulbright, you know where to find me. What do you want to do with your bio degree?”

“Eventually, I want to teach on the university level, always did. But I can’t take the pay right now so I’ll be looking for a job in industry. After I save enough money, I’ll go to grad school, because even though I already have a master’s, I need a doctorate to make any money in my field.”

“Me, too, I want to teach on the university level. Don’t care how much I make. Never had that much anyway so I won’t miss what I never had.”

Charles looked aside for a moment. What Mitch had said before was just beginning to sink in. “Hm…traveling through Europe. Sounds intriguing.”

“If we can stand each other by May, you might want to come with me. I’m dying to go to Italy. Love Italian food and Italian women.”

“Italian women.” Now he knew why he was sizing Mitch up. “Boy, do I have an Italian woman for you.”

“Yeah, who?”

“Can’t tell you yet. Have to get to know you well enough to see if you qualify.”

The last week of May, Charles and Mitch sent their extraneous possessions home, and they each packed a light bag. The only book they brought with them was *Europe on Five Dollars a Day*. They carefully folded Rand McNally road maps of France, Germany, Switzerland,

Italy, and even one of Austria if they had the chance, and placed them in Charles's bag, the lighter of the two.

Charles was down to thirty-seven dollars, but he tried not to appear worried. "If we go broke we can wait on tables in each town to pay for our meals."

"Or wash dishes."

"I can't wait to cross the Channel. It reminds me of all those World War II songs, and movies I saw as a kid." He hummed the song, "Bluebirds over the White Cliffs of Dover".

Mitch began swinging his shoulders. "And 'How're You Going to Keep Them Down on the Farm, after They've Seen Paris', but maybe that one was from the first World War."

"After reading Flaubert and Dumas, I want to see where Emma Bovary lived and find the lady of the camellias' grave."

"And where Louis Pasteur and Marie Curie did their work."

By the end of June, Mitch and Charles had hitchhiked their way through France, Germany, and Austria, back through Switzerland to the Italian border. The map told them Lake Maggiore wasn't too far away so they thumbed a ride. After spending a full day at the lake tanning themselves and overhearing what seemed like Italian idle conversation, they decided to hitch their way to Florence the next day.

When they arrived late in the afternoon, after the siesta, they found a *pensione* on the outskirts. Not until the next morning did they realize they'd park themselves there for at least a week.

"Jee, this whole city's a museum," Mitch said.

Charles felt goose bumps forming from his toes to his hair roots. "I could spend my life here, just absorbing the David. Felt like an idiot when I first looked at it, tears pouring down my face."

"An incredible work, got me emotional, too."

"Let's go to the Pitti Palace tomorrow."

"I think I read it's being restored."

"What isn't? Then let's try for the Palazzo Vecchio."

"You're on."

When they finally got to Rome, Charles and Mitch had learned how easy it was to get girls on Vespas to give them rides. The young ladies also provided sight-seeing tours and lodging. Chaperoned.

He, Mitch, and their female guides spent a full day in the Vatican Museum with Charles vowing he would go back sometime, spend a week, maybe the rest of his life in those halls. The next morning, they passed by the Castel Sant'Angelo. Charles didn't want to go in. The fortress was part of the setting for *Tosca*, and he didn't want to be reminded of his father's substituting Zia Palma's name in that infamous line in that opera. But they did manage to spend time in the church of St. John Lateran. Heaven forbid two designs on the mosaic floor should be the same!

In the afternoon the Borghese Palace was on their agenda. There Charles stood mesmerized before the "Paolina". He disregarded the tourists' rules not to touch any of the artwork, by touching Paolina's mat. How could Canova have chiseled such soft-looking lines from a piece of marble?

The next few days were filled. Window shopping on the Via Condotti reminded Charles how poor he was. But he did manage to splurge by treating Mitch and their female guides to gelato and cappuccino at Doney's on the Via Veneto. Even thought he saw Jayne Mansfield pass by on the other side of the street.

Charles, with Mitch panting behind, fled up the steps of the Capitoline Square, the smallest of Rome's seven hills, to overlook the bronze-turned-green horse mounted by a bronze-turned-green Marcus Aurelius. Both rested on what appeared to be a huge three-dimensional floor, like a large bulging egg, the genius of Michelangelo's geometric design. A reason or excuse to come back to that spot one day was to visit the Capitoline Museums, the oldest public collection of works in the world, so the guidebook said.

When they completed their two-day jaunt to Naples and Pompeii, he and Mitch returned to Rome, to St. Peter's Square, to attend an open air Mass celebrated by Pope Pius XII himself. After Mass they found a taxi, almost impossible on a Sunday, to speed, with no encouragement from them, to Fumicino and their Pan Am flight back to New York. But not before they had the taxi stop at the Trevi Fountain so they could toss a coin over their shoulder.

Mitch rushed up the ramp to the airplane. Just before boarding he turned around. "Every goddam inch of this boot is a work of art."

Charles grinned. "And our textbooks told us that you people had done it all."

Mitch saluted before tipping his imaginary hat. "On behalf of all the WASPs, or maybe in my case I should say WASCs of the world, I apologize."

"I'm glad you're going to stay with us a few days before you go back to Boston, Mitch. I want you to meet my family, feel we've been together so much this year that you are family."

With a three-hour delay in their flight, even after boarding the plane, it was already late Monday afternoon when his mother greeted Charles at the stoop, hugging him, pushing him away, passing her eyes over him, and hugging him again. He felt embarrassed with her clinging to him while standing in front of the building.

When she let go, he said, "Mama, I'd like you to meet Mitchell Broderick."

"I heard so much about you I feel you're my son." His mother was quick to give Mitch a bear hug which he returned.

"I am, anytime you want to adopt me, especially since Charles's told me about your cooking."

"Music to an Italian mother's ears," she said. "Let's go upstairs."

Charles wouldn't dare tell his mother, but what he really had a craving for after being away so long was a White Castle hamburger, and a tall orange drink and a hot dog drenched in mustard from Nedick's.

They climbed the three flights. At the third landing Charles said, "Mitch wants to teach at a university, too."

"But," Mitch said, "only after I've saved enough money to make the change from scientific research."

"Whatever makes you happy," his mother said.

Nothing had changed in the apartment. The floor waxed to its usual slipping state. Blue-white embroidered curtains on windows so clean that even when closed, they looked open. An ever-present trace of Lysol.

Charles ran through the hall shoving his head into all the railroad rooms. "Where's everybody? I'm away for a year and nobody's here to greet me?"

"Frank's registering today, his last year, thank God, and this was Anna's first day of class." She turned to Mitch, her face beaming. "My daughter's going to be a lawyer, next June. It sounds good, no? My daughter, the lawyer. Make yourselves comfortable. I'll bring you a drink." She excused herself.

"Don't mind her, Mitch. For her it's a big deal for anyone to even graduate from high school."

"Don't be so apologetic. You'd feel the same way if you'd been brought up in her generation."

No sooner did Charles put his laundry in the hamper when he heard Frank thump into the room.

"Can't believe it." Frank said. "Got all my classes just the way I wanted and the professors I...Charles! Didn't think you'd get in today." Frank hugged him and gave him a kiss on each cheek. "Want to be continental."

Then Frank moved him away. He opened his hand, counted how many times it fit around Charles's waist. "Hey, the last time I heard from you, you were complaining about how much weight you were losing eating English food."

"The last month I spent in Italy."

"That explains it, probably made up for it in spades." Frank turned to his guest. "You must be Mitch."

"And you, Frank. Hi." They smiled, shook hands.

"I'm so impressed being in the company of two Fulbright scholars."

"Don't be," Mitch said, "some of the biggest jerks in the world are scholars."

Frank rubbed his chin. "You know, I think you're right, too insulated from the real world."

"I shouldn't let you get away with that," Charles said. "Don't want you to find an excuse to slough off and not get into law school. You don't want to deprive Mama of saying, `my son, the lawyer,' too, now do you?"

"Wouldn't think of it. The old lady worked hard enough to___"

"Who are you calling an old lady?" His mother frowned, giving Frank a light tap on the cheek with her index and middle fingers. "And tell me," she said, facing Charles, "I just noticed the clothes falling out of the bin. How come, Carlo, you can be away a whole year, do your own laundry, and the minute you come home you expect me to do it for you."

"You do it better than I do, and I want you to feel that I'm home."

His mother squinted and twisted her fist toward him. "Smart aleck."

"When's dinner, Mama?"

"Carlo, what's the matter with you. Don't you want to wait for your sister?"

"No, put hers in the oven, I'm ravenous."

"All right, we'll eat. I don't know when she's coming home anyway."

His mother served in the dining room, something she always did when even one guest came. The glass on the breakfront glistened, revealing both the sparkling stemware with gold trim, and the rest of the china not being used for this special occasion. No one would have been able to tell from this distance that the stemware was purchased in the local hardware store.

This place is a far cry from the flats in London," Mitch said. "It's very warm and homey."

Charles stretched his arm toward his mother and squeezed her hand. "That's my Mom, nothing expensive but she has the touch that makes it look rich."

The four dug into the lasagna, salad, and chicken piccata.

"I never saw salads with so many ingredients till I went to Italy," Mitch said.

Mama smiled broadly. "I try to get a lot of things for the salad, different kinds of lettuce, chicory, radicchio and endive. But most of the stores here don't carry endive or radicchio, it's too expensive. I have to pick it up in the neighborhood where I work. What kind of dessert do you like, Mitch?"

"I'm so stuffed I have no room for dessert."

"Give him a little taste of everything you have," Charles said.

His mother's face lit up. She disappeared into the kitchen and in a few minutes reappeared with a smattering of spumoni, Italian cheesecake, cannoli, and a cream puff, all on one plate which she plunked in front of Mitch. "It wouldn't be a homecoming if I didn't get my son cannoli."

Mitch took in a deep breath which he let out with a wispy sigh, though he seemed to be aiming for a grunt. "If I eat all this, I'll be comatose."

"Eat each of them slowly," Frank said. "Let your tongue absorb the flavors. Watch how I do it."

His mother brought out two more plates with the same combination and Frank demonstrated beginning with the cheesecake.

"What about you, Mama," Charles said.

"I'll watch you eat for a while, then make the coffee. American or espresso, Mitch?"

"American."

Do you take sugar and cream?"

"Just cream, thank you."

Without speaking, he, Mitch, and Frank ate their dessert, worshipping every morsel.

Only a voice interrupted their adoration. "Well, you'd think you'd wait for me before attacking the food."

Charles didn't take another bite before getting up to give Anna a kiss and bear hug. She hugged him back very hard.

Then he introduced her to Mitch. Charles noted the way they greeted each other, she blinking occasionally, Mitch staring perpetually. Just as he had anticipated.

He knew after Mitch's absorption with the beautiful face of the woman on the excavated mosaic at Pompeii that he would fall in love with Anna at first sight.

As he hurried down the hall, Charles glanced into his mother's bedroom. He stopped, did a double take. "What're you going to wear for the wedding, Mama? This is only the engagement party and you're dressed to the hilt."

"Carlo, I'm so happy about those two I wanted to wear something elegant to show my happiness." After prancing in front of the mirror, she adjusted her zipper, then her hair.

"I know what you mean. I had a feeling the first time I met Mitch that he and Anna were made for each other."

"I know two other people who were made for each other," she said, batting her eyelashes.

He sat on her bed. "Yeah, who?

"You know who I mean."

"No I don't, think I'm a mind reader?"

"Come on, you know, you and Claudia." His mother tickled him under the chin. "You two remind me of something my mother always said. It sounds better in Italian but she used to say that God makes them, and He mates them."

"Claudia's kind of cute."

"She's more than that, Carlo. She's pretty...Charles. Big brown eyes. Same color hair."

He slanted his eyes toward her. "Twenty-five years I'm Carlo, all of a sudden I'm Charles? Now I know you want something from me."

She continued speaking as though she was not paying attention to most of what he was saying. "Besides, all your friends are married, even your brother, younger than you has a steady girl. Now Claudia would make you a good wife, she's got a lot of good qualities."

"Such as?"

"You know," she said giving him a gentle nudge. "The way she types all those papers for you, wants you to get your doctorate. Brags to everybody about your scholarship, awarded over an Irishman at Holy Cross no less, she keeps telling them. And she's a family girl, loves children, can do everything in the house yet she's got an education. Would make you a good wife, Carlo. Charles. Listen to your mother. It would make me happy if you two would get engaged next. And if you like the way I look for this party, wait till I dress for your wedding!"

"How do you know if she'd like to be my wife?"

"She worships the ground you walk on. Everybody knows it except you, stupid. You'd better hurry up before someone smarter than you gets her."

"I'll take it under advisement."

"Never mind the fancy words. Just do it."

Anna and Mitch led the bunny-hop with Claudia and Charles directly behind them. They were all panting by the time the music stopped. Anna and Mitch returned, hand in hand, to the bridal table, and flopped into their chairs.

Charles's feet hurt. He kicked off his shoes before searching out two chairs with soft seats, and something he could use to elevate his feet.

"That dance could really give you a workout, could use a glass of water," Claudia said.

"I'll get you one, then we can do the next slow dance that comes up after I take a breather." He signaled a waiter.

"Getting me water?" she said in a caustic tone, most unusual for her. "You're spoiling me with your generosity."

"Some people should be spoiled. Maybe you prefer some other drink?"

"No, water's fine." She was back to being herself.

The waiter brought the ice water-filled glass. Charles wiped the condensation from it with a napkin and handed the glass to Claudia who lifted it gently from him.

She touched the rim to her lips, then lowered the glass. "What did you mean, some people should be spoiled?"

"Finish that drink and let's dance."

She took a few sips. "You should have some water, too, you're in such a sweat."

"I need something stronger than water."

"It's my turn to get you a drink, what do you want?" She snapped her fingers at a passing waiter.

The waiter turned around, but Charles, after forcing his shoes back on, pulled Claudia back to the dance floor. "I want to talk."

"About what?"

"About my mother."

"Your mother?"

"Yeah. I think now that Anna's married my mother wants to get rid of me, too. That way she'll only have Frank to deal with."

"So?"

"She thinks I should get married."

Her steps slowed. "I suppose she also has someone in mind for you."

"As a matter of fact she does."

"Who?"

"You."

Claudia stood still. "Well, now I've heard your mother's point of view. What's yours?"

"I hate to admit it, but I agree with her."

"So it was her idea?"

"I'm sorry, Claudia, I'm very bad at this. Never did it before, and am doing it without a drink."

"Why do you need a drink to discuss this?"

"I'm nervous."

"About what?"

"That you'll say no."

She tightened her lips, shook her head. "You know, Charles, I've read all the papers you've written, all your interpretations of literature, and every damn one of them was romantic. Very romantic. But right now you sound like a real clod."

"You're right. It's not me, let me start again." He cleared his throat. "Claudia, I'd be thrilled if you'd do me the honor of being my wife." He took her hand and kissed it.

He knelt in the middle of the dance floor. One by one the couples stopped dancing to form a circle around the Romeo and Juliet they must have looked like. Charles didn't want to take the limelight away from his sister and new brother-in-law. He stood up quickly.

"That's better," Claudia said. "When did you first think you wanted to marry me?"

"When I realized that if I married you, I'd have a lifetime supply of cannoli."

"That's funny, but it's not."

"Can't you see I'm embarrassed, Claudia? Everybody's looking at us, I have to make jokes."

"Let's go." She walked out.

He followed her.

When they had reached the gardens which surrounded the catering hall, Claudia was still way ahead of him. He shouted, "Say, yes, Claudia." She came to an abrupt halt.

Honeysuckle aroma roamed throughout the air, and with it roses and lilacs.

No. Too late for lilacs. Just roses. The mixture of scents, or maybe the pollen, made him sneeze. He felt dizzy, and the humidity didn't help.

Claudia kept her back toward him. "You asked me to marry you but you never said that you loved me." She bent down, picked up a daisy, and began plucking the petals. "He loves me, he loves me not, he loves me, he loves me not." She kept plucking until she had only one petal left. Then she yanked it, opened her fingers, and let it flutter its way to the ground. "He loves me not," she said glumly.

He ignored her. "I knew I had feelings for you the day you gave me feedback on my paper on Fitzgerald."

She lifted her eyes. "What did I say?"

"That he and Zelda should've legitimatized their relationship. If it was strong enough, they should've played by the rules, done it the hard way. And it wasn't so much what you said but how you said it."

"And how did I?"

"With strength and commitment. And now I'm asking you if you'd commit yourself to me."

She finally turned around, looked directly into his eyes. "I love you, Charles, and think I fell in love with you the day I first saw you behind the counter, the day I picked up my mother's shoes."

"How could you be in love at thirteen?"

"If I had been five or ten years old, it wouldn't have made any difference. When you love someone, you just know."

Maybe his mother was right.

God makes them and He mates them.

CHAPTER 8

PAUL WATCHED ALEX with anticipation. His eyes bandied back and forth between her face and the edge of the door he always managed to leave open a little. She was immersed in her reading for a long time, void of any facial expression. Even though she had only a page or so left, he said, "So, what did you think of Charles's first sexual experience?"

Her eyes moved from the pages to over his head. "No comment."

"Come on, you must've had some reaction."

"It didn't seem real, didn't seem that any boy that age would hesitate at the opportunity of having sex with any female, young or old."

"Maybe, but didn't you find it entertaining? And you told me entertaining was what we were about."

Alex continued reading the last pages. "One thing I must compliment you on is that you didn't dwell on specific sexual acts and references to anatomy Charles and Angela were engaged in. If you do that it's titillating for the reader but good writing lets the reader fill in details from his or her own imagination what's only been suggested by the author."

"I noticed you did that in your novel."

"Now, Dr. Barone, if you did that because I did, I will take that as a compliment for isn't imitation the sincerest form of flattery? But it still seems to me that scene was gratuitous. We're going to have to cut, add, restructure anyway. As of now, I have the sense that we'll have to chuck Chuckie."

"Well, we'll see."

She browsed through a few more pages. "It's good you included real places, real products. Editors like that. But did we really need a tour of Italy? But make sure you don't overdo the actual products or brand names, it'll look as if you're quoting from the Sear's catalog. And now that I've read enough of your chapters, you may want to change the name of your main character to one that doesn't end in s. I'm getting dizzy reading all those s's possessives for Charles."

"Actually putting the apostrophe and s after a name that ends in s is one of those gray areas in English. You could just leave it as s apostrophe.

"Well, I will be sure to take that liberty, and please do so, too. And that scene with what's her name, uh, Cynthia."

"Claudia."

"Oh yes, Claudia, it was sweet, Paul, but for some reason Charles seemed prodded into that marriage."

"What makes you say that?"

"Because if he felt passionate enough about someone, he wouldn't need his mother to bring up the subject of marriage. He'd do it on his own."

"Suppose he's shy?"

"I don't get that impression from reading about him, and before I forget, why did you select that example from Fitzgerald? He's part of American lit and Charles is an English lit buff."

"Don't biology majors take chemistry and vice versa? You're not confined to one science, and all English majors have to take some courses in American lit." He sucked in his lower lip. "Guess I didn't do too well this week."

"No, you did fine, I'm just being picky. And while I'm being picky, Anna and Mitch's engagement, it came awfully fast, don't you think?"

"Probing their relationship may not be germane to the story, so far at least." He was growing irritated with her comments, but no one learned from always receiving compliments. "Not to change the subject, but how's Steve progressing?

Alex handed him the text. "Would I ask anyone to do what I didn't? So here are my two chapters. Read on."

* * *

Finally, a half-day off. Dr. Arcuri browsed around Howard's clothing store. He could use a few new ties, and his shirt cuffs were getting worn. Father's Day had just passed and his birthday was months away. Besides, he'd rather select his own clothes.

He picked up a shirt on the counter, felt the fabric between his thumb and index finger. A rich percale. He had the salesman check for his size, 16 1/2, 34. Two were available and he was disappointed there weren't more. He was just about to pay for the shirts when he glanced toward the window.

Oh, no. Just now.

Should he freeze like the manikins, or just duck behind one of the jacket racks?

Sister Mary Joachim, with Sister Mary Ruth trailing behind, was approaching the store. Maybe he could find a quick rear exit.

He put the money back into his wallet and muttered to the salesman, "Put these shirts aside for me, I'll be back later."

He started aiming for the back of the store when he heard, "Why Dr. Arcuri, it's been just about a year since I last saw you."

How did they get in so fast, especially with all that paraphernalia they wore? He turned around and smiled. "Oh hello, Sister Mary Joachim, Sister Ruth, now that there are no Arcuris in your school anymore, we haven't had any contact, at least not since Steve's graduation."

"How's she doing in that," Sister Mary Joachim tightened her lips and slid the rest of the words out between her teeth, "science school?"

He was about to go through the Inquisition so he decided to defend himself before his case came to trial. "Extremely well, and guess what? She hasn't lost her faith yet, in fact it's stronger than ever."

"Still goes to Mass on Sunday?" she asked with both brows raised.

"Of course, we go as a family."

"And the holy days of ob___?"

"And the holy days of obligation."

"And what about Lent? Discipline in Lent helps you learn to control impulses. Did she remember to give up things and do good works?"

Should he bother to remind her that in the Roman Catholic Church, it was the Italians who made the rules that only the Irish obeyed? If he started on that one, he'd never escape. Better leave it for a more opportune moment.

Sister Ruth moved away and began examining some of the merchandise as though she was trying to avoid being drawn into the conversation.

"Sister Mary Joachim," he said, "you'd be so proud of her. Steve said the Stations of the Cross every Friday during Lent. She gave up her favorite meal, pasta. Didn't touch it, even on Sundays and on St. Patrick's Day. And wait till you hear this." He moved closer. "One day during Lent she stayed over her friend's house. They served pasta for supper. Steve wouldn't eat it, and went to bed hungry. How's that for discipline, sacrifice, and controlling impulses?"

Sister Mary Joachim nodded her approval. As she untightened her lips, he thought he saw the potential for a smile. Instead, her brows became one. "You can't be too careful these days. There are many temptations out there, and a girl must be prepared."

"I must say, Sister, of all my daughters, and remember the other two are still in Catholic schools, Steve's the one with the greatest will power. Her sisters would tease her, knew she also gave up ice cream, candy, and cake for Lent, so they would deliberately dangle an ice cream cone or parade chocolates in front of her, and eat them temptingly while describing how delicious they were. But Steve wouldn't give in. It seems the more of a challenge they presented her, the more she liked it."

"Now you remember, Dr. Arcuri, if she's enjoying what she's doing, then it is not a sacrifice. Her reward is an earthly one, not a heavenly one."

No way could he win, so he said, "She also did a lot of charitable works, contributed her own money to buy cans for the Easter food drive, and spent an afternoon each week reading to the blind."

"How's she doing academically?"

"Top of her class. Surpassed Ira Goldstein and Seth Weissman who were second and third."

"Hm, Goldstein and Weissman." Sister Mary Joachim rolled her eyes. "That's really an achievement, but it doesn't surprise me."

"And this summer she'll be fourteen. She's getting a job so she can help save for college."

"But Dr. Arcuri, I'm sure you can afford to___"

"That's beside the point, she has to earn what she gets so that she will learn to appreciate it. Things shouldn't come too easy to children. By the way, Sister, what brings you to Howard's? I see Sister Ruth's looking at handkerchiefs."

For the first time in their encounter Sister Mary Joachim's eyes became bright. "This is the best men's store on Fordham Road. Father McCabe's birthday's coming up, his fiftieth, and the community's giving him a surprise party, so if you see him, don't give it away." She covered her mouth. "And don't tell anyone how old he is, he's sensitive about that."

"Kind of silly, especially for a priest. But you know what they said during the war, `The slip of a lip can sink a ship,' so mum's the word."

She turned as if to continue her shopping, then returned to her prior position. "Just tell me one more thing, Dr. Arcuri."

"Sure, Sister."

She straightened her glasses. "What's the biggest difference that Steve's noticed between going to public and Catholic school?"

He thought about it for a moment. "She had more homework in Catholic school and even though she has good teachers now, she thinks her other teachers were more dedicated."

Sister nodded her head and appeared pleased.

He tipped his hat. "Goodbye, Sister Mary Joachim, Sister Ruth. Be sure to give my best birthday wishes to Father McCabe."

The alarm clock's high-pitched clanking raised Steve to consciousness only after she felt her hand around it long enough searching for the alarm button, knocking over the slide rule and pen on her night table.

It had been a lost weekend with preparation for three exams leading to her falling asleep face down right into her trigonometry book.

She had awakened with a full bladder at three in the morning, not seeming to be worried about the trig exam, sure that her experiences with the erector sets had made her see the rotations more easily than the other girls and even boys in her class. Yet she must have had some concern about the test because when she finally crept into bed, she felt herself rotating like the geometric figures until five. And now it was six o'clock. Time to get up and start a new week.

Lingering in bed was unusual for her, but today her mind was not on school work. She felt like a stranger in her body, a person suspended above it, not inhabiting it. Maybe it was the jolt she had received from the alarm.

Slowly she slid out of bed, shuffled her feet into the bathroom to draw a bath. She removed her pajamas, and with her eyelids half-closed, happened to glance into the mirror.

Then the lids flipped open all the way. The glance became fixed.

Who was this person?

She moved close to the mirror, her face almost touching it, then back to get a clearer focus on her whole body. Steve circled her hand from her forehead down her cheek to her chin back up to her forehead. "My God," she said, "This person I'm looking at, whoever she is, is lovely." Radiant skin, surprisingly clear for her age. And all her features, which had originally taken their own direction, seemed to have come together in a carefully planned design. She couldn't help notice the envied nose she had inherited from her mother.

This is what her father had promised her, the missing link he had called it, to complement her intelligence and personality. Why had she ever doubted him?

While she removed her underwear, she kept staring at herself. Slowly, she stepped backward. The right and obtuse angles had formed arcs, the two grapes surrounded by soft, pulpy tissue.

She touched her skin. Pulled it. Released it. Resilient, like a rubber band. She viewed herself sideways, then faced her back to the mirror just turning her head toward it. Only the stream of overflowing water from the tub made her unglue her image from the mirror.

That Monday morning Steve languished in her bath. She circled the Ivory soap all over herself, discovering parts of her body she had never known existed. She was pleased that the soap floated, so that when it eluded her, she didn't need to search far.

But today her prolonged use of the Ivory, especially when she held it under the running faucet, had produced many bubbles. Steve punctured each one, and as it popped, she felt a new sense of discovery. After luxuriating in the tub, sloshing around, twisting, and turning within the liquid, she finally stood up, and like a ballerina, lifted first the right, then the left leg, landing safely on the mat. She unplugged the stopper, watching the bubbles collect and slowly disappear down the drain.

Steve faced the mirror again. Instead of rubbing the towel over her body the way she usually did, she patted it dry, a soft eggshell not to be treated roughly but gently coddled.

By the time she was ready to put on her clean underwear, she had made an important decision. She would let her hair grow so that it would flow with the contour of her body.

She went back into her room and made her bed.

Something was missing.

She rummaged through the drawers, trying to find the key to the closet. She located the key under a pile of sweaters. The brass key had turned green but was still able to unleash her dolls, her babies. Some had closed eyes, others semi-opened. After giving them each a kiss, the dolls, like Sleeping Beauty, opened their eyes all the way.

She shook the dust off them, and arranged them on her bed. One of the Dionne quintuplets was wearing a frumpy, pink dress, a tarnished necklace engraved with the name, Emily. Then there was the googly-eyed Lenci doll her father had made to order from Turin because it looked like her. Its Bohemian glass was still in tact but the molded felt hand-painted skirt had become even more stiff.

Now came the doll which was to occupy the place of honor. Shirley Temple. Before making Shirley the centerpiece, Steve placed Shirley's cheek on hers. She looked in the mirror. Remarkable resemblance! Same reddish-brown hair. Same nose. Same green eyes. She couldn't rip herself away from the mirror.

That Monday was the first time she had ever been late for school.

Steve watched her father peruse the applications, searching his face for the first signal of approval.

"Well done, Steve," he finally said. "One of these schools should accept you. Your community service, grades from a highly competitive high school, and SAT scores should be enough."

"But most of the other students play musical instruments and I don't."

"Your creative writing is probably better than theirs."

"I don't know what creative writing has to do with pre-med courses. Besides I hate writing."

"You'd never know it by reading your essay. Creative expository writing, the best of both possible worlds."

"It's all useless, all I'll probably end up writing is prescriptions. If I'm lucky."

"Not true. Reports, letters for insurance claims, letters for people who can't do jury duty."

She shifted her mouth to the side, then wrinkled her nose. "Sounds exciting, I can hardly wait."

Attending college in Manhattan. Wow! Steve was thrilled, especially since she'd be living on campus. Barnard, located close enough to the middle of the city, was accessible to so many cultural activities—theater, museums, opera. And the college offered a challenging environment, especially for the five pre-med students in her class. They followed the same schedule, carefully programmed and sequenced to fit in all the mathematics courses. Already worried about the men who would be her competitors for medical school, Steve decided to give herself an edge. She was the only one in her group to major in both biology and chemistry, spending many extra hours in the lab. She kept thinking that for all the time she'd have to attend cultural events in the city, she might as well have been in college in South Dakota.

The number of credits and hours involved were so restricting that she wasn't able to fit Introduction to Literature, a course required of sophomores, until junior year. She dreaded the course, which covered plays, novels, poetry, with long reading lists in each category. Time consuming readings, corresponding papers, and a twenty-two credit course load, including sixteen hours in the lab, didn't mix.

Dr. Sean Clancy never walked into the literature classroom. Rather, he trotted in with an enthusiastic smile. An atypical professor, he was always meticulously groomed, wore different color-coordinated outfits, a collection of stick-pins to match each tie. Steve figured he was independently wealthy; therefore, for him teaching was a labor of love.

He seemed tolerantly polite toward science students, favoring the English majors who would congregate with him after each class to discuss in more detail the assignments they had received as well as novels on the *New York Times* best-seller list. Where did they get the time to do all that reading? Or did they just skim the novels or use Cliffs Notes?

Dr. Clancy had a way of making English come alive. He was the masked reader in *Antigone*, the bereaved father in "The First Snowfall," the type of teacher who loved teaching and his subject to the point of contagion. Steve found herself reading books and poems not required, just suggested by Dr. Clancy.

Words took on new meanings when Dr. Clancy described a passage in a novel or read a Shakespearean sonnet. Steve began to look at the world differently from that of her concrete biological, chemical, and mathematical one. She was forced to think of the world metaphorically.

Mid semester Dr. Clancy read aloud Marvell's "To His Coy Mistress" with the students following along in their anthology texts. He then gave each member of the class the assignment to write a poem in response to Marvell.

Steve reread the poem several times. Who the hell did Marvell think he was? Of all the tricks guys used to get girls into bed, "Then worms shall try thy long preserved virginity" was undoubtedly the most imaginative.

She could rarely keep her temper under control, so why not let off steam and tell Mr. Wise Guy Marvell off? She sat at her desk, twiddled her thumbs, but twiddling gave her no inspiration.

Brain-dead.

She closed her eyes and tried to think of a different subject for a while. Something like when she forgot what she was just about to say, and if she didn't try to remember, it would eventually pop out.

Really, she didn't have much time to devote to this, but she had to hand in something. God damn it, she stank at writing, especially poetry.

She picked up her pen and began to scribble whatever gibberish came into her head:

If there were no eternity
And none to whom we must account,
We could love illicitly
As fleshy, earthy, passions mount.
But we must face eternity
Though that should be no problem here.
He taught us how to live and showed
That life in Him brings joy not fear.
So let us water our conflagration,
And say a prayer our lust to dim,
Resist that cruel, that luring temptation
And rest our restless hearts in Him.

Yuk! No talent.

A poet she was not.

Quite a rotten piece.

Boring, juvenile, dull, so devoid of creativity that she had to dip into of all people, St. Augustine, for some inspiration. She didn't even know if she'd used the right punctuation, but she felt better having told Marvell a thing or two, however horribly expressed.

The following week Dr. Clancy returned the poems to the students. On hers, no grade, no smear of the pen, no big red X right across the page, nor did he say anything to her when handing back the assignment.

She waited.

Still, no comment.

Worse than getting an F.

After class she passed by Dr. Clancy's office. He wasn't there, but the door was open about 45 degrees. She peeked in. Desk cleared. Speckless blotter, not a millimeter off dead-center. Pens lined up on the blotter in size order. Not one book out of place. Every one of them facing the same direction and in size order. She didn't want to be late for her next class, so she left.

At the end of the semester, as she was about to hand Dr. Clancy the extra blue booklet she didn't use for her final exam, she hesitated to consider whether she should've taken the advice one of her professors had offered to his students. "If you're not sure of the answer to a specific question, write all you know about the subject. That should be worth some points."

Her thoughts were interrupted by Dr. Clancy's question offered in a muffled voice. "Miss Arcuri, did you go to Catholic school?"

She was surprised by his question, but immediately answered, "Yes."

He began organizing the blue booklets into two piles, those with blank, and those with filled-in covers. He said with a tone of resignation, "It shows."

Did he think he was going to get away with making a comment like that without an explanation? "What shows?"

He continued sorting the booklets. "I thought about your poem to Marvell."

"That was a good six weeks ago, what about it?"

"It sounded as though it was written by a girl, a woman who's... who's anal-retentive, you know, tight-assed...repressed," he whispered.

She had never heard a college professor, any of her teachers use that kind of language. "Tight-assed. Repressed!"

"Please lower your voice, some are still working on the exam."

A time bomb started ticking in her, about to go off at any second. She'd try to control that big mouth of hers that always got her into trouble. But today she was so overtired her fuse was too short. Five, four, three, two, one. "Dr. Clancy," she whispered back, and then a gleam came to her eye. "'Tis an Irish name now, 'tisn't it, laddie? Irish, the synonym for tight-assed?" Granny Phelan would've been proud of the way she mimicked her brogue.

"Miss Arcuri!"

His shocked expression was enough to make her gloat. "I may be Miss Arcuri, but half of me is Phelan so I know first hand from whence I speak." She tilted her head and flipped up her eyes. "That sounds Shakespearean, doesn't it now?" She had to swallow her laughter. "And if being repressed as you put it means I won't jump into bed with anyone I'm not married to, you may call me repressed, but I call it having high standards. Now you have a pleasant summer, Dr. Irish, oh, forgive me, I mean, Clancy." She strutted out of the room.

With an office like his, who the devil was he to call her tight-assed?

She was half-way down the hall when....

Shit!

She had left her pencils and pens on the desk. Her Parker pen, her favorite.

The hell with it, she'd be damned if she'd go back and get it.

She resumed her walk down the hall, first in a huff. Then she began to slow down.

For it suddenly occurred to her. At the dawn of the age of ball-points, would only a person who was tight-assed be still writing with a fountain pen?

Back to studying science, where she belonged.

Animal physiology.

She chuckled. If there was anything she knew about God, it was that He had a sense of humor. For who else but Someone with a comedic bent could have raccoons, opossums, mate the way they did. And the skunk, emitting an odor to attract its mate? There had to be something stupid about the female species, letting out an odor to attract a male.

That day, Steve made a solemn promise to herself never to be so ridiculous as to ever wear perfume.

The last guests had finally left. Bows, streamers, gold and silver paper, and paper printed with flowers and lace had accumulated on the oriental rug in the middle of the living room floor. Steve held on to her mother's arm, gripping it, releasing it, and gripping it again.

"What's wrong with you?" her mother said. "This is supposed to be a happy occasion."

"I'm happy for Daria, but I'm going to miss her."

"It'll be a year before she's married."

"Just knowing she's going to leave us is depressing."

"She seems so happy, and she can't stay with us forever. And neither will you." Her mother cuddled her, pushed her hair back, and kissed her forehead the same way she did when she was a child. "You have to accept the fact that things change."

She pulled away from her mother and plopped on the sofa. Mom joined her.

"Mom, I've been meaning to ask you this for a long time, ever since Daria told us she was going to marry Bill. How do you know you're not making a mistake, that the person's the right one?"

For the first time that evening Mom's face looked alive, like the face of a mischievous leprechaun. "Why, Steve, have you met someone?"

"Oh, lots of guys, especially from Columbia, they're always hanging around. But you know I can't become serious with anyone. I still have to finish college and go to medical school. But I really want to know."

"There are no guarantees in life, Steve. And it's immature to think that anyone's perfect. You just have to decide which imperfections you'll be able to live with. Marriage takes commitment, work, risks. I don't have any brilliant answers to your question, I doubt that anyone has. It's like my father's business. Investments. Do your homework before buying any stocks, and then decide which ones have the most potential. If you wait for certainty, you'll wait forever, and miss many good opportunities."

Her mother stopped speaking, lowered her eyes. Then she looked straight at her. "All I can do is advise you how to minimize the risks. You don't change people. What you see is what you get." She paused and looked away before continuing. "Two things that come to mind in what you should look for are how he treats his mother and how he behaves when he doesn't get his way because a lot of marriage is not getting your way. And while you're looking, don't deceive yourself. It's very easy to practice self-deception, difficult to analyze a situation objectively."

"Self-deception?"

"Yes, I mean so much of life is what you want to believe. That justifies a lot. And believing what you want instead of what really exists is a double-edged sword. There are some people who say that denial allows us to go on, that if people ever had to face the truth about what they really were, they couldn't handle it. Yet, if they could face what they were, they'd be able to take advantage of their most valuable assets. Is this making any sense to you?"

"Sort of."

Her mother stood up, remained standing for a few seconds, then almost fell back on the sofa. "It's funny. I've heard a lot of my friends say that what attracted them to their spouses in the first place is what drives them crazy now."

"What do you mean?"

"Well, Carol said she admired Doug because he was such a hard worker and would be a good provider." She paused to catch her breath. "And now he's so busy working hard, they're never together."

"And if he didn't work so hard, she'd be complaining she doesn't have anything?"

"You have the idea, but what's really critical is to make sure you have the same values. Values are so important. They're like...like hooks. When you're floating around not knowing what to do, you hang your problem on your value hook and everything falls into place.

"And pay attention to how a man drives. You will note whether he is reckless or careful. It's very telling." She seemed to wander off for a while. Then she said, "One of Daddy's medical school classmates always said that a man shouldn't get married before age twenty-four, because before then, men are guided by their penises more than their brains."

"Twenty-four. I'll try to remember that."

Strange. Her mother was wearing a deep pink taffeta dress, yet she looked pale. Most likely the stress of the evening. And all this running around for the party was making her lose weight.

"Now, Steve, you've been exposed to strong values from our family and our religion. You know what's right and wrong...and there'll always be the self-deceptors around who'll try to lure you into going against your values, the false prophets, the ones who promise easy solutions to difficult problems, try to justify anything without thinking of the consequences." She stopped speaking, closed her eyes. In a few seconds she went on. "Be on your guard against them, and make sure the person you marry knows right from wrong, too." She paused and looked askance before facing her directly. "Basically, it all comes down to the advice my mother gave me. Whenever you come to a fork in the road, go right."

Her mother forced herself up by pushing down on the pillows, then walked toward the steps. She held on to the banister. "I'm tired, Steve. This engagement party was a lot of work even if we did have help, so I'm going to bed. Your father's smart. He's already there." She dragged herself up the steps before turning around half-way. "But getting back to your original question, remember, how does the man treat his mother, sister, women in general, and always check on how he reacts when he doesn't get what he wants."

"I won't forget, Mom, and thanks, I love you."

Mom blew her a kiss. "I love you too, baby."

CHAPTER 9

MEDICAL SCHOOL CATALOGS were accumulating on Steve's desk. She read them, reread them, tossed them on the floor. She really didn't have much interest in spending her life poking into people's orifices.

Disgusting.

And blood!

Ickey. The years she spent her Saturdays assisting in her father's office had confirmed that. The taste of acid, hydrochloric acid, backing up into her throat. Why was she always so goddamn clinical? Why couldn't she just be plain nauseous?

But Daddy seemed more at ease when she was there working with him, less haggard. And besides, after a while she could get used to, immune to dealing with blood and other body fluids.

Maybe.

Steve kept up the cycle of picking up the catalogs she had thrown on the floor, skimming through them, throwing them back.

Then her eyes fell on something.

It looked like another catalog, still in its brown wrapper, tucked under a stack of books on her desk. If it was a catalog, how had she missed it?

She ripped the wrapper. Boston University. Interesting. A special program...five years instead of four, and she could come out with both an M.D. and a Ph.D. She could cover her bets, maybe practice, do research. And teach.

Teach.

She had never thought of teaching with a medical degree. But with a Ph.D.? It would give her an edge at the university level.

What chance would she have of getting into that program? The second female curse. But what did she have to lose? No chance if she didn't apply, and it would be years before she'd have to decide on a specialty or research topic.

But suppose she actually did get into medical school, any medical school? What would she do when she saw her first cadaver?

Faint?

Puke?

How could she touch it, dissect it? Going to funeral parlors, looking at the dead always gave her a sickening feeling, the creeps. And when she was in elementary school and Sister St. Joseph showed a film in the auditorium on the life of Christ, Steve remembered crawling under her chair, covering her eyes and shivering when Jesus called Lazarus from the dead.

Why worry about cadavers? She might not be admitted.

But her MCATs were at the 97th percentile, her grades excellent, a 3.9, thanks to the B she received from Dr. Tight-assed Clancy. She had come this far, and for this she had to give up a lot of dates, fun. She...

A knock on the door.

Firm.

Rapid.

Megan and her mother were out for the day. Who would be knocking at this hour? She hastened to the door.

"Daddy!" She gave him a long tight hug, while glancing at the clock. "What are you doing home at two in the afternoon?"

He didn't answer. With eyes glazed over, he found his way to a chair.

Her heart paused. "Daddy, are you all right?"

"Sit down, Steve."

She didn't like the tone of his voice. She sat at the edge of her bed, her stomach now knotting itself into a ball.

"I'm afraid I have bad news, don't know how else to break it to you."

His face was so twisted and pale it looked like a thick, unbaked pretzel. She stood up and clutched his hand. "What is it?"

"Your mother has a lump in the breast, the size of a walnut and just as hard. I checked it out because I didn't want to alarm anyone until I got the lab results and was sure. It's...it's malignant and has spread to the lymph. I haven't told your sisters yet. I told you first because with your background you'd understand what has to be done and what the prognosis is."

"Daddy," her voice broke, "how long have you known?"

"About a week."

"And you didn't tell me, even to just get it out of your system? Does Mom know how bad it is?"

"She didn't ask and my guess is she doesn't want to know."

Wasn't it her mother who said not to deceive yourself? Advice much easier to give than take. "Is there anything you want me to do, Daddy?"

"There's nothing anyone can do. Just make whatever life she has left as pleasant as possible."

She bit her lip until she could taste the salty blood. "When will you tell Daria and Megan?"

"Soon, I'll tell them soon."

She wouldn't dare cry, especially in front of her father.

She had to be his strength.

Steve pulled from her purse the holy remembrance card she had removed from the small wooden table next to her mother's coffin. A Byzantine picture of the Blessed Virgin Mary holding the Christ Child. On the back it read, "Patricia Phelan Arcuri, March 7, 1956," followed by a prayer. She didn't read the prayer. Instead she carried the card into her mother's room, wedged it into the corner of her parents' wedding picture, and sobbed until the last tear had been dredged from her.

Then she took out the letter she had just received, faced the letterhead toward the picture, and began reading what she had already memorized.

"Dear Miss Arcuri,

We are pleased to inform you that you have been admitted into the M.D./Ph.D. program at the university..." She hurled the letter up into the air, careful to catch it as it drifted downward, not bothering to read the rest. That was all her mother needed to know. Somehow, though, she had the sense her mother already knew.

Steve yanked from the wedding picture the holy card, carefully wrapped and folded the letter around it, making deep creases on the folds with her fingernail. "Did you hear that Mom? I was admitted. A girl, Mom. Your baby. Not that I believed for a single second you'd doubt I'd make it. Steve. Your girl, your baby."

She sat on her mother's bed and re-read the letter. Another city environment. Just what she needed after Barnard. Why couldn't Boston University be in the suburbs, with a farm sprawling around it or directly on an ocean? But with what was ahead of her, it wouldn't make any difference where she was. Whether surrounded by prairies, deserts, or lakes, there'd be no time to enjoy any of it.

Five years it would take her. She'd be twenty-six, if she lasted. An old lady. A little more than half her mother's age.

She'd last all right. Would do whatever it took. She closed her eyes, visualizing the future, to see the day she received her diploma. Tears surged again because her mother wouldn't be there.

Now she had two reasons to push herself to the max.

She wanted her mother to be proud of her, and...

She could never, ever, forget her father's comment about the mustache.

One of her classmates passed by the lab. Rick Mazza looked as weary as she felt. "Are you still working on that corpse, Steve? It's seven o'clock."

"What do you mean, corpse. Cadaver, and her name's Martha. Besides," she sang, "I've grown accustomed to her face. She always makes the day begin." She stopped singing, then laughed. She sang a few more lines, then cried a cry which came from her gut. All work and no play were making her a dull girl.

"Hey, you'd better take it easy. You have battle fatigue...look punchy."

"I've got to do well on these anatomy and physiology exams."

"If you don't get enough rest, you're not going to do well no matter how much time you spend with Martha. Come on now, get some sleep." Rick pulled her by the arm. "But before that, why don't you come out with me for a pizza?"

Oh, Rick was cute, good-looking. Actually, handsome. The greatest harvest of thick, brown hair she had ever seen, a perfect set of pearly-white teeth, surrounded by full, luscious lips. She wanted to have a pizza with him, spend more time with him. She wanted...

"No way, have to study." She had to rewrap Martha in plastic and return her to the refrigerator. "Did you ever think about getting married, Rick?"

He rushed over to her, his fatigued eyes finally glittering. "Are you proposing, would certainly give it serious consideration."

Her half-opened eyes moved around the room. "If I were, I would do so in a more romantic, livelier place. I was just wondering if I'll ever have a normal life, find the type of man my mother told me about."

"Do you want to clue me in, I promise to try my best to be the type."

"Can you be serious for a change? Mom told me to check on how a man treats his mother and sisters, a good indicator of how he'll treat his wife."

"My father gave my sister different advice."

"What advice did he give her?"

"He told her to watch what a man does when he picks up a newspaper. If he goes for the sports pages first, he's a loser, will never amount to anything, so dump him. Not that sports aren't important, but they shouldn't be the only thing he reads, or the first. And my mother told her to avoid anyone who can't pass a water fountain without taking a drink. Anyone who has small tight handwriting, or who ekes out the last squeeze of toothpaste." He paused, wrinkled his forehead. "But you wouldn't know about the toothpaste unless you were already married."

"I'll add those to my list."

"For your information, Steve, I read the front page top right section of the *Times* first, and both my mother and sister will attest to the fact that I treat them royally."

"Oh, go to bed, you big oaf."

"Care to join me?"

"Get lost. Even if I wanted to, I wouldn't have the strength."

Back in her room Steve opened the anatomy text. First she carefully reviewed muscles, bones, tendons.

Then lips. Mere mucous membranes, excited because they're filled with sensitive nerves, touch sensations represented by a large part of the brain. She fingered her lips, then ran her tongue over them.

Rick's lips. What did they taste like? Had to have lots of sensitive nerve endings.

Maybe she should let him make love to her. Just once. But why lose your virginity over someone you didn't love, someone just sexually attractive? And who would want to be in anyone's active or faded memory as a one-night stand?

She opened her hand, placed it on the back of her head, and pushed it back into her books.

Next section. Breasts.

She laughed so hard she had to wrap her arms around herself. What a joke Mother Nature had played on us! How many men would be turned off if they knew they were obsessed over a pair of modified sweat glands?

Steve tittered about all the organs until she tittered herself to sleep.

Steve couldn't wait for her second year of medical school to be over. She'd be through with the theory, and get into the more practical part of medicine the following fall. Just now she was looking forward to the brief two-week summer break when she could be with her family, spend some time with Daria and her baby daughter.

Steve kept asking herself if she would ever marry, have children. To have that happen she'd first have to find more time for dating. She considered the dates she'd had in college, in medical school. No one who would pass her mother's test, no one who really interested her. What might a man she could fall in love with be like? He'd have to be bright, cultured, have a good sense of humor, and high moral integrity.

Someone like her father.

She wanted to share some of her time with Daddy. She missed him so much, even though she wondered where she had found the time to miss him. With Mom gone, and Megan now also married, her poor father was alone.

She would cook him a meal herself, when the two of them could have a kitchen dinner together. Might as well start practicing cooking. Sooner or later she'd need to do it, and Daddy would be a receptive guinea pig.

On her second night home for the short summer break, she decided to surprise him. She went to the market to buy fresh vegetables, the ones she knew he loved—zucchini, broccoli rabe, artichokes. The artichokes she had no clue how to deal with, so she left them in the refrigerator. Then she prepared the other vegetables, mashed potatoes, and a veal roast. Selecting one was a problem. She knew nothing about the different cuts of meat, assuming that the most expensive one would be the best, the most tender.

This was the first time she had ever cooked a roast. She followed the recipe in the cookbook. Make slivers under the skin of the meat. Insert garlic and parsley into the slivers. Season the outside of the roast with mustard and black pepper. To get the full flavor be sure to use freshly ground pepper corns not pepper from a shaker. It all smelled so delectable.

Steve removed the garlic odor from her hands by rubbing them with Comet to oxidize the odor, now leaving her instead with the smell of bleach. The floral-scented lotion she kept in the medicine chest would remedy the situation.

She set the table with a white linen cloth she ironed to eliminate fold creases, took out the expensive china and silverware from the dining room hutch. She placed fresh roses and two candles on the table, hoping it would remind Daddy of the meals her mother had made for him, especially when he came home late, and Steve would peer in on them from the top of the staircase, squeezing her face between the spindles.

The table looked too good to be in the kitchen. She should move the whole setting into the dining room.

No. The two of them would get lost in that room.

That evening Steve put on a starched white linen dress and let her auburn locks cover her shoulders. She didn't wear any makeup. It wasn't a date, just her father. And he was already familiar with what she looked like when she woke up in the morning.

When she came downstairs, she realized she had forgotten to put wine glasses on the table. White wine with white meats and fish, and red wine with red meats, she'd been told. While searching for the glasses in the china closet, she debated with herself about which red wine went best with veal. She was hopelessly ignorant on the subject.

She waited patiently. Six o'clock, six-thirty, seven. Why was he taking so long to come home? The meat would get dry, and she was no expert in preparing it to begin with.

She lit the candles, something else to do while she waited. Watched them flicker, drip. Observed the waves in the air above. Examined the cone inside the flame, yellow, not like the blue cone of the Bunsen burner indicating its more efficient use of oxygen. Damn it, why did everything she thought about eventually be hooked in some way with science?

Finally, the sound of metal scratching metal. Her father was hardly able to turn the key before she rushed to the door, turned the lock herself, jerked the door open, and embraced him.

"Steve, you're all dressed up. Going out tonight?"

"No, Daddy, I have a surprise for you."

"I'm all for surprises, what is it?"

She reached for his hand, led him into the kitchen. "I cooked a special dinner just for the two of us."

The smile he greeted her with wavered. "Oh, baby, that was wonderful, so thoughtful of you. Smells so good in here, but, but I, I didn't know so I made other dinner arrangements."

She felt as though her rib cage had collapsed. "Other dinner arrangements?"

"I have an eight o'clock appointment and just about enough time to shower and change. But don't look so disappointed." He circled her cheek with his finger. "Put it all in the refrigerator and we'll have it tomorrow. I'll come home early for our dinner together, even if I have to cancel patients. I promise."

She drifted over to the table to blow out the candles. Couldn't believe how short they had gotten. With her chin against her chest she mumbled, "Okay, we'll have it tomorrow."

Her father went upstairs. She heard scattering back and forth, and a minute or so later, the shower running.

First she sat at the kitchen table. Then she looked at the stove. The food was already out for over an hour. Better get it into the refrigerator. She wrapped several packages and placed them on the lowest shelf, the coolest.

She had lost her appetite, so she cleaned up the kitchen and went up to her room.

Ten minutes later she heard her father descend the steps, the door close. He didn't even say goodbye, or tell her what time he'd be home. Something he always expected of her.

He was probably going to the Fanellis, patients who had become personal friends, who always invited him to dinner once a month. Or maybe he was meeting with his colleagues for a night out where they discussed the latest in medical advances. It was selfish of her to have assumed he'd be free.

Eight-fifteen. Still about fifteen minutes until sunset. Might be a good idea to go for a walk, see if Mary Lou Bucci was in and would like to join her, or stay at her house and chat about the usual nothing. Just the name Mary Lou Bucci brought to mind those kissing games in her basement. Steve decided to go for a walk by herself.

That evening was the best that late spring in the city could show off. Azaleas, some scrawny, in the meager front yards of the wood and stucco row houses. Too beautiful an evening to spend indoors. Others must have picked up on the same idea, since she found herself accompanied by many people drifting through the streets, just taking in the charm of the oversized almost copper setting sun, bulging out to prove itself a sphere, promising another hot day tomorrow.

She looked into the seductive lit-up windows of the closed clothing shops. She assumed the stance of one of the manikins in the window, trying to project herself into the same outfit. She'd look ever better in it, since she had a better figure.

A few stores down, people were lined up to buy ice cream cones. Bells from a Good Humor truck getting ready to park at the curb summoned the people on the line to shirk the idea of cones, go for ice cream pops instead. Should she have one at all? She hadn't had any supper, didn't want to end up with a sugar high, but so what? This was vacation time, and precious little of it. She bypassed the Good Humor truck, got on the ice cream store line, ordered a chocolate cone with chocolate sprinkles, took an extra supply of napkins and wrapped several around the bottom of the cone so she wouldn't get on her white dress any of the ice cream which was already beginning to melt and drip.

She licked the sprinkles off the ice cream and pushed them up to her palate. Yum, yum. Delicious. Should've had the cone double-dipped.

It appeared as though every light in the Sorrento Restaurant was on. A few people in the lobby were waiting for tables. Large picture windows with white lace curtains framed by gold satin drapes tied back with gold tassels made the place look so romantic. The lights were Victorian, with those large translucent bulbous bulbs, but shouldn't they have been crystal?

Steve couldn't help smiling as she peeked in the window, observing the couples enjoying their...

She dropped the ice cream cone she had just placed near her open mouth, ready to take another bite. Even the napkins didn't prevent the chocolate from making a skid mark down the front of her dress.

A sudden chill passed through her. Maybe she should've taken a sweater to cover her shoulders. Shouldn't have eaten ice cream without having supper.

No. The cold feeling was from something else.

She was finally processing her father dining with Al Giordano's widow, her hand on the table, his hand over hers.

Steve couldn't move, her eyes stuck on the two of them. She finally turned around and accidentally stepped on the ice cream cone, causing her to slide over it and land on the pavement. Several people came to assist her but she ignored them, pushed herself up, and limped as quickly as she could all the way home.

Steve closed the door behind her. Her ankle was killing her but she managed to hobble up the steps to her room and flop on the bed, massage her ankle before elevating it on two pillows.

Mrs. Giordano.

Who did that bitch dare think she was, going out with, dating her father?

And where did her father get the audacity, the nerve, to date another woman?

Steve held her head, then thunked it onto her pillow. She had to block out the image, her father smiling, his hand on the widow's.

Why didn't he tell her where he was going, sneaking out of the house like a teenage boy, going to pick up his girlfriend, maybe even anticipating the back seat of his father's car.

Oh, God, she slapped her forehead, is that what they were planning after dinner?

How could he do this to her mother, to all of them? How could he be so ungrateful to Steve for following in his footsteps? Her stomach was tight, contracted. She felt like throwing up and rushed into the bathroom, heaving repeatedly with nothing coming out.

She washed her face with cold water and flopped into bed again. When she calmed down, she began to think more rationally. Her father was a widower, two years already. Mrs. Giordano, a widow. What was wrong with their having dinner together, or in having a friendly relationship?

As long as it remained friendly.

Yet, what if they decided to marry? There was nothing wrong with that, either.

But why did the whole idea make her feel so crushed and deceived?

The semester before her fifth year of medical school, Steve had to focus in on a research topic for the Ph.D. part of her program. A field that fascinated her was genetics, its potential for good, and evil. A real challenge. What about creating a microorganism that could live in the mouth and feed on tartar and plaque? A low calorie fruit, a deer, a rabbit that ate only weeds. Better yet, find a genetic cure for cancer, the kind her mother had.

The dean of the medical school recommended that for a mentor she contact Dr. Edward Marchese, who was teaching a course there, had a successful medical practice, and who himself had published in her area of interest when he continued to study for his Ph.D.

She made an appointment to meet with him and beforetime prepared some possible topics for research. She also made sure she'd look the part, so she donned a lab coat.

Dr. Marchese darted into the office fifteen minutes late. "Sorry. There was an emergency." He motioned her to a chair.

Always the excuse of an emergency. Secretaries primed to use that word. Her experience with emergencies was doctors' spending too much time in the hospital at lunch not wanting to interrupt their discussions about patients or procedures or the government's possible involvement in health care. At least, that was what Senator John F. Kennedy was proposing if he became President.

She decided not to waste any more time, be direct. "Thank you for offering your time to help me with my research."

"If somebody didn't volunteer to help me, I wouldn't be where I am. I'm sure some day you'll do it for someone else, too, maybe more than once."

"I'd really enjoy that." She had to overwhelm him with her seriousness of purpose, be more serious than the men would be. "What I have in mind are several possibilities…altering genetic makeup by drugs, isolating genes which cause different kinds of disease, tracing DNA in prehistoric animals." She opened her briefcase and lifted the pounds of papers she had accumulated and neatly categorized with large paper clips.

He removed the clips and index-fingered through the papers. "Your preliminary research is quite impressive, what's your name again?"

"Steve Arcuri."

"Very impressive, Miss Arcuri."

He leaned back in his chair, put on his glasses, took his time reading one of the topics. "I have to admit that when I first met with Dr. Epstein, he was my mentor, I didn't have a clue as to what I wanted to do."

She really wanted to stay focused on her own work, but it couldn't hurt to seem interested, be cordial. "What did you finally settle on?"

"The effect of different types of mechanical procedures on bone healing. That's how I ended up in orthopedic surgery."

"Orthopedic surgery! I thought you were a geneticist."

"My love is genetics, keep up with it as much as I do with my field. Such potential for curing diseases." He rose. "It's been my experience that if you're interested in one of these topics more than another, it'll be easier for you to cope with the research it entails. So I must ask you, Miss Arcuri, which is of the most concern to you now and possibly in the future?"

Steve looked away then returned her eyes to him. "Probably something to do with gene identification."

"Then let's go for it. Let me look over more carefully what you already have and I'll call you with suggestions within a week." He returned the gene identification research pile to her after he replaced the paper clip. "Write your phone number right on the top page and I'll let you know when we can meet again."

Why couldn't she just tell him and he write it? Damn doctors, used to being catered to. But she scrawled the number, then gave him back the papers which he placed into a folder.

"Don't want to wait too long," he said. "These things can drag on and we have to get you finished by February, preferably before."

She counted on her fingers. "That'll give us the summer and seven more months. But you're right, the sooner we start, the better." She stood up, and so did he.

"Before you go, Miss Arcuri, would you mind if I asked you a personal question?"

"Of course not."

He paused. "You're an extremely feminine woman. Why do you call yourself Steve?"

The response she knew by heart. Had reiterated it often enough. All she had to do was spew it out again. "My real name's Stefania, after my paternal grandfather. I was the third daughter. After my parents named my two older sisters after my father's mother and mother's mother, they probably thought they'd never have a son which they didn't, and my grandfather, Stefano, would have no namesake." She found herself speaking too rapidly so she stopped. After a brief pause she said, "Are you following me?"

"I am, but I asked you why you call yourself, Steve. My mother's name was also Stefania and that's what we called her."

"Yes, but when she was born her father probably wasn't as disappointed as mine that I wasn't a boy."

Dr. Marchese took a long look at her. "I can't imagine anyone being disappointed about that."

Steve looked back at him, feeling herself turn crimson. She didn't know what to do so she immediately collected her remaining papers categorized perpendicular to each other, reordered them parallel, and filed them into her briefcase.

She shook his hand. "Thank you, Dr. Marchese, for agreeing to take me on. I hope I won't disappoint you."

He still had her hand in his. "I'm sure you won't."

Two days later Steve received a message. Dr. Marchese had checked some additional research on her topic and had a proposal she might like to consider.

She made another appointment to meet with him, and was sure to wear her lab coat again. This time he wasn't late.

"Miss Arcuri, I had these articles in my file cabinet at home. They should give you some contextual background."

"Thank you, and since the last time we met, I found a few more articles that were just published. They helped me concentrate on a topic I think could use more research."

"It's interesting, coincidental that you came up with that because it's strikingly similar to the one I'm suggesting."

He allowed her to read what he had already written as if to prove what he had just said.

"Well, they say that great minds run in the same direction, so let that be a compliment to both of us."

"I agree. Now that we have a topic to work with, you have to fine tune it, and we have to discuss in detail how you're going to implement it."

"I spoke to Dr. Atwell yesterday. He expressed interest in my topic and'll make room for me in his lab."

Dr. Marchese's brows edged up an inch. "He's an excellent scientist, but keep your eye out for him. As long as you will be my mentee, I feel responsible for you so I must warn you___" Dr. Marchese stopped abruptly. "Maybe it's not professional for me to say this, and you never heard it from me, but I must warn you that he has a reputation as a womanizer."

She acknowledged his comment with a nod. "Do you always feel responsible for your mentees?"

"Actually, yes, especially since you're my first female mentee, just as responsible as I felt for my mother."

"Why your mother?"

"She was an extremely attractive woman when she was younger and was widowed early so I had to keep the men away from her."

"She never remarried?"

"No."

Suddenly she was thrust back in the Sorrento Restaurant, staring into the window. Her father and the widow, Mrs. Giordano, holding hands. "How did you know she didn't want to get married again?"

"She told me so, because if she had, I would've helped her out."

"You mean you would've screened the candidates more carefully."

"Precisely, just as I'll do with anyone who offers to work with you."

"Just what I need...another father."

He looked skeptical. "Don't you and your father get along?"

She gasped. "Of course we do, we're very close. I'm even going into medicine because that's what he wanted, and I can help him with his practice."

"So he's a physician, too." He hesitated. "Is that why you said you didn't need another father?"

"No, that just slipped out. You're not like him at all."

"We've only spoken in total a few minutes and you already know what I'm like?"

"I didn't mean that, either. It's just that I probably started out in medicine because I wanted to please my father, but now that I'm in it, I want to please myself. And I'm sorry, it wasn't fair of me to imply that I knew what you were like. I really don't know that much about you."

Dr. Marchese clasped his hands, placed them under his chin. "How would you like to remedy that, future physician?"

She looked down. "Well, since you're going to be my mentor, we'll be working closely, and maybe that would help us understand what's expected from each other."

"I totally agree. Why don't we start by having dinner tomorrow evening?"

In her anxiety to impress Dr. Marchese regarding her seriousness of purpose, she hadn't bothered to really notice him. But when he stood in the lobby of the dorm to greet her as she came down the steps, she observed behind his dimpled smile, sturdy teeth that had to have been raised on Italian bread. His nose was well carved, his hazel eyes had a charming sparkle, and his light brown, almost blonde hair looking as though he had just returned from the barber shop. His clothing was so well coordinated that she wondered if he did it on his own or if someone else laid it out for him.

"You do look different without a lab coat," he said.

"Better or worse?"

"Much better. Infinitely better."

"That's a good start to the evening. Don't want to spend the whole time talking about DNA."

"No way, what kind of food are you in the mood for?"

"Chinese, I'm a cheap date." Oops, she hoped he wouldn't take that the wrong way.

He simultaneously opened his mouth and took a quick breath. "Do you expect me to take you into the red light district?"

Her hand fled to her face. "Is that where the Chinese restaurants are? Goes to show how much socializing I've been involved in the past four years. But really, I have such a craving for Chinese food, could we go anyway?"

"I'm in the mood for Italian, but Chinese is fine with me."

Why did she suddenly find herself testing him according to her mother's criteria? After all, not getting your way about the choice of restaurants wasn't really earthshaking. But she had already noted that his driving from the dorm to the restaurant was very smooth and cautious.

Fung-Fang's had the most colorful window display of all the restaurants on the block. Inside was no let-down, either. Huge different-designed hand-fans were strung along one of the walls. Silk prints, most with peacocks, adorned the others. Hanging from the ceiling, tinkling metal mobiles. Tinkling subtly. If the restaurant actually was in a red light district, she couldn't tell from the inside.

"This is the only Chinese restaurant which has a full bar," he said.

"Then you've been here before?"

He nodded.

"In the red light district?" She smiled when she said it so he wouldn't feel as though she was trying to entrap him.

His response was a laugh from the belly.

Column A and Column B presented their choices. Steve wanted all of them but settled for wonton soup, egg rolls, fried rice, and moo goo gai pan. Ed ordered chicken chow mein, spare ribs, and moo shoo pork. She needed to instruct him on a proper diet, but what she was eating was no model, either.

The waiter asked if they were expecting anyone else to join them at their table for four. They shook their heads. He removed the two additional place settings.

A daiquiri and a scotch on-the-rocks arrived at the table. She had no idea what a daiquiri was. It was the first drink to enter her head when the waiter asked what she wanted. She deduced that Dr. Marchese's was the drink with the ice cubes. She couldn't hold any liquor, fell asleep immediately when Daddy had made her his cough medicine concoction with whiskey, honey, and lemon. It was the sleep that cured her. But tonight especially, she didn't want to appear like a stick-in-the-mud. She hoped she wouldn't make a stammering fool of herself.

"I'd like to propose a toast," Dr. Marchese said, lifting his scotch. "To Crick and Watson, without whom we wouldn't be dining together this evening."

She smiled and raised her glass to click his. "To Crick and Watson." She touched the drink to her lips, pretending to take a sip of the daiquiri that smelled like a lime. Harmless enough.

When the food arrived, Dr. Marchese requested chopsticks. The waiter brought two sets on a tray. Dr. Marchese picked up his set. She indicated to him she didn't know how to use them. He returned his chopsticks to the tray, then picked up a fork. They immediately tasted each other's choices, blending little by little half their meals on each other's plates.

Strong tea diluted the hot mustard. Steve's eyes were tearing, her nose running. "When I pass the boards, I'm going to recommend hot mustard to all my patients who have sinus conditions."

"Never thought of it before, but sounds like another of those natural Chinese cures. Miss Arcuri, you'll make a great physician."

"I hope so." She paused. "How long have you been a physician?"

"Since 1950, spent some time in Korea after that."

"Oh."

"Bet to you it seems like a long time. You think I'm old, don't you?"

"That's not really why I asked."

"Then why did you?"

"You don't look old enough to have the experience to be a mentor."

"I'm thirty-four, is that old enough?"

"I...I guess so."

"So tell me, Miss Arcuri, you seem old enough to have a boyfriend. Someone as attractive as you surrounded by all these men. You could have your pick."

She was getting woozy, wished he'd go to the men's room so she could dump the rest of the daiquiri into her water, or into the bud vase with the carnation, though it might be a dead giveaway if the flower suddenly wilted. "I've had to stay focused, didn't have time to get serious with anyone. Maybe now that the end's in sight." She bent her head and made sure her eyes were anywhere but connecting with his. "And how come someone thirty-four isn't married?" No sooner did she say that when her father's medical school classmate's advice that a man shouldn't marry before age twenty-four came back into her head.

"Was engaged once, but it didn't work out. Besides, my mother was very ill, needed my attention. She had worked very hard to put me through medical school and between building my practice and taking care of her and my sister, I had too many obligations for a personal life."

"Your sister?" Had he eavesdropped on the conversation with her mother? How does he treat his mother, his sister? Did he have more than one? And he certainly didn't seem like the type Rick Mazza had warned her about, the kind that headed for the sports pages first.

"Her husband was a pilot, killed in a plane crash. She has two kids and I sort of substituted as a father for them."

"Is that how you see yourself, as a father?"

"That depends on who I'm interacting with, certainly not toward you."

She didn't know how to respond so she pushed her plate away. "I can't believe how much I ate. The only thing I know is I'll be starving in an hour."

The waiter delivered two fortune cookies on a small round silver platter.

Dr. Marchese handed her the platter. "Take one."

She picked the cookie on the right. He took the other. They both opened the cookies and quickly glanced at their messages.

"What does yours say?" Dr. Marchese said.

"Won't tell you, read me yours first."

"Not fair, you picked first."

"No."

"Come on, that's why I wanted you to go ahead of me."

"Absolutely not."

He puffed out a quick breath. "Well, if you must know, it says, `Romance is around the corner.'"

She was certain his eyes were a little too probing.

Dr. Marchese tabled his message directly in front of her, facing it upward. Did he do that because he thought she didn't believe him, wanted her to check it? She didn't look at it, just said, "I trust you."

He waited a few seconds. "What does yours say?"

Blood rushed to her face. She couldn't speak the words, just handed him the slip she had squeezed closed between her thumb and index finger immediately after reading it.

"I'm beginning to think that the woman I'm mentoring doesn't know how to read." He opened it. "New love will come into your life." He took her hand. "Do you think this waiter knows us?"

She squeezed his hand. "Why don't you ask him?"

Dr. Marchese summoned the waiter. His name was embroidered in red, on his white jacket, which surprisingly, with all the activity in the restaurant, had not even a speck of food on it. "Yen, do you know us?"

"Know you? No sir."

"How did we get these particular fortune cookies?"

Yen's eyes floated around the restaurant. He moved his head in all directions before whispering, "I'm not supposed to tell anyone this but everyone knows it anyway. Experience tells me how people feel about each other by the way they eat, and the way they look at each other. We have a lot of different messages in the back, and the way you two look at each other told me which ones to stick in the cookie."

That evening Steve noticed Dr. Marchese left Yen a most generous tip.

The weather couldn't have been more perfect. Warm sunshine. No clouds in the blue sky, not even the fair weather cumulus variety.

Ushers, formally dressed, handed the parents, relatives, and friends their programs before guiding the early-comers to their folding chairs, the rest of the guests to the bleachers on the football field of Boston University. It seemed as though the film and camera manufacturers had struck gold, with most of the guests carrying one, and sometimes several cameras. A white tent protected the platform for the dignitaries.

The day was one of elation for Steve. Too much to handle for one day—her M.D., her Ph.D., and the engagement ring, with a marquise diamond from knuckle to knuckle Ed had placed on her finger just before the ceremony began. She kept searching the audience for her two favorite men.

Guests fortunate enough to have anticipated how cruel the sun could be over an extended period of time carried umbrellas. Others sheltered their faces and heads with the white, 8x11 programs. One by one, umbrellas opened until a sea of them made it impossible for Steve to locate the section where she knew her family would be.

Daddy and Ed had spoken to each other on the phone several times, even before he had asked her father's permission to marry her, but this was the first time the two would actually meet. With her family arriving just before the ceremony, she hadn't had a chance to introduce them to each other herself, but had pre-arranged that they would all meet afterwards at Marsh Chapel.

As the undergraduates were awarded their degrees, Steve kept herself entertained reading the program. Next the degrees were conferred to the graduate students. Only fifteen people received the M.D. and Ph.D. degrees and she was the only female. Her eyes became blurred. All she could think of was her mother. "I know you're here, Mom," she murmured. "I can feel how proud you are of me, and I'm sure you'd approve of Ed. He measures up to all your criteria."

She kept feeling the horizontal black velvet strips on her sleeves, and moving her left hand to the appropriate angle to catch the sun so that it would make her diamond refract a rainbow on her program. She had predicted her future.

A perfect career, a perfect marriage.

And most important of all, her father was ecstatic about both.

It took a while after the ceremony to forge through the crowds to find Megan, Daria, their husbands, her father, and Ed.

She hugged and kissed each one in turn.

"It seems that after all these years I'm not going to have another Dr. Arcuri too long," her father said. "I can wallow in it for only a few months before you become Dr. Marchese." He forged his way between her and Ed and extended his arms around their shoulders. "I'm so happy for both of you."

Steve moved her shoulder from under her father's arm and turned to clutch him so hard that she could feel his heart beating. So excited and tearful, she hadn't seen him very clearly at first.

But something about him was different.

What was it?

She moved him away.

Then the tears cascaded when she realized that this was the first time she had ever seen him without a mustache.

CHAPTER 10

PAUL RAN HIS finger through all the pages they had written, already worrying about the really time-consuming part, the revision. As he stared at his office door which he made sure was always slightly ajar when he and Alex were together, he forced himself to put thinking about revision out of his mind. "These last four chapters seem to flow. I really enjoyed reading that scene where Steve sees her father, even though he's a widower, dating another woman and she flips."

"When you're used to seeing two people together all the time, especially in a loving relationship, that can be a shocker."

"Not such a shocker as having a father involved with another woman while his wife's still alive." He shook the papers in his hand at her. "And far be it from me to tell a published novelist how to write, but you criticized me for matching up Anna and Mitch so quickly, and it doesn't seem so far that their relationship will be as important as Steve and Ed's. I mean, there wasn't much of a buildup. Slam, dunk, they're engaged."

"Make a note in the margin. After we get the whole story on paper, I'll reconsider if we need more detail."

He penciled in "detail" followed by a question mark.

"Congratulations, Paul, I noted that you finally kept the cumbersome s's out of the possessive when referring to Charles."

"I thought we'd agreed to take that liberty, even though it's not quite kosher. Didn't we?"

"Indeed, we did."

"Well, they're all grown up, settled, now what?"

"What I told you before, about your passion. How they react to the cultural change that's coming. Use your imagination. Take risks. You know that statistically academics in general don't tend to be risk-takers, so we'll have to buck that trend along with all the conventional wisdom. Maybe it's time to blend the stories."

"Fine, but if we do, we can't do it independently anymore. We'll have to schedule more meeting time and write it together." He looked toward the door, routinely checking whether it was still open a few inches. "Suppose I try to come up with something from his point of view, you do it from hers. There's got to be something we've written already that can connect them, make the stories come together. Let's read through what we wrote and find the link. Look hard."

"Good idea, then we'll run with it. And, Paul, we have to give hints as to what's coming down the pike. That keeps the readers hooked."

"Hints?"

"Hints."

"Okay, let's get to work."

* * *

Dr. Wayne Ashley sent for Charles. Wayne kept reading the pages in his hand, slowly placing one page behind the other until he was back to the first. "Thank you for forwarding this resume, this Broderick fellow looks like a highly qualified candidate."

Charles was delighted. "He is, I met him in London when we were both on Fulbrights, and he's a great guy, too. Always wanted to be a college professor, has a strong background in biology and good experience in industry."

"I noticed he listed your name as a personal reference."

"I certainly can vouch for him, he's my brother-in-law."

Wayne's eyes became slits. He turned down the volume on his voice. "Now, Charles, I wouldn't let that be common knowledge around here, especially before he's hired. Even later it may not be good for you, both of you, especially before tenure. So let's eliminate your name as a reference."

"Never thought about it, but you're probably right. Now I want you to know that Mitch is very much like Dave, has the same strengths, would be a wonderful replacement."

"Dave'll be difficult to replace. It's tragic what happened to him, leaving a wife and young family like that. He'll be missed." Wayne closed his eyes, drooped his head, and shook it sideways slowly.

"Having his office next to mine makes it even worse for me. Dave'd come in and chat, a great friend. But when you meet Mitch, you'll find he has many of the same positive attributes as Dave."

"Good, the faculty can be the bane of existence for an academic dean. It'll come back to haunt me if we don't get the right person, end up with some pain-in-the-ass. We have enough pains-in-the-ass around here already, so do the impossible. Take your time, but get a replacement as soon as possible. It's tough when this happens mid-semester. Those adjuncts are holding things together for the moment but Chester's on my back to move on this quickly and settle it before Thanksgiving which brings me to another problem, Charles." He removed his glasses and massaged the top of his nose with his middle finger. "I can't get the Democratic Convention out of my mind."

"What about it?"

Wayne rolled his chair next to where Charles was sitting. "I'm sure you recall what a ruckus the Women's Political Caucus made at that convention this summer. I can feel the rumblings around here already, like to pride myself in being ahead of the times, anticipate the future, avoid problems. So I thought that for this position we'd interview some women, if any should apply. You know, keep up appearances, let it look as though we're seeking them out, giving them a chance. This way if the subject ever comes up, we can verify that we interviewed them but didn't find them as qualified as your brother-in-law." He winked at Charles while nudging him with his elbow.

"Some conniver you are. Now I know how you got into administration and have stayed in it so long."

"We have to do a search of course." Wayne's voice became almost inaudible. "But you know how these things go. We already have the person we want in mind but have to go through the motions. It'll be on record, documented, that we were open and gave these broads a chance. Shut'em up." Wayne put a hand on Charles' shoulder. "Now this is how I see it. We'll get a committee together, self-nominating. We'll have to include Bob Lucas because he's the chairman of the science department, maybe a few others in the department, and you know how that department feels about having women. You'll volunteer to serve, get your cronies to do the same. When they ask you to chair the committee, first you put up a fuss, then reluctantly agree. Everybody hates to chair these damn things. Once the committee's in place we'll put an ad in the *Times* and the *Chronicle*, make sure your name goes into the ad as the person they can forward their vitae to, and give them a week for a deadline. You can screen them first, maybe eliminate or," he put his hand over his mouth, "conveniently misplace some resumes that may seem competitive with your brother-in-law's, interview some people, especially the women, very rigorously if any show interest, and the rest will be in your hands. The committee'll pick up your enthusiasm about your brother-in-law and he'll be a shoo-in." The gleam in Wayne's eyes disappeared. "And remember, we never had this conversation. If you bring it up, I'll deny it."

"What conversation?" Charles stood up, turned on his heel, and left the office holding an extra copy of Mitch's resume. He'd have to tell Mitch to provide a different copy, one with someone else's name to replace his on the personal references list.

The resumes kept pouring in, two hundred three all together. Looking over them, Charles did feel some guilt. Suppose he was in the same position, sending his resume as he did when he first applied to Graham. Wouldn't he be upset if he knew that after coming in for the interview and anticipating getting the job, someone else had already been lined up?

But this was the way the system worked. Besides, he knew Mitch was outstanding, so committed he would be willing to give up an $8,000 a year salary differential to teach in a college. And of paramount importance, Mitch was family.

Charles perused the resumes, eliminating those candidates who didn't have doctorates. That brought it down to one hundred forty-seven, still a monumental task. In that group three were women. After reading their resumes, only one was qualified for an interview.

Born in the Bronx. Probably spoke with a Bronx accent. Thirty-eight years old.

Strange that an Italian-American female would have a doctorate, two doctorates.

A female scientist, cold, clinical. A physician. A ghoul.

He looked further. Married to a physician, probably a pathologist. Another ghoul.

Two children, a girl nine, a boy six. He could see the kids already. Looked like their parents. Stubby, with pasta bellies. Thick glasses, dark black hair.

Damn it. He hated when people stereotyped him. Why was he doing it himself, and to somebody he'd never met?

Charles threw the woman's resume into an empty space on his desk, creating its own separate pile.

The committee of five men including Charles reviewed the remaining resumes, and ranked them in order of interest. The five applicants with the highest rank were scheduled to be interviewed. Among them was Mitchell Broderick.

And Stefania Marchese.

Charles thought he might spill some coffee on her resume, smudge it up a little, but he didn't think it necessary. He just made sure her resume was on the bottom.

The walnut paneled walls and coffered ceiling always made the conference room, customarily used for interviews, look dreary even with all bulbs burning. Of no assistance was the mahogany, chevron-patterned wood floor. Even the wall tapestry with its bright blues and greens had little chance of becoming faded. What made the room appear richer, if not bright, was the burgundy Persian rug, so expensive it would be true to its genes, and wait many decades before showing a hint of becoming threadbare.

The session would be grueling, with all candidates coming on the same day. The committee engaged the dean's secretary to usher the candidates in and out in a timely manner, careful not to have them bump into each other.

Charles had to remember Wayne's directive to be quick about the selection. Charles scheduled interviews for nine, ten, eleven, one, and two, with a twelve o'clock lunch break. He was confident that before day's end, the committee would come to a decision.

Mitch's interview was arranged for one o'clock, when Charles figured the committee would be refreshed after the first three hours and candidates. Mitch was already sitting outside the door when they returned from the cafeteria. Wayne introduced him to all committee members including Charles, who began the questioning. "Dr. Broderick, would you please tell the committee something about yourself."

"Surely." His tone was most pleasant. He summarized in less than two minutes his experience and education.

Good. To the point.

Pete Stratton picked up on the questioning. Pete always looked like the friendly version of the MGM lion, never snarling, always smiling. Every time he moved his head, his mane followed a second later. Only today he seemed unduly serious. "What kind of research are you involved with in your company?"

Mitch responded in a very serious and authoritative tone. "Our team developed a drug currently on the market, levodopa, which stimulates the brain to replenish depleted supplies of dopamine in patients with Parkinson's disease. Levodopa is successful in restoring muscle control, but has the side effects of nausea and vomiting. So we went back to the drawing board and came up with another drug, carbidopa, which when used in combination with levodopa, delays the conversion of dopamine until it reaches the brain, thereby decreasing the amount of levodopa needed so patients don't experience as many side effects."

"So is that combination the standard treatment for Parkinson's patients?" Bob Lucas asked.

"Pretty much," Mitch said, "but as you probably know, the drugs wear off in advanced patients, metabolized before they have a chance to work. So we're now looking to find new medications that would act on different parts of the brain, to determine if when given alone, or in combination with levodopa, these medications would overcome the on-off syndrome of symptom control."

The committee was silent for a few seconds. Charles was confident Mitch sounded so in command of his research, he had to be impressing the group.

Bob Lucas probed further. "According to your resume, you don't have any teaching experience."

"Not in a formal sense. But I've been a research team leader and in that capacity have demonstrated skills that are needed in teaching, such as organizing content and materials and conveying content to my team verbally."

Stan Lubich turned to the second page of the resume, put the tip of the first page between his teeth through which he spoke, almost indiscernibly. "What research did you do for your doctoral dissertation?"

"I studied the behavior of the box turtle under varying conditions."

"What was the most difficult part of your research?" Pete asked while examining his fingernails.

"Believe it or not it had nothing to do with biology, it was dealing with my mentor. He was impossible to find, wouldn't return my phone calls, and when I finally caught up with him and asked him a question, he'd jump on me as though I was already supposed to know the answer, and responded by asking me what the answer was to my own question."

"Having someone like that for a mentor can be tough" Pete said with considerable empathy. "Mine was no piece of cake either. How did you get through the dissertation?"

"Another member of the department guided me," Mitch was quick to respond. "He didn't get along with my mentor either, thought he was senile and should've retired years before. Told me that even when he was younger though, he was always nasty. But I worked hard and survived."

Charles was pleased with the procedures thus far, sure that Pete would vote for Mitch. Yet, much to his dismay, Fred Wachsman and Bob Lucas spent several minutes discussing the woes they had with their mentors. As subtly as he could, Charles signaled them to get back on track and they finally stopped the irrelevant discussion. Then the rest of the team continued the guided questioning for another thirty minutes.

Fred asked the final question, the last one Charles would allow if he was to keep to the schedule. "Tell us why, Dr. Broderick, you'd be willing to accept a drastic cut in salary to obtain this position."

"I always wanted to teach, think it would be more satisfying than working in a lab." Mitch's voice conveyed sincerity.

The committee kept filling the blank spaces under each structured question. Charles was thrilled the interview seemed to be going along so well. It didn't need his intervention. Mitch would've done well even if Charles hadn't given him the questions in advance. After the first three candidates they had seen that morning, all boring, Mitch stood out, way ahead of the pack.

Charles read the body language on the other four committee members confident that his brother-in-law was well received.

At five minutes to two they all shook hands with Mitch, and he left without giving Charles any special attention.

Wayne's secretary led Mitch out the rear door.

Steve had spent some time that morning deciding what to wear. She was used to playing a man's game. That would necessitate her looking business-like. Would it be a pants suit which was just becoming fashionable, or a regular one? Didn't want to hide her great legs so she chose the latter outfit this crisp fall day. Parallel gold buttons joined by thin gold braids running across the jacket of the woolen emerald green suit deepened the color of her eyes and contrasted with her hair, the front with a soft wave, the back gathered in a My-Fair-Lady twist which she steadied with brown hairpins. The thick shoulder pads, power shoulders they now called it, would have the same effect as the pants suit anyway. She had just the perfect thin gold chain, not at all the flashy kind she loathed, which would encircle her throat right above the scoop neck. After digging through her drawers, she found the white lace-edged handkerchief to fit into the off-center chest pocket, giving her a touch of femininity. Black pumps would complete the outfit.

She put on the suit, looked into the mirror. The jacket zipped in the back and came to a point in the front. The gold buttons and braid made the outfit look military.

Self-confident.

In charge.

She planned her makeup to be subdued, conservative, while carefully playing up her eyes and cheeks. She was keenly aware that eye contact had to be used effectively, so she made sure the lipstick wasn't so pronounced that it detracted from her eyes.

Steve practiced her handshake by grasping firmly onto the throat of her son's worn stuffed giraffe. But that was really no way to determine what effect she had. So she shook her left hand with her right enough times to ensure that it exhibited the Goldilocks effect...not too hard, not too soft, but just right. While repeating the process, she kept eye-measuring the angle between her thumb and closed fingers, making sure she avoided the limp, wishy-washy, dead-fish hand offering she herself had experienced with men and women alike, giving away their corresponding personalities. Or the tight raised hand which tilted downward proffering only the fingers, and fingers stuck to each other at that.

The list she wrote of all the questions she could possibly be asked fell from the dresser to the floor. She picked up the list to read again before turning it over to check the questions she wanted to ask to demonstrate how much she had studied the college, its mission, and the science department offerings. A list of catch-words she could interject at the appropriate time describing how she would fit into the environment was crunched on the bottom of the page.

Steve found herself with a bad case of nerves, not realizing until now how much she wanted this job. Perfect for a woman with children, the younger just entering the first grade. She had always wanted to teach and this job gave her the time and flexibility to set up a limited practice, or help Ed with his, if she should decide on that in the future.

On the hall table rested the black leather briefcase she had packed the night before containing extra copies of her resume, a working pen she had checked several times, and a note pad.

Again, what was it she had to remember in the interview strategies guidelines? Be on time, direct, positive, enthusiastic, confident. Being on time was inherent in her, and so was her ability to be direct. Too damn direct. It was also in her nature to be positive, enthusiastic, and confident. But she had to make sure to keep her attention focused on all these attributes, as well as the other five in the guidelines, so she created a mnemonic. ODPEC. Not long after staring at it did she realize that if she reordered the letters, they spelled COPED, which is what she hoped to do, and do well, during the interview.

And above all she had to remember the Three Twelves Rule. The first impression you make comes when you're twelve feet away, the second when you shake hands twelve inches away, the last from the first twelve words you speak.

Steve appeared at the interview at exactly two o'clock. She sat outside the dean's office repeating COPED to herself confident, on-time which she could now forget, positive, enthusiastic, and direct, her list of questions, and the Three Twelves Rule.

She hoped the guidelines were right, that if the interviewer was experienced, he or she would spend the first few minutes in chitchat.

Chitchat was what she desperately needed right now.

Charles placed the last resume in front of him. He leaned his elbow on it, inadvertently causing it to slip off the table and flutter to the floor. Several of the pages scattered. When he bent down to collect them, he heard Wayne's secretary say, "Dr. Marchese, this is Dr. Stratton...Dr. Lubich...Dr. Wachsman...Dr. Lucas...and___"

Charles was still collecting papers from the floor. He placed the pages back in numerical order, stood up, put the resume on the table again, and before he had a chance to be introduced, the woman said, "By process of elimination you must be Dr. Pastore, who signed the letter requesting me to make this appointment." She smiled while shaking his hand with a firm grip.

He met her eyes a split second, then them turned away. "That's right."

"Thank you for the opportunity of having this interview with you." She relaxed her hand, removed it from his and took her seat in the witness stand, the seat reserved for her at the head of an oval table surrounded by five more chairs.

Nobody spoke.

Charles noticed that all the other men were busy looking at her, instead of at her resume.

The silence was unnerving.

Had to get rid of her quickly. He cleared the tickle in his throat. "Did you have a hard time finding the campus, Dr. Marchese?" That sparked the others into attention.

"Not at all, I live in Westchester and've passed it several times. A beautiful place."

"Yes, we're fortunate to work in such an aesthetic environment. The Grahams were avid horticulturalists and made sure that their home would be surrounded with prize specimens which have all been left in tact even when Mr. Graham added buildings to the property."

"I noticed the huge Japanese maple on the lawn. That alone must be valued in the thousands," she said.

"It is magnificent, a symbol of the values the college stands for."

He held the structured question sheet with her name on top. "Speaking of the college, we're pleased that you're here, Dr. Marchese, and would like you to begin by telling us something about your background."

She leaned forward slightly, distributing to each committee member the same amount of attention while addressing them. Her presentation was clear and succinct.

The group asked essentially the same types of questions they had asked the other four candidates, but didn't grill her as hard. Yet, even he had to admit to himself her responses were very articulate and knowledgeable.

The more he tried to hurry the interview along, the more the others kept probing her with categories of questions not on the list. Already the interchange had gone a half-hour over schedule. Maybe if he hadn't scheduled her for last he could have gotten her out sooner.

Then Pete surprised him by saying, "Dr. Marchese, how did you get along with your mentor?"

She grinned. Then, with a coy expression, she looked directly at Pete. "It must've been very well. I married him."

That brought chuckles from everyone including Dr. Marchese.

At 3:30 the committee excused her.

The committee remained in the room to discuss the candidates. Charles was worried. Ticked. The woman had a keen intelligence, and a good wit. Absent was the Bronx accent. A tinge of Boston, perhaps. All in all, she was a damn good candidate. No, outstanding.

"I'll be perfectly honest with you," Pete Stratton said, "I had no intention of giving this woman any consideration at all, but I must say she was most impressive. And absolutely charming."

"We don't hire people by charm," Charles retorted with a cautioning fist, "we hire them on their qualifications and I think that Dr. Broderick is much more qualified than she is."

"How can you say that?" Stan Lubich said, his voice conveying the same irritation that was on his face. "Her research is more current, she's published regularly since getting her degrees, and certainly research in gene identification is much more timely and critical than the life of the box turtle. And I am sure that genetics will some day overcome Parkinson's and many other diseases. But most important for our department, she'd give us more flexibility, she can teach chemistry as well as biology."

"You're right," Pete said. "She also has both an M.D. and a Ph.D., graduated first in her class at Barnard and third in medical school out of a highly select class. Good P.R. for the college and the department. And," he winced, "if I ever get a little shoulder pain, I have someone I can go to."

They all laughed.

"Besides," Pete added, "I think that her personality makes her a good candidate for teaching. We need vibrant people on this faculty. Vitality is contagious."

"I don't believe this," Charles said, "she's surely captivated this whole group. You weren't as hard on her as you were with the other candidates, and I don't even think you asked her much of what you started out to."

"We didn't have to," Fred Wachsman chimed in, "I could tell immediately she has great control of her subject and would be a tremendous asset to the college...very competent."

"The only control she has is over all of you," Charles said, feeling blood rush to his head. He turned to Bob Lucas. "You've been conspicuously silent through all of this, Bob. You're the chairman of the department, what do you think?"

Without hesitating a second Bob said, "I'm putting my money on her. It's about time we had a woman in the science department. Now that we're coed, it'd be good for our female students to have a female science teacher. And a bonus I hadn't anticipated is that she can advise the students in the pre-med program we're trying to build up. I think we should give her a chance."

Charles could see where all of this was headed. "Is there any further discussion?" He looked around the table.

Dead silence.

Then he said with some trepidation, "By secret ballot let's rank the candidates." In front of each committee member he tossed a paper slip mimeographed with the numerals one through five. He was sure to give himself one, also.

He collected the folded ballots. After mixing them up and opening them in front of everyone, all but one ballot had that woman's name listed first. He had no other choice but to recommend Dr. Stefania Marchese to the dean for the position. At least his job, as commissioned, was done quickly, even if bungled. Only one problem remained.

What was he going to tell his sister and brother-in-law?

CHAPTER 11

STEVE ARRIVED ON campus at 8:00 A.M. with several cartons of books, a separate carton containing a can of Endust, Handi Wipes, a roll of Viva towels, a spray bottle of Windex along with a refill, and several hand-painted pots brimming with philodendra and coleus. She rolled up her tape measure, just about to place it in the top middle desk drawer she had just pulled out, when....

Crud, all over the place. Then she opened all the drawers. More crud. Pencil shavings, broken rubber bands, bent paper clips, clumps of dried glue. The drawers didn't need to be cleaned, they needed to be sandblasted.

She turned all the drawers upside down over the wastepaper basket, then placed them side by side over the desk, sprayed them with Windex, let it soak, then cleaned the inside of the drawers with several Viva towels. When the drawers were almost dry, she sprayed, and cleaned again.

Her tape measure had become unraveled. She rolled it up again, put it in the top drawer in a section designed to hold something the size of paper clips. Had to keep that tape measure where she could see it. Had to stay trim. Medical school was weak in nutrition education but she had already done her research and would be wary of fats and starches in cafeteria food. Time, maybe, to consider bringing her own lunch.

David Benson's nameplate had already been unscrewed from the door. His books were gone, his file cabinets empty. And even though the maintenance staff had cleaned the windows and floor, the bookshelves and other furniture needed scrubbing. How sloppy men, no, people, could be.

She estimated how much drapery would cover the windows, then remembered the tape measure. It gave her a more accurate idea. And the desk, it had to be refinished and protected with a glass top like the one she had made for her dining room table. The walls were impoverished, could use some pictures, some Shakespearean quotes. She'd have to decide which ones. And of course, the first thing to go up would be her favorite poster, "Will the World Be a Better Place Because You Have Lived in It?"

Steve gazed out the naked window. The leaves were just about hanging on, battling against the slightest wind. How would the trees look come spring?

"It seems as though you're settling in here, dearie. Welcome."

She turned to find a cheerful round face with devilish blue eyes, a blotch of orange rouge on each cheek, matching orange lipstick already journeying up the lines above her mouth, and hair that was once blond braided and folded on top of the head. Demarking the face from the neck, a makeup foundation line.

"Oh, hi, I was just imagining what the campus would look like in the spring. I'm Steve Marchese." With her hand she outlined the office through the air. "David Benson's replacement."

"I'm Alice Cronin from the English Department, one of the few females in the old boys' club. And I hope you don't have the same fate as Dave."

"I promise to be careful driving. Don't need any head-on collisions, especially at this point in the semester. My children are too young to be without a mother. Please come in and sit down. Sorry I don't have a coffee pot set up yet, but when I do, you'll be the first one invited."

"I'm a teetotaler myself, carry my own bags, so all I need is hot water, very hot water."

The devilish twinkle in Alice Cronin's eyes told Steve that hot water was probably what the woman enjoyed being in.

"Please sit down, Alice, take this chair." She wheeled it over. "I just got through scrubbing and polishing it."

Alice sat down, almost sliding off. Must've been the silicone in the Endust.

"What did you polish this with? I should've brought a seat belt."

They both laughed.

Alice sat up straight in the chair, holding on to the arms. "I must tell you how great it is having yet another woman on campus. You know I wanted to be on the search committee for Dave's replacement, but didn't get voted in."

"To tell you the truth, I wasn't surprised that an all-male committee interviewed me. I've always lived in an all-male world. I was just surprised I got the job."

"We have to stick together. I'm going to teach you the ropes, I like you already even though you're not Irish."

"I'm half-Irish, will that do?"

"Better than nothing. But," Alice snapped her fingers, "that must be it. Liked you the second I laid eyes on you. And my first impressions are usually correct, at least ninety-five percent of the time."

"Good enough to reject the null hypothesis at the .05 level of confidence." How could she be polite without being taught the ropes? She didn't want anyone else's attitudes to taint her. She wanted to be open-minded, assess each situation, and form her own conclusions. "How long have you been teaching here?"

"Longer than most, the first token female, even though there are a few more today. But Graham's a great place, small enough to give you a lot of freedom and really get to know your students, and they, you."

"I read about the mission of the college in the catalog. Commitment through scholarship and leadership. Seems as___"

"Don't ever believe what you read in the catalog. I'd be willing to bet that most of the professors here have never even read the catalog, don't know what the mission is, and neither do the students. If you ask them, they look at you as if you belong on another galaxy. Then don't ask them what a galaxy is, either. I'll tell you what this place is all about in a nutshell."

Alice wiggled around in her chair as if she was trying to pinpoint the exact location on the seat where she'd be most comfortable, an indication that she intended to spend quite a bit of time there. "You see, the Grahams were very rich, made their money in beer, but since they never had any children, they designated their estate be used as an institution of higher learning of excellence where the youth they never had would be educated. They stipulated that all the faculty offices be off the center of a circle with no department member allowed to be next to another member of the same department so there'd be more intermingling socially and intellectually, which is what they did in their own offices in the breweries. Even left an architect's plan for the building. Claimed the more their employees mixed with each other, the better the communication, the more productive the company became."

"I noticed that the administrative offices, the secretaries and conference rooms are in the hub of the circle, just opposite the faculty offices."

"And the cafeteria's in the shape of a circle, an expanded hub, one flight down. We can't escape each other. Have to be in contact with each other, even if we don't want to."

"Communication, open, honest communication is critical."

"That true so I'm going to communicate to you what to look for and watch out for in the faculty."

Steve had a lot to do. She wanted to experience interaction with the faculty herself. How could she shut the woman up? No use, she was on a roll.

Alice squinted. "Can't believe I'm telling you all this. Never would do this with someone I had just met and would certainly criticize someone else for doing so. But I have a good feeling about you, really good vibes, want to protect you, give you a heads up.

"That Bill Foster, head of the history department, he's the person you go to when you have a problem. Clear-headed, honest, most helpful. I've been to him a lot myself. Very trustworthy. Sure what you tell'im will remain confidential, a good family man, works well with the students.

"Now if you have a problem make sure you go to Bill Foster, not Morty Drucker, head of the psychology department. He's on his fourth wife, and all his kids are in therapy. A fifty-year-old still trying to find himself.

"And keep an eye out for the other female on campus, Cleo Babbitt, a typical liberal, loves embracing humanity but can't relate to a single human being, a real bitch, blames her own inadequacies on everyone else, especially men being prejudiced against her because she's a woman, not because she's the bitch that she is. Campaigned for busing, but her kid's in private school. Is one of the open ones, but move out of the way, dearie, if you don't agree with her. Makes it tough on women like us who really produce."

Good news. She was already viewed as a producer. How could she get rid of Alice?

Alice revved up the talking machine. "And the most dangerous ones are Hugh Campbell and Sy Fisher, a wacko team. They instigated the students to riot, spit on the American flag, and steal files in the administrative offices a couple of years ago when that behavior was considered chic, only to idiots, of course. Real radicals, gave a seminar on how to construct bombs. Smoked pot with the students, even bedded some of them. Can you imagine! Parents send their daughters to be educated and instead of giving these kids moral guidance, they take advantage of their naivety. Contemptible pricks, they are."

Steve's head was swirling. She didn't appreciate being saturated with all this gossip, not to mention the conglomeration of names. How could she remember any of them without associating them with faces? But there was no halting Alice.

"Then there's that group that believes in free speech, always talking about it, unless your speech doesn't coincide with theirs. Frank Bowman, Lloyd Fredericks, and Jim Dunbar. Shouted everybody down when we had discussions about Cambodia, encouraged the students to do the same. Never allowed open dialog about anything. All they know how to do is suck up the intellectual oxygen, indoctrinate, yet they consider themselves scholars. Despicable characters, the whole lot of them. Come to think of it, they're probably more dangerous than the wacko team. Their danger's more subtle."

What in the room could she use to gag Alice?

"Now who, excuse me, *whom* have I left out?" Alice twisted her mouth to the right then to the left. "I don't want to bombard you with too much."

She had already done that but the old biddy appeared to be winding down so Steve let her finish.

"Oh, yes, our pop sociologists, Morris Fields, we call him Moe, Henry Burdens, we call him Hank, and Jeff Hoffman, we call him, well, you know what we call him. They're always together, so they're known as the Dynamic Trio. Actually, the trio, they are brilliant, and so amusing to be with. Always spewing, a better word might be spinning, sociology facts. Keep you entertained."

Steve asked herself how these sociologist, pop-sociologists Alice had called them, could always be together with their offices so deliberately distant from each other.

Then Alice's voice became hushed. "And the one whose office is next to yours, on this side." She turned her thumb to the wall. "Charles Pastore, a decent sort. The voice of reason and balance on this campus. Well-respected. Just up for tenure which I'm sure he'll get, but even though he didn't have it all along, he always stood up for what he believed in, even if it wasn't what the rest of them wanted to hear. Beautiful family, sweet wife, two fine boys."

At least Alice started and finished with something positive.

She figured her lesson to be over when Alice said, "Watch that dean, that Wayne Ashley, a real politician and a sniveling sneak. Do you know what some of us in the English department call him? Reed-That-Bends."

"Why Reed-That-Bends?"

"From *The Last of the Mohicans*, an Indian who lacked courage."

"Never heard that before, but then, I never read the book."

"Says one thing to your face, another behind your back. Thinks he's real smooth...really smooth, have to watch out for the lingo or is it jargon of the day. Told him off a couple of times myself. Doesn't like me because I'm one of the few who tells him the truth...according to Cronin." A laugh erupted from her belly.

Was this what it was going to be like having an office in a circle, across from the hub?

"Don't know what got into me today. What did I have for breakfast? Or it must be my gift of gab, my sense of trust in you." Alice started to get up, then sat down again. "And, dearie, let me give you a quick lesson on how to be a college professor. Now you make sure you read the *New York Times* from cover to cover every day and at least one weekly news magazine like *Time*, *Newsweek*, *U.S. News and World Report*, and especially the *Times* Sunday Magazine. The trick is to find the times, excuse the pun, during lunch discussions when you can quote, I repeat, quote from them. They're very impressed by that. You can even make up your own quote but if you say it's from one of those sources, they'll brand you as an intellectual. Now how's that for disgusting?"

"Thanks so much for your input, Alice. I'll be on the lookout for all the characteristics you've described and make sure I renew all my subscriptions."

"Good, then you'll be ahead of the game."

Steve was very suspicious of Alice Cronin.

Alice was the kind of person Steve would give only the information she wanted everyone else to know.

"Charles, I know how you must feel about your brother-in-law," Wayne Ashley said, "but you know about best made plans. We did our best trying to hire him. And now that we're stuck with this woman, and I must confess she's highly qualified, and hate to admit, more qualified than your brother-in-law, with that I'd have to agree with the committee, we've got to make the best of it. Now here's what I'd like you to do."

Just what he needed, more advice from Wayne. But that was just what Charles was about to get anyway.

"Since you chaired the committee that recommended her, go along with it. I want you to get her on your Curriculum Committee, make it look as if you're supporting her. She needs to get involved in committee work if she's going to build up her file."

"I thought you didn't want that to happen to her, a chance to build a file. You didn't want her on board, but it looks as though you're already setting her up for promotion and tenure."

"Don't sound like such a sore loser, Charles, you're not going to be happy to hear this but I like her. A lot. Even Chester likes her." Wayne began to snicker. "Is going to write you a thank-you letter for your good work. She's most attractive and charming and frankly, just what the students need."

"A thank-you letter from Chester! She even has the president charmed. You guys all sound alike. Charm. Is that a requirement for a full-professorship now? We should all go to charm school instead of graduate school."

Wayne slanted his eyes to the side. "Considering this crowd, that might not be a bad idea."

"Jesus Christ, Wayne, you're just as bad as the rest of them, charmed by the very woman you didn't want hired in the first place."

He trudged out of the office.

Charles waited over two weeks after his conversation with Wayne before inviting Dr. Marchese to his office. He couldn't help laughing to himself when he saw her. The clip of a pen which had to be red felt hugged the outside of her chest pocket. The pen had run into her lab coat, leaving a large red spot and streaks, making it appear as though she had a bleeding heart.

He offered her a chair. "Dr. Marchese___"

"Please call me, Steve. Everyone does."

"Why, Steve?"

"It's a long story, we'll save it for another time."

"Okay, Steve, but I must say the name really doesn't fit you. Now getting back to why you're here, Wayne's made a great suggestion. He thinks it'd be a good idea for you to get involved in committee work."

"What does he have in mind?"

"He thinks you'd be perfect for the Curriculum Committee, a powerful, influential committee. Serving on that committee will look good when you collect supporting data for your annual review, advancement, and eventual tenure. He thinks your input would be valuable and that it would be good to get a woman on that committee to replace Sam Plotkin who resigned, bring another perspective. He thinks that your background in science would bring more balance to the work we're doing now."

She gave him a look he couldn't quite interpret.

"So far you've told me Wayne thinks this and Wayne thinks that. As chair of the committee, what do you think?"

"W...why of course I agree with him."

She leaned toward him. "Are you prepared for someone who calls the shots as she sees them?"

"Sure, that's what we need with this group."

"It's pretty dreadful, I've been reading the minutes you circulated, a lot of garbage being proposed."

"We have some very liberal people, actually radicals on the committee."

"Who? The ones I've heard about who protested against the war and instigated the students? They've never had an honest discussion about it and won't allow any other opinions to be heard. I think the war was wrong myself, but the way a lot of these professors gave into... academics in general gave into some of the demands of students has been unconscionable. I mean, the faculty here must have voted these jerks into these committees in the first place."

"You know faculties, and though you haven't been here long enough, you can probably guess. All you have to do is use words as compassion, the poor," he looked at the red pen blotch on her chest pocket, "have the bleeding hearts parading the posters, appeal to the emotions, and the faculty become so morally outraged, get such a guilt trip they'd vote for Godzilla."

"The ones who must feel morally superior, you mean?"

"You're on the mark, and now this group's trying to revise the curriculum according to the students' demands. We're in the *relevant* stage now. `Is it relevant' is the cry of the day."

"I'm really worried about what a shot science is taking. Professors discouraging students from studying science because it's part of the military-industrial complex. Very short-sighted. And blaming science for polluting the environment, for its potential for evil, forget the good, and even developing technology for the benefit of the capitalists. Discouraging research and development? Where's that going to leave this country when it comes to competing in an ever competitive world?"

"That's also one of my concerns, though science is not my field. Also about declining standards in coursework, the fact that the moral compass has been turning and is beginning to definitely point south."

"Charles," she said, looking as if she was about to grab his arm but then put her hand down, "that scares me to death. I've a girl almost ten. Some of these experimental lifestyles being proposed, all this liberal sex, it all has to have a detrimental effect on the family. And just you wait, eighteen, twenty years from now the professors will all being bitching that the students don't know anything, and complaining about the emotional problems their students are having, caused in great part by the very policies they're now promoting."

"You know, Dr. Mar...Steve, I think you're going to be just what this Curriculum Committee needs.

Students buzzed around the lab, working industriously on their experiments. The centrifuge hummed, mortars and pestles worked overtime, Bunsen burners flared under test tubes and under beakers placed on asbestos-topped tripods.

Steve kept circulating among the students in the laboratory session of her chemistry class. Her charges seemed to be pursuing industriously the lab activity for the day. An occasional hand went up, and she offered assistance in the form of answering questions or adjusting equipment.

Gretchen Murray was the only one who seemed a little distant from the material. She was sitting on a chair with a spindled back, her legs elevated onto a stool, almost completely blocking an aisle between lab tables. Safety had to be Steve's main concern. What if other students might try to pass through the aisle and trip?

She meandered in her direction. "Hi, Gretchen, you're not your usual self today." Then she lowered her voice, "Please move your chair and stool in a little closer to the lab table."

The straggly-haired, reddish blonde twisted the upper part of her torso toward her. "I really want to, but I have terrible leg cramps."

"You're not on the track team, are you?"

"No, unfortunately, I wish I were, anything but in Dr. Dunbar's class."

"What does that have to do with leg cramps?"

Gretchen massaged her right calf. "Dr. Marchese, if I told you, you wouldn't believe it. It's something you have to see for yourself."

"He teaches history, doesn't he?"

"If you can call it that. Really, go down to his class and take a look, he has a second section of the same course I just came from." Her freckles seemed to be more prominent today, literally jumping out of her face. "You won't believe it."

The last thing she needed was to hear more rantings from Jim Dunbar. She had read some of the rot he'd been sending around to everyone's mail box, and Alice Cronin had already given her an earful about him. Leaving class, even for a few minutes, wouldn't be the prudent thing to do, especially in the middle of a lab. Yet, Jim Dunbar was also on the Curriculum Committee. What could he be up to?

After about twenty more minutes had passed, Steve could no longer squelch her curiosity. She asked the class if they had any other questions or problems. Since everything seemed to be running smoothly, she decided, against her better judgment, to sneak away for a few minutes.

If anyone got hurt while she was out of the room, she would be in deep trouble.

According to the schedule, Jim's class was in room 119. She walked briskly down the hallway, then two flights down. The door to the room was paned half-way on the top with chicken-wire glass. The door was closed but the light was on. She put her face close to the pane. An empty room. Maybe he dismissed his class early. She shouldn't have waited so long to come down.

She turned the knob and opened the door.

Voices. But where were they coming from?

Her eyes skimmed the room, starting with the walls, settling on the floor. There, under a huge round table, a leg, with frayed bell-bottom dungarees, a heavily scuffed combat boot. She gasped, rushed her hand to her chest. Then she ran to offer her assistance.

She shoved the table aside, preparing to kneel over the body, maybe administer CPR, or whatever.

More bodies, scrunched underneath, knees up or Indian-style, supporting notebooks, an occasional hand with a pen.

The denim-covered booted leg slid out from under the table with Jim Dunbar's head still bent from ducking under it. He remained on the floor, not moving as much as a micrometer. "Are you lost, Dr. Marchese, can't find your classroom?"

She could hardly find his face for his unkempt beard and uncombed greasy hair. "What's going on?"

"A lesson you can well learn, as we in this class are all well learning," he said with the zeal of the apostles after Pentecost. "In this class, we are all equal, a model for society. No one is above the other. The student is not better than the professor, nor the professor better than the student. I do not feel it's my place to stand over the students and conduct my class in any way that is not egalitarian. We all remain under the table."

To describe him as a schmuck would be too euphemistic. Did he ever hear of sitting in a circle, or would that be too innovative an idea?

Poor students. Is this the gobbledygook they were getting for their tuition? How could any of these innocents be suckered in by this horseshit? For she sadly noted corroboration, acceptance on some faces, yet hope in the shaking heads and rolling eyes of others.

To even give this misguided idiot a response would be a reward. He was the one who couldn't find his classroom, or his class for that matter. He was the one who was lost. She had to give Gretchen Murray credit for not wasting her breath telling her about it, and even more points for telling her it had to be seen to be believed.

Steve scurried out of the room and returned to the lab, where there was still a scintilla of sanity in academia.

Later that day when Steve packed her briefcase, she considered how fortunate she was to have attended college at a time when logic and reason prevailed. This was now the time of sloppy dress, sloppy speech, sloppy writing, sloppy thinking, sloppy manners, not to mention, sloppy morals.

The worst that had happened to her in college was that Dr. Clancy had suggested, no indicated, that she was tight-assed. And maybe he was right. At least, at the time. Would he have understood how targeted she had to remain, and why?

Tranquility momentarily was restored to the campus, and she welcomed the walk to her car. She picked up her briefcase, car keys in hand, just about to lock her office door when...

Screams, unrelenting.

She ran to the window. The shrieks seemed to be coming from the parking lot.

She shielded her eyes from the glaring sun and looked outside. A crowd. Gathering around a woman. And a car.

Was the woman injured?

Steve made a dash for the parking lot, catching a glimpse of her own car in the distance. With a breaststroke motion she shoved the crowd aside.

On the ground, Leslie Wagner from the Philosophy Department, stretched on her back. A petite woman whose size was overcompensated for by her brain. Her briefcase open, books and papers strewn about.

Purse on the floor. She was breathing rapidly, her carotids registering close to 200 on Steve's fingertip.

Steve lifted Leslie's head. The woman's face was flush. She didn't speak, kept motioning to her car door. What did she need?

Steve lowered Leslie's head and gently placed it back on the concrete.

Bill Foster had just arrived. Thank God. Someone sane. "Bill, she keeps motioning to the car. Maybe she wants something in there."

"Sure, is it locked?"

"Check before I search her purse for the keys."

Bill opened the door. The stench that came out of the car was unbearable.

Dung. Fresh dung.

Bill slammed the door. "The feces of a large animal, a dog, or dogs, on, on the driver's seat cushion she props herself up with," he said covering his mouth and nose with a handkerchief. The murmuring crowd covered their noses and quickly began to disperse.

"How do you read it, Bill?"

He made a gargling sound before spitting into his handkerchief. "The thank-you from those who support the radical feminist doctrine, for the brilliant opposition paper Leslie circulated in everybody's mailbox yesterday."

Would she find a thank-you in her car, too? She approached it cautiously. It was still locked, something Ed had always cautioned her to do.

Welcome to academia. If today's examples were any indication of what she was going have to face on the Curriculum Committee, she had her work cut out for her.

After several months, the Curriculum Committee had concluded its work, ready to present majority and minority recommendations at a specially scheduled faculty meeting where they would discuss the recommendations and make a final decision.

Steve noted that Frank Bowman, Lloyd Fredericks, and Jim Dunbar came in together, and sat together. The three were wearing bell-bottom dungarees and wrinkled lumberjack shirts with rolled-up sleeves. Frank and Jim donned beige suede fringe-bordered vests.

Charles was speaking at the podium. "The committee's studied the Black Studies and Women's Studies programs at many other universities. We, the minority, weren't too impressed. We're willing to consider a Black Studies and Women's Studies program here if, and only if, they meet the standards of all the other curricula, and so far, in our opinion, they haven't."

Catcalls. From the audience.

One person yelled, "Those are white standards."

Another called out, "Racist pig."

Yet another heckler shouted, "Elitist."

Steve saw the three fomenting the agitation. The next time she wouldn't shirk Alice Cronin's observations off so easily.

The turmoil and jeering continued until Frank Bowman stood up. "Dr. Marchese's been very quiet during this entire meeting, or is her silence an indication that she is a racist snob like the rest of you? Do tell us, Dr. Marchese, what does our female scientist faculty member think?"

The sarcastic tenor of his voice was still reverberating through the room.

Should she keep her mouth shut? She was new on campus, a long way from tenure.

Damn tenure.

Who she was as a person was more important. Bowman had charged her, insulted her before her peers, and she was already losing her calm. Besides, how could anyone who was half-Irish and half-Italian remain calm about anything, especially an accusation like this?

What was coming over her? She found herself walking up to the podium. Charles, who was still standing in front of it, stepped aside. The face of Isabel Burke, that snotty little bitch sore loser who had made fun of her because she didn't look like a girl but would still crown the Blessed Mother, was sneering at her. She hadn't thought about Isabel in years, yet the same sensation overcoming her at the time attacked her now. It was less important that her name was pulled out of the cigar box than that Isabel's wasn't.

Now it was Frank Bowman's turn to lose.

Steve moved her face close to the microphone. "Your female scientist faculty member agrees with you, Dr. Bowman, there is, indeed, racism on this campus."

A sudden drop in the auditorium temperature.

Shock waves pulsated throughout the room.

Charles backed up a few steps ensuring her the floor.

Bowman, Fredericks, and Dunbar acknowledged each other with winning smiles, and thumbs up.

"Let me give you some examples that I witnessed after having completed just my first semester here," Steve said. "There are too many black students getting A's for work which you'd give white students C's or D's, if not F's. They're not being challenged. Instead, they're being praised by a lot of professors giving these students a false concept of their achievement. When they get rewarded for not having earned something, it's more debilitating long term than the discrimination used against them over the years.

"Our own Teacher Education department here at Graham tells its pre-service students that there is a considerable body of research which supports the fact that students, people, rise to the level of expectation. It's condescending to blacks when we don't expect the same standards of them because the subtle message we send is that they really can't achieve. You're expressing the bigotry of low expectations.

"Professors patronize these students and I think it is insecurity professors feel doling out these inflated grades because they fear so much being called racists. And when you call people by that label for demanding and expecting excellence, you only divert the argument from the tough issues. So you see, there is racism on this campus. Worst of all, Dr. Bowman, the male social scientist, it's people like you and your ilk who are institutionalizing it."

The audience gasped, followed by murmuring.

She felt as Leslie Wagner must have felt on the concrete parking lot floor, her pulse rate had way passed normal.

She tapped the microphone. Silence returned.

"And while I'm at it, let me tell you a few other things. When the Women's Studies curriculum can be judged according to the same standards as all other curricula, or identify its own standards, then I'll consider it. And if being a snob means that I want to raise everyone to excellence instead of bringing everyone down to the lowest common denominator, promoting a culture of mediocrity which some people," she directed her stare at Bowman, "seem to enjoy wallowing in, then please forgive me for being so selfish, and thank God I'm the snob and elitist of the century and damn proud of it."

A smattering of applause.

Soon an ovation with foot stamping.

"It's about time," and "Glad she told them off," were a few yelps she could hear above the din her remarks had created.

Frank Bowman jumped out of his seat, made a gagging noise that sounded like the death rattle, and walked out, as did the other committee members who proposed the standards changes. Somehow, though, Steve had the feeling they wouldn't go out permanently with a whimper.

There didn't seem to be any point in keeping the meeting going any longer, and she hoped Charles would conclude it. The tickle in her stomach told her that when it came to a vote, the faculty would support the minority opinion in demanding the same high standards.

Immediately after the meeting, many of the faculty surrounded Steve, Charles, and the committee members who supported the minority position, spending time even though it was late, congratulating them for their work, shaking Steve's hand, patting her back, shoulder, even hugging and kissing her.

Way after the faculty disappeared, Steve was still stewing, and felt if she didn't keep moving, she'd explode. She began collecting the leftover position papers they'd brought to distribute to the faculty, put the papers in order, tapping them into neat piles. She leaned her left hand on the remaining pile, and with the right rubbed her forehead to relieve a tension headache.

Charles placed his hand over her left hand, and squeezed it. "Steve, I was so proud of you. Reed-That-Bends, oh, I mean Wayne knew what he was doing when he recommended you for this committee. For that he had courage and I shouldn't call him that name anymore. Maybe you should call me Reed-That-Bends. I'm the one who should've retorted on the racist accusation."

"I'll be damned if I ever submit to racial blackmail, female blackmail, or any other goddam group blackmail." Her eyes were beginning to moisten. This was no time for tears, so she stopped them by placing her tongue between her teeth and biting down.

"As chairman of the committee, I should've confronted that crowd myself, expressed what I was feeling, but you did it so well, better than I ever could. I was in such shock, for a moment I couldn't think, didn't know what to say. You took over with such ease, Steve, that...that you saved my life."

His hand was still over hers. She paused, then pulled her hand from under his. This was the first time after her outburst that she faced him directly. "There's an old Chinese proverb that says once you save someone's life, you're responsible for that person forever."

Alice Cronin was pacing in Steve's office, her rouged cheeks only slightly more red than the rest of her face. "Bravo. Oops." She covered her mouth. "Brava. I'm proud of you, dearie, stood up to all of 'em."

If the old biddy called her dearie once more, she was going to slug her.

Steve picked up the rhythm of Alice's pacing. "Maybe I should've tried to control myself more, but I just couldn't help it, didn't know what was going to come out of me when I heard that garbage."

"Listen, it took a female on this campus to show some balls. The faculty was in awe of your little shall we say, tête-à-tête with Bowman. You told him what that bunch of pussies could never say, so today they got their rocks off through you, and loved every minute of it. Those three have been getting away with a lot because nobody stood up to them." Alice dropped herself into Steve's chair.

"Rocks off, Dr. Cronin? In what masterpiece of literature did you read that expression?"

"In my father's. Everything was rocks with him, especially on the rocks." She looked askance. "I stand corrected. Everything was straight with him, straight up." Alice blurted a laughter so contagious it made Steve relax.

She stopped pacing, slid a chair toward Alice, and sat opposite her. "You never know how people are going to react to things. But today I didn't care, I just had to be myself."

"Let me tell you, you're well-liked on this campus already. The students have told me, and you know how good I am at prying things out of them. That they enjoy your classes, that you make the difficult easy, and that you're real. I've heard comments from them even without asking, and from the faculty. The students think you're a great teacher, very professional, caring, a good sense of humor, a great sense of balance, and a lot of common sense which, as everybody says, isn't very common."

"That's good to hear, but what does real mean?"

"That you're on this planet, someone they can relate to, not some spaced-out professor who has no contact with the world outside academia. And the others think you can make anyone from the janitor to the president feel comfortable."

"And who might those others be?"

"Those who really know what's going on. Who else but the secretaries. Said you'll sit down and have lunch with them while Cleo Babbitt, the great white liberal, not only never sits with them, but never even says hello, makes believe she doesn't see them.

"But while I'm giving you the dirt, let me warn you about something else." She leaned forward, signaling Steve to do likewise. The usually bellowing voice modulated to a whisper. "Don't think that everyone's your friend."

"What are you trying to tell me, Alice?"

"I told you about this one next door?" Alice directed her thumb to the wall exactly the same way she did the first time she came to Steve's office, as though she had perfected the movement through practice. "Even though I said good things to you about Charles and really do like him, I heard through very reliable sources that...that he was the only one on the search committee who argued against your appointment."

Steve stood up abruptly. "I can't believe that."

"Well, believe it, dearie, because I overheard Pete Stratton say that the vote was four to one in your favor, and Charles must've been the one who voted against you because he didn't want a woman, kept pushing for some guy named Broderick for the job."

"Broderick? Are you sure?"

"Absolutely, because I implied to Lucas and Stratton that I already knew what went on, and when they were positive I had all the details, they expounded more on the topic really giving me the scoop."

Sneaks.

Alice, as well as Charles.

"Thanks for clueing me in, Alice. Some friend he is."

"That's what I heard, that he really argued for Broderick. Just be careful, Steve."

When Alice left, Steve sat at her desk, her eyes scanning the wall that insulated her office from Charles'. What if she knocked all that artwork off his wall? What if she kicked the wall down?

No. Bombing it would be better.

That phony bastard. Had the genes of a chameleon.

Making believe he was her friend.

Putting her on his committee.

Bringing her personally to meet the president.

Didn't want a woman, didn't he now! Wouldn't mind if he said so to her face. That she could respect, but all this be-kind-to-Steve junk, you-saved-my-life junk, made her stomach turn.

She wheeled her chair back with such force that she felt like a teenager burning rubber. She stood up and put her hand on the wall.

Vibrations.

She replaced her hand with her ear.

Voices.

Too goddam bad. More voices, louder ones would be heard before she was through with him.

She stormed into the hall.

His office door was closed.

She knocked on the door.

A pause. "Come in."

Charles was seated at his desk with Pete Stratton sitting across from him.

She went up to Pete and whispered in his ear loud enough so Charles could hear. "Something really important has come up. I would appreciate it if I could speak to Charles in private."

Pete looked at her, then at Charles, who nodded approval before Pete quickly obliged.

Steve slammed Charles' door shut.

A wall picture fell. Too bad it wasn't one with a glass cover.

She kicked the undaunted picture aside, folded her arms behind her back, and forced it up against the door.

Charles was still reeling from her bursting into the room. He didn't speak, just kept watching the inflamed face, emerald darts shooting from her eyes, her heaving breasts, her mouth open to assist her nostrils in getting enough air.

She finally closed her mouth and said through gritted teeth, "Who's Broderick?"

"Broderick?"

"Don't pretend you don't know what I'm talking about. Who is he?"

The tone of her voice, the fact that she heard the name, told him she already knew. He attempted to appear nonchalant, so he stood up casually and walked to the front of his desk and leaned his butt against it. "He's…he's one of the five candidates we interviewed for your job."

"That part's true. So tell me now, what about his candidacy in your opinion made him more qualified than I was?"

"The work of the search committee is private information, something I can't discuss."

"Don't give me that. Private my eye. If it's such private information how come everybody on this campus seems to know what went on there?"

The way her eyes were stabbing his made it difficult for him to concentrate. She was waiting for an expert answer, and it had better be a damn good one. He moved away from his desk and said. "He had several years of experience in industry."

"So what? I had several years of clinical experience. And?"

"He was a Fulbright scholar."

"Big deal."

He couldn't come up with any more reasons.

As she slowly moved toward him, he correspondingly stumbled backwards.

She opened her hand as though she were going to place it over his chest and push him, but she stopped, leaving her hand in the same position. "Did Broderick graduate first in his college class?"

He paused before answering. "No."

"Does he have two doctorates?"

"N…no."

"Did he graduate third in graduate school?" she said, angling her hand and shaking it as though she was slicing the air.

"No."

"Did he have my undergrad and graduate grade point averages?" Yet another shake of the hand, this one losing its steam.

"No."

"Did he have more publications...recent, *relevant* if I may use that word without retching, publications than I have?"

"No."

"Could he have taught two and probably more sciences?"

"No."

"Would he have been as effective a teacher as you now know I am?" Her words were becoming more breathy.

"No."

"Would he have been as hard-working?"

He glanced at the wall, then returned his eyes to her. "You'd probably be even on that score."

"So, Dr. Pastore, all things considered, what makes this male so qualified that you preferred him over me?"

"Where did you get that wacky idea?"

"Never mind, and please, please don't patronize me my fair-weather friend, or insult me further by lying." She moved within ten inches of him, her face ablaze. "Well, damn it, give me an answer." Her eyes kept hurling green darts as her still opened hand flew up high in what appeared like a deliberate move to strike him.

He hesitated, not knowing what to say and whether he should be prepared to duck. At this point he had no choice but to tell the truth. "If you must know, and no one else on campus knows this except Wayne of course...and I'd appreciate it if you'd keep it to yourself." He put his head down. "He's my brother-in-law, my sister's husband."

She finally lowered her hand as the urge to smash his head with her fist, something, his bookends, anything, subsided. At least the situation didn't have to do with the fact that she was a woman competing in a man's world.

"Dr. Pastore," she said after some silence, "I have many faults, but the difference between you and me is that I don't pretend I'm something I'm not. So when I say I won't reveal that information to anyone, you can count on it."

Contempt was gliding all over her face, not finding a place to land. "So after all that sanctimony you exude, I find that nepotism wins out over principle. Under that obsequious assistance you proffer is...is the lowest form of invertebrate to become extinct during natural selection." She might not have won the spelling bee when sarsaparilla, with its insidious elusive 'a' in the middle vanquished her, but she received satisfaction in the fact that time studying the dictionary had helped her retrieve appropriate vocabulary for this moment.

Steve was sure that if she spoke another word, she would choke, so she dug her heels into the floor, pivoted to face the door, twisted the door knob and tore the door open. She marched out of his office turning only to slam the door hard enough so that it vibrated on its hinges.

She drove home with a lead foot on the accelerator.

CHAPTER 12

ALEX WAS BUBBLING over with excitement. "Paul, I can't believe it. Two chapters, and we wrote them together."

For some reason he couldn't share her excitement, just kept staring at the aggressive vine which looked as though it would at any second burst through the concrete under the window sill, creep along the floor and throttle him.

"Biology professor, do you know the name of that vine?"

She wasn't looking at the vine, only at the door always slightly open. Eventually, her eyes found the vine she seemed to study for a moment. "Well, you really heard what I just said, didn't you? But if you must know, and I don't remember it from any botany course I ever took, I read it in the Graham annual report. Kudzu. Such a hard name to remember, I took time to check the spelling. Those in charge of the Grahams' estate ordered it as something they thought the Grahams might like, a hardy exotic species which is overtaking everything from Florida to Maine."

"Yes, kudzu, for some reason I can never remember the name." Paul felt the kudzu was overtaking him. He removed his handkerchief, wiped his brow, and blotted the rest of his face. "I, I really was paying attention to what you said, yes, we did do the two chapters together, and we brought the stories together pretty well. But maybe like the kudzu, Steve was too aggressive."

"I don't think so. She was aggressive from the beginning so how else could we have written it?"

"Maybe we can find a more subdued way for her to challenge Charles, question her appointment." He scratched his head. "Anyway, let's keep going. Where do we go from here?"

"We have to introduce conflict. Conflict is what keeps readers turning pages. Now, two more chapters, Paul." She opened her appointment book. "We have to arrange to meet an additional day, or we're not going to make it by the deadline."

"Instead of writing anything new, maybe we should start revising what we have. You know some writers revise chapter by chapter."

"What's with you, you seem to have an obsession with revising."

"Maybe it's insecurity, I just want it to be good."

"My God, Paul, I still find sections in my novel I'd like to revise, it could go on forever. There comes a time you have to stop and we're nowhere near getting to that point yet. No, we have to keep going, get everything down. We'll revise later."

Two days before their next scheduled writing time, Paul picked up the phone. "I have an advanced case of writer's block, Alex, the kudzu is wrapped around my head. I don't think I can make our next appointment."

Silence came from the other end of the line.

"Alex, did you hear me?"

"Writer's block, let me think." She was quiet for a while longer, then she said, "I once took a writing course, and the instructor told us how to deal with it. He said to go to the zoo and look at an animal, really look at it as though you were looking at it for the very first time. Study it carefully, and you'll be cured, inspired."

"The zoo?"

"Well, it doesn't necessarily have to be the zoo. It could be a flower, a cup...any plant, animal, or mineral at all. Even a picture. The idea is to get your juices flowing. Then all you have to do is let it rip, or, as they say now, let it all hang out."

He'd give it a try. But even more important, what conflict could he let hang out as they continued to write together?

* * *

Early the next morning Charles went to his office. He was sitting at his desk before classes, red pen in hand, reading students' papers, writing comments, circling spelling and grammatical errors, when he heard the door click closed.

As he looked up, he dropped the pen on his trousers, not bothering to check if it had smeared them.

Steve was standing in the same position she was the afternoon before, her arms behind her back, her back pressed against the door.

He remained fixed, staring at her.

She didn't speak, just looked at him. An alluring, sensual look. What was she up to?

Her eyes were exactly the way they were the previous day, piercing his, her breasts rising and lowering under her blouse, her lips slightly parted to let in more air than her nostrils seemed able to accommodate. She kept probing his eyes. Probing, probing.

He couldn't stand it anymore.

He stood up, letting his chair roll to the side.

Her eyes changed from blue-green to dewy emerald, as they swept over his body.

Tantalizing, beckoning.

The silence between them amplified the probing, the pulsing. She slinked closer to him, opened both hands, and pushed them against his chest with such strength he almost fell.

He straightened out. She pushed against his chest again with equal force. This time he had anticipated her move and was steadier on his feet.

Her palms were facing him, ready for the next attack, when he grabbed her wrists and forced her arms behind her back.

In a split second he was pressing against her, brushing, then rubbing his lips over her face, taking tender bites before obliging her succulent lips. No way could he get enough of her. She nibbled on his lips without piercing his skin.

She wedged herself further into him, bent her head back, her wrists still behind her. It gave him the signal to glide his frictionless mouth down her neck. Her heaving breasts were still shifting, up and down, up and down. He was sure the nipples under the blouse had to be the palest of pink.

She yanked away both hands he had interlocked, moved them to the back of his head pressing it down hard against her breasts, pulling his head up by his hair, returning his mouth to hers. She dug her nails into his back while swirling her tongue over his lips.

He was so enraptured by the sensation, and so stunned, it took him a while before he was able to capture her tongue.

She was sighing, moaning. He was sighing in sympathy, groaning, gasping, more moaning, more...

"Wake up, sweetheart." Claudia was shaking him. "You're having a nightmare."

Charles was on his back still in an ecstatic state. When he opened his eyes, the nightlight informed him his hardness had elevated the sheet covering him into a pyramid standing alone in a desert. He sat up swiftly, lifted his knees, while wrapping his arms around them.

Claudia put her hand on his shoulder. "You're in a sweat." She reached for some tissues on her nightstand to blot his face. "I've never seen you like this. Must've been a terrible dream."

Charles let his head freefall into his knees. "Oh God, Claudia, it was. The worst dream I ever had. Horrible." He quickly contorted toward her. "What was I saying?"

"You weren't saying anything, just moaning, making strange noises. And panting. I never heard you make noises like that before."

"The worst dream. Just awful."

"Why don't you tell me about it? Would make you feel better."

What the hell was he going to tell her? He was so startled by the dream he couldn't think.

"Claudia, please," he gagged on his saliva, "I hate to bother you in the middle of the night, but please, get a washcloth, soak it, really soak it in cold water, wring it out, tight, and bring it to me."

"Of course, I'll be right back."

He knew his erection had disappeared the moment the shock of his dream hit him, but he kept his knees up anyway, hugging them tightly, resting his cheek on them.

"Here," she said.

He took the washcloth, folded it in fourths, forced it against his forehead while hyperventilating to give himself time to conjure up a nightmare.

"It...I think it, it must've been that TV movie I caught the end of, muggers stopping my car, taking my car and my money, beating me in the head with their guns. The pain was killing me. And. And I had to chase them on foot, running, running, couldn't catch my breath." He pressed the washcloth deeper into his forehead, then on his mouth, hoping to stamp out Steve's tingling lips.

Claudia rested her head on his arm. "If that ever happens to you, let them have the money, the car, anything. Don't fight it, give in. Even though it's not right what they're doing, don't fight it. You could get hurt, have a heart attack. And," she clasped her hands around his head, moved it against her chest, "if anything ever happened to you, if I ever lost you, I would die." She borrowed the washcloth to wipe her tears.

Too late.

He was already lost, didn't need a review course in Freudian psychology, or a psychiatrist to help him fully understand the dream. Something he'd repressed, didn't want to face from the second he'd laid eyes on Steve, voting against her only when he was sure she'd get the appointment anyway. Wanted her there more than Mitch.

He held Claudia.

His head was a mess.

Don't fight it, she had said. She didn't know what the "it" was. He had to fight it, and his torment over not wanting to hurt her.

The pain he felt for his mother the night he caught his father and aunt in illicit fondling returned. He felt the same pain for his wife. "You'll never lose me, Claudia."

But as he was saying it, he also knew, that after that night, he would never be the same when he was anywhere near Stefania Marchese.

Charles was about to leave for work the next morning when Claudia asked him to pick up on the way home from campus a pair of leaded glass panels she had ordered for their entrance door.

"Don't you think leaded glass is kind of expensive? We could've gotten away with using plain glass."

"The panels are expensive but they're in the entrance, set a tone for the whole house. Not that they really go with a Cape Cod, but Charles, I don't ask for many luxuries, and besides, you said you'd install them yourself, and that would save some money." She handed him an open map, and had already traced in red the route from the college to the factory and circled its location.

"Very well organized. Done like a school teacher."

"They emphasized the necessity of being organized in our education courses. Our survival in the classroom would depend on it."

"Do you miss teaching?"

"Sometimes I do, but I can't go back till the boys are older. Even though they're in school now, they still have lots of activities afterwards that I have to attend to."

"Whatever you want, Claudia, whatever makes you happy."

"You're what makes me happy". She kissed both his cheeks and hugged him so hard he felt she might pass through him. "Please, promise you won't have any more of those scary dreams. You even frighten me with them."

"Well, you know people can't control their dreams. But I promise I won't watch any more violent movies."

She hesitated, wrinkled her forehead. "I didn't think you ever did."

What did she mean by that? She was right. He never watched violent movies, hardly watched any movies at all, just political shows, and only those when he wasn't reading. Did she suspect what had really happened?

Charles spread the street map on the table. He took a closer look at the roads, tracing with his finger the route Claudia had outlined. If he picked up the Sprain, that would lead to the Taconic and to the exit at Underhill. His finger backtracked to Briarcliff Manor, the finger circling the area until it came to the street he remembered on Steve's resume. Hickory Lane. There it was, a few blocks off the Pleasantville Road exit.

"Daddy, daddy." Philip and Louis jumped on him, hugged him.

He let the map fall onto the floor. "Don't you two look handsome. And I bet you're smart, too."

"Our class's going on a field trip today," Philip said.

"Where?"

"Don't you remember, I told you last week. To the Hudson River Museum, the planetarium they have, to study the constellations."

"Philip made a constellation box and showed it to me," Louis said. "When I get older, I'll go to the planetarium, too, and find the same stars."

"You don't have to wait that long. Daddy'll take you to the planetarium this weekend."

"Oh, I love you, Daddy, you're the greatest." Louis picked up the map. "You dropped this. I'll put it in your briefcase for you." The boy had considerable difficulty trying to refold the map. After several futile attempts he squashed it together and stuffed it on top of the papers already placed in the open briefcase.

Charles stared at the map, the Pleasantville Road exit, and Hickory Lane jumping into his brain. He then snapped the briefcase closed. "Thanks, kid." He rubbed the top of Louis' head. "Don't forget, you and I have a date. This weekend."

Louis put his right thumb up.

Charles dragged himself into his six-year-old Monte Carlo. This morning, going to work was a chore. He had slept less than half the night, and even that part was restless.

But lack of sleep was the least of his problems. What was he going to do when he saw Steve? He'd have to find a way to avoid her, avoid looking at her except in the most casual way. Maybe talk to Wayne and come up with some excuse to have her office, or his, moved. But then, there was the hub.

While steering with his left hand, he tapped his forehead with his right. Was it in a book he read or in a movie that he remembered the saying that three things you couldn't hide were love, smoke, and a man riding on a camel? What difference did it make where he heard it as long as he hid it? He placed his right hand back on the wheel and steered with determination. He would hide his love and he would begin by practicing in the rear view mirror.

The aloof look.

The irked look.

The detached look

He was still practicing when he arrived on campus, lucky that he got there in one piece.

He walked into his office, thinking of what he would say to her.

Her door was open, the light on, but she wasn't there.

It might be possible to slip into class before she came back.

Charles emptied his briefcase on the desk, un-crinkled the map, then folded it properly. He filed a few papers before going through his mail.

He was just about to open the notes for his first class when he heard, "Charles, I have to speak to you." The tone was soft and mellow, very different from the taut intensity it communicated the day before.

Her voice made his head spongy.

He remained still, not wanting to look at her.

Oh yes, how he wanted to look at her!

He planted the aloof look on his face, tightened his lips, and braced himself to turn around. She was wearing a silky, long-sleeved shirtwaist dress, turquoise, her neck bare of the thin gold chain she had worn the day she was interviewed. She was leaning on the door with her arms behind her, the way she had the day before and in the dream, this time, though, looking more like a guest who wasn't quite sure she was welcome.

He avoided her eyes, remained silent.

"Charles, I had a chance to think about what I said to you yesterday. I think I overreacted. You have to understand that after all the work, the struggling I've done, to think that a male would get a job over me if he wasn't as good or better just pushes my button...not that I think that automatically giving your brother-in-law a job was justified, but at least it was a family matter on your part, and not that I'm a woman. I'm really sorry I attacked you the way I did, and I apologize. Shake?"

His dilemma. If he didn't take her hand, it meant he was holding a grudge, a stupid grudge. And if he did take it, it would hit his nervous system like an atomic blast.

How could he conceal his trembling hands?

He covered the hand she offered with both of his, keeping his fingers in motion. "Steve, I don't blame you for acting the way you did. I thought about it all the way home, and I wouldn't've liked it if someone had done that to me. What's important now is that you're here, he's not, and so far, you and I seem to be getting along. So let's forget it."

She withdrew her hand from both of his. "It's forgotten."

"I have to get to class."

"So do I, see you later."

"See you later." Charles added another folder from his briefcase to his notes and headed for class.

He wouldn't see her later.

He was seeing her now, and God help him, every waking and sleeping second.

Charles packed papers into his briefcase, planning to leave directly after his last class without returning to the office.

During lunch he deliberately placed his back toward the table where Steve was sitting. She was having lunch with Wayne. They seemed to be engaged in a light-hearted conversation.

Imagine. All of a sudden he was jealous of Wayne. A man at least twenty years his senior. A man who wore a toupee which never quite set right on his head.

Back to the business at hand. The leaded glass panels. He headed for his car, turned on the ignition, trying to recall the route to Underhill without referring to the map. As soon as he got onto the Sprain, he put on the radio. Had to find a way of distracting himself, but didn't want to miss the exit on the Taconic. A male voice was singing, "I know that your lips are sweet. But our lips can never meet."

He changed the station.

"Go away little girl," the same voice sang. "Go away little girl. It's hurting me more each moment that we delay. When you are near me like this, you're much too hard to resist. So go away little girl, before I beg you to stay."

He flipped off the radio. God in heaven, what are you trying to do to me? What are you trying to do?

This situation was utterly ridiculous, immature, infantile. It would pass. He'd find a way to get rid of this stupidity. He'd...

A mirage. Had to be. He had turned off the highway and found himself on Hickory Lane.

He jammed on his brakes, held his head in his hands and wept, disgusted with himself for behaving like an immature pathetic adolescent, a stupid love-sick puppy. He took out a handkerchief, wiped his face, blew his nose, his foot still hugging the brake.

According to the dashboard clock, five more minutes had passed. He turned the wheel and found his way back north on the Taconic.

Nothing could surpass a breakfast of bacon, eggs, and coffee anticipating the dunking of buttered toast. Saturday was the only day Claudia would allow Charles his cholesterol treat, and though he had just devoured more than his quota, his eyes couldn't let go of the two leftover crisp pieces of bacon curled up on the griddle, trying to decide whether or not to give in to the temptation. The two pieces of bacon forming a perfect 69.

Charles smacked himself in the head.

It was a good thing his wife had picked up some dishes and was heading toward the sink.

"Claudia, I've been thinking. I've been teaching at Graham for almost eight years now and I'm getting restless. Maybe it's the seven-year itch syndrome, time for a change."

Claudia returned to the table the dishes she had just picked up. One side of her fuzzy pink bathrobe was coming off her shoulder. She adjusted the robe back on her shoulder, then the belt, and sat down. "Charles, you just got tenure. If you change jobs, you're going to have to start all over again."

"I never worry about tenure, I'm sure I can get it somewhere else."

"But there are so few jobs for English professors now, the market's glutted with Ph.D.s in English."

"How about in another city, where we could get a bigger house, more land for less money?"

"You mean move, just when the children are adjusted to school?"

"They're young, more flexible."

"And what about your family, mine? I'll miss them. You know family is everything."

Family.

Family is everything.

His stomach became a knot. He couldn't tell her why she needed to be more flexible, but he had planted the seed. He'd bring up the subject again another time.

Maybe he could find a job in college administration elsewhere. There seemed to be more openings in that area than there were for professors. He would miss his literature, but if he were going to preserve his sanity, he had to get away.

He would apply for that sabbatical leave he was due for but hadn't yet taken. And even though he was the breadwinner, he'd take the sabbatical for a year at half-pay instead of for a semester at full pay. That choice would give him the edge over his competitors and the approval of the administration. It'd be tough, a big sacrifice now that he had a house, but in a year he could dig up some project, work part-time to make up the difference, forget Steve. A leave was one of his options. He'd check the *Chronicle* for more.

That evening Charles went to the one room he himself had finished in his basement, his place of refuge where he could immerse himself in literature.

He had always believed and tried to teach, successfully he thought, that literature, great literature, could provide insights into life. His hand swept over the neatly categorized shelves. It stopped at Elizabeth Barrett Browning. He pulled out a book and flipped through the pages to read a passage he had underlined.

> "Who so loves
> Believes the impossible."

Could it be that in the impossible situation he was finding himself, there was some chance he and Steve could be together? What made him even think that she felt the same about him? If she did, could she leave her husband, her children? Could he leave Claudia, the boys? Too many complications.

He replaced Browning, pulled out Jean Anouilh, searching for any section of the text he had marked. "Oh, love is real enough; you will find it some day, but it has one archenemy—and that is life."

Life did interfere with love. Life, with its twists and turns, its tricks. Life that creates one situation in which you feel comfortable, then left hooks you with another.

He didn't want to read any more of Anouilh. Too depressing.

But Dostoevsky might have the answer. He read out loud an excerpt from a page he had folded. "With love one can live even without happiness." Hearing the words accentuated his agony.

What on earth made him think that Steve loved him? Did she? Could she? If not, he'd have neither love nor happiness. Perhaps that best described his situation.

He hurled Dostoevsky onto the floor.

Sparks between Steve Marchese and Jim Dunbar were already jetting across the room, bouncing off the walls when Charles arrived at the Curriculum Committee meeting ten minutes late. He unpacked his briefcase, checked the minutes of the prior meeting he hadn't had a chance to review.

Jim was speaking non-stop, and Charles noticed Steve looking up at the portrait of the Grahams who, nestled in the wood paneling, appeared uneasy. He could read her mind. She was most likely thinking that the Grahams would be turning over in their mausoleums, listening to the proposals offered by the more radical professors.

"We have to drop the core curriculum in favor of courses that are more relevant," Jim said.

"And what might those be, Jim," Steve asked, "some of those gut courses that make the students feel free and happy but know less by the time they graduate than when they entered?"

Jim gave one of those impatient thrusts of the hand. "You have to trust the student to make his own decisions, you___"

Steve interrupted Jim with an air that said time was too precious a commodity for her to put up with his prattle. "We're supposed to be a community of scholars. While I value student input, I don't think they have the experience or expertise to know at this stage what literature they should read."

Jim was quick to respond. "They think Shakespeare is rubbish."

Steve had that if-eyes-could-kill look. "They think, they think? Stop right there. They can't think for themselves because people like you tell them what to think, don't model how to think rationally. They've come to that conclusion without ever having read Shakespeare, and sometimes I wonder if you have."

"Shakespeare and all that Western culture is very ethnocentric," Jim said.

Steve stood up, rested her palms against the glass-topped conference table, and leaned closer and closer toward Jim as she spoke. "Tell me which group isn't ethnocentric, which group doesn't think its culture's the greatest. And giving up reading the literature that has withstood the test of time, having universal application shouldn't be dropped in favor of the literature of the moment."

"Western culture is the culprit that fostered imperialism and the oppression of women, blacks," he retorted, his voice rising.

"I took only one history course at Barnard, and the most important thing I remember is that the professor, I can still see Dr. Dobbs scowling while shaking his fist, constantly reminding us that the greatest mistake of history is judging the past in terms of the present." As she spoke, she shook her fist the same way Dr. Dobbs must have. "Grow up, Jim. It's culprits like you who don't want the students to understand the history and culture of this nation, what made it great. All you really want is a curriculum that pleases the students instead of educating them. This way you'll be popular. You can go for popularity but I'll go for respect. Students crave leadership, develop only contempt for those who give in to their infantile demands. The students don't have to love me, I have enough love in my life outside this campus."

Those words went right for Charles' chest.

"They have to respect me," she went on, "and I'll be damned as long as I'm on this faculty if I succumb to some of the rubbish people like you propose. If students in their infinite wisdom want their educational experiences fragmented, want to eliminate grades, their whims catered to, run the universities, let them be presidents and deans elsewhere, and you and your ilk go with them."

"Don't let the Board of Trustees hear that," Jim said. "Everybody's concerned about enrollment."

Steve's voice was getting higher in pitch and amplitude. "The hell with the Board of Trustees. Besides, excellence and quality will always win out, just as it does in business. When you go for profit, you don't get it, but when you go for quality, profit follows. So if you're worried about enrollment, go for quality." She plopped into her chair.

Charles kept listening to Steve bombard Jim. Every word she uttered was an aphrodisiac.

Then Steve stood up again, addressed everyone on the committee, looking at each person face to face. "Let's not destroy the solid liberal arts program we've built here so when we realize we've made a mistake, after we produce a generation of robots and shallow ignoramuses, it'll be ten times harder to rectify the problem and re-institute a quality core program." She turned to Bob Lucas. "Bob, why don't you say something?"

Bob had been staring at the wall. He looked at Steve. "I'm listening. You're doing very well on your own."

"You're not open to new ideas, Steve," Jim said.

"I don't feel that things have to stay the way they are because that's the way they always were, and I am fully aware that change is the first step toward progress. But I am not for change for the sake of change. When I change something it has to be for the better, and I'm not open to anything just to be open. I'm open to seeing what literature you think would be adequate in replacing the Great Books. Put your literature on the table and explain to us how you're judging it. You justify it. I'm open to a lot more than you. I'm open to reasonable discourse. Therefore, I don't have my students forming conclusions before they even know what the problem is. I don't indoctrinate them and don't introduce courses with half truths or outright lies, those where propaganda substitutes for omissions and myths for truth."

Charles watched Steve knock the wind out of Jim. She was speaking so fast it was hard to keep up with her.

"And it kills me when people like you think they're open, open to everything but disagreement with your ideas. When people don't agree with you, you resort to your moronic virtue, or is it just plain lawlessness like the time Frank Bowman kicked down the bookstore door because it wasn't open all day and night, had bourgeois hours, so after he knocked the door down the students just went in and took whatever books they wanted. And let's not forget what happened to Leslie Wagner, who when she refused to go along with radical feminist doctrine, found feces dumped on the driver's seat of her car. You're all open all right."

Jim retorted, "We believe in equality. The student is equal to the professor."

"Equal to someone like you? You're wrong. The student is better. But I don't consider the student my equal, at this point in life the student has done nothing to warrant scholarly equality. And while we're talking about equality, let me remind you how much of a farce you made of this idea when you conducted class under a table so no one would be higher than the other, come on now. Pretty soon you'll be proposing that Congress pass legislation mandating that we all be of the same height."

Jim's face was the same color as his matted magenta shirt, the veins in his temples visibly pulsing. Steve had instigated everyone else in the committee to gang up on him.

Charles was titillated watching the show.

Steve Marchese was something else.

After the meeting Charles approached Bob Lucas in the hallway. "Bob, I know you hate meetings, but today you looked as though you were staring into space, really disturbed about something."

Bob's eyes made a bee-line for the floor. "Does it show that much?"

"I know how you feel about dropping the core curriculum."

"I can't understand why they'd want to dump the truly great literature for passing trends. Even though I was a science major, I read the great masterpieces in college and they've had a permanent, and I might add, positive effect on my life."

"Do you want to resign from the committee?"

"Hell, no."

"Then why are you so upset?"

Bob walked into Charles' office while beckoning him to follow. Bob closed the door and sat down. He crossed his legs, clasped his hands over his knee. His eyes remained low, and he didn't speak.

"What's the matter with you, Bob. Don't you feel good?"

"No, I don't feel good. As a matter of fact, I feel like shit."

"Maybe you should go for a physical."

"I don't need a physical. I need a shrink." He finally raised his eyes and looked directly at Charles. "I know I can talk to you in confidence."

Charles patted Bob's back, then sat at the desk. He folded his hands under his chin. "Of course you can, you know that, what's on your mind?"

Bob was silent a few seconds. Remaining in the same cross-legged position with hands over his knee, he began to rock back and forth, back and forth. "It's about a member of my department who serves under my chairmanship no less."

"Who?"

Bob hesitated. "Steve."

"Yeah, she can be a tough cookie. When she believes in something, she really pushes for it, and when she does, get out of the way."

"It's not that, Charles. I find." His eyes rediscovered the floor. "I find that I'm...I'm...I'm attracted to her."

The silence that followed was disquieting. He wasn't sure which urge to comply with, clutch Bob in an empathetic embrace, or beat his face to a pulp. He had difficulty choking out, "You mean, a...a sexual attraction?"

"More than that, Charles. I enjoy her company, love when she's near me, when we're together. I even look forward to the curriculum committee meetings when she's there, and you know how I hate that committee. She's wonderful. And yes, Charles, I am sexually attracted to her, very much so. In fact, Charles, she's such a breath of fresh air that I feel invigorated in her presence, and...Jesus Christ, Charles, I think, I think I'm in love with her, with the whole person."

Why did he suddenly feel like the statue of Saint Sebastian, the one in his old church, with arrows pierced all over his body? Charles unfolded his hands from under his chin, moved them under the desk and clutched them. "Bob, how can you be in love with her? You're a married man, she's married, too. Get a grip on yourself. I'm not sure I can give you sound advice on this matter, you should probably talk to Bill Foster. But the fact that you've come to me, to anyone at all, the fact that you've admitted the problem to yourself is a good first step."

How good-looking Bob was! Full head of black hair, deep blue eyes, chiseled nose. Never noticed before.

Charles stood up feeling that if he didn't do something more constructive with his hands, he'd end up pummeling Bob. He grabbed the back of his chair, and shook it. "I really don't know what to tell you,

I wasn't prepared for this, especially from you, but as you spend enough time in this job you get to view the world through your own discipline."

Charles rolled his chair from the back of his desk, and skidded the chair next to Bob. "Sex is a powerful force. What immediately comes to mind, because I did my dissertation on Lawrence, is what he describes as the phallic hunt. He was concerned with contrasting the mental with the phallic consciousness, and how the two may be reconciled, probably because he was trying to reconcile it for himself and it's universal to all men. Am I making any sense?"

"Yeah, something like the Yiddish schmuck."

"Right, stupid, but if you know it's stupid, at least you're thinking. You're aware of the fact that the phallus needs to be regulated. Bob, you're walking in very dangerous territory. Very dangerous. It's insanity. You have a lot to lose. Maybe it's just what they call middle-age crazy. At our age we want to feel as though we're not losing our youth. We drive silly sports cars, look for younger women, you know what I'm talking about."

"I don't remember having this barrage of hormones when I was a teenager. I keep thinking, thinking we made a mistake when we hired Steve, should've taken that Broderick fellow."

"Moot point. As for hormones, man has to maintain an intelligent control over hormones or he is no better than the beast." He gazed at the ceiling. "These things don't happen to people who are happily married." His gaze abandoned the ceiling for Bob. "You are, aren't you?"

"I thought I was."

"You've got to get a handle on this, it can ruin your career, your family, your life. Now this sometimes happens when men and women work together. Probably more so now that women are striving to compete with men in the workforce. But people like us, you and me," he moved his hand back and forth between them, "we know the rules. I mean there are vows we've taken and we have to take them seriously."

"Charles, even you, Mr. Stability, have to admit she's unique."

Charles felt that leeches had attached themselves to his head. He couldn't understand how he was able to resume speaking, but managed to smile through clenched teeth. "There are lots of unique women, but you can't fall in love with all of them. Do...do you think she knows how you feel? I mean did she ever give you the sense that she may feel the same way, maybe...maybe come on to you?" He held his breath in anticipation of the answer.

"Never. What the hell's the matter with you, you know she'd never do that."

That last remark slugged him in the chest. He sighed, hoping that by his sighing, Bob would think it was relief for his situation.

"I know it's crazy, Charles, but whenever I'm on campus, I search for her in every room, scan it with my peripheral vision. When she's not there, I get this aching feeling. I arranged the course schedule so we'd both be free at the same time. Then I'd know she'd be in the cafeteria, an excuse to have lunch together. Bob covered his mouth as he continued to speak. "I...I...even followed her home one day."

"That was risky, did she see you?"

"Hell, no. I keep asking myself how this could happen. Maybe because I married my high school sweetheart. Didn't have enough experience with women before I got married. Steve reminds me of one of those girls in high school you always desired but knew were untouchable, knew they'd never look at you, the kind that just floated around campus, and you choked with desire each time they passed by. Charles, I've been over this again and again, and I don't know what to do."

What advice could he possibly give him? "Look, Bob, I'm not a psychologist or a priest. You should see a therapist, a marriage counselor without your wife of course, at first. You know we men are supposed to need a variety, more stimuli, they'll explain it to you because I can't be of much help."

"You've been so much help already, just listening to me. And I know I can trust you to keep this to yourself."

He pressed his hand into Bob's shoulder. "Absolutely."

Who the hell did Bob think he was feeling for Steve the way he did? What gall!

While driving home, he regretted not being able to tape record his rage-controlled, Oscar-winning conversation with Bob. Advice that had come out so freely.

Advice he should have played back to himself over and over again.

Steve felt more than a twinge of discomfort sitting in the reception room of the president's office. Her eyes examined the walls. It seemed as though there was a different portrait of the Grahams in every important office and room, and this one was no exception. When did they ever find the time to pose? But today the Grahams were staring at her with a scowl.

Why did Chester's secretary, Mrs. Grant, who was always so cordial, sound so stern over the phone when she asked, no demanded, that Steve come to the president's office? And why was Mrs. Grant giving her such a cold shoulder today when she was always so expressive and gracious?

Steve's grades were in on time, she was never late, conducted classes the students enjoyed and learned from. She did have a habit of parking her car in front of the library, but that could've been handled with a brief memo.

There wasn't much more time to consider this meeting before she found herself being ushered into Chester's office by his silent, stone-faced secretary.

Chester Finlay was sitting behind his desk, fiddling with the collar of his turtleneck. His face, hung over by gravity, shouted deep smile lines even though he wasn't smiling. Accessible to his right hand was an oval goldfish bowl, brimming over with M&M's. The only bright spot in the office came from the reflection of light from his bald head. The room didn't appear so imposing the day she came here to meet with him before receiving her contract.

He rose, moved a chair to face the front of his desk, resumed his position behind it, then motioned her to sit. "Dr. Marchese."

What happened to the Steve he always called her?

Chester selected a few yellow M&M's, popped them into his mouth before he clasped his hands and moved to the edge of his seat. Then he unclasped his hands, lifted a pen, and brandished it at her. "It has come to my attention you stated publicly that you think students should go elsewhere and that the Board of Trustees could go to hell."

Ha! So when the open, liberal, sniveling snitches wouldn't confront her on the issues, they reported her to the president. Really ballsy. She decided to let Chester finish before responding.

"I'm sure I don't have to tell you that colleges are becoming very competitive for students, especially now that the society is moving toward equality, and the attitude of many students is they should go to a city or state college instead of a private one like Graham. They don't want to be associated with anything that's considered remotely elitist. The last thing we can tolerate is professors' encouraging students to go to our competitors. Attrition is bad enough." He nestled himself into the back of his chair, and with the pen he was no longer waving at her probed for more yellow M&M's, directing them to the top of the bowl. When he collected a handful worth, he shoved the M&M's into his mouth all at once. "Now I'd like to hear your side of the story," he said while crunching them, "so what do you have to say?"

Her nature was to explode, but if there was ever a time she had to remain calm and rational, it was now. But above all, she had to be honest. She leaned toward him. "First of all, thank you for inviting me to tell you what you call my side. Only I'd like to think of it as our side. What you heard was taken out of context. I don't know what you mean when you say we're moving toward equality because I don't know what that word means anymore. I only know what quality means. Jim Dunbar and I had a, shall we say for lack of a better word, a discussion during the Curriculum Committee meeting about dropping the core requirements, something he was for, and I, against. He wanted to replace the core with courses the students want but he wasn't, still isn't able to give me the criteria for judging the courses except in a most superficial way. He's also supporting history courses that are fantasy, not fact. And I said that students who want that kind of education should go somewhere else.

"I believe that parents who spend a lot of money to send their children here should get excellence, not fads and mistruths. Chester," she leaned closer to him and pressed his wrist as her eyes interlocked with his, "a degree from Graham has to mean something. When the perception out there is that it does, that we demand quality and can deliver it, students'll be banging on our doors to get in. We don't need courses that have students feel good about themselves and not learn anything substantive."

The strain on Chester's face disappeared. So did the white imprint of her fingers on his wrist when she released it. He dug deeper into the goldfish bowl, with his entire hand this time, stiffening and stretching his fingers to pick up a few, increasing more elusive yellow M&M's. "We have to remain open-minded, Steve."

She must have been making points with him. He was back to calling her Steve, and for the first time in their encounter, he offered her some yellow M&M's, which she refused. Did the yellow ones taste different, or did the color have some other significance? "Scientists are trained to be open-minded. We change our opinions all the time, but that change must be based on solid information, facts. As a professor, assistant professor though it may be, I am ashamed at what some of my colleagues are trying to pass off as scholarship. Now I know it's easier to be scientific with more tangible, empirical data that we in the biological and physical sciences have access to, but the social scientists want to use our methods, too, and that's fine with me. But," she said slowly and deliberately, "the politics must not guide the science, and that's exactly what's happening."

What was the matter with Chester? His eyes were closed. Damn it. Was she boring him to death? She raised her voice. "Chester, are you listening to me?"

His eyes popped open. "Of course I am, heard every word you said, can repeat it verbatim. I can concentrate better with my eyes closed, it blocks out other stimuli." He closed his eyes again.

Did he close his eyes during a Board of Trustees meeting? This was no time to test him, so she continued with an overdrive effort to retain her composure. "As I was saying, the politics must not guide the science. When they won't consider any hypothesis they don't like before it's even tested, push conclusions and opinions and present only information that supports their ideas, won't look at new evidence, they should be exposed for the unscientific thinkers they are. The result is knee-jerk education, students sop up and can spout on command opinions they've been told, but they can't back them up with facts, don't even know how to begin finding them. They need the analytic tools to help them cope with making intelligent decisions."

Was it the gab genes she'd received from the Irish or the Italians that wouldn't make her shut up?

"Chester, it's one thing to have adolescent students, that we expect. But adolescent faculty? I still can't imagine that you didn't suspend or have Bowman and his students charged with breaking and entering when they destroyed the door to the bookstore, invaded the place, and stole books because the bookstore had reasonably scheduled hours, something they interpreted as bourgeois. They were rewarded for their despicable behavior and that only encourages more of the kind including the faculty's getting away with intellectual dishonesty, especially under the guise of academic freedom. Believe me, Chester, they're not being academics, and they have no clue what freedom entails.

"We should encourage exposure to new ideas. Investigate them. Test them. The university is the last haven for inquiry. If we don't do it here, and do it right, we might as well fold up our tents and move on, because we're all frauds and should be sued for malpractice."

"Can you give me an example of what you're talking about, what they're promoting and just how they do it?" He opened his eyes again, but this time kept them that way.

She looked straight into his pupils, firmed up her voice. "Are you sure, really sure you want to hear it?"

He squinted, then blinked. "I want your input, about what I just asked you, and, and about anything else that's on your mind."

She moved her face very close to his. "Absolutely sure?"

"Shoot."

Had she known they'd end up with this discussion, she would've been prepared. But now that she had the president's ear, by God she'd fill it with all the issues jammed up in her. She waited to begin, hoping that once she started, the dendritic connections in her brain wouldn't fail her but would trigger others.

"Lately, Chester, I've been feeling that I'm watching a play in the theater of the absurd. The cast of characters includes some of the faculty and their student followers. The play's theme is we don't believe in the old values anymore, or any moral authority for that matter. We believe in the earth. The creation, not the Creator. God is dead. *Time* magazine has told us so. And with no moral authority, let's believe anything, the anything being all lifestyles and values are equal including leading to equal results. Success is good only if everyone can have it equally, whether or not they've invested the same effort. We can't be judgmental even if we've had the experience to know better. And do you know why we can't be judgmental? I mean, do you get it, Chester?"

"I think I get it, but tell me anyway."

"So this feel-good society can feel good about their weaknesses instead of confronting them head-on. With the rules gone we don't have to be accountable for our behavior. And with God dead, we have new gods. The god of drugs. And the god of sex who preaches that casual sex doesn't lead to illegitimate pregnancies, emotional consequences, venereal diseases, and take it from one who knows, there are new ones lurking in the future. Let's ridicule couples committed to their marriage. The most bizarre behavior is considered normal. It seems as though the country has become inoculated against common sense. Where do people think this is all going to end? Do they think beyond the moment, or think at all? Even Charles has constantly complained to me about this."

"Which Charles?"

"Pastore."

"A good man. A little pompous, full of himself, but otherwise a good man." Chester pursed his lips while nodding. "Smart as a whip."

She was shocked that the president would make such personal comments in front of her about another faculty member, but it gave her time to pause, catch her breath, and inhale another deep one. "Last week I picked up the catalog to refer to for advisement purposes, and my eyes happened to fall on the college's mission. Have you read it lately?"

He shook his head. "I know what it says."

"Commitment through excellence and leadership. Commitment through excellence and leadership," she repeated slowly and emphatically. "And sadly I found myself laughing. These are just words, empty words, and they've become a joke. What is excellent about an education that doesn't expose students to all points of view? What leadership can they exhibit, and what could they be committed to with such an unscientific education. Do you want me to go on, or have you heard enough?"

He rolled his arm as though trying to increase the volume of an orchestra he was conducting. "Please continue."

"You know most of the other issues such as relaxing standards, pushing gut courses, accepting Black English, and eliminating grades. The only standards now are double standards. Free expression unless someone else's values are being expressed. Choices for women unless they disagree with the choices of the radical feminists, and I can go on.

"Now take the case of pot. We don't know the long-term effects of smoking it, all we know so far is that it can lead to harder drug dependency. Yet some faculty, too many actually say it's perfectly safe, even though the evidence just isn't there, and a few of them are smoking pot with the students. And don't get me started on mind-altering drugs in this imbecilic tune-in, turn-on, drop-out, experience-everything generation. Let me ask you, Chester."

He moved closer.

"In the balance of things, which is better, living in a single or two parent household, getting promoted for achieving grade level or not?"

Chester must have known the questions were rhetorical, for he didn't respond, just kept staring at her.

Why did she feel she was having a transient ischemic attack, her blood leaving her brain for her feet? She had worked herself up into such a state, she thought she might faint. For many seconds she allowed silence to remain between them before winding herself up again. "Now this has nothing to do with the examples you asked for but I've noted a lack of civility on campus. I can't understand why professors can't express themselves with the vocabulary of educated, professional people instead of adopting the sophomoric language of the students with speech such as `pissed off', `suck' and its rhyming word becoming commonplace with them especially in the classroom. The terms," she paused hoping her next words would sink in, "consequences and responsibility, have been eradicated from the dictionary. The only vocabulary expansion I've witnessed on the part of both students and faculty is that ass has become asshole.

"And as long as we're having this discussion," she brushed aside several pens on his desk with some of them rolling off, "I think it's an absolute disgrace that some professors are sleeping with their students. Parents trust their daughters to our care and they end up being compromised by a bunch of middle-aged jackasses who need their egos stroked. They're all against power and authority but they want to exert their power and authority over these young women."

"What would you expect me to do about it? The girls are the age of consent."

She got up, moved toward him and stood over him. He remained in his chair. "There's a difference between what's legal and what's good judgment, like...like the difference between the First Amendment and pornography. You're like Nero, Chester, been sitting on your fanny in this office too long, fiddling around fund-raising while Graham is burning. Get off your butt, mingle with the troops for a while, talk to people, the faculty, students. Visit classrooms, listen, and above all, visit the dorms. You'll begin to get a sense of what's really going on."

Should she be bold enough to say what she was thinking? Why not seize the opportunity? "You asked me for my input, what I would expect you to do about their sexual activity? You know I'm a physician." She began pacing. "In that capacity the first thing I would suggest is that you eliminate, or at least cut your intake of M&M's in half. Besides increasing your chances for constipation, they give you a sugar high quickly followed by a sugar low, which makes your brain spongy. Then, after really assessing the academic and social situation on campus, go have your testicles examined."

His eyes bulged, his chin fell into his chest, and his bald shiny head reflected red.

"When you've been assured they're still there and functioning," she continued, "call the culprits in. One at a time, not all together. That part's important. You know who they are, and tell them you'll have them fired if it ever happens again."

Good. He seemed flustered by what she was sure was her reference to his private parts. About time someone pumped his brain with some shock therapy. But he needed some more.

He shook his head. "But...but they're all tenured."

"So you *do* know who they are!" She gave him the most piercing stare she could muster. "Chester, I assure you if you take a strong stand, don't cave in on this issue, it'll go away. Now before you call them in, do your homework, consult with the college's lawyers so that when the lechers play the tenure card, you can describe in detail exactly how you can have them thrown out. They're such wimps you'll have to call the janitor to clean up after them. Now if you want to lose students, just let the word get out to the parents that some of this nonsense is going on. Would you want your daughter subjected to it? I wouldn't."

Chester leaned his elbows on the desk and remained silent for some time. Finally, he shoved aside the fishbowl of M&M's, and got out of his chair. "I have to tell you, Steve, I was furious with you when I heard about that comment you made at that meeting. I should've known it was misconstrued." He faced her directly, then looked askance. "Sometimes I think you're a little too blunt, can use more tact, but I know you're a straight-shooter, and I thank you for your input. I'm going to think about what you said, talk to Wayne about it. Not sure how I'm going to handle it yet."

"I trust you'll come up with the right thing."

He offered his hand which she pressed between hers.

With his free hand he squeezed both of hers. "Can't believe what they said even registered with me."

"Consider the source, Chester. Consider the source."

CHAPTER 13

STEVE LEFT CHESTER'S office shaken, sure that her blood pressure had passed 200. All the way back to her office she kept talking to herself, mulling over their conversation. Social sciences. Social sciences. Soft sciences they were. Who did some of these social scientists think they were usurping the methods of the hard sciences, bastardizing, contorting, and maiming them? How dare these same social scientists not only destroy objective knowledge, but worse, destroy the methods of discovering it.

The hard sciences belonged to her, and she'd be damned before she'd let these agenda-promoting twits get away with twisting her sciences, her methodology to suit their own purposes. These new gods were churning society into their own image and likeness, and God help the society when the churning was over.

Whoever heard of coming to conclusions before one ever entertained a hypothesis? Whoever heard of a plausible hypothesis being discarded before being tested, if one didn't want that hypothesis to be validated? And as she had told Chester, teach conclusion they want and then find only the facts which supported them.

What should she do about it? Be like too many of her colleagues, accede to the ridiculous to avoid dealing with the real problems? Talk and complain about it and do nothing, expect and hope that others would do something? With all her failings, and she acknowledged she could list them on at least two sheets of paper, typewritten, single-spaced, on both sides, being a fraud wasn't one of them.

A revolution was gripping academia, one that had nothing to do with scholarship, and everything to do with propaganda. The time had come for a counter-revolution. And did any revolution ever get going unless someone started it?

She paced around her office for a while, then slumped into her desk chair, pen in mouth. So this was why professors sucked on their pipes! Perhaps oral gratification fed inspiration.

The drooping plants around her room seemed to have picked up on her feelings. They needed an infusion of water. And what the students needed was an infusion of intellectual honesty and analytic skills.

What could she do?

Form a truth squad?

Too tacky.

How about establishing a club? That idea was more practical, more subtle. How much time would it take away from her family? Who might even be interested in joining? What would she call it?

A catchy name would be desirable. The Truth-Seekers Club? Gads. So sanctimonious she could see the members coming to meetings wearing halos. The Anti-Propaganda Club? Too much like promoting its own propaganda. The Rodin Society. Would anyone get that it was promoting thinking?

She removed the pen from her mouth, opened the top right drawer, and pulled out a sheet of paper. She closed the drawer, then opened it again and removed a few more sheets. She scrawled the words, think, think, think.

The pen was back in her mouth.

She tore the paper in half, then in quarters, and threw it into the wastepaper basket. On the next sheet she wrote, think, be alert, wake up.

Worse than the first try.

She also attempted to toss that paper into the wastepaper basket, but it landed on the floor. She let it rest.

On the third sheet she wrote, "Are you tired of being told what to think instead of being exposed to how to think?" She read it over, then underlined what and how. Then she read it out loud. It had a good ring to it. Now what club title would correspond to the copy? It would take good scholarship to be an effective thinker. Good scholarship. She snapped her fingers. By Jove she got it. The Scholars Society. Did she need an apostrophe after the s? Was it the club of, by, or for scholars? That wasn't the pressing issue now. Expanding upon the copy was. Come join The Scholars Society, where you and your professors will deal with real issues and analyze scientifically how...

A crash came from the room next door. She held on to the paper and rushed out of her office.

As she approached the doorframe to Charles' office, she saw that a bookcase had overturned, split into several pieces, books scattered all over the floor. She began picking them up. "What happened?"

Charles was breathing heavily as he removed the books from her arms. He placed the books on his desk. "Please don't bother, I'll fix this mess as soon as I calm down."

"Was the bookcase out of balance?"

A lot was out of balance in his life. "No, I shoved it over myself. In a tantrum."

"A tantrum? Aren't you a little old for that? That's a monopoly for two-year-olds. What's wrong with you lately anyway, you've been acting strange." She frowned, then cowered. "Are you still angry with me for blowing up at you?"

He was shocked that she would even entertain that idea. "Do you think I'm the vendetta type?"

"Since we never had a disagreement before the one about your brother-in-law, nor since, I don't know what to think."

He stooped over to examine the bookcase. "I really did a job on this, seems irreparable." He tried to match up some of the pieces. "Even if it holds, it'll never be the same. I'll call maintenance, let them take it away. Maybe they have another one, a better one in the storage room, donated by some corporation for a tax deduction."

"Good luck. And whatever possessed you to turn it over in the first place?"

"Frustration. Frustration aggression. Or," he paused., "maybe the psychologists would call it sublimation. An incident in class made me furious."

"Do you want to tell me about it? You don't have to if you don't want to." Her tone and face conveyed genuine concern.

What the hell, why shouldn't he? "You know that blowhard, Barry Klinger?"

She shook her head. "I heard his name before but never had him as a student."

"Even if you haven't, you can't miss him. Same old story. Constantly parroting what he hears in class. Beating up on Shakespeare, Western civilization. Speaks with such authority on matters about which he knows nothing. Never an original thought, or any thought for that matter in his head, and I've had my fill of him. But today he pushed me over the top and I guess, I guess, my way of gagging him was to punch the bookcase. I had no idea how fragile it was."

"So," she said, squinting, hands on hips, "what are you going to do about it, huh? Wreck another bookcase? That'll really accomplish something!"

"Just before I had my little tantrum, I was sitting at my desk trying to come up with some type of organization which could weed out that type of thinking, or maybe I should say the non-thinking being shoved down these students' throats. I started to___"

She removed her hands from her hips, and offered him the paper she was still holding. "Do great minds run in the same direction or what? I was going to put this flyer in everyone's mailbox, invite everyone, students, faculty, administration. It's only a first draft, but it's the concept that counts."

He read the heading out loud. "The Scholars Society."

"Does scholars need an apostrophe, English professor?"

"No, in this case it's considered a plural not possessive."

"Good, I didn't put one in. I was feeling the same frustration so I came up with the idea. Want to co-sponsor it with me, put your money where your mouth is? A great way to vent our frustration."

What could she know of his frustration? What he needed was less, not more contact with her. "How would we do it?"

"Not sure yet." She hesitated. "For starters, suppose I give them instruction in critical thinking, then let them practice it in groups with a problem of their choice. You could help me circulate among the groups and see what types of questions they come up with, add some of your own. And, and if you want to reverse the procedure, you give them instruction in critical thinking, and I'll assist you with the groups. That would be fine with me."

"Either way, it's a big commitment."

"Anything worth doing is."

The day the club was scheduled for its first meeting, Steve entered the conference room a half-hour ahead of the posted time. She complimented herself for reserving the Blake Room, the smallest of all the conference rooms. It was like booking a concert hall. If just a few people showed up, the place wouldn't look vacant, the performers less embarrassed. And tonight of all nights, she didn't want to play to an empty house.

Sitting all alone in that room was eerie. The Blake Room was just as mahogany paneled and dark as the other conference rooms, even darker since it had only two windows. The reddish hue in the wood, if it added anything at all, made the lighting slightly more mellow.

She had arranged for a portable blackboard, and tried to decide where she should rest it by wheeling it in several different directions to catch whatever light was not being absorbed by the walls. Out of her tote bag she unpacked a board eraser and a box of chalk, just in case.

Torrential rain with a driving wind kept blowing so much water against the windows she was sure they would cave in, with the chairs in the room floating soon after. The temperature was hovering around 36 degrees. She hoped it would stay above freezing, not have to drive home in the dreaded ice. Would anyone venture out in this weather? The propagandists knew what she was up to, and would gloat if the occasion ended up being a no-show.

Ten minutes later she was still alone. Not even Charles was there. She should've cancelled, maybe postponed the meeting.

She kept looking at her watch, checking it against the hexagonal brass wall clock. She stepped up to the blackboard and erased it even though it was blank.

Twelve minutes later, a young man entered, soaked. He was followed by Charles, who looked around the room, his face displaying the same anxiety that she felt. He acknowledged her, sat a few seats away, and removed some pads from his briefcase.

Seconds later a few more students dribbled in, umbrellas creating rivulets on the chevron wood floor. She would start promptly even if no one else came.

By the time the minute hand pulled itself to eight o'clock, seventeen students had gathered, none of them hers. Why weren't any of her students there? She was about to begin when another five poked their heads in, then disappeared for a few seconds before carrying in more chairs to add to the circle she had arranged. Not bad. Especially in this crazy weather. Twenty-two students so far out of a student body of two thousand. No other faculty showed up.

She rose.

The room became quiet.

Then, sensitized to the notion of equality Jim Dunbar's charades had stamped into her, she sat down. "Before we begin, I'm curious to know what dragged you all out on such a stormy night."

A young man raised his hand. "I was curious about the club."

"Please tell me your name."

"Jack."

"It's not necessary to raise your hand, Jack, this is not a class, it's a club you will all eventually run yourselves, as soon as you learn how to do it properly. Just tell me what you were curious about."

Jack began lifting his arm again, but instead squeezed his eyes before placing his hand back in his lap. "I know what the word scholar means, at least I think I know, but I'm not sure what scholars do."

A smile crossed her face. "Well, we're about to find out. You have to remember first and foremost that to think like a scholar, or to put it another way, to think scientifically, it is imperative that you do not fool yourself. The big problem here, and you will have to keep reminding yourself of this, is that *you* are the easiest person to fool."

Silence followed. She allowed the silence for some time to let her last comment sink in. "What we're going to do will not be easy, at least in the beginning before what we learn to do becomes habitual. We're going to practice some scientific thinking, use analytic skills to help us solve problems, make intelligent, informed decisions. The fact that you're here on this dreadful night demonstrates that you are motivated enough to succeed."

"I'm here because I think the name of the club has snob appeal," shouted a young man wearing a Make Love Not War T-shirt so worn Steve could just about read the words.

Most of the other students booed.

A girl who looked as though she should have been cast for the role of Jennifer in *Love Story* called out, "One of my professors told me that only suckers would come to this meeting, join this society."

"Well, you be the judge. Tonight will be a sampler, you don't have to come back. Now let me ask you what recent events have captured your interest?"

"Watergate," a girl sitting near the door offered.

"Do you have a particular problem about Watergate you'd like to bring up?"

"No, but give me some time, come back to me later."

Steve surveyed the seating circle she had created. Strange that everyone in the group was wearing glasses…aviator, French, horn-rimmed, and those with huge frames. Did the types of glasses selected identify personalities, politics? "Anyone else?"

"Suppose we do, how about whether the eighteen-year-olds should have gotten the vote," the potential Jennifer said.

"That may be interesting. What's your name?"

"Jennifer."

How was that for coincidence? "Let's have some more suggestions before we decide."

The man next to Jack adjusted his chair. "I was always interested in whether or not we should've gone into Cambodia."

Charles, who had been watching her carefully but had remained quiet, finally interjected, "What we could do is examine the information we had at the time, which if I recall correctly was May of either 1969 or 1970...actually," he thought for a while, "1970, and the information we have now, then compare and contrast the decisions we would've made under both circumstances."

Steve kept looking toward the door. Where were the radical faculty tonight? Would they pop in at any moment with their antics, disrupt the meeting, or were they all sugar plums? Then a stomach-sinking thought passed through her. Were these students sent as plants? Snoopy surrogates?

A black-haired, dark-eyed young man just about jumped out of his chair, his sudden movement chasing the weird thought out of her. "What about whether or not drugs should be legalized?"

Nods followed raised eyes.

She went back to the woman who wanted to discuss Watergate. "Have you come up with any problems about Watergate yet?"

"No, the drug question is fine with me, it's better than my idea."

"Well, if you want to pursue some Watergate questions, we could do it at another meeting. I get the feeling there's consensus about the drug question." She waited for objections but there were none.

She had done her homework, prepared for this meeting. And it had been pure self-discovery. Never before had she attempted to teach the content her homework had revealed, and she was now ready to take a chance at what might follow.

"Before we begin our discussion tonight, I would like us to undergo a little exercise as a prerequisite to scholarly thinking, and for everyday decision-making. We all have biases, and tend to rely on our emotions when making decisions. When our emotions take over, we sift through facts and have a tendency to select only those we want to consider. To maximize the quality of your thinking, you have to first become an effective critic of your own thinking. Then you have to practice, practice, and practice some more until effective thinking becomes a habit. The first critique deals with the problem of egocentric thinking."

Payback time. The social scientists had used, or maybe she should say abused her discipline. Now she would use their subject, only, she hoped, with honor.

But now came her dilemma. Should she present an overview of what was to be accomplished so that they could see how each part fit into the whole, or should she just go step by step and not overwhelm them? Keeping them too late, especially on a night like tonight, would be self-defeating, so she chose the latter.

"I am going to ask five questions, write them all on the board. Then we'll go over each one individually." She selected a piece of chalk from the box she had brought with her and walked up to the board. She sectioned off a space on the top, drew four vertical lines underneath, each leaving an equal amount of space in between, at least as her eye could gauge. "As I write these questions, I want you to try to be honest with yourself, and think of answers to each question as they relate to you personally. Now we all do these, but it is imperative that we know we're doing them. The first is, what do you believe is true because *you* believe it?" She wrote, 'What do you believe is true because' in the top space, then 'you believe it?' at the head of the first column. She underlined 'you'.

The students looked at each other as though she had asked a trick question.

"Could you explain that a little more?" The voice came from a fair-skinned, blonde man with the stubble on his face trying desperately to become a beard.

"Basically, the question is asking what you assume to be true, about any subject at all, your politics, your morals, that kind of thing, even though you have never questioned the basis for that truth. To put it another way, can you give an example where you assumed others were correct because they agreed with you, and incorrect when they didn't? Now you'll have plenty of time to consider each question, but I want to bring them all up first. Okay?"

No objections. Only perplexed faces.

"The next question is, what do you believe to be true because *we* believe it?" She pointed to the question already in the space at this top, then wrote 'we believe it?' at the head of the second column, making sure she underlined 'we'. "This one is different from the first in that it is more social. It asks what you assume to be true because the group you belong to, your friends, your religion, your culture, believes it, but you have never questioned the basis for that truth."

Were they getting this, or was she wasting her time? Maybe she should have ignored this part, and gone straight to the drug problem they suggested.

No. They needed this first, and with practice, would make the connection.

"The third question is, what do you believe is true because you *want to* believe it? While writing 'you want to believe it?' on the board, she had a vision of her mother sitting on their Victorian living room sofa, and recalled that Mom had warned her that in making decisions, so much was what you want to believe.

"Only two more. The next is, what do you believe is true because you *have always* believed it? She wrote the appropriate part of the question at the head of the fourth column underlining the words she had emphasized. "Our behavior indicates that we more readily believe what coincides with long held beliefs. So what beliefs have you long held, even though you have not seriously considered the extent to which, given the evidence, or if you've looked for any evidence at all, that those beliefs are justified?"

She checked their faces for understanding. All she could read on them so far was concentration. And that was good because they were at least paying attention.

"Finally, what do you believe is true because it is *in your selfish interest* to believe it?" She completed the fifth column heading. "What beliefs do you hold fast to that justify your getting more money, power, prestige or other personal gain, even though these beliefs are not grounded in sound reasoning or evidence?"

From under the window came a voice, hardly audible, competing with the beating that the water was giving the panes. "Could you give us more details on the third question?"

Steve checked the board for column three. "Are you dating someone you know to be intrinsically selfish, but you want to believe you can change that person? Can you provide some situation when you wanted to believe something because it felt good, supported your other beliefs, or when what you wanted to believe didn't require you to change your thinking in any significant way, or admit you were wrong?"

"Thanks, that helps…somewhat," the voice responded.

They were all still staring at the board, even Charles. All participants seemed oblivious to the vociferous storm.

"Dr. Pastore will pass out some paper." At the sound of his name, Charles jumped out of his seat, began ripping paper from his pads and distributing it.

"What I'd like you to do," she continued, "is write at least three answers to each question, examples of your beliefs that fit under each category. Do some honest soul-searching. Mull it over, it will be a real challenge. I'm not going to collect the papers, only you will see the answers. Your responses should help clear your head for receiving objective evidence when examining problems The Scholars Society will tackle. Let me review the questions once more. What do you believe is true because," she placed her hand above each column respectively, "you believe it, your group believes it, you want to believe it, you have always believed it, or it is in your selfish interest to believe it. So are you ready?"

The only response she received was from the wind whistling up and down, up and down, like someone practicing a glissando on a cello. As for the students, they remained dead-panned. She and Charles shared some inquisitive glances. Where was he all night, just gaping at her, hardly injecting any input, behaving more like an observer than a co-sponsor?

Then one by one students' pens were in mouths. She recalled her own experience. Oral gratification feeding inspiration. Some intense seat squirming before a few began writing. Gradually, more students started scrawling. Eventually all were busy writing.

Ten minutes into the task she requested that they stop working. "Now take those same questions that you dealt with in a general way, and apply them to the drug problem. For example, what do you currently believe about the legalization of drugs though you never questioned that belief. Looking over at column three, what do you want to believe about drug legalization? Do this with all five questions. There are no wrong or right answers, just your own honesty and open-mindedness. And this part is critical." She made sure all eyes were on her. "Think. Think of how your current beliefs might color your answer to the drug problem before we even consider it. If you need more paper, let me know. Now begin."

A long pause before more writing.

A fusillade of rain attacking the windows didn't seem to distract anyone. Even Charles was writing what she assumed to be his own answers to the questions.

She kept her eye on the clock, allowing ten more minutes for this set of responses.

"Time is up. If you have more to write, that's fine, you can do it on your own, but now we have to move on. What is important is that you should have a sense of your own biases and beliefs which may not be based on objective investigation, and you should do this exercise often, in fact every time you consider making a decision."

The body language in the room was encouraging, the students leaning forward instead of stretching back in their seats. And it appeared that in just these few minutes the blonde man's stubble had matured. "Put your private papers away."

They quickly complied.

"Now what I'd like is for everyone to be part of a group. We're, we're," she paused to check, "twenty-two people, so we can have, let me see, three groups of four, two groups of five. Let's shift our chairs around."

She waited for the scratching noise to subside before picking up more pads on Charles' desk in the event that the students needed more paper. "The problem we've decided to consider is should the United States legalize drugs. All we want to do tonight is the first step, make sure we fully understand all the terms in the problem. First identify the key concepts, then brainstorm within your group to come up with as many questions about the concepts as possible, not letting the biases you just uncovered impede any questions. Remember, in scientific thinking," she said slowly and deliberately, "asking the right questions is more important than having the right answers. And select someone in the group to record your questions."

She handed Charles the pads she was still holding and he distributed one to each group.

"Dr. Pastore and I will circulate, see if you have any questions, how you're progressing, then we'll do the exercise ourselves."

For a few minutes she and Charles moved around the room, answered a few questions. When all interaction seemed to be progressing smoothly, Charles faced two chairs opposite each other. She and Charles sat down and arched their heads over a sheet of paper. They prepared a list of questions they wanted to be considered regarding the key terms in the drug problem.

With the humidity in that room high enough to squelch any fire, she smelled wood burning. The project seemed to be humming along with no one seemingly distracted by the battering and thrashing the windows were receiving, the leaking coming from them, or the roaring wind which was causing a draft in the room. She opened the door for some more ventilation before the air, so saturated and heavy, would put everyone to sleep. She'd have to advise the maintenance staff that the windows needed caulking.

Fifteen minutes later she requested that they stop working. Most seemed reluctant to end the discussions, but as she stared at them in silence, one by one they rested their utensils.

She stood in front of the portable blackboard and erased the belief questions. Then she re-adjusted the board once again to ensure it was in the best possible position to catch the light the dark walls were usurping. "I'm going to ask the recorder in each group to read the questions you've come up with. Would the recorder for the group by the door please begin?" She picked up a piece of chalk.

"We've come up with so many questions," the recorder said, "they won't fit on that board."

"So did we," said another.

Poor planning. She should've anticipated that her meager blackboard wouldn't do the job. "Then next time we'll reserve a classroom." She rested the chalk on the ledge. "So why don't you all just read your questions slowly, give us time to absorb them."

They began the reading. When they were finished, there were sixty-one different questions, and those conjured up within only a short period of time. Charles added two that he and she had come up with, which the students hadn't covered.

"We've completed the first step. Pass me your papers, I'll prepare a list of your questions which didn't overlap for the next session. We'll review them and see if we can come up with any more. The fact that you should have by then an in-depth idea of the problem will make it easier to develop hypotheses to solve it. But," she made eye contact with everyone in the room, "the hard part is yet to come. Checking out all the hypotheses, and something special I'm going to ask all of you to do. Prepare arguments for the position you are personally against."

Groans and sighs. Some snorts.

She wanted the meeting to end on a positive note. "Cheer up, I have good news and bad news. The good news is, if what I've been reading is correct, computers will be doing most of the hypothesis checking for us in the future."

The clapping of a few hands.

"But the bad news is that since the future is about twenty years or so away, we'll have to learn to do it ourselves."

A student massaged his temples. "It never occurred to me, Dr. Marchese, that I had already formed a conclusion regarding the drug problem before I even examined my own prejudices or understood the ramifications of the problem."

"That, young man, is one of the problems in decision-making, jumping on the bandwagon before you fully understand your personal relation to the bandwagon, what it stands for and where it's going. And if you're alert in class, you won't allow any of your professors to shove a bandwagon down your throat."

The young student closed his eyes. "I have a headache."

"So do I," another male student said, also massaging his temples.

She didn't bother telling them she had a headache, too. A big one. "Good," she said, winking, "it means you're thinking."

CHAPTER 14

THE SIXTH FACULTY Forum of the year, Wayne Ashley's brainchild, was scheduled for that afternoon. A time for sharing projects, research, expertise. Steve had skipped all the forums except the first when she had to give her presentation to the faculty. Alice Cronin had warned her not to miss too many, especially during her probation period, because spies in the audience took attendance and reported to Wayne, then he to Chester, those who showed up and those who didn't. So elementary-schoolish, it was probably a figment of Alice's imagination.

Should she go or shouldn't she? Besides, she was still ticked at Charles for being a rather passive co-sponsor at the first Scholars Society meeting, letting most of it all fall in her lap. And she was already ten minutes late and had a million things to do. But Wayne was right about something—there was a need for the faculty to learn from and support each other. How would she have liked it if after all the work she had done in preparing her Forum lecture, it had been poorly attended.

She'd go for a while, perhaps ask a question, if for no other reason than to verify her presence, then leave early.

She was tired, and hungry from having had lunch at eleven instead of twelve. She could rest in the auditorium while listening to the lecture. She had never read *Lady Chatterley's Lover*. For her, the discussion would be abstract, boring.

Steve pussy-footed into the auditorium and slinked into the next to the last row, careful not to interrupt the presentation. As luck would have it, she dropped a nine-pound biochemistry text on the floor. The crash resounded throughout the auditorium.

Charles interrupted his speech for a few seconds then glanced in her direction. Everyone turned to look at her. If nothing else, there'd be no need for the dean's supposed spies to look for her, check her attendance.

Then Charles resumed speaking. "Whether or not the novel is great is still being debated. But one thing critics can certainly agree on is that it is lush."

Bad enough she hadn't read the novel, but now she was late and out of context.

Charles went on. "It's replete with religious imagery and symbolism, with some reviewers believing that it's a blasphemous parody of the Gospels."

What time was it? She hoped nobody saw her yawn.

"Look at the way Lawrence describes Connie's freedom, her spring," Charles said with enthusiasm. He read,

> Constance sat down with her back to a young pine-tree, that swayed against her with curious life, elastic, and powerful, rising up. The erect, alive thing, with its top in the sun! And she watched the daffodils turn golden, in a burst of sun that was warm on her hands and lap. Even she caught the faint, tarry scent of the flowers. And then, being so still and alone, she seemed to get into the current of her own proper destiny. She had been fastened by a rope, and jagging and snarring like a boat at its moorings; now she was loose and adrift.

Steve had to remember to buy Cheerios and what was on the list she had left on her desk in her rush not to be later than she already was. Did Cheerios have sugar? Some. But they were still more wholesome than Froot Loops. Anyway, she'd double check the ingredients on the label.

"Most agree," Charles went on, "that the novel is about the worship of the phallus, but I think Lawrence is doing more than that. He wants to remind us the world is alive and that is what is worth cherishing. But we must admit we have a sexual nature, too, and one can only go on truly living when there is harmony between the mind and body."

Was the dry cleaning ready? Time to check her ticket. She smacked her forehead. Christopher's violin lesson! Oh good, that was tomorrow, Thursday.

She tried to listen, but her eyes kept closing. She forced them open. Saints in heaven, was he still talking?

"The relationship between the characters is what Lawrence calls `the tremble of life'. He tries to show us how we are strangers to our intellectual selves by showing us concrete sexual desires. What does Lawrence mean by desire? It's illustrated in the scene where Connie, escaping Clifford, heads toward the gamekeeper's hut and bends down in front of a chicken coop. She starts feeding the pheasant chicks who are huddled among little birds and cries."

Charles lifted the text.

Who was Connie, and who was Clifford, and who cared?

Steve looked at her watch. Is he going to read again? How could she sneak out comfortably?

Charles looked out at the audience. His eyes seemed to have settled on her. She remained still, and tried to pay attention while he read in a way that appeared to give him utter delight.

> The keeper squatting beside her, was also watching with an amused face the bold little bird in her hands. Suddenly he saw a tear fall on to her wrist.
>
> And he stood up, and stood away, moving to the other coop. For suddenly he was aware of the old flame shooting and leaping up in his loins, that he had hoped was quiescent for ever. He fought against it, turning his back to her. But it leapt, and leapt downwards, circling in his knees.
>
> He turned again to look at her. She was kneeling and holding her two hands slowly forward, blindly, so that the chicken should run into the mother-hen again. And there

> was something so mute and forlorn in her, compassion flamed in his bowels for her.
>
> Without knowing, he came quickly towards her and crouched beside her again, taking the chick from her hands, because she was afraid of the hen, and putting it back in the coop. At the back of his loins the fire suddenly darted stronger.
>
> He glanced apprehensively at her. Her face was averted, and she was crying blindly, in all the anguish of her generation's forlornness. His heart melted suddenly, like a drop of fire, and he put out his hand and laid his fingers on her knee.
>
> 'You shouldn't cry,' he said softly.
>
> But then she put her hands over her face and felt that really her heart was broken and nothing mattered any more.
>
> He laid his hand on her shoulder, and softly, gently, it began to travel down the curve of her back, blindly, with a blind stroking motion, to the curve of her crouching loins. And there his hand softly, softly, stroked the curve of her flank, in the blind instinctive caress.

Charles allowed the raised text to descend slowly.

A mesmerized silence filled the auditorium.

Steve rummaged through her pocketbook for the dry cleaning ticket. She pulled it out, read the date. The clothes were ready but she'd pick them up tomorrow.

When Charles resumed speaking, she gathered her books, threw her pocketbook over her shoulder, slipped out of the room hearing him say, "In a conventional novel we find our customary views about unrequited love reinforced and seem to find some kind of reward in our feelings of despair over the tragedy of a loveless world. We..."

Should she go back to the office to get her grocery list, or save time and just try to remember it?

Forget the list.

She was much later than usual getting home that afternoon. In the car she kept thinking that she should've skipped the Faculty Forum, used the time to go to the supermarket, fill her empty refrigerator.

Charles' description of Connie went through her head. "She was fastened by a rope...now she was loose and adrift." He did seem enraptured by his own reading.

Tonight dinner would be late. Ed and the children wouldn't die of starvation.

After supper Ed went into his study, and Victoria and Christopher helped with the dishes. "Dry the pots and don't put them down, put them away," Steve said. "Don't leave them on the drain board."

Victoria exhaled with her usual puff of air. "They'll dry anyway on the board, I'll put them away later."

Steve recognized the adolescent act of rebellion, Victoria always making sure she left out at least one part of a task. Steve wouldn't make an issue out of it this evening. In general, Victoria was a decent kid.

At 7:30, her neighbor, Mrs. Fabricant, picked up Victoria and Christopher to take them to a performance of *Peter Pan* in her son's school. With the children out of the house, and Ed busily delving into his medical journals, Steve began to relax. She went up to her bedroom to catch up on some reading, but soon began to feel unusually tired. She looked at the clock. Only 9:00 but it seemed like twelve. Had an eight o'clock class the next day. The way she felt, it would be best to retire early.

She gathered a fresh nightgown, underwear, and a pair of terry cloth slippers, rested them all on the hamper, and searched in the cabinet under the sink for a new bar of Dove.

She undressed, slid open the tub enclosure door, stepped inside the tub, closed the door, and adjusted the shower water. When it felt tepid, she stood underneath just absorbing the cathartic flow of liquid. Then she turned the shower massage to pulsating. With its rhythm pouncing on her back, she already began to feel invigorated.

She circled the soap between the palms of her wet hands, working it up to a rich creamy lather. Charles' reading came to her. "...he put out his hand and laid his fingers on her knee."

She closed the water. With the Dove she whipped up more lather, transferred it to her skin while she closed her eyes and massaged her body.

What was it he read? "He laid his hand on her shoulder, and softly, gently, it began to travel down the cure of her back, blindly, with a curving motion, to the curve of her crouching loins."

Steve worked up more foam between her hands and passed it over her thighs.

The Dove slipped out of her hands onto the floor.

More of Charles' readings passed through her mind. "And there his hand softly, softly, stroked the curve of her flank, in the blind instinctive caress."

Charles' hands were all over her, creating even more foam as he slithered both his hands from her abdomen up her arms and shoulders to her neck and over her breasts.

She flipped her eyelids open.

What was the matter with her?

Was she losing her mind?

Yet even with her eyes open she could still feel Charles' circling, swirling maneuvers.

She stumbled backwards, and in so doing slipped on the soap that she had dropped on the tub floor. Instinctively, she tried to break her fall by grabbing onto the knob, inadvertently turning on the hot water full blast. Instantly, the scalding water was pouring all over her but she was so paralyzed by her fall that she couldn't move, remaining slumped on the floor. The gushing liquid kept penetrating her skin, burning and burning but its intensity still couldn't extricate the sensation of Charles' hands.

As soon as she was able to catch her breath, she screamed.

Within a few moments Ed scurried into the bathroom. She could see him vaguely through the steam.

He slid open the shower door with such force that it thudded at the end of its track.

Ed turned off the water which had already drenched his sleeve and the front of his shirt.

She was gasping for air as she watched him.

He grabbed a towel, just about to dry her. "Steve, you're badly burned."

He turned the dial from shower to tub, adjusted the water to warm, lowered the stopper, and turned on the water again. "Stay under here till the tub fills, then sit in it, keep yourself submerged." He searched the medicine chest finally removing a box and throwing what she knew had to be baking soda into the tub. "I'll find some sterile ointment." Ed pulled open the cabinets. "Where do you keep it?"

"I…it's in the cab…cabinet...on t…top of the stove, where…where you would usually get burned."

"Make sure you stay under the warm water till I get back, don't want you to go into shock."

She remained still, the water slowly enveloping her.

It seemed like forever until Ed was back.

He let her soak for several minutes then patted her dry before spreading the ointment over the blistered skin.

"Hold me, Ed, hold me."

"I'm afraid to touch you. Maybe you need a..."

"No, don't be afraid, I, I don't need anything. Just hold me. That'll take away the pain."

"This was a terrible accident. How did you fall? How long were you exposed to such hot water?"

"I…I was so tired I slipped on the soap I dropped, and, and grabbed onto the first knob I could as I was falling. Just my luck it was the, the hot water knob I turned on. I was, I was so stunned and hurt by the fall I couldn't move."

"I think you're working too hard. Just like you, and you thought having your own practice would be tough. Tomorrow morning before I leave I'm going to adjust the hot water temperature." He paused for a moment. "And…and maybe we should take a vacation, just the two of us alone."

A vacation.

That's what she needed. But it wasn't the kind he was thinking of. "That sounds wonderful."

He slowly helped her into the bedroom. He held her, and she cried.

"God, Steve, how I love you. It pains me so much when you're hurt."

She squeezed him making her pain both more intensified and relieved at the same time. "Keep telling me that."

"I love you, adore you. I always will." He put away the nightgown and underwear she had brought in with her, laid a cotton sheet over the bed, and rested her on it. He covered her with another cotton sheet, placing it gently over the blistered areas. He lay next to her, kissing her hand, caressing her face.

She couldn't stop crying. How could this have happened? Except for her father, Ed was the most wonderful man in the world, so wonderful she wished she could do what the geneticists were saying was coming. Clone him. "You're so good to me."

After some more time passed, she wiped her tears, opened her eyes. From where she rested she had a good view of the room. She'd redo the bedroom. The molding and powder blue flock wallpaper had to go. She needed more contemporary walls. The drapes? Dust collectors. She'd replace them with vertical blinds, give the room a more open feeling.

All night she couldn't sleep. The pain she was now experiencing was still not able to take her mind off the pleasure she was receiving just before she fell.

She felt she was in a freefall as she kept asking herself if her whole life was a lie.

After so many years, whatever made Roberta Winslow come to mind, a classmate she hadn't seen or thought about since graduating from college. What was it that Roberta had told her? She was engaged to this boy and then one day, as she was standing on line in the supermarket, she turned around, her eyes fell upon the man standing behind her, and everything changed.

The next day was the first time Steve missed classes. She needed to heal before she could move. She asked Ed to call the college, inform them only that she was ill, not say explicitly what was wrong with her, and left assignments for the students and a schedule when she would make up classes.

Steve lay in bed trying to determine her next move. Now it was she who was a character in the theater of the absurd, she who was the fraud she'd accused others of being. She was attracted to Charles but her conscious self would never let her admit it. There was something about his smile, the way he looked at her, the passion he conveyed every time he spoke of literature, the time he covered her hand with his. She had ignored it all.

But now the message ticking in her head was to leave the college. Having the job she always wanted and now couldn't keep. One of the curves that life could throw. For after last evening, seeing Charles would be different. With their offices next to each other, the situation was impossible. And there was still the rest of the year to contend with, not to mention The Scholars Society.

She'd get control of it, go to her office very early on Sundays before Mass. She could get more work done with nobody around, especially Charles. Her free time during the week between classes she could spend in the lab or in the library. And once the students started developing their own analytic skills, they could run The Scholars Society without her or Charles alternately mentoring it.

Sunday morning Steve rose early, dreading the reams of mail and messages she'd have to attend to after missing classes for two days. She put on loose clothing, then went into the kitchen, guzzled down a cup of coffee so hot she could feel it scarring its way down through her esophagus. Just what she needed. More scalding.

The short drive to campus was most pleasant with the position of the sun telling her it wanted to leave winter behind, but the temperature warning, not yet.

When she arrived on campus, only one car was parked in front of the office building, one she didn't recognize, probably belonging to a custodian. She parked directly opposite the car, fumbled for her keys, but soon found she didn't need them. The building was unlocked. She scrambled up the steps and followed the curve to her office.

What she had not anticipated was how cold the building would be on Sunday, with the heat turned down so low.

She felt so sore her chills made the burns feel worse, her blood nurturing them less, abandoning her skin seeking warmth in deeper parts of her body.

Oh, Christ.

Charles' door was open, the light on.

Should she run away?

Silly. Probably just the custodian cleaning up.

She didn't have time to give the matter more consideration before Charles stepped out into the hall, his head slightly bent. Over his white shirt and red tie he was wearing a heavy gray cardigan with thick cable stitches.

"Steve! I was wondering who was making that commotion. What are you doing here on Sunday?"

The shock of seeing him made her drop some books.

He picked them up and held them. "Dropping books is getting to be a habit with you."

She didn't answer, just unlocked her door.

He followed her in, placed the books on her desk.

Finally, she said, "Never mind what I'm doing here, what are you doing here? I didn't see your car."

"Took Claudia's, it was already in the driveway."

Steve began flipping through the piles of envelopes on her desk, noticing not enough of it was junk mail. "I missed so many days I wanted to catch up on the mail before tomorrow."

When she finally faced him, he was looking at her neck.

"What happened to you?"

With his eyes on her like that, she felt weak, couldn't think. Why not make light of it? "My husband beat me."

Charles moved closer, his face glaring concern. "My God, Steve, your skin's raw. And it looks more like a burn than a blow."

He lifted his hand as if he was going to touch her.

She stepped back clumsily, almost tripping. "Did you think I was serious about the beating? A...a cooking accident. Was making...French fries, got water in the pot and the oil splattered all over me. But don't worry. Remember my husband and I are both physicians and we took care of it right away."

"Maybe so, but it still looks awful."

Standing so close to him, she regretted not wearing something that covered her more, even if it rested on the blisters. "Really, Charles, it's nothing."

Why was he still staring at her?

"I noticed you came to my lecture Wednesday."

Did he have to bring that up? "How could you have avoided noticing? I came in with a bang." Why did she use that word? "We...we should support each other. Knew how I would've felt if there was poor attendance at my DNA presentation."

"But you came late and left early."

So he noticed that, too. "When you go home everything's taken care of already, but even though I have help, there are lots of things mothers have to do themselves."

"What did you think of the part you heard?"

"Had I read the novel, I would've connected with it more. But I'm curious." She kept speaking without looking at him, shuffling some more envelopes. "Why did you select that novel to present to the faculty?"

"I don't know if I told you this or not but I did my doctoral research on Lawrence. *Lady Chatterley's Lover* was censored until the late Fifties. It was published in 1928, by a Florentine bookseller."

"Leave it to an Italian."

"But in 1959 it was finally published in America, the unexpurgated edition. The next year the British ban was challenged and the novel was finally allowed to be sold in England. I never had a chance to read it myself until after I finished my doctorate."

"From what I heard it's nothing compared to what's being published today. It's certainly not what could be considered obscene."

"You're right, not for today, but in 1928 it was shocking." His eyes were beaming. "I love the intensity of its imagery, the tenderness it conveys. People can learn a lot from it about relationships."

She began categorizing the stacks of envelopes. "Charles, I don't want to be unsociable, but I have a lot of work to do."

"I can take a hint. I should be working, too, that's what I'm here for."

He strolled out of her office.

She put her coat back on in case he came in again and tried to examine her neck, but more timely, to protect herself from the penetrating cold in the building.

An hour or so later she placed the mail that needed stamps into the post office basket, and her papers into a briefcase. She piled some books to take home with her, picked them up, and pushed the light switch down with her elbow. By now the cold in the building had gotten to her and she was shivering.

Charles must've heard her moving around. He came to the door, looked at her hand holding the office keys. "I'm finished, too. Why don't you let me carry some of your things and put them in the car for you?"

She didn't have a chance to protest before he was taking the briefcase and books from her.

They walked out of the building together. He accompanied her to the car, handed her the books and briefcase, which she put on the back seat.

"Thanks," she said without meeting his eyes. "Enjoy the rest of the day."

"You, too, see you tomorrow." He headed for his car.

She turned on the ignition. The car had cooled off, blasting cold air from the heater. She was so chilled she wanted to get out of there quickly. She didn't bother locking her doors. Without looking behind, she shifted the car into reverse, force-fed the accelerator.

Within seconds she felt a thud as her head banged against the wheel.

She opened her eyes. The door on the driver's side was open. Someone was holding her face, touching the part of her forehead that had been pressed against the wheel. At first she wasn't sure who it was until she smelled the after shave, and as the blur became clear, her eyes fused with Charles'.

"Are you all right, Steve?" he said in a breathy voice.

"I...I'm a little foggy. What happened?"

"We rammed into each other."

"How long, how long have I been like this?"

"Not long, just a few minutes, do you want me to call your husband?" He kept passing his hand gently over her forehead and her cheeks.

"No, please, please don't, I'll be all right. Just let me sit here for a while and you make sure I don't pass out."

She was limp from the smack on her head, but more from his stroking, as if the shower she had taken on Wednesday were a premonition of this moment, instead of an expression of her desire.

"I can't let you drive home alone. I'll drive you, just tell me how to get there."

"No, no, Charles, I can take care of myself." She knew it was foolish to drive home alone after blacking out, but she couldn't be alone with him in a car, or near him any longer. "If I wasn't sure of it, I wouldn't say so. Now, I'm going to close my eyes. When I open them, just tell me if my pupils are dilating."

She closed her eyes. When she opened them, his face was only a few inches from hers, and he was looking at her with an intensity she had never seen in a man, in anyone else before. It was one of those moments when every atom in her body told her this was her destiny, yet at the same time those same atoms struggled to tell her it was wrong. "Well?"

Her question interrupted his stare.

"Do it again, I want to make sure."

Her lips started to swell. She recalled the anatomy and physiology courses she had studied so clinically. Lips. Mucous membranes loaded with sensitive nerve endings.

She closed her lids for at least ten seconds, asking herself if when she opened her eyes, she would see him gauging the willingness of her lips to welcome his.

She opened her eyes a second time.

He was staring at her mouth when he said, "Your pupils are fine."

She tried to conceal how rattled she was by the sensation of his breathing so close to her by placing her hand over her mouth and raising her brows. "Did I damage your car?"

"I don't think so, but I was so anxious to see if you were okay that I didn't look. Besides, the car's not important, but judging from the way we hit, our bumpers may be merged."

Their bumpers.

The way he kept staring at her, stroking her face, placing his finger on her burn, she had a sense he might've known he was responsible for it, and it might be more than their bumpers that were merged.

He continued looking at her, his hand still on her face and her neck, drawing over them with tenderness. Her blood had returned to her skin and she felt warm, aroused.

"It's all my fault, Charles. I didn't look behind me when backing out. I'm sorry."

"The cars don't matter. It just matters that you be okay."

"I think I'm okay now. Want to go home, have to get to Mass."

"Maybe you should get some rest instead."

"The last thing you should do when you get a bump on the head is rest, especially if you may have a concussion. You have to keep moving."

"Sorry, Doc, I'll call you tonight to see how you are."

"You don't have to."

"I do have to."

He finally removed his hands from her face and closed the door. "Let me check the car." He disappeared for a few seconds, then spoke through the door. "The bumpers are crushed against each other but not stuck. There's an indentation on the bumpers, easy to repair, but no damage to the body. All you have to do is go home." He patted the door. "You're excused."

She drove away, his image in the rear view mirror shrinking as he stood looking after her.

She felt so torn. How could she explain what was happening to her? Was she spoiled, had things too easy, first from her father, then from Ed? Maybe it was infatuation. What exactly was infatuation?

It had never occurred to her when she first came to the Graham to replace Dave Benson that she might be destined to have the same fate. But if she weren't careful, she, too, would be headed for a head-on collision.

And this one would have nothing to do with cars.

Charles slipped into the Pinto. He had gone to campus on Sunday to avoid Steve. At least he tried, but only got more entangled. He couldn't help thinking that he wouldn't be in this pickle if he had destroyed her resume in the first place, or had sent her a form letter stating that her resume would be kept on file should another opening occur.

And it was some joke! Directions she would have to give him. To her house. A place he could find from anywhere in the universe. He had driven past that house numerous times, in the evenings, fighting against his better judgment, looking for lights in that smaller version of Tara, especially in the upstairs where he knew the bedrooms had to be.

When they were lit, he envied the interaction between husband and wife. Was she teasing him, were they laughing, sharing problems?

When the rooms were dark, he felt the horror of their being together in whichever bedroom was theirs, Steve alone with her husband in the night, in their locked room, with his touching her, kissing her, possessing her body.

How could he stop thinking like this? Time for some distraction.

The radio.

He could use a little Burt Bacharach, but the dial was set for WQXR which was broadcasting a recording of *Tosca*, and he had already missed the beginning of the first act.

He listened, then sang the duet with Tosca in the best tenor he could muster.

But the baritone was soon in charge, in control of the scene and the music.

The lascivious Scarpia. Charles had heard his father play the record often enough.

His father.

Probably inherited his genes, his personality flaw.

This was the first time since catching his father and aunt in their hand and leg tryst under the dining room table that Charles was ever able to feel some empathy with his father.

For this time, when the chorus sang the "Te Deum," it was Charles who sang along superimposing the name on the blasphemy, *Stefania, mi fai dimenticare Iddio.* (Stefania, you make me forget God.)

Steve hurried into kitchen, out of breath. Good. Everyone had finished breakfast, and no one was still there. Even the sink was clear of dishes. She opened the freezer, removed some ice, wrapped it in a dish towel she shoved into her briefcase, and practically flew up the steps to her bedroom.

Thank God Ed was in his study so when she called, "I'm home, honey," he answered, "Okay" from a distance.

She opened the top vanity drawer, shoving aside brushes and tubes.

Scissors.

Just what she was looking for. Not as sharp as barber scissors, but good enough for her immediate needs.

There, tilted obliquely next to several upright bottles, was the makeup foundation she had to put on her forehead to conceal the remnants of the contusion she was trying to shrink with the ice.

Steve sat in front of the mirror staring at this new woman, her amygdala sparring with her cerebrum. Which one would win?

What kind of creature was behind that face? What kind of craziness was happening to her? These things didn't happen to people like her, only to those who looked for it, loose women, bored women, those who'd never achieved anything in life and were searching for some wild gratification.

Could it be that she was pushing forty and afraid of losing her youth?

Ed called up the steps. "Are you ready?"

"I'm ready," Christopher shouted, "but as usual, Victoria probably isn't."

"What do you mean I'm not ready," Victoria shouted back.

"It takes you forever to get out of the bathroom," Christopher said.

"That's enough from you two," Ed said. "Start being civil to each other, remember we're going to church."

The last thing Steve wanted to do just now was go to church. It was the nuns' constant mantra, "There are a hundred sixty-eight hours in a week. You can give at least one to God," that gave her the impetus to change into something more suitable.

At a time when hats had gone the way of virginity, dare she wear a hat? Would she draw just what she wanted to avoid—too much attention? Then, was there a choice today? The large-brimmed black hat designed to dip to the side was perfect for the occasion. She adjusted the hat slightly so the dip would cover more of her forehead than her cheek.

She stepped out into the hall. "Let's go. All I have to do is put on my coat." She walked down the steps aiming the side of her face with the camouflaged forehead away from Ed and the children.

Just as they arrived at the church, Christopher rushed up the steps way ahead of them. Not until they reached the vestibule did they see him trying to fill his water pistol in the holy water font.

Ed took the toy away from him, gave him a dirty look, and emptied the water back into the font. After shaking the water out of the pistol some more, he placed it in his pocket.

During Mass, Steve's head was pounding. She couldn't concentrate, and she couldn't read the missal.

The music was particularly deadly today with some unkempt blonde-haired chunky grandmother-type in front of the microphone, facing the congregation alternately bleating and screeching.

Get a voice and pick a pitch. The only way to improve the woman's singing was with a laryngectomy.

And what was this, second grade? If the woman ever again repeated the hymn number, hymn five thirteen, in individual digits, five, one, three, Steve was going to hurl the hymnal at her.

Where did the Church dig up these people? And the squealing woman's moaning, squawking male counterpart. Did he ever hear of phrasing? He wasn't supposed to take a breath every second or third note. Probably recruited him from the emphysema ward.

How could anyone have hired an organist with amputated fingers? Missed more notes, played everything like a dirge. The musicianship of a cabbage head. If he pulled out all stops, he could drown out the squeaking soprano. And if he played one additional verse of anything, she was going to smash him with one of the pipes.

No wonder hardly anyone was singing. What was this supposed to be, a spectator sport? Were these people here because religion was a ritual, or a commitment?

What was it for her?

Why couldn't there be music the way it was in the Protestant churches? Alive. An integral part of the liturgy with everybody participating in music as prayer.

Her mother had told her that the Irish always had to practice their faith surreptitiously, quietly, to prevent the English from knowing Mass was being celebrated. And now with the American Catholic church under Irish dominance, the tradition of little or non-participation in the music persisted.

The last thing her throbbing head needed was the homily by Father Keenan. She had nicknamed him Father Coda. His sermons, one continuous ending. Just when she had her fingers crossed that he was concluding, he'd begin all over again. He needed a trip to the Newark Cathedral to read the inscription on the pulpit. "Be bright, be brief, and be gone."

Who was this Catholic Church anyway? Always telling everybody what was right and wrong. Rules, rules, rules. Spilling over into every aspect of life.

She had to force herself to stay awake by making her eyes travel all over the church. The walls were barren, not with the Baroque decorations of the Italian parishes, their statues dressed in warm colors, brocades, or velvets glitzy with gold, silver, and semi-precious stones.

Christopher kept flipping the pages of the missal with both her and Ed cautioning him to stop, and Victoria giving her brother a stern look which he returned with a giggle.

Steve caught a glimpse of the statue of the Blessed Virgin Mary, Our Lady of Lourdes. Her thoughts returned to her childhood, when she tripped climbing up the ladder while holding the flowers to crown the Virgin. Farthest from her mind then, and even so far as a week ago, was the tripping she was now engaged in. She hoped she wouldn't fall.

Then the stained glass window next to the pew where she was sitting attracted her attention. Its inscription read, "In loving memory of Terence and Maura Donovan." Steve asked Maura if she ever had feelings for a man other than Terence. If so, did she ever tell him, or was she too ashamed to let him know? Did he know anyway? Did she give it away by her behavior? How much suffering did Maura bring on him?

Did Terence ever have feelings for another woman?

Did Ed? He had a lot of female patients, but it had never occurred to her until now that Ed might have been attracted to any of them. How would she feel about it?

She opened her purse, then her wallet. She pulled out the holy card with her mother's name on it, now faded and so frayed at the edge. Who did Patricia Phelan Arcuri think she was anyway? How did she have the nerve, the audacity to die? Where was she, especially now, when Steve needed her most? Her mother had never prepared her for anything like this. Watch how he treats his mother and sisters, how he drives, and how he behaves when he doesn't get his way. This advice was not enough.

Maybe she married Ed because she was always obsessed with pleasing her father. Maybe men in science were too boring, straight-laced, conservative. It was those in the arts who could lose themselves in passion.

Lucky were those who married the true passion in their lives. And luckier yet were those who didn't meet their true passion after they were married.

Father Keenan interrupted her ramblings. "Let us offer one another a sign of peace."

Ed turned to her and said, "Peace be with you." He proceeded to kiss her, then Victoria and Christopher, while shaking their hands respectively. Then those in front of and behind them were also offering their hands to wish them peace.

Peace.

This handshaking. Whose idea was it? People coughing, sneezing into their hands. Blowing their noses, picking their ears, their eyes. Didn't the hierarchy know that one of the best ways to transmit germs was through the hands, worse than saliva? Sweaty, grubby, sticky, filthy hands. Thoroughly unsanitary and disgusting. She'd write the Cardinal.

Then her eyes wandered to the red and white banner hanging high on the side of the altar, probably pieced together by students preparing for Confirmation. "I Have the Strength for Everything through Him Who Empowers Me."

She had the faith.

She'd get the strength.

Father Keenan held up the host. "This is the Lamb of God who takes away the sins of the world. Happy are those who are called to His supper."

The parishioners responded, "Oh Lord, I am not worthy to receive you, but only say the word and I shall be healed."

Down her cheeks tears were beginning to drip. She immediately wiped them away with a tissue. Say the word, God. Please say the word. I need all the healing you can give me.

Later that evening Charles dialed Steve's number.

A man answered. Charles assumed it was her husband.

"This is Charles Pastore from the English Department, one of Steve's colleagues at Graham. I wanted to know how she was feeling."

"It was a serious burn but she's on the mend."

"I don't mean the burn, I mean the bump on her head."

Silence traveled through the wires. "The bump? Hold on, I'll let you speak with her. I didn't quite catch your name. Charles Broderick, did you say?"

So that was his connection!

"No, Charles Pastore."

"Sorry, I'll get her, Charles, just a second. Good to talk to you."

Evidently, Charles Pastore wasn't a household name.

This was the first time he had ever spoken to Ed. Disappointed he was so pleasant. Wanted him to be nasty, a tyrant. Some son-of-a-bitch prick bastard Steve could learn to hate or, hopefully, already did.

"Hi, Charles."

The sound of her voice alerted every cell in his body. "I told you I'd call, how are you feeling?"

"Other than a pretty bad headache, I'm fine. Besides, if I have any aftereffects, I probably won't get them till tomorrow. Or Tuesday. But what about you? You must've gotten shaken up, too?"

"I doubt it, but as you said, if I get any aftereffects, they'll come later. Though I think I let the cat out of the bag."

"Which cat is that?"

"Your husband seemed surprised when I asked about your head. Didn't you tell him?"

"No, I didn't want to worry him unnecessarily. Backed the car into the garage so he wouldn't notice the bumper until I can get it fixed. He's still trying to get over my burn. But now that you've mentioned it, I'll have to tell him, and he'll get on my case about working on Sundays."

"Sorry if I'm causing any trouble."

"No big deal. He's very supportive and understanding, just a very concerned person, is like that with his patients, too."

"It's encouraging to hear there are still doctors out there concerned with their patients."

"Well, it's reassuring to know one of my colleagues is concerned about me, too. Thanks for calling."

"I told you I would."

"I really appreciate it. Thanks again."

"See you tomorrow."

"See you tomorrow."

"Ed, I've been thinking," Steve said. "How would you feel about moving to a new place, trying something new in a different city?"

The newspaper he was reading slid out of his hand, landing on his lap. He removed his glasses. "I don't believe what I'm hearing. You were the one who always wanted to live in this area. That's why I gave up a lucrative practice in Boston and joined with partners here to build a new practice. We've been planning this new clinic and are just about to open it. You know how much money I've invested in it, and you're the one who always wanted to teach. You have a job you've been telling me you love and now you want to change? And what about the children?"

She knew how much Ed had given up to accede to her wishes to be near her family. It was one of her mother's criteria, being gracious and accommodating if not actually sacrificing. Taking the medical boards in a different state. Building a new practice.

"Suppose I join you in your new project, you know I'm a damned good physician."

"It's too soon, we don't know how the concept's going to work yet." He paused, then his brows met the top of his nose. "You know, Steve, you haven't been yourself, ever since you had that accident with the hot water. You don't have to work if you don't want to. We have more than enough money to lead a most comfortable life and take care of the children's education. Maybe you should take a leave of absence."

"I couldn't do that, not now." She took his hand, pressed it against her cheek. "But you're right, Ed. I haven't been the same, probably still in shock. But you know how I'm always looking for new opportunities."

"Well, let's see how the old ones play out first." He pulled his hand away. "You seem very restless lately." He put his glasses back on, scrutinized her face. "You're behaving strangely, even look different."

She rushed her hand to her forehead. "It's a compliment that I look different, it means you noticed my new hairdo. I'm wearing bangs."

"Bangs?" He paused. "They look good…but then you always look good."

Thank heaven he picked up the newspaper again.

"As far as your working, do anything that pleases you," he said without looking at her. "If you're happy, that's all that pleases me."

"You're so understanding." She kissed his cheek. "I'm so lucky to have you."

CHAPTER 15

"AS I READ this over, Alex," Paul said, "I think what's missing are some scenes depicting in more detail the relationship between Steve and Ed, Charles and Claudia. It doesn't seem realistic that Steve and Charles would have this attraction for each other if there weren't some void in their relationship with their spouses."

"I told you the real work was in the rewriting. And, and I didn't tell you this yet…but wait till we have to read the whole damn manuscript out loud, to pull out even more kinks. Though we can't let that hamper us now, we have to keep plugging." She ignored his raised eyes as he mimed 'out loud'. Besides, using up so much mental energy had made her famished, so she finally began taking large bites of the turkey sandwich she removed from her thermal bag.

When she finished more than half the sandwich, she said, "Well, Paul, you certainly overcame your writer's block. If you keep letting yourself go as well as you did, you should get writer's block more often."

"You told me to look at something in a way I had never looked at it before, and it worked."

"Well, what was it?"

He hesitated. "I'm not telling, let it suffice to say that whatever it was helped me get over it."

The sandwich she had almost finished left her mouth dry. She pulled the flap on the Diet Coke can and took a sip. "That's not fair. Suppose I get writer's block. If it happens to me, I want to be able to anticipate what I could thoroughly examine in a new way."

"Then all you'll have to do is what you said I should do, it could be any animal, plant, or mineral. What's important is how you look at it."

"Come on, Paul, tell me what it was."

He looked down at his shoes. "Maybe when we're finished, besides I'm mad at you for not telling me beforehand that we had to read the entire manuscript out loud."

"*Mad* at me, Dr. Barone, eminent professor of English and diction?

"Okay, *angry* with you."

"That's better." He was probably tired after this session, and justifiably so. She had really pushed him with the writing, surprised him with the oral reading, and wouldn't try to pry any more information out of him. "Next week we have to try for four chapters, even if we have to work an extra day."

"Four chapters in two sessions shouldn't be insurmountable, especially if we think about them in advance."

She covered her yawn, finished off the rest of the Coke, and collected the pages of the manuscript. "Same time, next week. Think up some more conflict."

* * *

Victoria ran into the house perspired and flustered. She was still trying to catch her breath as she spoke. "Mom, I...have to. . .have to. . .do a report...a report on *Jane Eyre* and the book's not in the school library... or in the Briarcliff library. The librarian told me the person who has it isn't due to return it...for two whole weeks. It could be tomorrow or two weeks, if it's returned on time.

"You mean they have only one copy?"

"Guess so."

"When's the report due?"

"Friday."

Steve placed her hands on her hips. "Now, Victoria, I told you so many times not to wait till a few days before assignments are due before getting the materials you need. Last minute work is rarely excellent. Just this once I'll bail you out, I'll check the Graham library. If they have it, I'll drive you over to pick it up, so you can start reading it tonight. You can use my card so you can keep the book longer than you could in the public library if you need to hold on to it."

Her day had started early, there were a million things left to do, and Steve had no idea what she was going to make for dinner. Going back to campus was the last thing she needed, but she made the phone call anyway. Why did she always have to empathize with Victoria's assignments? "They have the book, but first take Chopin out for a walk."

"Do I have to?" she answered in a flippant manner.

Steve wanted to slap her face. Hard. "Yes you do, that was one of the conditions for you and Christopher getting a dog, and now you have to live up to your commitment."

When Chopin heard the leash rattle, he jumped off the sofa and shook himself, his ears making a whipping sound. Steve was pleased they decided to get a miniature instead of a standard poodle, and a dog that didn't shed.

Steve backed the car out of the garage, then waited in the driveway for Victoria to return with Chopin, deposit him in the house, and lock up. She jumped into the car with such a broad smile it caused Steve to wonder how a child who must have broken the record for thumb-sucking could have ended up with such perfect teeth.

It was most unusual to be so foggy out this late in the day. The air was heavy, dull, and depressing, and driving was particularly dangerous. One could hardly see the tail lights of the cars ahead. She tried extra hard to be alert.

Steve was used to her daughter's being quite chatty, but on the way to the library Victoria was silent. Too silent. That usually meant something was on her mind though she wasn't yet ready to talk about it. Steve let the silence continue. Maybe Victoria felt guilty that she was making her drive back to campus. Maybe...

"Mom, is there any sex in *Jane Eyre*?"

She jerked the wheel then steadied it. She slowed down. Cars were beginning to pass her. "Probably, but that's not what I remember most about it."

"What do you remember?"

"It's the scene where Mr. Rochester, that's the man Jane works for, asks her to live with him even though his wife, insane as she is, is still alive. And Jane, who loves him, is tempted to say yes. But she knows who she is and tells him that laws and principles are not for the times when there is no temptation. And if laws could be broken for individual convenience, they would be worthless."

Why of all the scenes in the novel would she have remembered this one? Was this what Dr. Clancy meant when he suggested she might be tight-assed?

She had to get back to Victoria's original question. "Why do you want to know about the sex?"

"This girl in my class, Roseanne, she told me whenever she has to read a book, she looks for the sex scenes first."

She'd had conversations about this with Victoria before, but for some reason today's seemed more urgent. "It's perfectly normal for people your age to be curious about sex. In fact, every generation thinks it has discovered sex. And it has, for them. But sex has been around a very long time, ever since...since the protists and for good reason. Sex keeps the species going." Oh God, she sounded as though she was in a classroom, giving a lecture, but she sensed that was not what Victoria was really asking her.

She stopped talking and drove another mile or two, cars still passing her. "Victoria, I don't think I ever told you this before, but when you were little, around seventeen, eighteen months or so, anyway, before you were two, you were playing on the floor in the kitchen, playing with blocks, and plastic jars and caps, screwing the caps, unscrewing them, trying to put into the jars anything that could or even couldn't fit, unscrewing the caps again, dumping out what you had just put it, and doing this over and over again. And before I had a chance to notice, like in a split second, you were in the cabinet under the sink, had unscrewed the cap on a bottle of Lysol, just about to drink it, and I ripped it away from you so quickly and furiously."

For the first time, Victoria abandoned her straight ahead look-out-of-the-window pose, and turned toward her. "No, you never told me that before."

Steve reserved her eyes for the road. "At the time, you couldn't think logically, and if you could think at all, it was probably that I was the meanest Mom anyone could have, taking away what you wanted at the time. You couldn't possibly have understood that the Lysol would've killed you. It's now that you have more experience and maturity, you know what poisonous substances can do to the body." She took one hand off the wheel, and grasped Victoria's hand. "When I think of what damage that could've done to you, it grips me right in the gut, and I still want to cry."

Victoria removed her hand from under Steve's and kissed it.

Steve kept that hand off the wheel long enough to filter through her purse for a tissue to blot her eyes. "That day I had a long talk with myself. I was an irresponsible mother because I hadn't removed everything in your reach that could be dangerous."

"You're not irresponsible, Mom." The voice which could be so surly suddenly sounded most compassionate.

"Well, what I did, leaving that bottle where you could get to it, was irresponsible, and then, after I finished the conversation I was having with myself, I decided that in raising a child, especially as she grew up, I was going to carefully select which dragons I was going to attack. Do you think you know what that means?"

For a while Victoria was silent. Then she said, "I think, I think it means you would have to pick what's really important enough to fight for. Am I right?"

"Right on. When you were in your high chair, you used to pick up things from the tray, especially food, and drop them on the floor. You would spill juice and milk on your tray, put your finger or squish your hand into the liquid, spread it around. It used to bug me but I knew that these were things you had to do to learn and develop. And you know, Victoria, there are little things you still do that annoy me, like leaving the pots on the drain board, not putting them away, or leaving the bathroom a mess, and I try not to make an issue out of them. But sex, that's a damn big dragon."

"What do you mean?"

"First you have to understand that the emotional brain evolved before the thinking brain, and biologically our sexual development comes before our full potential for reasoning, and that's a big problem.

"Also, the male species has different hormones which give them a different sex drive. When boys reach puberty, they spend most of their time thinking about sex, and as a result think with their penises. They will do anything to have sex. It's not that they're evil, they just have difficulty controlling these hormone surges. Even Chopin, if we didn't have him neutered when he was a puppy, would be trying to sneak out of the house to chase any female. In the army there's a saying that summarizes it. It's crude but it makes my point. 'A stiff dick knows no conscience.' Guys'll tell you they love you, that you're the best thing that's come into their life. And, at that time, in the heat of passion they really believe it." Was Victoria listening or blowing her off?

"Some girls in my school are having sex."

Steve had all to do to keep from swerving off the road. She wished the sun would come out, dry up the fog, and add some light, some hope, to this conversation.

"Victoria, I'd be willing to wager that those girls don't have a high self-esteem, that if they had ever accomplished anything or had strong fathers as you have, they wouldn't need to be having sex at this age. "Remember," her hand was firmly over her daughter's again, "we're a family, a proud family, and everything each of us does reflects on all of us. How would you feel if your father ran around with other women, or if I did the same with other men?" Charles' hands were all over her again, as they were in the shower.

"You know I would hate it." Her voice came across with the same disgust that showed in her screwed-up face.

"Well, we would hate you having sex when you're too young. Always remember, it's like the Lysol bottle. At the time you may think it's a great idea, but it would really be detrimental. Many times you'll be tempted, but remember this." She paused long enough to ensure Victoria's attention. "'No is power. Saying no gives *you* control."

She slowed down and looked for a place to park, eventually finding a wide shoulder. She didn't turn off the ignition but kept her foot on the brake. "Many years ago, my mother and I had a long talk, not about sex but about something she warned me against. She called them the false prophets, those who tell you all enticing things that you tend to believe and want to believe at your age, or any age. But remember, they are false prophets."

Steve hadn't realized how fast she was talking. She stopped to take a deep breath while pushing back Victoria's hair. "You understand that all behavior has consequences, something that has gotten lost in this generation. If you eat too much, you'll gain weight, if you don't study for a test, you won't do as well as you could've and might possibly fail. Some of these are reversible. But sex, and we've had this discussion before, has a lot of consequences, most of them emotional consequences, especially when there isn't any deep commitment in a relationship."

She didn't want to discuss the subject any more at this point because it seemed as though she was starting to preach, and that, she knew, drove teenagers crazy. But she was stunned when Victoria said, "Mom, my teacher told us that girls tend to model their mothers, and I want to be just like you."

A sickening feeling came to her stomach. She hoped her daughter would never be like her, that Victoria would never have the same feelings she had been experiencing. It was truly remarkable how Dr. Stefania Marchese, the great advisor, and the phoniest bitch of all, hadn't choked on her own words.

She took her foot off the brake and steered back onto the highway.

When they pulled up to the library entrance, Steve handed Victoria her card. "Take your time. See if there's anything else you'd like to take out while I check my mail and messages."

"Where'll you meet me?"

"Right here," she looked at her watch, "in about a half-hour. That should be enough time, but if you need more, I'll wait."

"Thanks, Mom."

Charles put on his reading glasses. That came with the territory of passing forty. He double checked the list he was about to hand the reserve librarian. "Seems this list gets longer and longer each year. Hate to give you more work."

"Don't worry about it, Dr. Pastore," Mrs. Winthrop said, "It gives me a chance to read all the extra books you put on, sometimes twice. Gives me something to do in between helping the students. I always enjoy the books you select, they offer the students a good sense of balance while exposing them to quality writing."

She was wearing a floral print dress, the kind his mother wore, so stylish in the Forties. "Coming from a person with your background, I'll take that as a compliment. It takes a lot of effort to___"

Was he seeing things?

He blinked, frowned, then took another look.

He was right the first time.

A girl.

A younger version of Steve Marchese. About that there was no mistake.

He watched her carefully. She entered the library with a slip of paper in her hand. The walk was the same. She looked confused, moving her head around and referring to the paper. Steve, a child, just entering the challenge of adolescence, about to blossom at a moment's notice.

He grabbed the edge of the counter, had to resist the urge to run up to her and cradle her in his arms, reassure her, protect her, tell her not to worry, that at this stage in her life, everything seemed insurmountable, that he was there to care for her.

He was always curious about how Steve might have looked as a young girl, but now he felt he was participating in her growth, her development. He could even meet her before she met Ed.

Ed.

Charles walked over to the girl. "Is there something I could help you with?"

The green eyes, auburn hair and pink skin were slightly less like her mother's than her smile. "Oh, thank you, I'm looking for the fiction heading. Want to find a copy of *Jane Eyre*."

"No problem, just follow me."

"And would you tell me where I could find a critique of the novel?"

"Sure, in the 800 section over there." He pointed to it. "And you're in luck, young lady. I teach English literature here and have an excellent critique of *Jane Eyre* in my office." As soon as he made his offer, he realized how strange it must've sounded to her having someone she had just met offer his personal book.

"Oh, I thought you were a librarian. You know, my mother teaches here, too. Dr. Marchese, do you know her?"

Did he know her?

"Yes, as a matter of fact, her office's right next to mine."

"That's where she's now, in her office."

"Well, let me help you find some critiques and if there's nothing you like, you can borrow my book."

"That's kind of you, what's your name?"

"Charles Pastore."

"Charles Pastore. Charles Pastore. Never heard that name before. But I'll remember it now. I'm Victoria Marchese." She offered her hand.

He took it as he thought, never heard the name Charles Pastore.

He could feel the air leaving his lungs.

How come Steve didn't speak of him at home? Wasn't it important that she did, or didn't she dare?"

"Now that I look at you, you look exactly like your mother."

He watched the girl browse through the bookshelves. She removed a book. Even from a distance, he knew it was *Jane Eyre*. But she seemed less successful in the critique section. He walked over to her, noticed that the shelves he recommended as sources were deplete.

"It looks as though I'm going to have to take you up on your offer," she said.

"That's fine with me. But under one condition. Promise me to read the novel and critique it yourself first before you read the opinions of others."

"I promise." She said it with such innocence he had all to do not to embrace her.

"Let's go to my office, we can meet your mother there at the same time."

Charles walked shoulder to shoulder with Victoria. He was on a high being near someone who was made up of half of Steve, feeling that he was in a different time, a different place.

The kind of place where he and Steve could begin all over again, but with a different ending.

Steve sat at her dressing table, still in her robe.

"Hurry up, Steve," Ed said. "The hosts have to greet everyone, can't be late." He stepped out of the room, a trace of shaving lotion following him.

She took her time looking into the mirror. Never did she come out of a beauty shop looking the way she wanted. Going to the hairdresser earlier that day had been a waste of time. She rearranged the hairdo she wasn't satisfied with. Now she had a softer look. There had to be a better way to communicate with beauticians, maybe bring a picture of a hairstyle, if she could find one.

Spread out over the bed was her dress. Expensive. Suitable for a physician's wife, especially for this occasion.

She tried not to think of it, but she knew Charles would be there.

With Claudia.

He had never seen Steve in anything except business clothes or in a lab coat. How would he like this creation? Off the shoulder, pink petals lining the scoop neck, tight waist, a flowing silk organza skirt. She hadn't realized until now, that when she purchased the dress, she wanted Charles to like it.

Why was she thinking like this? Her life had been going according to plan…the perfect education, the perfect husband, the perfect family, the perfect job. Until Charles had to throw a monkey wrench into everything. How messy life could be!

Perhaps after tonight, Ed would have so many new patients she could join his practice, or run the clinic. That would separate her from Charles once and for all. She'd never think about him again.

Ed called from downstairs. "Are you ready, Steve? We're going to be late."

"I'll be right down."

She took one last look into the mirror, and was about to get up. Her eyes drifted toward the numerous still sealed bottles of perfume, gifts from relatives and friends. She remembered when studying animal physiology in college, her amusement about the female species, especially the skunk, letting out an odor to attract her mate. She recalled how ridiculous she thought it was, and her promise to herself never to wear perfume. And so far, she had kept her promise.

But now, just before putting on her dress, she ripped the wrapping from a bottle of Chanel, and dabbed its contents behind her ears and down her neck.

Ed's two associates and a few early-comers were already in the lobby of the clinic when Steve and Ed arrived. Servers were passing out hors d'oeuvres, and the bartenders were straightening out the liquor bottles and arranging glasses according to size. One was slicing lemons, limes, and oranges and sorting them into different containers. An ice sculpture of the three physician hosts with their medical garb, one holding a stethoscope, another a sphygmomanometer, and the third a reflex-testing hammer served as the centerpiece for a huge round table.

Shortly, three waiters balanced a platter in the shape of a huge fan which had to be in her estimation about six feet long. Each fan rib separated a space for a different vegetable—carrots, radishes, beets, black and green olives, broccoli florets, tomatoes, celery, scallions, and lettuce.

The caterers were just arranging the carved turkey next to the roast beef and ham when four other servers began to uncover trays of Italian meats and pastas and place them over chafing dishes. Steve waited for the varieties of cholesterol-saturated pastries she had personally selected to fill out the display. A certain feeling of anxiety she had definitely acquired from the Italian side of her family began to overtake her. Would the food be enough?

"Glad we made it before most of the guests arrived," Ed said.

No sooner did he finish the sentence when Wayne Ashley and his wife drifted in.

Steve greeted them, then brought them to Ed. "I'd like you to meet our academic dean, Wayne Ashley, and his wife, Thelma."

"I must tell you, Ed," Wayne said, "you have in incredible woman here. We were hesitant about hiring her, but she's performed beyond our greatest expectations."

"Stop reminding me about her competence in anything she does or I may eventually ask her to join our group."

Wayne raised his hand as if he were going to push Ed. "Don't you dare. We won't put up with losing her."

After exchanging a few more pleasantries, Steve introduced the Ashleys to Ed's partners. More guests wandered in, and the bartenders began taking orders. Steve tried to keep herself circulating so the time wouldn't drag before Charles arrived.

Tracy Robbins came in alone. Steve was quick to walk up to her and take her aside. "How are things going?"

Tracy stretched a plastic smile. As she spoke, she kept pushing back with her fingers her long center-parted straight brown hair that persisted in falling over her eyes. "Not too well, but this is not the time to talk about it."

"Why don't you stop in my office Monday? You teach a class then, don't you?"

"Yes, it ends at two. I'll drop by then."

"Good, now let me make sure you meet everyone. I'll introduce you to some people you may not know from the college."

"Why don't you first let me meet your husband? Which of those men standing in the lobby is he?"

"The tall, good-looking one at the end." Steve put her arm around Tracy's shoulder and approached Ed, who was chatting once again with Wayne. "This is Tracy Robbins, an adjunct in our department. I mentioned her to you, she teaches General Biology."

"Of course I remember, heard a lot of good things about your teaching. Hope you have a great time this evening, have you had something to eat?"

"I'm not hungry."

"Well, then how about starting with a drink? Stay here, I'll get it for you. What'll it be?"

"How does a martini sound? Double."

"Sounds good to me." Ed walked over to the bar.

"You're lucky, Steve," Tracy said. "Seems like a most pleasant guy."

"He is, but if you want him to stay pleasant, make sure he sees you eating something before the night's over. You know how Italians are about food. It's in their genes and by God one day I'll isolate whichever ones they are and get the Nobel prize."

"Then even if I'm not hungry, if it would make Ed feel better, I'll put something in my plate and wave it in front of him."

"Good, but put a lot in your plate."

Ed brought Tracy her double martini. She took it, and moved to a corner of the room to chat with the Strattons.

"That woman's very unhappy," Ed said. "Does she always look like this?"

"You're very perceptive, sweetheart, she's having a bad time with her marriage. Split up with her husband recently, and there's a child involved."

"That's always tough, but if you're really a friend, convince her to get some counseling. I don't like the way she looks."

"Yes, Doctor." She caught a glimpse of another entering guest. "Oh, no" she whispered in Ed's ear, "Alice Cronin's here. Make sure you get her involved with other people or she'll bend your ear all night."

Ed turned around. "Don't tell me. You must be Alice Cronin. After what Steve's told me about you, I could spot you anywhere." He kissed both of Alice's rouge blotched cheeks.

She blushed making her cheeks more deeply colored. "Why, you Italian men are all alike, know how to make a woman feel special. If I had met one of you early enough, I would've trapped you, even if I had to learn how to cook, and I wouldn't be a shriveled up old spinster."

From a distance Steve noticed a gentleman entering the room by himself. "Well, tonight you may get lucky. I want you to meet one of Ed's colleagues, an ob-gyn man, Leo Mc Cann. Sorry he's not Italian. Lost his wife two years ago." She pinched Alice's cheek. It left a film of red-orange between Steve's thumb and index finger. "I'll introduce you and you go charm him. Who knows where that will lead."

She deposited Alice with Leo.

Steve was just about to greet Bob and Estelle Lucas, when Ed whisked her away.

"Steve, I want you to meet Marvin Epstein, the professor who mentored my dissertation."

She gave Dr. Epstein a full smile and a firm handshake. Then she reconsidered and also gave him a kiss. "How can I ever thank you for helping Ed so much. If you hadn't helped him, he would never have helped me, in fact we would never have met. So you see, you're responsible for us, and in a large part for this association of doctors and full-service clinic."

"It was easy to help Ed. He was a willing student. But I must confess, had I known how he was going to meet you, I would've mentored you myself."

"I might've ended up with a better piece of research." She winked and kissed him again.

Ed slipped his hand into hers. "I'd better take her away from here, you two look too cozy."

Steve was still beaming when she turned around and...

A strained smile.

His hair in its usual side part, combed back, the intractable curl ever falling into his part. Charles' eyes immediately shifted past her. He kept moving his head as if he was searching for someone in the crowd.

She was grateful to be holding Ed's hand, for she was able to compress it as she said, "Ed, these are the Pastores, Charles and I believe, Claudia. That is," she said, facing Charles directly, "if you're not bringing a date other than your wife this evening."

They all chuckled except Charles, who looked as though he was trying very hard to smile.

"We've spoken on the phone, once I think," Ed said, "but now we've finally met. It's a pleasure. And I must thank you for putting up with my wife. She can be quite a handful and I know your office is next to hers. Hope she doesn't pester you too much."

"Steve's an ideal colleague. Never whines, works hard, and has a lot of common sense. She's no trouble at all."

So Ed was taller than he was, not much, maybe an inch or so and had more hair than he pictured him to have. Wavy, too. Ed was dressed in a three-piece suit, good quality. His shirt cuffs protruded just enough from his sleeve to reveal monogramed initials. And just knowing that Ed was holding Steve's hand was enough to make Charles bristle, clench his teeth.

"It must've been quite a project to set up this clinic, Ed," Claudia said.

"Been a dream of mine for years. There was a lot of stress involved, but as they say in medicine, there's bad stress and good stress, and this one was good. Later one of my associates'll take you on a tour to see the facilities and equipment. Do tell your friends about it. They'll get comprehensive service, quick results, and excellent care. Someone'll be on call twenty-four hours a day."

"We certainly will," Claudia said, "and we wish you every success."

"Thank you, now make sure you have enough to eat."

Charles was pleased the interchange was over. He couldn't look at Ed too much longer without revealing his envy, and he had only caught a glimpse of Steve, keeping his eyes off her lest they sink into her skin, burn her more deeply than the scalding she had received from her burn.

He decided he wouldn't speak to Ed again that evening but lose himself in the crowd, place his back toward him if he came near them again, completely ignore him. Ed didn't have to worry about the price of leaded glass doors, could give Steve anything she wanted. Ed had money and would have a hell of a lot more after this clinic was opened—formidable competition for one on a professor's salary. Ed had prestige, good looks, a warm personality, and worst of all, he had Steve.

Ed, Ed, Ed. He wanted to blot the name out of his mind.

Charles spotted Bob Lucas standing alone in front of the bar, sipping a drink, his head slumped. He left Claudia with the Strattons, then went over to Bob. "How are things going?"

"Which things?"

"The ones we discussed in my office." He lowered his voice. "In private."

Bob gulped down the rest of the drink. "When I look at her all dressed up like that, with her husband next to her, I have all to do not to smash him right in the face, throttle him. Fields, Burdens, and Hoffman were just here. After a few drinks our Dynamic Trio started spouting off their pop sociology again. Tonight they told me just what I wanted to hear, that there are four things that tell you about a man—his house, his car, his wife, and his shoes. Well, I certainly know about the first three, but that son-of-a bitch's wearing shoes that had to have been imported from Italy, and now I loathe him more than ever.

"Right now I've just finished my drink, and I'm going to have a lot more before the night's over. Estelle's busy talking to Thelma. They've always gotten on, and I'm glad Thelma's here."

"Did you take my advice, speak to a counselor?"

"As a matter of fact, I did."

"What did he say?"

"He was a she, and she said that I have to remove the stimulus, replace my inappropriate stimuli with realistic ones, something they call cognitive restructuring. A fancy shmancy way of telling me I have to avoid Steve. How the hell am I going to do that? I'm chairman of her department, on committees with her, her boss. Can I fire her? I might as well fire myself. Can I leave my job? At my age it'd be tough, one thing if I was just out of graduate school.

"When I told her I didn't understand how to remove the stimulus, she came up with having me think of one of my children whenever I think of Steve. Have a visual image of one of my kids. I tried that and then my mind wanders to thinking how much I'd like to have a child with her. Jesus Christ, Charles, I see the image of her child, our child. I can describe exactly what the kid looks like."

Bob ordered another drink.

Charles took out a handkerchief to wipe his brow. "I'll have a drink, too."

The rest of the night he needed to avoid both Ed and Bob. Charles left Bob drowning himself in his fourth scotch and soda, drifted over to the corner with his double J&B, neat, and stared out the window at the dark, considering how much better he would have done financially if he, like his brother and sister, had become a lawyer. Maybe he could go back to school at night and do it now.

He was still considering how having an English major as a background would play so well into law when a hand touched his shoulder. "Hi, Dr. Pastore."

His head twisted toward the voice. "Why, Victoria, how are you?"

"Just wanted to say thank you once more for lending me your book. I got an A on the critique. Did you get my note?"

"I most certainly did, but I would've loved to have read your critique."

"I'll send you a copy, only six pages, with all my teacher's remarks on it."

"Is there anything about the book that stands out in your mind?"

"Oh, yes."

"Good, what was it?"

"The part where the married Mr. Rochester asks Jane to live with him and she tells him in no uncertain terms that if we could pick and choose the laws we'd like to obey, they'd have no worth."

He felt a lump in his stomach and remained silent for a moment before reacting. "My God, Victoria, if you were as old as my students, I could understand how you might remember that scene so vividly. But at you're age, I'm shocked."

Victoria put on a less than innocent look. "To be perfectly honest, it might've gone right over my head. But before I read the book I asked my mother what she remembered about it, and that's the scene she described, so I was sort of expecting it, waiting for it, and when it came, it stuck with me."

If that was the most important scene for her mother, what hope did he have? A creeping paralysis was overtaking him, and he was grateful to Claudia, who joined them and said to Victoria, "You have to be Steve's daughter, you look just like her."

"That's what everyone tells me. My brother looks like my Dad, though. We didn't want Daddy to feel left out. Are you Mrs. Pastore?"

Charles was trying to overcome his inability to move, staring at Victoria in her virginal long white dress, lace over the bodice up to her neck, her auburn hair tied back with a matching lace bow, her radiant face, to be thinking of etiquette.

"Oops, this lovely lady's my wife, Claudia."

"Mrs. Pastore, your husband was very kind. He let me borrow one of his books to do a report, and I got an A."

"What was the report about?"

"*Jane Eyre*."

"Did you enjoy it?" Claudia said.

"Yes I did, and now I'm going to read the other Bronte sister, maybe compare them."

"You should be proud of yourself," Claudia said, "I didn't read those novels till I was in high school."

"You should be proud of your husband for helping me."

"I am proud of him." She placed her arm around his shoulders. "He's an inspiration to his students, and to me."

A young boy came over and pulled Victoria's arm. "Aunt Daria and Uncle Bill are looking for you."

"This is my brother, Christopher."

Like his father, he also was wearing a three-piece suit, which was shifting around seeking a place to settle on his body. Charles' eyes jetted down to the boy's shoes. Loafers.

Christopher put up his hand as though he was taking an oath, then waved and gave him and Claudia a quick handshake. "Hi, now hurry up, Victoria, they're waiting."

"It was a pleasure to meet you, Mrs. Pastore," Victoria said. "And thanks again, Dr. Pastore, I promise I'll send you the report."

Christopher tugged her away. "Bye."

Claudia watched them wade through the crowd. "What poise for a girl her age. She's lovely, makes me regret I didn't have a girl."

"We can still fix that."

"No, two is enough, besides, with my luck it would be another boy. I'll have to settle for some nice daughters-in-law. But that young lady is really something, just like her mother. Then they say that girls usually are."

Charles' chest was all bunched up. He wanted to end the conversation. Thinking about and seeing Victoria and Steve made his feeling of isolation from their lives more intense. "Let's go chat with Wayne and Thelma."

Steve kicked off her high heels before melting into a gold plush tufted bedroom chair. She rested her feet on the ottoman, hoping that placing herself in this position would alleviate the throbbing in her groin.

She kept thinking that Charles was almost rude to Ed, snubbing him, hardly looking at him as he was speaking. What had gotten into him? How dare he treat her husband like that!

And Claudia. Alice Cronin was right describing her as sweet. Sweet to the point of saccharine. What a boring bitch! Pretty. Pretty plain, pretty prim, a pretty proper prude.

What did that say about Charles, his wife an extension of himself?

Didn't Claudia know that no one was still wearing pompadours in the Seventies? That dress, boring brown, up to her boring chin, as though she was hiding the scar from a tracheotomy.

Steve could see it already. The same menu for every day of the week in the Pastore house. Monday, lamb chops, Tuesday, chicken. Everything in their life by prescription, super-organized.

Ed walked into the room.

"I must say the party was a success," Steve said.

"I agree, and the way you handled yourself and our guests added the extra touch."

"The children were great. I never knew they had such social skills."

"Well, Victoria at least. Christopher still has a long way to go, and he seems so out of place in a suit."

"Don't be too hard on him. He's a boy, still a little klutzy, and very shy. He'll outgrow it."

Ed moved close to her and whispered, "You know, sweetheart, I was looking at Victoria tonight. I'm thrilled that she's so much like you. It's as though God knew I loved you so much, He had to send me more of you to love."

"Ed, how touching." Hardly realizing what she was doing, she unzipped his fly.

In an instant he moved closer, kissed first her shoulder, then her neck, ear, lips. "I've been meaning to tell you all night, you smell wonderful. What are you wearing?" He began unbuttoning the back of her dress.

"Why, Ed. After the crazy day you had today, aren't you too tired for this?"

"Remember, you're the aggressor, you started it, and I love it. I was tired before, but when we're alone and I have the time to absorb you, look at you, smell you, my adrenalin begins to flow."

"Adrenalin, Dr. Marchese?"

"Sorry, Dr. Marchese. Testosterone, I have to remember whom I'm making love to." He pulled her over to the bed.

She was sure Charles and Claudia were still making love the same way, by prescription, by appointment, on Saturday night if they didn't have somewhere to go. And if they did go out and came home late and were too tired, maybe they'd grab a quickie on a Sunday morning, before the kids barged in.

Bet they didn't even kiss when they made love. Anyone responsible for the stiff starched collars and stiff starched overlay on the buttons in Charles' shirts couldn't possibly know how to kiss Charles until he choked. Routine. No spontaneity, surprises.

Ed gasped, "What are you trying to do to me?"

Claudia didn't know that lovemaking in the evening started early in the day with seductive, coy looks, innocent smiles, and subtle manipulations.

"Don't stop," Ed said, sighing.

Did Claudia ever sneak up behind Charles, kiss the back of his neck, crawl her fingers up the back of his head, pinch him lightly all over his body, nibble on his ear?

"I love when you do that," Ed said, "it's my weak spot."

What did Claudia know about foreplay, about how to move her lips over Charles' body?

Did Claudia ever try this?

Or this?

Ed's breathing quickened.

Steve knew enough about anatomy to jet Charles to another galaxy, make him barely conscious to the point at which he would have no choice but to lose himself in her.

Ed stopped quaking, remained still.

Many silent seconds passed. Then he murmured, "The hell with the clinic. I have to take time off so we can do this more often."

"That's a wonderful idea."

She rolled over on her back, squeezed her eyes hoping that it would squelch her thoughts of Charles.

Then, she froze in horror.

What if? What if she were in a car accident, and in a coma. What if, God forbid, when she came to, the first word she said was Charles? What would Ed, who would certainly be at her bedside, say, think? How hurt would he be? Better if she'd be killed, silenced, than give Ed such pain. She turned around and sank her face into the pillow to absorb the tears.

Yet, Charles was suddenly there in the room, lying next to her.

Oh, God. She was becoming so unhinged. Had to stop thinking this way.

Was it time to take Alice Cronin's advice, talk to Bill Foster when there was a problem? No, he'd see right through it when she tried to pass off her situation as a friend's.

She tried tightening her eyes again.

But no matter how she tried to distract herself, the thoughts kept returning. She couldn't stop the thinking.

The thinking.

Then she received consolation in what she had read once in a psychology text.

We can't control how we feel.

We can control only how we act when we feel.

Monday afternoon at two, Tracy Robbins knocked on Steve's open door. The woman appeared strained, her brown eyes bordering on black, especially with the dark circles underneath.

"I've been expecting you, have a seat." Steve pulled up a chair and made sure to close the door. "How did class go today?"

"Class's fine, great therapy."

"We all need therapy at one time or another, even if it's just talking to somebody."

"Well, I need to talk to you."

"I'm more than willing to listen. Just hope I can help. How's Kim?"

Tracy pushed her hair back, first with her fingers, then with her entire hand. "She seems to be surviving fairly well. I'm the one all this seems to be coming down on. Steve, I was sure that having Kim would save our marriage, but it only made things worse."

"Where's Kim now?"

"This week she's with Alan, next week with me."

"How do you manage that logistically?"

"With great difficulty. Alan's moved back with his parents in Riverhead. Every weekend we meet midway on the Long Island Expressway. He brings Kim and I take her, the next weekend I bring her back so he can have her. Did you ever hear that the LIE's the greatest parking lot in the world? And if you've ever driven it, you know what a nightmare that can be, weekdays or weekends, very time consuming. I've already told you I'm taking courses, need time to study. And I'm already dreading that expressway in the summer when Manhattan empties out and heads for the Hamptons."

"I don't want to get personal, but you're getting only an adjunct's salary for the two courses you teach. How are you managing financially?"

Tracy didn't answer for a while, then put her head down. "I'm...I'm living with someone."

Several moments passed before Steve said, "You didn't bring anyone with you to the party, so I didn't know. Who?"

"We had a fight that night and I walked out. He didn't want to come with me, and I don't like going out with his friends." She fidgeted. "You know, it's okay to live with someone now, maybe not ten years ago, but now it's okay. He's financially secure, and good to Kim when she's with us." She took turns twisting and pushing back her hair. "And he's going to marry me...after he divorces his wife. He owns the house we're living in, and he'll keep it after the divorce because he can prove he paid for it himself without her assistance. It's all going to be fine. He knows I want to continue going for my doctorate so I can teach in college full-time and spend more time with Kim. It'll take me a few years, but he'll wait. We argue a lot, but he treats me okay."

"What do you argue about?"

"Nothing important, just silly things like what or where to eat."

Steve stood up and began pacing around the office. She looked out the window, then sat down again. "Tracy, I don't want to sound like an old fuddy-duddy, but there had to be something about Alan that attracted you to him in the first place, something that made you love him enough to marry him, commit yourself to him, have his child."

"He was a fun guy. My father's a minister, very straight-laced, and Alan was just the opposite." Tracy picked up a pen that was on the desk. Then she began to spin the pen over the desk. "It was like being free. Being me." When the pen stopped, she whirled it again. "Whee."

"And this gentleman you're living with, is he a fun guy, too?"

"Sure, a great fun guy. And," she stopped speaking a few seconds, looked askance, "we have great sex, not the way it was between me and Alan."

"It's so easy to fall into this divorce culture, Tracy, but you have a child that will be caught in the middle. Wasn't there more to Alan than fun? Didn't he have other qualities, salvageable qualities that could bring you two together again?"

"Not that I can think of, and even if he did, I was so obnoxious to him that he's seeing someone else, too."

"Do you still love him?"

The question brought moisture to Tracy's eyes, and within a few seconds, tears streaming down her cheeks. She held her head and cried, a yelping cry so loud that she tried to smother it by removing both hands from her head and transferring them to her mouth.

Steve leaped out of her chair and put her arms around her. "Cry, Tracy, cry all you want. I'll hold you until you're all cried out. I prescribe it, it's good for your system."

Tracy was so bent over in her chair that her head was almost on her knees.

When she finally lifted her head, Steve handed her the box of tissues she always kept on her desk. "Are your parents giving you any support?"

"Not financially, they never wanted me to marry Alan, so now they're punishing me. The only thing they'll pay for is counseling."

"Then why don't you go? If you can't get Alan to go with you, go alone, give it one more try. If you want, I'll go with you to the counselor, wait outside. Hate to see a marriage break up if there's another way."

"I'll think about it, but I really believe Alan's deeply involved with someone else."

"As I said, even if you have to go alone, it has to help. The longer you procrastinate, the harder it will be."

"I'll see."

Steve watched Tracy, her nose swollen, her eyes lost in her skull, leave the office, then knock on Charles' door.

She probably needed a male point of view.

CHAPTER 16

ONE OF THOSE days again for Steve. Sloppy papers handed in, most ripped out of loose leaf or spiral notebooks. Whatever happened to pride in one's work? Past participles, if they came from irregular verbs, were things of the past, had pulled a disappearing act.

Atrocious spelling. A real problem with sentence structure, and worst of all, the inability to write an introduction, middle, and conclusion to any essay or report. Where was a thought process evident anywhere? And if she were to assign a name to this doing-good-walking-slow-writing-neat generation, it would be the adverbless generation.

She'd return the whole lot of papers, not accept them until they were presentable and thorough, including the English. Everyone on the faculty was complaining about the English, talking about it. Talking and moaning. If everyone else on the faculty refused to accept the garbage too many students were turning in, there would be no problem.

She had a crushing headache. She opened her desk drawer, and after looking under the tape measure, boxes of paper clips, and staples found the small bottle of Bufferin.

What was happening to her, to society? She was trained to solve problems. Why couldn't she comprehend this problem with Charles? If only she could bring it up with Bill Foster. Maybe he could give her some insights into the society at large, give her a context for her predicament so she could figure out how to disentangle herself from it before it swallowed her up.

Her thoughts returned to the astronomy course she had taken in college, the only elective she was able to fit into her saturated schedule. Everyone should study astronomy, she had thought even then. It made all our problems so insignificant, so miniscule when pitted against the vastness of the universe. She wanted to reflect more on the majesty of the universe, how her turbulence with Charles paled when she compared her situation with the cosmos.

She'd go to the library, or a bookstore, read some psychology text, some self-help books. But the growling in her stomach told her it was time for an overdue lunch.

The smell of hamburgers and onions permeated the entire building. Cholesterol and calories. Not exactly what she felt like eating, but nothing else appealed to her at the moment. Besides, the cafeteria was no gathering place for honed taste buds anyway.

What luck! Just what she needed. Bill Foster was sitting by himself, the remains of the poor man's surf and turf, tuna salad and a hot dog, on his plate, and another plate with a not yet broken into piece of apple pie. She sat at his table and he appeared delighted to see her.

"Bill, today I'm in my pessimistic mood. Believe it's all in the genes, and I'm not usually a person who feels dejected, but you've got to help me out on this."

"What is it, Steve?"

"Why don't you finish your lunch first? It'll make me feel less guilty about bothering you."

Bill patted his belly. "I don't have to finish, and I certainly don't need dessert." He pushed the pie aside.

"You know how Italians, and part Italians are. You never interrupt us when we're eating. We think everybody's like us, can only think when we're sure we've finished the last morsel. So at least finish your coffee."

Bill picked up his cup.

Before he had the chance to swallow the first sip, she leaned toward him. "Tell me, Bill, as a historian, your assessment of the Sixties on our society."

He slowly lowered the cup back onto its saucer, then adjusted his horn-rimmed glasses. "Wow, that's a biggie, so much so I'm collecting material to write a book about it. For me the Sixties was a shock, because we went a long way from the panty raids and trying to see how many people we could fit into a telephone booth or a car, which they did in my time, to carrying arms, bombing buildings, and stealing secret files."

"I know what you mean," she said. "The worst thing we did was step on each other's white bucks."

At first Bill laughed. Then he became very serious. He tinkered with his fork, flattened out his napkin, made some indentations on it with the fork's prongs. For a moment Steve thought she was watching a rerun of *Spellbound*. Only Bill didn't quite look like Gregory Peck.

Bill raised his arm. The face of his watch was on the underpart of his wrist so he had to twist his arm to see the time. "I have a class in about ten minutes and don't have the time to discuss this in depth now, and I don't want to give you a simplistic view of something that's highly complex. But...but if I had to put my finger on it, I'd say that what gave the impetus to the Sixties was TV."

She responded immediately. "What does television have to do with it?" Then she covered her mouth. "Ed tells me I should've been a lawyer, always questioning. But I promise not to interrupt you anymore, just listen."

Bill made a circular motion with his arm. "Feel free to interrupt. But to get back to your question, TV began to show us that all was not right with the world. People were starving, Negroes weren't being treated fairly, not that we didn't know it, but it has more of an impact when you actually see it. The threat of nuclear war. Remember the political ad the Democrats used against Barry Goldwater, the nuclear bomb, the little girl with the daisy? On TV it was communicated to millions in an instant.

"Jee," he wiggled in his seat, "I'm glad you asked me to discuss this. Just getting these strands of information out helps clarify my thoughts so that some day soon I may put them together coherently in writing. In fact, I'm so excited I'm using up a lot of energy, getting hungry again, going to finish my dessert and get some more."

She winked. "You don't need an excuse to get extra dessert."

Bill took back the plate of apple pie he had pushed aside and left the table returning shortly with another piece of pie. "You really have my juices flowing...now. . .let's see, where was I?" He attacked the pie again. "The Baby Boomers were getting ready for college. They were brought up in a world that was financially secure. Kids wanted more of a say in what happened on campus, wanted universities to be more responsive to what they perceived their needs were, and there were so many youths that they found their strength in numbers. They could change the world."

Bill finished his first piece of pie and began digging into the next. She couldn't believe how much energy he seemed to be consuming.

He spoke while chewing. "Now I'm sure you know that student revolts have existed as long as there were universities. But this group began to sense the power they had, and started to organize for the different causes they believed in. And if I have to give them credit for anything, I'll give them credit for their fight for civil rights."

"Amen." Images of Martin Luther King, the freedom marches zoomed through her head giving her a warm feeling.

"There's also the fact, and I have documentation for this, that the student revolts in the beginning weren't that strong, rather sporadic. But when the media put these kids on TV, it encouraged students in other universities to do the same and network among each other. They believed the publicity about being idealistic. How could the side that was for the poor, racial justice, the end of nuclear war be wrong about any of their ideas? Even many of their professors were telling them how great their ideas were. The message of the Sixties was enticing. Fads and clichés solved everything. There were simple answers to complex problems, but here's the rub."

Bill took another large chunk of pie, shoved it into his mouth, and didn't continue speaking until he swallowed. "Oh yes, the rub. The students' willingness to believe this consumed their reasoning ability. They developed a false sense of superiority over humanity. They were the virtuous ones. Only their morals were worthy of consideration. Self-deception substituted for thought."

Patricia Phelan Arcuri came to her mind. "Self-deception. Now where have I heard that before?"

Bill didn't appear to have heard her comment, and if he did, it was so personal with her, he probably wouldn't have understood it anyway.

He stared up at the ceiling. "It was at this time I said to myself, 'Hey Bill, whoa, slow down. This is not the way liberals function', and I considered myself a liberal in those days."

"You, a liberal? But you're so conservative."

"You know what they say. The staunchest conservatives are former liberals. But I'll do you one better." He stopped speaking, probably to ensure her attention, and looked directly at her. "I was a Marxist."

"Come on now."

"At the time I went to school, being a Marxist was intellectual, just like being an atheist. After that I became a liberal. You have to remember, Steve, that liberals had always fostered..." He pressed on the table each finger of his right hand consecutively as he enumerated the list. "Individual liberty, reason and argument, civility, representation in institutions, the rule of law. But what I saw in a lot of the behavior was not law but anarchy, and in many cases like wishing victory for the Vietcong, outright treason, and inhumane behavior in the name of promoting humane objectives. And I'm waiting, just waiting now that the war's over, and I'll probably have to wait till doomsday, for the outcry of the moralists over the atrocities the North Vietnamese are now performing to see if they'll admit that the victory they were hoping for was a victory of a new tyranny." Bill's brow went up when he looked at her. "Have you heard the outcry?"

She shook her head.

He put his fingers in his ears. "They're so quiet, the silence is puncturing my ear drums."

Steve started asking herself how all of this related to her situation. Bill was speaking so fast she didn't have a chance to reflect on what he was saying, yet she made sure to keep listening attentively.

Bill tightened his lips. "The universities were totally unprepared for the student onslaught often reacting to it timidly, caving in to the most ridiculous demands. Universities always existed to test ideas, to be places for reasoned discourse, and in the Sixties they made a 180 degree turn, started to, and are still are promoting an ideological agenda."

He paused for a few seconds, then resumed speaking. "It's only now that I realize the youth of the Sixties had a love-hate relationship with the war. They wanted the war to end, yet they didn't. For the war made them special, allowing them to perform every license. When you're for the end of oppression, and for all kinds of lofty ideas, you can rationalize your way into justifying your own behavior, especially personal behavior."

Personal behavior. Was he now getting close to her predicament?

Bill picked up his fork, then put it down again. "And when I stepped back and tried to make sense of it, I concluded that most of the students I knew couldn't handle the fact that life wasn't perfect. There were no utopias. Human nature was what it is. And when they actually began to understand what the real demands of the freedom they were all demanding were, they chickened out and began to run from the challenges by demanding group identities dictated by ideology."

There wasn't enough air in the room to feed his enthusiasm as he continued to speak. "There was also the perception that we were so affluent, that we had unlimited resources. We could fix any problem by just hurling money at it. Money could solve anything. As though they had forgotten that John F. Kennedy had told them to ask not what their country could do for them, but what they could do for their country." He looked aside, frowned. "I often wonder if or how the Sixties would've been different if he hadn't been assassinated."

"He was certainly able to channel the energy of the young. You know that youth must have a cause. In my day it was the anti-vivisection movement, but in the Sixties it was the Peace Corps that gave youth a purpose."

"It seems after he died the intellectual community turned on the American experiment itself. And now, more than ten years later, it's not at all as JFK suggested. We're all entitled to everything. Welfare, an education without working for it, just paying tuition and showing up, breathing.

"Some groups saw the Constitution as flawed because it didn't promise respect and love for any group, only that individual rights be protected. The Civil Rights Act was designed to ensure equality, and if you read the text, it specifically states that nothing in it should be interpreted to grant preferential treatment. Now that was before the culture of liberation took over the idea of equality."

"When I think of what some academics, even here have done to exacerbate the situation, I get livid."

How could she worm from him what she wanted to come from their conversation?

Bill was so wound up he didn't seem to be able to stop talking. "Only the insecure people, those who wanted to be popular with the students, were the ones who contributed significantly to the nonsense. Tear down the institutions and replace them with utopias. The students never learned that there were no utopias and the nations whose governments they were encouraging like North Vietnam were the most repressive regimes. Or if they knew it, they ignored it. They were so busy pursuing perfection that this immaturity stood in the way of their realizing that nothing in life is perfect, including the U.S. government."

"They felt the government had to be compassionate."

Bill slammed his hand on the table, rattling his two pie plates. Then he straightened his bow-tie. "If the left thinks they're compassionate, they'd better take a long, hard look at what suffering their policies of compassion have produced, including producing a culture of dependency with people stuck in a quagmire they can't get out of. You know, Steve, emotions can really hijack the intellect."

And didn't she know that!

"And that's what they do," he continued, "appeal to the emotions. But this was just a part of it. It was a time of romantic notions, the belief that accomplishing something truly of merit was easy. And the academics went along with them."

"The whole thing is so antithetical to anything in my medical training that I'll never understand it."

"I thought about what I had seen in academia. Professors fighting for their principles by attacking the principle of majority rule. Faculty, not all but too many, willing to support any outrageous act or idea to confirm their own self-worth, feelings of guilt, or self-doubt."

"I read about a lecture a professor at another university gave, Dr. Edward Shils. He described what happened in the Sixties as a tidal wave that rolled over the nation, then slowly rolled back, depositing debris on the beach. Great metaphor."

"And debris not only in the universities."

Now maybe he was coming to it. But she prodded anyway. "How has all of this affected the society, all of us?"

He paused, scratched his head. "Well, the Beatles stated it very well, something like there's no more black or white, only shades of gray. The Ten Commandments have become like a buffet at a restaurant. Choose what you like; pass over the rest. To put it another way, there's no such thing as wrong. Love debased into impulses, what's right is what feels good at the time. As long as it doesn't hurt anyone else, and even that's up for grabs. There are no consequences for behavior anymore."

Impulses. Right is what feels good. She passed her hand over her face.

Bill stopped speaking long enough to adjust his bow-tie again. "We live in an age of oxymorons, Steve. Open marriage, easy abortions, free love, easy learning, easy divorce. Any little thing can cause you to break up with your spouse. No commitment, no trying to work things out for the children's sake. Not that I think it's that simple, but you won't see the effects of this family disintegration until the next decade, if that long.

Steve put her head down and spoke into the table. "We have to ask ourselves if what's being passed off as acceptable is what makes us free, or what helps us avoid facing life's imperfections. I think about this a lot because I'm worried about my children. Experience everything. It's all right to take drugs. If it feels good, do it. And kids are having sex younger and younger, even before they know their partners' names. You're liberated this way they're being told."

"But this is the key, Steve, liberated," he then continued slowly and deliberately, "but...not...free. Because there's no responsibility. What people don't understand is that this so-called liberation is the worst form of repression. It would never occur to them that sexual fulfillment can conflict with higher values. And all that young people are encouraged to reject—religion, routines, postponement of immediate gratification—those are the very vehicles they need to deal successfully with their lives. Let me tell you, Steve, the world belongs to those who can postpone immediate gratification."

"You're preaching to the converted, Bill." She considered all the impulses she had. She had to be able to control impulses, or she would never have survived college and medical school.

Bill checked his watch again. "Christ, I have a two o'clock class, I have to stop this rambling, have to run, you really got me going on this, but remember this was just an overview. Don't want to leave you with the impression it's this simple, I had only ten minutes to describe it."

Most lucid rambling she'd ever heard. What could he do if he had been prepared for her question, or delivered a course on the Sixties? What else could he have told her?

He placed his two pie plates on the tray, opened his hands as if he was going to pick it up, when he stopped dead. He looked at her so seriously she felt knives penetrating her pupils. "Our students are fortunate to have a professor like you, Steve, to guide their thinking. You have the reputation for showing the highest standards of morality, for being an all-together person, stable, and trustworthy. It's a pleasure to have you as colleague." He picked up his tray. "We'll talk about the Sixties and even the Seventies and what may be left of it again. Take care."

His accolade wrenched her gut.

Moral.

Stable.

Trustworthy.

He should only have known why she tried to get him to talk today. All she could say was, "Next time let's invite those who don't agree with us to get their interpretation and input. It'll be a good test of our ideas."

"You're on." Bill scuttled out of the dining room leaving her to digest their conversation.

Steve regretted gulping down her hamburger. It was already backing up on her. When she finally lifted her cup, the thought of the cold coffee attacked her with waves of nausea. She put the cup down again.

The cafeteria was becoming quiet, just a few people lingering, the clanking of utensils dwindling. She'd just sit there and relax for a while, try to think about what Bill had said.

Responsibility. Consequences. Sexual fulfillment interfering with higher values. Her head was spinning. She needed...

"So here's where you're hiding. Where have you been?"

She didn't have to turn around to see who it was. Her skipped heartbeats had already responded to the sound of his voice. "Here and there. Busy," she said almost reflexively.

"I haven't seen you in days.".

"What are you doing here? Lunch is over." She spoke in a tone which she recognized as caustic. She had to control her blinking before she finally faced him.

"I was passing by," he said, "saw the back of your head, noticed you were sitting alone."

"I haven't been alone too long. Bill Foster was just here, and we had a great conversation."

"About what?"

"About the Sixties."

"Is that why you look so drained?

She ran the outer part of her hand across her forehead. "Actually, I don't feel so good, choked down my lunch, and its playing havoc with my stomach. Sorry I snapped at you, Charles, but since you're here, sit down, let me ask you something."

He sat across from her.

She looked straight at him. "Do you believe in life after death?"

He looked back at her, a perplexed expression on his face. "Is that supposed to have something to do with the Sixties, with your conversation with Bill?"

"Not directly, but what do you think?"

He seemed irritated with the question. "Why are you asking me this? You know what I think, I think the same way you do. It's an important part of our religion."

She looked away. "Of course I know, it's just that sometimes we accept things without thinking about them. Actually, I don't know what I'm saying, just babbling."

"I'm sure Bill told you what the Sixties had to say about religion. Anything that had rules had to go. I have to tell you something that infuriated me. Ken Sullivan, an old friend of mine from high school, went to Fordham. As all institutions, they're always requesting contributions from their alumni. He vowed never to send them another cent from the time he heard they removed the crucifixes from the wall to get Bundy funds. And I don't blame him, those two-faced Jesuit bastards.

"My alma mater, Holy Cross," his voice cracked, "keeps requesting donations, too. Can you imagine a college with that name ever removing crucifixes? They'll keep getting donations from me until I find they've rolled over, given up what they stand for to get some government handout."

"Yesterday I was speaking to the head of that federally subsidized program for those studying here who didn't make the entrance requirements but whose teachers felt had potential even though they hadn't yet achieved. The fellow they hired a few months ago, Ronald Williams, I think his name is. He told me that the students in that program who seem to be making it so far are those who have religion."

"That's probably because religion gives some structure to their lives."

"Or because those who seek structure also seek religion."

"Steve, will you ever stop being a scientist?"

She was confident he wasn't expecting an answer, so she asked, "Do you believe in a utopia?"

"What's with you today, asking all these silly questions? You know there's only the mythical utopia—freedom from traditions, rules, laws," he lifted his eyes, "complete self-determination, the triumph of the individual self."

It seemed that all she knew, but never thought about consciously suddenly came to light.

She raised her still full cup of coffee, which she had no intention of drinking. "To utopia, the real utopia." She swirled the cup, allowing some of the coffee to spill. "The real utopia is coming to grips with yourself, your weaknesses, strengths, values. The real utopia, Charles, is within."

CHAPTER 17

BY THE TIME Steve headed back to her office, it was almost two-thirty. She passed Tracy Robbins in the hall. "Hi, have you given any consideration to my recommendation?"

"I did, but things are going so well now, I really don't think I need it."

"I still think it'd be a good idea to talk to a professional. Remember, I volunteered to go with you."

"I feel so great now. Everything's going to be fine, getting everything in order. Never felt so peaceful in my life."

The woman seemed so upbeat, it was heartening. "That's good to hear. How's your graduate work progressing?"

"Great, handed in my papers, already preparing for finals. That'll leave me with only twenty-four more credits. They add up quickly. Have to run, good to see you."

"Good to see you, too." She called out to Tracy's back, now disappearing down the hall. "Don't forget, I'm here if you need me."

Steve was just about to start packing her books when she heard a knock on the door.

"Dr. Marchese, I know it's not your office hours, but I have to talk to you."

"Of course, Jill, come in."

"Do you mind if I close the door?"

"No, if that'll make you feel more comfortable."

Why was it that she felt this was going to be another of those days when she would be more of a therapist than a teacher? Her head was still pounding from the lunch discussion with Bill Foster, her stomach a disaster, and she didn't know how much, if any rational thinking was left in her.

"I don't want Dr. Babbitt to see me here," Jill said. "Just got out of her class, and she'll probably figure out why I'm talking to you."

Steve saw an image of Cleo Babbitt as though she was standing right in front of her. Always dressed like a flower child, but with shoes only Minnie Mouse would wear. She choked down her chuckle. "I really don't want to get entangled in a problem between a student and another professor. If you have a problem with her course, the professional way to deal with it is to approach her yourself."

"I will, but I want to talk about it first. Maybe there's something wrong with me, but I'm getting increasingly uncomfortable in her class. I feel that what we're getting exposed to is not intellectually honest."

"What course is it?"

"Women's Studies."

"What's not intellectually honest about it?"

"First of all, in your class we're encouraged to come up with as many hypotheses as we can. Then we test them. In her class, if someone comes up with a hypothesis that doesn't fit into her scheme of things, she laughs at it, ridicules you."

"Can you give me an example?"

Without hesitating Jill said, "Sure. In one of the offshoots of an article she assigned, the discussion came up that girls didn't score as well as boys in math in the SATs. A girl in the class had read somewhere some possible reasons for this. I don't remember them all but some were that girls didn't play with blocks when they were small as boys were encouraged to do, girls didn't take as many math courses, there weren't enough female role models teaching math. All of these are plausible. But one of the other suggestions was that at a certain point in the embryonic stage, boys had a higher level of some hormone that affected the growth of the part of the brain which was related to mathematical functioning. To me this was also plausible, but when it was offered as a possibility, she refused to discuss it, discarded it as biological, and went on with other hypotheses. In other words, she had already formed her conclusions before she had even tested the hypothesis because she didn't want it proved true if it would've been." Jill stopped talking before taking a deep breath. "Did you follow that?"

"Oh, yes, most scholarly."

"And it's the same with everything else. Everything we hear is one-sided. And it doesn't necessarily coincide with my experience. All I hear in that class is how oppressed we women are. And, frankly, I don't feel oppressed at all. You know how you're always telling us that science is more about asking the right questions than having the right answers?" Jill searched Steve's face in a way that sought agreement. "Well, I've taken that seriously. If I ask questions about how we're oppressed, instead of answers I get accusations, or something to make me feel guilty."

"Such as?"

"Such as if you're not with us you're against us, or what's wrong with you, or you just don't get it. To be perfectly honest, I don't think *they* get it. Since high school I had always been led to believe that one studied literature, quality literature that is, because it was life-generating, exposed us to ideas that can often conflict with ones we already held, made us think, challenged us." Jill had worked herself up into a sweat, and was breathing hard. "But in that class everything we read is attacked with her ideology in mind, that only her way of interpreting anything is correct, that men are responsible for all the problems of women, and the way to resolve it is through social and political action. Sometimes I think they want to pass a law against menstruation."

"And child-bearing even though they'd like to pass that on to the men, also. Actually, they don't quibble so much against carrying and delivering the child as bringing it up, though I think it's wonderful that men are now taking a more active role in that department, and it's about time." Her eyes traveled to the window. "But now you're making me think of my experiences here at Graham. Not to say that women are always treated fairly in the workforce, but I have to honestly say that I've not been mistreated in any perceptible way by men here."

The confrontation with Charles regarding his brother-in-law came to mind. But that was more a familial concern rather than his being anti-female. "Then I don't think I portray myself as some kook who has such hostility toward men so that they end up being aggressive or patronizing."

Steve put her head into her hand for a few moments, then looked up. "If it helps you at all, Jill, be encouraged by the fact that whenever any group seeks to move upward, including women, it always goes through a period of adolescence, making ridiculous assertions and unreasonable demands. It takes a while for them to progress to adulthood. Is there anything she's willing to blame women for in that course?"

"No, in fact that's one of the questions I asked her that she attacked me for. And when I asked her if she believed in the First Amendment, she jerked her body as though she'd been goosed. Became indignant and said, `Of course'. And when I asked her how she reconciled that with her stand against pornography, I didn't get an answer but got another attack for not being sensitive to women who'd been raped."

Steve was amused as she recalled presenting that same pornography analogy to Chester the day he called her into his office. "Has she shown any examples of how women may've caused their own problems?"

"Never, that's not consistent with her ideology of oppression. And frankly, I'm confused. First I hear her say that feminism offers women choices. But one girl said she wanted to stay home and raise her kids herself. She was laughed down by the class, encouraged by Dr. Babbitt. That's a choice a woman couldn't make."

Cleo Babbitt, another person who's open unless your opinion doesn't agree with hers. Chalk up another one for Alice Cronin.

Jill removed a tissue from her purse, patted her face and neck. "And while they claim they're all nurturing, if you don't agree with them, they become vicious. When it's convenient we're the same as men, when it's not, we're different. We're the stronger sex, yet we've allowed ourselves to become oppressed by men.

"And let me give you an example of her feeling she's been oppressed by men. She wears sleeveless dresses or sleeveless whatever, and doesn't shave under her arms. If men don't have to shave under their arms, neither does she. And when she lifts her arm to write on the board, I want to barf."

Steve couldn't get involved pursuing that one. "I'd like to share with you a pet peeve of mine. When they wanted to have women's studies here, not just as a course, but as a *bona fide* part of the core curriculum, they claimed they didn't want to use male standards to judge it, yet they couldn't come up with female standards either. But I'm curious, Jill, it's unusual for young women to have so many insights about what's really going on in the society. You usually have to be considerably older to figure things out, if ever. To what do you attribute your gift?"

A sneer displaced Jill's inquisitive expression. "Don't think for one moment I wasn't tempted to join any of the revolutions that were going on, especially the sexual revolution. It was through simple observation and reflection that I wised up."

Steve lifted her brows and Jill continued. "A girl I went to high school with, class valedictorian mind you, tried to prod me into becoming a radical. She was free, constantly organizing demonstrations for or against anything, was into everything from drugs to orgies to living on a commune. You name it, she was into it. Having fun. For a while I thought it would be fun, too, until one day I took a good look at her. Her life had become vulgar...no, that's too good to describe it." Jill paused for a moment. "Depraved or sordid would probably be more like it. When the modesty was gone, so was the dignity. It was then that I said to myself, if the way she lived was being free, then shackle me in repression."

"What happened to her?"

"She left her boyfriend, the one at the time, after he put his hand on her crotch at a party indicating sexual possession of her. Her whole life came to a jolt at that one action. It woke her up. Haven't seen her since she left him, lost contact, but I was wise to the whole scene much earlier."

"Your perception is very interesting for someone your age. But getting back to the women's movement, be careful not to lump all women into one group. Some are pleased the way things are, some know that reasonable changes have to be made. Then there are the activists who find something offensive to them in every word, and finally, we have the violent."

Steve stared at the ceiling. "I don't think there's a woman on this campus who's had to compete in a man's world more than I have, and there's a lot that needs changing. Such as getting women access to credit, equal access to professional schools and jobs, if they qualify of course. Like, like control of property, lots of legitimate injustices. And I'm probably aware more than anyone else about the under-research on women's health.

"But when they get extreme, they hurt the feminist cause. When you're taught to see all of women's problems caused by the fact that they're oppressed, by men of course, then you have the perfect excuse to blame others. At first you may be enticed into feeling that politicizing these so-called problems of women is liberating, but like other things that are supposed to make you liberated, they only result in enslavement into a system of thinking that doesn't allow you to take charge of your life. It makes it very easy to run away from something that's extremely difficult to do...coming to grips with yourself, something my mother warned me about many years ago when I was about your age, but I didn't fully understand it then."

"They're so self-righteous. They, oh I have to be careful since you said not to lump them all into one category, the radical ones claim to have such humane objectives, but they're the most ruthless bunch I know, displaying all the traits they've scorned in men."

Steve, her head vibrating from all the topics she'd covered that day, stood up, hoping that would signal Jill to do likewise. "Stick to your guns, Jill. The sad part is that they'll have to hang themselves, and God help us many others, before they see the effects of some of the things they're espousing, but if you wait long enough, about ten years, maybe sooner, you're going to see many women jumping off the bandwagon so fast there aren't going to be enough orthopedists around to heal their broken bones."

"I don't think most women agree with them, but they're the squeaky wheels."

She was pleased her conversation with Bill Foster was current, fresh in her mind, and found herself expanding on his ideas. "Be careful of easy-way-out ideas, the tyranny of what's popular. They have a lot of appeal, often appear stronger than complicated old ideas. Right now having it all is the wonderful idea. Anyone who believes that is deceiving herself. Having it all is not only impossible, but if one tries to pursue it, it's more frustrating than the problems you're trying to deal with in the first place. And a lot of people get hurt in the process.

"Wouldn't give up motherhood and staying home with my children when they were young for all the degrees in the world. I know that's not possible for all women, but for me it was an experience I wouldn't change. Couldn't imagine anyone else giving them the values, the love, manners, and the speech I wanted them to have. Keep up the thinking and the questioning, Jill, and keep me informed."

"I will. Thanks, Dr. Marchese."

Later that evening Steve reflected on her day. Her chat with Bill Foster, her conversation with Jill. The agreement, the advice about what was right and what had to be done was there, but she herself was simultaneously succumbing to everything she felt was wrong with the society.

Time to think about something else. She went into the bedroom, opened her briefcase just about to pull out her notes for the next day's classes, when the phone jangled on the nightstand. She finally interrupted the fifth ring. "Hello."

"Steve?"

His voice gave her brain a shock. "Yes."

"It's Charles."

She closed her eyes. "Hi, what's up?"

"I, I don't know how else to tell you this, so I have to be direct. Are you sitting down?"

"No, but if you wait a few seconds, I will be." She dragged her vanity chair to the nightstand. "What's the matter?"

He hesitated, then said in a broken voice, "Tracy Robbins… is dead."

"What do you mean, dead? I spoke to her this afternoon right after her class." After she said that, she realized how ludicrous it sounded. She'd seen death enough times to know how quickly it could come, surprisingly, out of nowhere. "When? How?"

"This afternoon, about four o'clock. I was still in my office at four-thirty when the news came."

"What, what happened?"

"A bullet, through her head."

"Wait a minute. Are, are you telling me she was murdered?"

"No, self-inflicted."

"Self inflicted!" Steve put the transmitter against her cheek for a moment, then returned it to her mouth. "Where did she get the gun?"

"The guy she was living with, it was his. And she ran out to the middle of the front lawn of his house and did it right there, as if to call her pain to everyone's attention."

What Charles had told her had just hit her. She felt her tear ducts overflow. "Ed warned me about her the night he met her at the party. I should've insisted she go for counseling. And me, I'm some physician, I should've recognized the symptom. The minute she was so happy, so relieved, peaceful, saying that she had put things in order, I should've known she'd made the decision to kill herself." By now she was crying uncontrollably. "It's…it's…all…my fault."

"Stop blaming yourself, Steve, she came to see me, too. Heard from my students that the way I interpret literature helps them get insights into behavior. Guess she was hoping I could give her some insights into her situation. Evidently, I didn't help her much, either."

She blew her nose. "What did you tell her?"

"That you can't live outside of your value system. That's the only insight I could come up with under the circumstances she described.

And I really believe that, and I'm sure she did too, though she didn't want to hear it. She had a terrible conflict living the way she was."

"I, I never thought of it that way. But now that you said it, you're probably right. Can't live against your value system."

"I'll call her husband and see if there's anything I can do."

"Please tell Alan that if he needs someone to watch Kim, she can stay with us until he can arrange permanent plans he feels comfortable with."

"I'll tell him."

She had to blow her nose again, so hard it plugged up her ears. "Thanks for letting me know."

"I knew you'd want to hear it now instead of getting the shock tomorrow morning before class."

"Thanks again." She let the phone slip into its cradle.

CHAPTER 18

TWO WEEKS LATER Jill was sitting on the floor outside Steve's office when she arrived. The girl was reading a book propped up on her knees. She looked up and smiled but didn't say anything.

"Jill, how did you fare with Dr. Babbitt? Were you able to resolve your differences?"

"Not quite, but I know I've got her going. She's going to be more careful about what she's doing in that class, and the students are waking up, too. Just from some of the questions I'm asking, that whole class is turning around."

"It takes only one thinking person to do it. I'm glad it was you. Though I have to confess I was disappointed that no one from my classes joined The Scholars Society."

"Your students feel they get enough scholarly activities in your classes."

That was a relief to hear though she was still crushed that none of her students had joined the club. "Then, may I recruit you as a science major?"

"Not really. I love literature too much. Speaking of which, I'm waiting for Dr. Pastore. Do you know when he's coming?"

Steve checked the wall clock. It glared 9:16. "He's usually here way before nine."

"I had an appointment with him to go over my paper before class."

"Be patient, I'm sure he'll be here soon."

She unlocked the door, nudged it open with her foot, and made a bee-line for the desk where she deposited her brimming briefcase, and a reservoir of books which didn't fit into it. After prioritizing the pink message slips, she returned a few phone calls while browsing through the mail. Twenty minutes later she noticed that Jill was still sitting outside.

She stepped out into the hall, looked down each end. Charles' door was closed. "I don't understand why he's not here, Jill. He's never late for an appointment."

"Worse than that, he has a nine o'clock class and it's past nine-thirty already. I walked down to the classroom a few minutes ago, and students are there waiting, but Dr. Pastore didn't show."

Steve suddenly felt queasy. "Did you check the bulletin board outside the registrar's office to see if his class was canceled?"

"No, but I was so absorbed in this novel I'm reading, I think I should." She straightened out her knees, kicked her legs. She rolled over, and stood up. "Jee, my legs are stiff," she said while massaging them. Then she dropped her book and hobbled down the hall.

By ten o'clock there was still no sign of Charles.

Steve picked up the phone to dial the registrar.

After two rings a voice responded, "Registrar's office, Mrs. Thorne."

"Dr. Pastore didn't show up for class, and according to the students, you didn't post any notice. Do you know where he is? The students are concerned."

"Oh, I have the thumb-tack in my hand, just about to post the announcement." Mrs. Thorne choked up. "Who, who is this?"

"Dr. Marchese. What is it?"

"Oh, Dr. Marchese, thank God it's you. There, there was an accident this morning, just got a call from his wife, they're at the hospital, their son was in a car driven by a neighbor. They were hit, the neighbor and her son are dead, and their boy's in critical condition."

She remained stiff, trying to process the information. "Which hospital?"

"Queen of Angels."

She hung up without responding to Mrs. Thorne.

Charles.

In pain.

At the hospital.

She had to control every cell in her body from rising up and running to him, clutching him, holding him, wrenching the pain from his body. She opened her desk drawer, put her hands in the drawer and squeezed the drawer closed with her knee, trapping her hands with the agony which would prevent her from grabbing onto him, the hands which would shove Claudia aside, out of his life so that she couldn't share in his suffering. Why did she resort to masochism in a situation like this?

Their boy.

Charles' and Claudia's.

She couldn't go to the hospital. Couldn't watch them clinging to each other as they watched their son fighting for life, the life they created, the life that if it remained or not, reinforced their union.

That she couldn't face.

She'd stay at the college and go through the motions of holding class, and office hours, hoping that when Charles eventually returned, she would greet him with the usual pleasantries, conveying her concern in an aloof, casual manner not with the compulsion of leaping into his arms.

Her numbed hands felt free again.

She stretched her fingers before picking up the phone. "Ed, you have to do me a favor." Her voice was hardly in control of the trembling. He'd understand why, as a mother, she'd be upset. "Go down to Queen of Angels. Now. The Pastores are there. Their son was in an accident and is in critical condition. See to it that they get the best care, the best doctors. You've got to do that for me."

"That's awful. I'd be happy to do it but why don't you meet me there? Maybe you can reassure his wife while I check the medical procedures. Do you know who's working on the case?"

Reassure his wife. About what? That she didn't have any feelings for Charles and didn't pick up that Charles had feelings for her? One of those situations when both knew it, but it had to remain unspoken. "I have no idea, just got the news, please Ed, just go do it. For me."

"Relax, sweetheart. You're concerned because you know how it would feel if, God forbid, it happened to either of our kids. I'll leave in about five minutes."

"Good, go as quickly as you can." Steve hung up the phone a second time within the last few minutes.

Her hands were still hurting, but more painful was the torture of knowing how insignificant feelings between people like her and Charles became when there was a child involved.

Ed hurried into the hospital waiting room. "Charles, Claudia, Steve asked me to come down. I'm so sorry about your boy."

Charles held on to Claudia. Seeing Ed Marchese only added to his misery. "He's in a coma, was in a car accident. Mrs. Panzer and her son are dead. They went to school early, before the bus, to get a head start on a project they were doing." He pulled out his handkerchief. "It's... it's only because Philip was in the back seat…that, that he'll have any chance of surviving at all."

Ed patted his back, then put a comforting arm around his shoulder. "I already spoke with Dr. Thorndike. He went over the case with me and assured me that everything possible was being attended to immediately."

He wiped his face with his handkerchief and blotted his tears. "What are his chances? I already heard that from Thorndike but I want to hear your opinion."

"The next few hours are critical. He has several fractured ribs, very serious head injuries, a ruptured spleen and liver and a punctured lung. We have him on a respirator. But he's strong, has that strength and youth on his side. Even though he's in a coma, speak to him in a loving way. Hold his hand, massage it gently, encourage him. Sometimes that reassurance can make the difference. Who's taking care of your other boy?"

Claudia stopped sobbing and spoke for the first time. "I just called my sister, she'll pick him up from school. He, he doesn't know yet."

The sobbing returned then subsided. "Maybe she'll have to take him home with her because we can't leave here. She has her own children in school."

"I want you both to know that Steve and I would be more than willing to take him. In the morning I can drop him off at school before going to the clinic, this way his life won't be so disrupted. It's going to be hard on him, too."

"We appreciate your concern," Charles said. He meant it but still resented the power Ed had in this situation.

"It's the least I can do. What are friends for? Now rest assured that as a friend I'll be on top of every move these doctors make. Just their knowing that will keep them extra alert. What you two need is rest."

"We can't rest until we know what's going to happen," Claudia said. "Not knowing is the worst thing we have to deal with."

"Just think positively. Let that thinking be conveyed to your boy if just through touching him and talking to him, even if you don't think he can hear you. Your love alone will be worth more than all the treatment in the world. I'll do what I can, keep abreast of his condition, check the charts, stop by at least once a day. And remember if you need someone to take care of your other boy, just pick up the phone and call Steve. You know where to find her. It would probably be good for her, she's so upset."

Charles asked himself if she was more upset for the boy, or for him.

While waiting for news about Philip, Charles became very reflective. He tried to understand what had happened to his son, but couldn't. All he could come up with was that he was being warned, that Someone up there was trying to tell him something. Like the time the lamp came crashing down on his desk just a few seconds after Sister Stella asked him to move to another seat. Charles had to do something about his feelings for Steve or He would start picking on his family. The old Catholic school guilt.

He had thought about taking a sabbatical before, talked about it, but had never acted upon it. Now it was time to apply. Not for a semester, but for a year. A year was the usual time it took one to adjust to the loss of a spouse, or for any other loved one, and in one year he would get over Steve, this tyrannical grip she had over him. The instant he made his decision he felt purged.

For now, all he could do was wait.

Wait.

Wait and pray.

Watch the swinging doors which needed a generous dose of WD-40. The smell of antiseptics, of overcooked food, the dragging of carts by non-smiling faces. How long could he look at the sickening green walls, the sickening green uniforms? If only he could unplug that P.A. system. "Calling Dr. Roberts. Calling Dr. Feingold." His head was throbbing.

Everyone in the hospital was reluctant to say anything. He kept looking for some sign of hope on their faces, not daring to breathe lest he would read something less than good news.

His wife was little help. Not uttering a sound, just hanging on to his arm, while Steve was hanging on to his heart. Providing Claudia with support left him less time for worrying, less time for thinking about Steve.

Until he heard, "Calling Dr. Marchese."

Not much later Ed stopped in. Then every day, sometimes twice. Charles always tried to interpret his expression. Was the boy improving, getting worse, the same? Each second torture, torment. Even when Ed's face was far from uplifting, he would encourage him with something encouraging.

How could Steve ever give up a man who was so thoughtful, so kind? How could she...?

Wait. And pray.

For his boy.

And for himself.

A week later Charles returned to work. He almost sneaked into his office, looking straight ahead while passing the office next door, reassuring himself that a sabbatical would make him free of Steve.

She must have heard him enter. "Good morning, Charles," she called out from next door.

He put his briefcase down so that he could fortify himself to confront her. "Why good morning, Steve," he tried to say in a cheerful way while sauntering into her office.

"I know the news about Philip is good. Ed told me it was touch and go for several days, and even though he'll need a long recuperation period, he's going to be fine. You know how fast kids bounce back. I'm so happy for you." She rose from her desk, moved close to him, and hugged him without looking at him.

When she put her arms around him, he felt his skeletal system begin to dissolve. "Thank you, Ed was wonderful. I think all that talking we gave our boy, at Ed's suggestion, made a big difference."

"We know that in medicine there's more to healing than meets the eye. But you sound extra chipper, did you also win the lottery?"

"Better than that, I did a lot of thinking while I was sitting in the hospital. I'm going to apply for a sabbatical, have the perfect project in mind."

"That's great, do you mean we'll be rid of you for six months?"

"No, a year. I'm going to apply for a year so I'll have a better chance of getting it. The administration gives preference to those who apply for a year, because we take it at half-pay."

"A year then," she said with a flat voice. "What project do you plan on doing?"

"I'm going to go back to England to visit all the old haunts from my younger days, Piccadilly, the Tower of London, The Sherlock Holmes. Then I'm going to write an article, monograph, or whatever vehicle is appropriate, comparing the symbolism, the imagery in the "Song of Solomon" with that used in *Lady Chatterley's Lover*."

"Do you have to go to England to do that?"

"I can do it from here, but you don't get the same sense as when you're actually there. And," he brought his voice to a whisper, "I won't write this in the sabbatical application, but part of my hidden agenda is that I'm going to lose weight. I can't fit into my clothes anymore.

Gotta shed at least ten pounds, come home with a forty-inch waist. And England's probably the best place to do it."

"Is that so? I've never been to England and don't know enough about your literary project to have an opinion, but let's get some baseline data on your weight. I'll tack it on my bulletin board and see how you've improved when you get back. See how optimistic I am, note I've said how you've improved, not if. And we'll begin as of today before you even apply for your sabbatical. Get a head start. I don't have a scale in here, but I'll do one better."

She opened her top desk drawer, pushing aside the paper clips, removing the one that was clasped on her wound-up tape measure. She approached him while unrolling the tape. "Lift your jacket."

For a moment he didn't move. Then he did as she requested.

She surrounded her arms about his waist, pulling the tape measure along with her. "No cheating. Don't breathe in, relax and take a natural position."

He froze as the lightness of her fingers moved around his body. He should leave for the sabbatical right now, before he had even applied.

Steve drew the tip of the tape measure around to the point where it met the rest of the tape. "Forty-four inches! My God, you'd better make it more than ten pounds if you want to lose four inches."

He remained immobile.

"Scientists always check their results, so I'll have to do this again. Don't move and, above all, relax. Up goes the jacket, and don't try to pull in your stomach."

She put her arms and tape measure around him again. This time she lingered with her hands fumbling across his back.

His brain imploded.

All he wanted to do was free his arms from lifting the jacket, draw her to him, press on her cheek his lips which would unavoidably find her mouth. He had to suck in his lower lip and bite it to resist.

When she finally finished fiddling with the tape measure, she said, "A little better than I thought. Forty-three and seven eighths. But it'll still take more than ten pounds to get to your goal. And let me give you some medical advice," she shook her finger at him, "you must learn to listen to your body. It will tell you what it needs."

Great medical advice. If he listened to his body, they'd both be in deep trouble.

She rolled up the tape measure and returned it to her drawer. On a piece of yellow paper, she wrote the date, November 14, 1976, and forty-three and seven eighths inches. She removed a thumbtack from her still open drawer, placed the paper against the bulletin board, and stuck the thumbtack through both. "Are you sure you weren't holding anything in?"

"I'm sure," he said with quiet desperation.

"When you get back, we'll check again, but you should start the diet now. Now, Charles. It's like smoking. You have to go cold turkey."

At that moment he knew that even though he hadn't yet applied for the sabbatical, and even if it were granted for a hundred years, he already couldn't wait to get back.

Just anticipating that Charles would be away for a year left Steve in a state of depression. She wanted to be separated from him, yet she didn't. It would be best to use the time he was away to wrangle with what else she could do with her life, her career.

Even though his sabbatical wouldn't begin until the end of May, she already felt she needed to fill the emptiness of not seeing him by keeping busy. After class she returned to the laboratory to check how her student assistants had set up the materials and equipment for the following week's experiments.

The smell of peanuts.

What chemical could that possibly be?

She turned on the lights. On the floor in the corner, a leg with a dirty sneaker and a bell-bottomed jean.

The leg swirled around, followed by a mirror-imaged one. The two legs scrambled up, supporting Marsha Wright. She was eating from a paper plate a mixture of spaghetti and what looked like chunky peanut butter. In this age of experimentation, now Steve had seen everything.

Where did the girl get that combination? It made Steve's stomach curdle.

Marsha brushed the dust off her braless tank top.

Not another therapy day!

"Why, Marsha, I was just about to send you a note. You haven't been to the last two classes."

"That's why I'm here, I wanted to talk to you."

"What are you doing here in the dark? You should've come to my office during office hours. It's lucky for you that I came back to check the lab, or I would've missed you. Have you been ill?"

"Depends on what you mean by ill. I'm not sick or anything, I mean I don't have a fever or cold or something. I just don't feel like doing anything."

"Oh, and how long have you felt this way?"

"Quite a while, but it's only the last week I've really given into it."

"Did something happen a week ago, anything you can pinpoint?"

Marsha's brown hair kept falling into her face, covering her espresso eyes. She pushed her hair out of the way. "I had an argument with my mother. Not just any old argument, a super-duper one. I mean we argue all the time, but this one was too much, a real dilly."

Steve was in a hurry to get home, but she thought of how Victoria would feel if she wanted to speak to her teacher and was pushed aside, ignored, or handled abruptly. "Do you want to talk about it?"

"She's the cause of all my troubles, criticizes my friends, doesn't like my boyfriend."

"And what do you say to her when she does this?"

"What I know really drives her nuts, that I didn't ask to be born, so if I disappoint her, it's her fault."

This nonsense was pushing Steve to the limit, fraying her patience. "The last time I checked, I had a hard time locating anyone I know, or don't know, who ever asked to be born. But that expression is so hackneyed now, and it was never a heavy hitter to begin with. It's something young people latched on to without thinking. But I'm interested in your thinking."

"My thinking?"

"Yes, Marsha, I want you to think out loud about this whole situation, I want you to hear yourself thinking about the way you're thinking."

"Out loud?"

"Yes, why don't you begin?"

"Where?"

"Anywhere."

Marsha shuffled her books around, and leaving them on the floor, took a seat on a lab stool. "I have a test coming up on...Oh, I don't want to start there. My mother, I have it really in for her because she never forced me to play a musical instrument."

"And if she had, you'd be complaining that she did. Go on."

"She's a real pain-in-the-ass, always nagging me to get my hair cut, wear different clothes, wants to pick out friends for me. I told her she shouldn't've had me. She should've had someone like that Heidi Buck, a gorgeous blond, high grades and SAT scores, wants to be a lawyer, who lives across the street. And it's not my problem that she had me because I didn't ask for it."

Marsha slouched on the stool and stared into space.

"Go on, Marsha."

"Well, I didn't ask for it," she said, still looking upward.

"You said that already. You didn't ask for it, so now what?"

"I'm in this goddam world where nothing's ever right. I have to take exams and have to study, have no time for fun."

"So?"

"If I wasn't here on this creepy earth, I would never've known about it, and wouldn't have had to be bothered with anything."

"And now that you're here, what choices do you have?"

"Well...well for one, I could cop out." She picked a chunk of peanut butter out of her teeth, then swallowed it.

"That's one choice. How do you see your life if you cop out?"

"I could live on a commune."

"Describe what your life would be like there."

Marsha crumpled her face. "Well, well I don't know. Everybody does a little job here and there and everybody lives together...and you can have children with anyone you want to have them with and raise them with a lot of other people...and...and I don't think I want to do that."

"Well now that you know that, what other choices do you have?"

"Damn it, I knew that's what you were leading up to. I can drop out of school...and get a job...but not the job I want...or...I can finish my degree and see where it takes me."

"You have another choice. You don't have to do anything."

Marsha straightened up, pushed her hair out of her eyes once more. "I don't?"

"Right, you don't. You don't have to do anything...study, work, as long as you understand and are willing to accept the results, and don't expect the same results as those who do. Do you know anyone who has anything worth having who didn't have to be bothered, really bothered to get it?"

Marsha didn't answer. She sat with a pensive look and after almost a minute began gathering her belongings. "I guess I did sound like a clod. Maybe I'm just lazy, but it seems that everything's accumulating on me now. Have to be better organized, use my time better."

"Marsha, whenever someone tells you something, or you hear something like 'I didn't ask to be born', don't accept. Think. It sounds to me like you're thinking better already. Now stop thinking and act."

"But I___"

She moved her face less than ten inches from the girl's and grabbed her hard by the shoulders. "I have one more thing to say to you about not being asked to be born. At the moment you were conceived, one sperm out of 400,000,000 penetrated your mother's egg. Did you know that?"

"No, or if I learned it, I forgot it."

"Well, remember this. For you to be born, you had to win out over 399,999,999 other possibilities. You're a winner already, and you're unique. There will never be another person like you. No other species, only man, has the capability of improving its life. So use that capability well."

The girl was looking at her seemingly in total shock.

Steve was still holding Marsha's shoulders which she now shook. "Young lady, now hear this. If you don't stop acting like a brat, I'm going to be your surrogate mother, one who's not responsible for your being born, take you over my knee, and spank you myself. Now scat!" She released the girl's shoulders, then gave her a loving pat on the rear.

Marsha returned the pat with a broad smile, collected her books, folded her paper plate with the half-eaten spaghetti with peanut butter, and skipped out of the lab.

Nimbus clouds were hovering over the parkway as Steve drove home. Claps of thunder rolled throughout the area, creating so many vibrations it felt like a series of earthquakes. It appeared as though lightning bolts were on a timer to go off every thirty seconds. At three-thirty it was so dark it could have been midnight. Unusual to have this type of thunderstorm, any thunderstorm in late October.

She arrived at the house grateful no one else was home yet. Then she recalled that today was after-school soccer practice for Christopher, and community service day for Victoria.

Chopin was probably hiding somewhere. She called for him, even crinkled some wrappings from the dog treats, rattled his leash, but he was nowhere to be found. She searched the rooms for him.

Victoria's flute was disassembled on the music stand, next to the piano, the open flute case on the sofa. And on the piano her Chopin waltz book, open on the music rack to the Minute Waltz, her favorite piece from her favorite composer. Victoria loved Chopin's music so much she begged to have the dog named after him.

Christopher's violin was on the living room floor, the bow still tightened despite the warning inside the case, "Loosen your bow after playing." Rosin from the bow left dust on the carpet.

She climbed the steps and peeked into her son's room. Christopher had promised to put his books in the bookcase last night before going to bed, but they were still strewn all over the floor. She would have to dock the children's allowance.

Steve went into her bedroom. She threw herself prostrate on the bed without removing the spread, something she always warned her children and husband not to do. "Always take the spread off the bed before you sit or lie down," she had constantly nagged. But today she didn't care. All she wanted to do was die.

She hoped Charles would die.

Maybe they'd both die.

That would end this lunacy once and for all.

She felt her arms around his waist, how she wanted to keep them there and recheck and recheck and recheck his dimensions. How she wanted him to hold her until she was void of energy, void of herself, lost in him.

She couldn't help notice his eyes when she called out his dimensions. He wasn't even listening. All she could feel was the resonance between them, his tingling creating hers.

He looked at her with the same passion in his eyes he conveyed when he read literature, that silly hair sticking up, that curl either sticking up at the end of, or flopping into his part.

Think about the problem out loud, Marsha. This way you can hear what you're thinking, think about your thinking. What was good for Marsha Wright was good for her. Think about this situation out loud.

Rumbling.

From under the bed.

So that's where Chopin was! Back in the uterus where it was safe. And that's exactly where she wanted to be.

She knocked on the bed for him. While she was still knocking, he crunched himself out from underneath and jumped on the bed. "My hero." She hugged him and he snuggled his black snout into her armpit after licking her cheek. She remembered tears reaching her eyes when for the first time after months of squatting, he finally lifted his leg. Her little boy, all grown up. "My little hero, they say that you're man's best friend."

Chopin lifted his head, moved it up and down as if agreeing. Then he scratched behind his ear with one foot, another foot tapping simultaneously.

"You're not very brave but I know you can keep a secret. I'd talk to my father about this but you know he has a weak heart, and if he hears this, it would surely do him in.

"I told Marsha Wright, one of my students, to think about her situation out loud. So now I'm going to do the same thing. To you. Not even you will believe this, Chopin, but." She took a deep breath, held it, then forced the air out of her lungs. "I love...Charles...Pastore. There, I said it. It feels good that I said it. Isn't that crazy? I love another man. I didn't plan on it, ask for it, and I don't understand it, am completely stumped. I love Ed, too, but it's a different kind of love. Can I be in love with two people at the same time?" She grabbed the curly fur behind Chopin's neck to lift his head. "Do you understand what I'm saying?"

He tilted his head, looking embarrassed. Then he grunted.

"You do understand. I always knew you were smart, so now tell me, genius, what am I supposed to do? Me, the adviser of students, the role model, the reputation I have on campus, protecting standards, the values, the things I believe in. So what can I do? I tried ignoring him, making sure my schedule's so different from his, that we don't see each other or have lunch together. My husband fights me every time I tell him I want to move or change my job. I don't go to any campus affairs when I know Charles'll be there. I'm polite. Coolly polite, even though it's hard to be cool when I'm seething inside. What else can I do, Chopin?"

He made a whiny sound that modulated to low, then returned to high.

"So you don't know, either. Some help you are!"

She lifted Chopin's ears, held them up a couple of seconds, then released them suddenly. Another crackle of thunder sent him scampering back under the bed.

She was alone again, tired. Time to take her mind off Charles. The TV would help. She turned it on. "Charles of the Ritz will make you feel glamorous," the commercial said.

Damn the TV.

The nostalgia radio station would do it. She twisted the knob. Doris Day was singing "Secret Love." Just what she needed to hear! She shook the radio before switching it off.

What time was it? The digital clock read 4:17, the first three digits of Charles' phone number, a number she had occasion to dial only once, yet was still inscribed in her brain. She opened her hands and squashed them against her ears. When she finished compressing them, she yanked one of the decorator pillows off the spread, and hurled the pillow at the clock, knocking it over.

This situation was so utterly hopeless, ridiculous, and every other appropriate adjective she could think of. That it was. She had told Tracy Robbins to cry, that crying relieved the body of pent-up emotions.

She cried profusely while thanking the Creator for providing man with such a mechanism. And she thanked Him for something else. The infinite wisdom He had in constructing us in such a way that others wouldn't know what we were thinking. Not Charles. Not Ed. Not her children. God had the omniscience to...

Creaking.

Coming from the steps.

She had forgotten to close the bedroom door. Better run into the bathroom, drench her face in cold water, conceal her puffy eyes. Couldn't be seen like this. Could she make anyone, especially Ed believe she had a cold?

Footsteps. Headed toward Victoria's room.

A closed door.

Then quiet.

Victoria must've known she was home. Her daughter was always the bubbly type who bounced in and out of the house with a flourish, a person who exuded life, always making a point of greeting her, telling her about her day. But today there was something strange about the silence. What could possibly have happened at community service day? Probably worked with some poor kids, which always drove Victoria to tears and made her want to buy the little children things with her own money.

She stepped into the hall, pausing in front of Victoria's room.

Sobs so loud, she didn't have to put her ear to the door to hear them.

She knocked on the door.

No answer.

She knocked louder.

Still no answer.

She turned the knob. Victoria was lying face down on the bedspread, something she, too, never did. When her daughter became aware of her presence, she stood up, lunged at her, clutching her with a strength Steve was confident an adolescent couldn't possess.

Neither spoke as Victoria kept clutching and sobbing. Steve knew her daughter would begin the conversation whenever she was ready. But Steve wasn't prepared for the first question.

"Mom, do you still love Daddy?"

The question was a piercing one, so much so that Steve initially couldn't answer, because it was one she was still asking herself.

All she could say was, "Where did you get the idea for such a question?"

"From Karen Fuller."

"Karen Fuller? Who's she?"

"A girl in my class. She's sick, upset. Her parents are probably going to get a divorce. Karen told me she had no clue her mother was in love with another man, just took off yesterday and ran away with him. Her father didn't know, either. Karen wants to die, and I feel so bad, I want to die for her. And she and her brother want to run away from home, they think it's their fault, and if I were in their shoes, I'd want to run away, too."

What was the great adviser to students going to tell her daughter? "Victoria. Things happen in life. People get sick, have accidents, die. Married people sometimes don't get along. They might split up, or try to work it out. Sometimes they don't make it. It's not pleasant, but it's life."

"Do you still love Daddy?"

The question threw her nervous system out of whack. She closed her eyes. "Of course I do." And, in her own way, she did.

Victoria's face was painted with relief. She pulled a tissue from the Kleenex box, blew her nose. "That's good, because I know he loves you, and I know you, you couldn't leave us like Karen's mother did, and hurt us or Daddy."

"How could I ever do that?"

Victoria resumed clinging and crying, her warm tears pelleting Steve's arm. "I know you couldn't. It just makes me feel so much better to, to hear you say it."

CHAPTER 19

BY THE TIME Paul and Alex finished the last four chapters, it was almost midnight. Even though it was late and both of them were exhausted, they kept pushing themselves to peruse the manuscript.

Alex stopped turning pages and looked up. "This section with Bill Foster seems excessive. It's too long and if I say so myself, rather tedious and overbearing."

"Well, wasn't that the point of the whole book, our disgust with what's happening in this decade and our wanting people to understand what's going on?"

"There has to be a better way to present this material." She ran through the edge of the pages with her thumb, making a zipping sound. "Maybe we can find a place to put the same content, spread it around in different chapters. Do you think that readers will find this information dull?"

"I don't think so. Besides being entertained, readers want, or should want to be educated."

"You know, a lot of readers won't agree with Bill Foster's assessment."

"You mean won't want to agree. All I can say is that I have a deep commitment to the integrity of scholarship and a deep aversion to its politicalization. I will not be a party to politicizing scholarship nor should anyone who calls himself a scholar. And if they believe there's a different conclusion to what's going on in the society, then let them, like us, write their own novel and come up with the empirical evidence to support their point of view."

"Wow, you sound like someone who has learned something from the chapter we wrote on The Scholars Society. But I still think that we should have several people, several historians read that section on Bill Foster and get their feedback. It may take us longer to finish, but it would be worth it to make sure that section is accurate."

Paul ignored her. He seemed rather put off with her pursuing this discussion. Instead of answering, he kept on reading, re-reading, and adding comments in red to the margins.

She decided to press him. "And didn't we agree that we would avoid distracting readers by giving names to characters like the registrar, Steve's neighbor, the librarian, unless they were important?"

He didn't answer so she looked up. He had fallen asleep, arms outstretched over the desk, his cheek flat on the desk blotter, which was beginning to moisten from his perspiration. With his mouth open, he snored so loud, that every time he exhaled, his breath lifted from the desk a loose piece of white manuscript paper close to his nose.

It had been a grueling two days. Even though the air conditioner's compressor had burned out, causing the temperature in the office to reach 97, with the humidity probably just about as high, Alex was thrilled that they had persisted in completing the four planned chapters.

Now came the homestretch. They were nearing the end, almost ready to revise. That would probably make Paul happy, since he had expressed concern about revision so many times.

She didn't wake him, just opened his appointment book and scheduled two more sessions. She left the book open to next week's page, but wanted to make sure it was visible. She propped the open book against his family picture, and after searching around his desk, found the perfect item to hold the book up. The marble base of the penholder. After debating with herself whether or not to leave the lights on, she decided to reduce the heat in the room by turning them off.

Worn out herself, she tip-toed out of the room, and closed the door.

* * *

Steve noticed a group of faculty gathered around a small table in a remote corner of the cafeteria. They were probably involved in a meeting. She began to head in a different direction when one of the men at the table called out her name. Pete Stratton's voice. She turned around, and he signaled her to join them.

Charles and Bill Foster were also there.

"You all look as though you're plotting the overthrow of the administration," she said.

Pete had a sparkle in his eyes. "Almost."

She bent her head toward them. "What's so secretive? And why did you ask me to join in the conspiracy."

Pete held out a chair for her. "Well," he whispered, "the three of us got invitations to Morty's daughter's wedding, and we're trying to find out which others from the college were invited besides us."

"I got one, too," she said. "Would've been surprised if I didn't, after all the talks I had with Morty about his daughter."

Pete kept his voice low. "Everyone knows Claire has experimented with all kinds of lifestyles, but what finally made her settle down?"

Steve dragged her chair closer to the table.

"Morty's told just about everyone on the faculty this," Bill said, "so I know I'm not revealing anything he told me in confidence." The circumference of the group decreased. "It was when she got some venereal disease from going to all those nude parties. Then she moved in with this guy and found out she wasn't the only one he was living with. She told her father she'd had enough, her life had become so sordid, decadent that if she didn't get out of it soon, there would be no turning back. Claire finished her education, she had dropped out of college after two years, got a job as a journalist, and met what Morty calls a very traditional fellow when she went to interview him for an article she was writing. A lawyer, I think he said."

"Are you going to the wedding, Steve?" Pete said.

"How could I not go? Morty's so excited about it. He wants to spend more time with Claire and his future son-in-law, so he's giving up the chairmanship, is just going to teach psychology courses. He's finished with the alimony now that his first three wives have remarried, is collecting royalties on his book, *How to Keep a Marriage Together*, and is using this occasion as a double celebration. After all the pride Morty has that Claire has finally gotten it together, he needs us to reassure him, show that we share his joy."

Bill pursed his lips. "I guess Rita and I'll have to go, too. My wife loves going to weddings, says it's the only time she can get dressed up."

"Guess I'm going to have to find something to wear," Steve said.

Charles instantly responded with his first words since she joined the table. "Why don't you wear that flowing pink chiffon dress with the petals and the basque waist you wore to Ed's cocktail party?"

Charles and Claudia arrived at the reception early. The rectangular room was large enough to hold ten round tables which clustered at one end, leaving space in the middle for the dance floor, and a smaller space at the other end for the band.

When Claudia went to the powder room, Charles found his way to the entrance desk which held the cards with the names of the guests and their assigned tables. Theirs was table 4. He picked up his card slowly to give him time to survey the other cards.

Steve's table was also 4.

He put the card in his pocket, stepped over to the bar, and waited for Claudia without ordering a drink.

Within the next few minutes Peter Stratton, Bill Foster and their wives arrived.

Pete slung his arm over Charles' shoulder. "I'm glad Morty put us at the same table."

"So am I."

The women began to chat. Bill and Pete asked their wives what they wanted from the bar, then left.

As soon as Charles decided what he wanted to drink, Steve and Ed entered the room. Charles' blood pressure shot up. She was not wearing that flowing pink dress, but a royal blue, bare shouldered one that hugged her figure. She carried a silver clutch purse and silver shawl which she draped over her chair.

Ed shook his hand, then Claudia's, and Steve presented them with a handshake, smile, and a hello before proceeding to greet Lillian Stratton and Rita Foster.

Charles was pleased the Strattons and Fosters had arrived before Steve and Ed because the Marcheses were now relegated to sitting not next to but across from him, giving him a good view of Steve.

Pete and Bill returned with four drinks. Their wives each took one and Pete and Bill deposited the remaining two behind their respective plates. They both shook Ed's hand and simultaneously planted a kiss on Steve, Bill on her right cheek, Pete on her left. They performed with such timing, it couldn't have been better had it been rehearsed.

Pete picked up his glass. "I'll repeat what I just said to Charles. Glad Morty put us at the same table...and to complete our table and make this a perfect evening, here come Bob and Estelle Lucas."

Bob immediately plopped next to Steve.

Charles was hoping he wasn't going to have to at some point in the evening listen to Bob's tales of frustration about his feelings for Steve. Talk about how she looked in the dress, how her eyes picked up its color making them turn turquoise, how her skin glowed. To relieve his own tension, he thought he'd introduce something lighthearted. He turned to Bill Foster. "Why is it, Bill, that at every occasion you and I are stuck sitting with people from the science department?"

"Might've been fun instead to meet some new people," Steve said.

Pete shook his head up and down. "You're good at that, Steve. Always seem to be comfortable with anyone. It takes me a while to warm up to___"

"You don't have to warm up to everyone you're sociable with," she said. "It's just good to try to understand how different people think. I worry about having mind sets, that's why I spend most of the time listening."

Bill leaned toward Steve and started to snicker. "You could've gotten stuck sitting with Jim Dunbar."

"Frankly, I don't mind sitting with him as long as we're going to have a conversation, even an argument. But I can't stand eating with him, avoid it whenever I can. Most of his food collects in his mustache and beard instead of in his mouth, and I find that repulsive."

Charles made a conscious decision not to speak anymore. He turned his chair to face the dance floor, his back toward the group.

After several minutes in that position he heard Ed say, "Charles, you seem to be fascinated by the music, haven't said much."

He turned his chair back. Ed's presence in the hospital supervising Philip's treatment made Charles very grateful. But in the hospital, Ed was just Ed. Alone. Now the sight of him sitting next to Steve made Charles' stomach so twisted he couldn't even touch an hors d'oeuvre. He attempted a response without sounding flat. "I get a kick out of watching people dance. You learn a lot about people by watching them dance."

Ed looked curious. "What are some of the patterns you've observed?"

Charles faced his chair to the dance floor again. "Look at the couple over there, the girl in the green dress with the guy in the gray suit." He pointed in their direction. "There's very little connection between them. They're doing their own thing, I guess the expression is now. If they really cared about each other, they'd end up close for at least part of the time."

Ed pointed to a couple dancing directly in front of them. "What do you make of these two?"

He examined them for some time. "I figure them as momentarily out of touch. They like each other but've had an argument recently and haven't yet reconciled. They're dancing in a *pro forma* way and haven't talked things out yet."

"That's an interesting interpretation. What about the couple___?" Ed's beeper rang, just as the waiter delivered a tray of fruit compotes.

"Oh, no," Steve said. "The blessing and curse of modern technology."

Ed stood up. "I'll be right back."

Steve's head followed him.

The table guests spent some time exploring more of Charles' dance interpretations, sometimes offering conflicting theories.

During one of the offerings, Ed came back to the table. "I have to get to the hospital right away. They need me for a consultation, and depending on the situation I may even have to operate."

Steve picked up her purse, and the shawl draped over her chair. "Just now that I'm starving."

Ed put his hand on her shoulder. "No, Steve, there's no point coming with me. You'll just be hanging around, and I can't drive you home now, and someone has to be in the house so that sitter can go home at a reasonable time. So relax, have a good time." He looked around the table. "I'm sure someone can drop you off."

Bob Lucas was just opening his mouth when Claudia said, "We'll take her home, it's no problem."

Charles wanted to gag her. He didn't want to drive Steve home so he gently nudged Claudia's leg with his under the table.

Steve started to get up again. "But I can take a tax___"

Claudia nudged him back, then signaled Steve to sit. "Charles doesn't mind, do you sweetheart? It's the least we can do. Ed, you were the first to be at the hospital when we needed help."

Charles' pulse rose. "Of course not," he said with a smile which came from only his outer layer of skin, "no inconvenience at all."

"Enough of this discussion," Claudia said, "it's taken care of."

Ed thanked him and Claudia, waved goodbye to everyone, kissed Steve, and left.

Immediately after Ed hurried out of the room, Bob Lucas asked Steve to dance.

"Now that I'm the odd one at the table," she said, "you really don't have to pay any attention to me."

Bob made a welcoming gesture with his hand. "It's my pleasure, want to see if Charles can analyze our dancing style."

Everyone laughed.

Charles spent the next few minutes staring at Bob as he danced cheek to cheek with Steve, dancing so close he had to be rubbing against her breasts, assessing them for size and softness, feeling her pelvis swaying so close to his groin. What was Bob thinking, dancing with his eyes closed? Was he anticipating what she would look like lying next to him, or was he hoping to some way find his lips to her ear, her cheek, her...

"Make sure, Charles, you're not the only one who doesn't ask Steve to dance tonight, at least once," Claudia said. "That would be rude. She'd probably think you're annoyed at her for having to drive her home."

He covered his mouth while whispering, "For God's sake, Claudia, I see her every day, that's bad enough. Do I also have to dance with her?"

"Yes, you do, it's the gentlemanly thing to do. I know how I'd feel if I were left by myself without you, and the people at the table ignored me. So make sure it's the next dance."

"If it's a polka, forget it."

"Then and only then will you be excused. But the next slow one, no excuses allowed."

He was reluctant to dance with Steve. The only times he had been close to her were the day they bumped cars and he rushed to her, almost dying in the fear she was hurt. When she hugged him after he came back from Philip's ordeal. And the day she measured his waist, and he had all to do not to force a fusion between them.

Just as the next slow dance began, Steve got up from the table. Relief vied with disappointment. Maybe she wouldn't come back, but stop to chat with faculty members at other tables.

After the slow number, the musicians took a break...the signal that the entree was about to be served. The dancers found their way back to the tables.

And so did Steve.

All the while she slowly ate the prime rib, baked potato, and string beans almondine, Charles kept his eyes on the others sitting with them, wanting to appear to be listening to their idle conversation, occasionally joining in himself. He was careful to address his remarks to the men or their wives. He kept holding Claudia's hand as if to reassure himself that all was well between them, even kissed her in what he couldn't make up his mind was an attempt to reaffirm his love for her, or an act of challenge to Steve.

As soon as the waiters began removing the plates, the band leader announced, "It's Henry Mancini time." These musicians had a real knack for timing. He guessed it came with the territory. Applause from the guests, some of whom rose from their tables, and rushed to the dance floor, even though the music hadn't yet begun.

"It's your turn, Charles," Claudia whispered.

He hesitated, wanting to seem as though he was reluctantly granting her request. But then he noted Bob getting up, looking as though he was going to ask Steve to dance again. He had to beat Bob to the punch. "You've had several turns, Bob, now it's mine."

Bob gave him a dirty look.

Screw him.

Charles stood behind Steve's chair, moved his lips close to her ear. "Would you care to dance?"

She turned around, looked at him, then at Claudia, who smiled and said, "Take him off my hands for a while."

Steve stood up and aimed for the dance floor. He followed her, his eyes on her bare shoulders, her gently swinging hips.

When they both arrived at the center, she turned toward him, but didn't look at him.

They both just stood there.

Charles felt as though they were the only two people in the universe, the only ones ever created. He put his hand on her shoulder in a clumsy grasp, and weaved the fingers of his other hand into hers. They started moving to "Days of Wine and Roses" with her keeping him at arm's length, her expressionless face looking beyond him. He allowed her to remain far away for a while, but as the seconds increased, he moved her closer. He didn't want her to feel his heart palpitating so he swooped her over several feet. Another couple bumped into them, pushing them together, the top of her head settling on his cheek.

She smelled so wonderful.

The touch of her soft skin against his made his mouth open to fill his lungs more fully with the essence of her.

The sensation of her warm body conveyed to his brain the order to open his hand, press it against the small of her back toward him so she couldn't escape his grip, lest she dare attempt to move away from him. He wanted her body near his and held it firmly, grinding it against him, not caring who on earth, or even in heaven, was watching. It was an experience so erotic, no wonder the Baptists had banned it.

He dared not look into her face, for to do so, he would have to peel her away from him, and if she was still as expressionless as she was when they began dancing, he would ache in despair.

"Days of Wine and Roses" flowed into "Moon River". He and Steve danced with their feet plastered to the floor, shifting back and forth, from left to right, without budging from the center of the floor. He couldn't move her any more than that, lest the motion force more distance between them.

The band played a fanfare. Time for cake-cutting, and time to become unglued. He kept her hand tightly in his as they walked back to the table.

"Well, Charles," Pete said, "we analyzed your dancing."

His stomach clumped.

"We came to the conclusion that you are a man with clubbed feet who should frequent a Fred Astaire studio."

When everyone laughed, his body relaxed. Within a few minutes the waiters were serving coffee, tea, and whipped cream-topped wedding cake with chocolate and vanilla filling.

Claudia looked at her watch, then moved it closer. "My God, it's eleven thirty already. We have to leave."

At first Charles didn't stir. Then he dug into his pocket for the tickets the coat-check girl had given him. He picked up their coats. Steve had left her ticket with Ed, so she and Charles had to filter through the other coats to find hers.

He helped Claudia with her coat first. After Steve covered herself with the silver shawl, Charles assisted with her coat, rested his hand on her shoulder, then ran his index finger lightly from her shoulder across her back, stopping at her spine.

Just as the three of them reached the car, Claudia said, "It's later than I thought we'd be. If the baby sitter doesn't get home in time, her mother won't let her sit for us anymore. Would you mind, Steve, if Charles drops me off first? We're close by."

Steve shrugged. "It really doesn't matter, whatever's convenient for you."

Charles pulled up to his garage. He wished his house would retreat into the dark. He didn't want Steve to see his shingled, cookie-cutter Cape Cod, a bead in a string of homes squeezed into a long block, the leaded glass door panels out of place with the architecture, and out of place in the neighborhood, making his house even more of a sore thumb. Without ever having entered her house, he knew his would fit into the living room of the majestic columned colonial, her rich doctor husband giving her all the things he couldn't.

Steve bade goodnight to Claudia, and just as she left the car, he said, "I love you, sweetheart." She blew him a kiss.

He noted that the instant Claudia left, Steve shoved herself up against the door on the front passenger's side. If she had planted herself any farther away, she'd be riding outside.

After he drove away, a long silence followed.

Steve finally broke the ice. "If you get on the Sprain north, it'll take you to the Taconic, right to my house which is close to the exit."

"What exit is it?"

"Pleasantville Road."

"Warn me just before we get there."

"I will, it's not that far."

He continued to follow the path he could've driven with his eyes closed.

Another long period of silence.

He turned his head toward her. "Would you like me to turn on the radio?"

"Please, keep your eyes on the road...and, and frankly after all that loud music, I'm rather enjoying the quiet. By the way, what did you think of the wedding?"

"They're all the same to me."

"I feel the same way. After a while they all merge into one, and you can't tell which was which. And those amplifiers. Give you laryngitis if you dare attempt to speak to anyone at your table." She paused, yawned. "But this was a really important occasion for Morty. Hope it'll last. These days, people separate for any little thing."

"It's especially hard when they have kids."

"Kids always feel guilty, blame themselves for their parents' breakup. Charles," she pointed to the sign, "it's the next exit, I'll direct you from there."

She moved close to the windshield, looking as though she was surveying the road. When they reached the end of the exit, she said, "Go left at the stop sign, then right at the next stop sign. Hickory Lane is only a few blocks up from there."

As he approached the street, it took every atom in his being to make the final turn. He wanted to push way down on the accelerator and drive and drive, with her in the car as far away as they could go. A superlife. A superpower feeling crawling over him.

"It's the white house on the left corner," she said.

He pulled into the driveway. "Do you think Ed's back?"

"Probably not. This's happened before, many times, it usually takes several hours. I hope he won't be too late because he has to be in the hospital again early tomorrow."

"These are the evenings I'm happy I'm not a physician."

"I know what you mean." She started to open the door. "Where are you going?"

"I'm a gentleman. And in my day a gentleman opened the door for ladies, and walked them to their door."

She started to argue, but he was already getting out of the car.

He walked around, opened the door all the way. He took her arm and led her up the path to the front door.

"I'd ask you in, but I know you have to get back."

He didn't answer, but watched her remove keys from her purse.

"Thanks for the buggy ride," she said as she unlocked the door, the porch light illuminating the two of them. "Sorry I took you out of your way."

"Anything for a friend. A dear friend. A very dear friend."

She smiled.

He approached her and kissed her cheek. "Goodnight, Steve."

"Goodnight, Charles."

Charles returned to the car, backed out of the driveway. Dare he put the radio on? For a few miles he didn't. Then he switched it on. Just Barry Manilow singing a soothing song. But soon Barry was asking some pertinent questions in three-quarter time.

And tell me
When will our eyes meet?
When can I touch you?
When will this strong yearning end?

Charles put his hand on the dial, just about to twist it over to an all-news station, but his fingers remained still, and he wallowed in the lyrics as Barry continued,

And when will I hold you again?

Charles was dancing again with Steve's body against his. He mumbled, "And when will I hold you again?"

The children were already asleep. Steve checked the refrigerator door for taped messages. "Dear Mom and Dad, we love you," was the only note. It made her eyes well up.

She paid Cathy Wilson an extra ten dollars for staying so late. Cathy called her mother, and in a few minutes, Mrs. Wilson picked her up.

Steve climbed the steps, pulling hard on the banister. The TV was still on in Christopher's room where he slept, uncovered, on his back, mouth slightly open, arms extended like Christ crucified. Before closing the TV, she used its light to straighten his sheets and blanket and cover him. With the research now indicating that boys tend to be genetically more like their mothers, she hoped he wouldn't suffer the same disease she was now experiencing. She stared at the boy, immune, so far, from that disease. She ran over his face with her hand, kissed him, then went into her room.

She removed her dress, hung it in the closet, and pulled a flannel bathrobe off the hanger. She was about to put it on, when she hesitated. She returned the flannel robe to the hanger, took the pink lace with the plunging neckline instead.

She checked herself in the mirror, tightened the pink satin belt, and examined her figure. Not bad for her age. She spoke into the mirror. "Vanity, thy name is Steve."

She turned around, walked a few steps, stopping abruptly.

She returned once again to the mirror and let out a sardonic laugh. "Ah, no. Vanity, thy name is Stefania."

Stefania.

She lifted the lace hem to the middle of her thigh. No sign of spider veins. Just one black-and-blue on her leg, the height of the open dishwasher door.

As she studied her reflection, she couldn't help thinking what Charles would do if both of them were free? Would he ask her out to dinner? If so, what would be the appropriate amount of time he would wait after she had become widowed? When he finished his Manhattan, would he dangle the cherry stem with its attached fruit in front of her? Encourage her to bite into it with him? When their lips touched, would he...?

She let her hair down and brushed it. She pulled off the bedspread and began gathering clean clothes for her shower when the bell rang.

Did Ed forget his key? Not like him.

She didn't want the children to wake up, so she ran down the steps without taking the time to find an appropriate pair of slippers.

She turned on the chandelier in the entrance hall. "Ed?"

No answer.

A robber wouldn't announce himself by ringing the bell, but sneak in through a window or rear door.

She called out again, "Ed?"

Still no answer.

Why was she so negligent in not ordering a jalousie? She slid open the chain door guard. The door opened the length of the chain.

Charles!

One hand behind his back.

She was so stunned, she couldn't speak.

He didn't speak, either, just stared at her after his eyes followed with the speed of light their flight up the sweeping curve of the staircase.

She opened the door half-way.

With his other hand he pushed the door open all the way.

Never before was she more aware of the fact that she was a warm-blooded animal. She rushed her hand to her chest, stumbled backwards. Should've put on the flannel robe.

He stepped into the hall.

Very slowly, the hand behind his back appeared, holding in front of her a goblet, still in its three-sided white shadow box with white satin bow, the fourth side covered with transparent plastic. Through it she could read, Claire and Ronald, December 12, 1976.

"Your wedding favor, Madame Stefania, you left it in the car."

Stefania.

She reached to take the goblet from him, but withdrew her hand to return it to cover her chest. "You shouldn't have taken the trouble to bring it back, you could've given it to me Monday."

"Thought you might need it, in the event you wanted a night cap this cold evening," he said with what sounded like calculated innocence.

She put her head down. "I'm really sorry. It didn't fit in my purse, more of an evening bag."

"Well, are you going to take it, or did I drive back for nothing?"

As she took it from him, her fingertips brushed his hand. "Thanks."

His eyes were no longer staring at her face, but sweeping over her robe. "My pleasure."

She crossed the hand holding the goblet over her other hand, making an X over her breasts. "Goodnight."

"It seems to me we've been through this already this evening, but… goodnight."

The climb upstairs was even more difficult this time around. Charles' dead giveaway glassy eyes.

Steve needed Ed to come home.

Immediately.

She scurried to the telephone, called the hospital. He'd be at least another hour.

She prepared for her shower, dreading the thoughts that might enter her mind this evening. She made the water very cold so she would move quickly under it, holding on feverishly to the soap so she wouldn't have a repetition of the shower which produced the burns. All the while she was showering she kept asking herself what she would do if Charles really kissed her.

Remain stiff?

Push him away?

Act indignant and slap his face, or return his kiss, lingering over, sucking his lips till they melted away.

She folded the bedspread she had already pulled down. Next she overturned the blanket and sheets. She slid into bed, remaining on her back, slowly raising the covers up to her neck as if to protect her body from invading stimuli. But the covers didn't help. They couldn't eliminate the grinding of Charles' body against hers, the rotating, the mold he had etched on her back, of his open hand forcing her against him. The rotating in her mind between what she desired and what she knew was right.

Newton's first law of gravitation found its way into her memory. The force between two bodies was directly proportional to the product of their masses and inversely proportional to the square of the distance between them. What if the distance between them was zero, as it was during their dancing? Zero squared was still zero, and in mathematics, division by zero was undefined.

Undefined.

That's what this whole thing was.

And what was that spurt of, "I love you, sweetheart," that he had hurled at Claudia. Sounded like the man doth protest too much.

But most of all, Steve had been enlightened by Charles' kiss. For as his lips approached her cheek, with the porch light beaming on them, there was something she couldn't help notice.

His eyes were focused on her mouth.

The following Monday Steve checked the course schedule to find out when Warren Kent would be free. She needed desperately the affirmation she couldn't get openly from Charles. That would give her peace.

She looked up Warren's extension in the college directory. "Warren, it's Steve. I need about five minutes of your time. When can you see me?"

"I have a meeting at one-thirty and want to grab some lunch first, so, so how about now?"

Steve curved her way around the hub to an office not quite diagonally across from hers. The office was typical of one in the arts. Books wedged in between open files, papers on the brink of the desk, defying gravity, a desk jumbled with rubber bands, pens, scripts. The only semblance of order came from enlarged photographs of the plays he had directed on campus, one per year, about twenty-five all together, she estimated, arranged chronologically around the walls.

"Thanks for your time, Warren, I know you want to eat before your meeting so I won't keep you too long."

He pulled up a chair for her, removed a pile of papers from it, and dusted it off with the sleeve of his tweed. He waved her to the chair with the gracious gesture of an English gentleman, undoubtedly, a role he had often played. Then he bowed before taking a seat at his desk. "There's no rush, it's always good to talk to you. What's cooking?"

She didn't accept his chair, but remained standing, leaning her palms against the top of whatever space she could steal from his desk. In all the years he had been teaching acting, he was experienced analyzing verbal and nonverbal communication, and she was careful that he wouldn't analyze hers.

"If you were directing a play and there was a character in it, a male, of course, who was attracted to a married woman and tried to hide it, what would be some behaviors that would give him away?" Good job. It came out matter-of-fact. Neutral. She gave herself a mental pat on the back.

From a cynical smile on his face he squeaked out the words, "So you finally figured out that someone on this campus has a thing for you."

Her heart lurched into her throat.

The moment she'd been waiting for. He was about to verify what she sensed.

He would verbalize the unspeakable, the words she was so desperate to hear.

She could hardly collect the breath to ask, "Who?"

"Now, Steve," he said, his voice conveying skepticism, "you have to be a dunce if you don't know that Bob Lucas really has a case on you."

"Bob Lucas!"

Her heart eventually caught up with the beats it had just missed. She tripped her way to the chair she had previously rejected, not sure whether her sudden weakness was from the surprise over Bob, or her being crushed over the fact that Warren hadn't mentioned Charles.

"Warren, I'm…really in shock. If...if, my God, what you say is true, I, I really have to be a dunce, because I can't believe it."

"Well, then, if you didn't pick up on his feelings for you, it tells me that you don't give a damn about him, so maybe I was too quick to judge your motives."

"You were, Warren, all I really came for was an answer to my original question. Do you want me to repeat it?"

"No." He looked away, squinted, and put his unlit pipe into his mouth. "How old is the man?"

"Oh, maybe middle-aged."

"That shouldn't be hard. I've played many roles as a middle-aged man. And the woman?"

"The same."

"What about their socioeconomic status? I've interpreted roles from beggars to kings."

She hadn't thought about that. "Perhaps middle to upper middle class."

"How often do they see each other?"

"Frequently."

"In her husband's presence?"

"Occasionally."

"Now both the frequency of their contact and the presence of the husband have to provide some tension." He lit his pipe, sucked on it, and blew air out of his mouth while staring into space.

He was taking so long to answer she feared he was really asking himself whom she was talking about, to come clean and tell him what she suspected.

Then his eyebrows and mouth moved closer together. "Hm. Now if I was directing a play and there was a character in it who was attracted to a married woman and tried to hide it, I'd have him looking at her when she wasn't looking at him. And when she faced him have him twist his head in another direction, a twist, a real jerk, not just a slow movement." He acted it out for her, then winced. "Damn it, I think I just pulled my neck." He rubbed the spot. "But you get the picture. That conveys the tension, the guilt he's under."

Charles had done that too many times. "And?"

"He'd probably find some occasions to touch her hand, or some other part of her."

She recalled the times Charles had placed his hand over hers. Once after the Curriculum Committee meeting when he told her she had saved his life, and another in the cafeteria when he asked her if she wanted a cup of coffee. She was so thrown by his action, her instinctive reaction was to remove her hand, superimpose hers on his.

"He'd probably linger when in her presence, or leave, then find some excuse to return...probably immediately...but not necessarily immediately after leaving."

The night he really didn't have to return the goblet.

Warren stopped sucking on the pipe and began clicking his teeth over it. "And when they were close to each other, not too close, but close, he might move his hand, extend it toward her but not touch her."

The day they were both reading the same letter at the same time. "What about giving her a routine kiss on the cheek while looking at her lips?"

"That's self-explanatory."

Her skin began to prickle. "And what about putting his hand on her shoulder then gently running his finger across her back."

"My dear, I would call that a caress."

The prickling became a full-fledged tickle, accompanied by chills. "Is there anything else?"

"You sound as if you are directing a play."

"No." She crossed her fingers behind her back. "But my cousin's playing the part and his director's not much help, keeps telling him to act as he feels, but he's too young to have had those kinds of feelings. I mean, deep feelings."

"I'm sure I'll think of something else he can do. And if I do, I'll call you."

"Thanks, Warren. For being such a love I'm going to kiss your cheek, but my eyes will be looking at it, too."

He winked. "Too bad."

"You devil."

Though Steve was hungry when she went to Warren's office, she came out feeling so wound up, that now, nothing would go down. That comment about Bob Lucas, her chairman no less, had really upset her.

She needed her spirits lifted, so she headed for the cafeteria in search of the Dynamic Trio. They were sitting at a table in the corner with a few other faculty, and as usual, appeared to be having a jovial time as she joined them.

"Now I have empirical evidence that I'm middle class," Moe Fields said. Everyone at the table laughed.

She must have looked perplexed because Hank Burdens said, "Moe, tell Steve what you're talking about."

Moe placed a broad smile on his face. "We're discussing a study that just came out, in the *Journal of Pop-Sociology*. They report a new way to determine social class."

"Which is?" Steve said, anticipating what lunacy he would come up with.

Moe was quick to respond. "When two married couples go out together in a car, look at how they sit. If the women sit together, they're lower class. If they sit with their spouses, they're middle class. And if___"

"Let me guess," she said, "if they sit with the other person's spouse, they're upper class."

"Not very scientific but it makes for good lunch conversation," Moe said.

Steve lifted her brow. "Suppose that more than two couples, let's say three get into the same car."

Jeff Hoffman began to roar to the point of stomach-holding. "If they...if they...sit on each other's laps, they, they have *no* class."

She smiled, shook her head. "It must be nearing the end of the semester or they're putting something in the food here. But from now on, when I want to put on airs, I'll be more aware of how to sit in a car when Ed and I go out with another couple."

The three of them continued to eat, and joke, and share silly anecdotes with her. She still hadn't touched any food.

Then she returned to her office. Today her office hours were from two to four. Only two students showed up, so she used the remaining time to catch up on clerical work.

Just before four, the phone rang.

Where was the secretary?

Steve let the phone ring a few more times, then pushed her extension button. "Science department, Dr. Marchese."

"Is *he* also married?" a male voice asked.

For a moment she was caught off-guard. In a few seconds, she processed the voice. "Yes, he is, in the play, that is."

"Well, then you might find in the script that he praises his wife a lot or even shows signs of endearment toward her in front of the woman he's attracted to, and if that's not in the script, add it. And even if he's not married, he can recall every detail about her, what she wears, the way her hair is, every word she speaks."

"You're a love, Warren. Thanks."

"As they say, the play's the thing. And remember, a certain type of smile he gives her when he does look at her is another dead giveaway."

CHAPTER 20

IT SOUNDED LIKE a Greek diner at suppertime in the Pastore household that evening. Dishes scraping against each other. Utensils rattling. Missing was calling out the orders. But Charles was thinking about them anyway. Corned beef and cabbage, chopped steak with onions and mashed potatoes.

The aroma of the chocolate layer cake Claudia had baked still permeated the house. Even though Charles had devoured a large piece, he, despite the gentle slaps his wife kept giving his hand, insisted on slicing off another piece and picking at it as he sent Philip and Louis to their rooms to do their homework.

"Claudia, I'd really love it if you'd come with me. I'm asking you to come for only two weeks."

"I'd love to, but I can't leave the boys for that amount of time. Besides, with your cut in salary, we have to be more economical. We can't pay for extra meals, larger rooms, or additional air fare. And you know the only plane I like is one on the ground."

"But this'd be like a second honeymoon."

"Every day counts. You need the time to do your research without worrying about me, how I'm going to occupy myself while you're studying." She looked aside. "Actually, I might begin studying again too, update my skills. Soon, Charles, I'll go back to teaching, and then we'll have more money, that second honeymoon, third, and fourth. The same vacations, summers off, Christmas, Easter. I promise."

He needed her to go with him. To give him her undivided attention in the hope that what he felt had subsided between them could be rekindled.

He wanted her presence to distract thoughts of Steve, how Steve might react to a visit to Harrods, how her face would produce that scientific curiosity in the British Museum, how she would look in a hotel room in that pink lace robe showing her cleavage as she prepared for bed.

Charles' flight to London was different this time around. No lost luggage. No attempt to see from the aircraft the landmarks pictured in the travel brochures. The Pan Am 747 jetted across the ocean in five and a half hours instead of the twelve hours in the original propeller-driven plane.

He stood on line at the ticket booth in Leicester Square to buy tickets for as many productions as he could afford. He visited draughty dark dank libraries, a Chaucer exhibit, university archives, attempting to bury himself in research. But Steve cropped up in every book, every sentence, every word he read. It was Durrell who wrote, "The richest love is that which submits to the arbitration of time." Would he feel different about her by the time the sabbatical was over? If the emptiness he was enduring was any indication, his sabbatical, if taken for the purpose of forgetting her, was a waste.

On Charles' first day back at Graham after the sabbatical, he received in the campus mail a notice that confirmed the rumors he had been getting in letters from his colleagues. Now it was official. Wayne Ashley was retiring. A search committee had already been formed to find a new dean.

Charles scrunched up the notice and threw it into the wastepaper basket.

Then he reconsidered.

Hm. A job in administration. Wasn't the same as teaching literature. But after taking such a hit on his salary for the full year's sabbatical, in the first semester alone he'd make up the difference. He wouldn't be next door to Steve anymore, wouldn't see her so often, and maybe that would help. After some experience in administration, he could move on to another institution.

He removed the notice from the basket, un-crumpled the paper, and walked into the hall. Pete Stratton was walking down the hall. As soon as Pete noticed him, his walk became a gallop. They shook hands, then hugged.

"Great to have you back, Charles. We'll have to have lunch so you can tell me all about your England adventure."

"Sounds good to me." He held up the wrinkled notice he was holding. "But I just read that Wayne's retiring."

"We've been speculating for months now that it would happen. Wants to go back to the Midwest, has grandchildren there."

Charles pushed Pete by the arm into the office. "Pete, what would you say if I told you I'm thinking about applying for his job?"

Pete screwed up his face so much the space above his teeth showed. "I'd say you're nuts. Give up your summers, your hours, not to mention your love, literature. Come to think of it," he pointed to his temple, "I can't think of one damn good thing about it except for the fact that the pay's great. Besides, there's a committee already formed to find a new dean, a tough committee ordered by Chester to find someone good, someone he can work with. They're placing an ad in the *Times* and the *Chronicle* this weekend."

"Who's on the committee?"

"I don't know who they all are, but the ones I know are Stan Lubich, Alice Cronin, and," he looked up, "I know Bruce is."

"Who's chairing the committee?"

"Steve Marchese, and you know she'll be thorough and tough."

The sound of her name gave Charles a lump in his chest. He said out loud the name he had only thought of all year. "Steve Marchese." Just saying it made him feel his hair stand on end.

Pete got up. "I have a meeting." He headed for the door. As soon as Pete stepped into the hall, he turned around. "And speak of the devil, here she comes."

Dare Charles also enter the hall? He was already beginning to feel blood draining from his head, his eyes tense with anticipation when he walked outside of his office.

The voice was perky but pleasant. "Well, look who's back!"

She was not wearing the usual lab coat, but a short-sleeved white blouse this warm late August day, and a flowing white skirt with a gold metal belt. Her skin had a special glow which told him that she had spent some time in the sun that summer.

"Good to see you Charles." She gave him a hug and peck on the cheek. "When are we going to hear about your trip?"

"Whenever we have a month with nothing to do, but seriously we will have to make time to talk about it."

"If that's the reception he gets when he comes back from sabbatical, I'm going to take one, too," Pete said. "But I have to run. Why don't you two discuss what we were just talking about, Charles?" Pete then proceeded down the hall.

She had a curious look. "So, what's the mystery, what were you talking about?"

Pete's suggestion had taken the edge off his feeling of clumsiness about being alone with her. Charles motioned her into his office. "I…I thought I'd apply for Wayne's job."

He tried to read her face, but nothing was printed on it.

"I see. And someone evidently told you, probably Pete, that I'm chairing that search."

"As a matter of fact, he just did."

She hesitated. "I'm really surprised, Charles. You don't seem the type to want to go into administration. What happened to that passion you have, or should I say had for literature? I thought it would be enhanced, or at least rekindled in England."

"It's still there, will always be. That's one of the things I found out on my sabbatical. But look at it this way. If I get to be dean, I won't have to have my office next to yours. Just think about it. Instead of your being rid of me, I'd be rid of you."

She paced, then looked up. "First of all, I have to see if you pass the test to be dean."

"Which test?"

Her eyes crinkled at the edges. She left his office without answering him, and returned momentarily with a piece of paper and a tape measure in hand. "Lift your jacket and keep it up." First she referred to the paper. "Forty-three and seven eighths inches." Then she wrapped the tape measure around his waist.

Her touching him weakened his arms. He let the jacket go.

With her arms still around him, she looked into his eyes. "If you can't follow directions, how the heck would you qualify to be a dean?"

Her smile relieved his tension.

He lifted the jacket again, this time holding it up until she finished measuring.

"Not perfect, but not bad. Forty and a half inches. You're half an inch away from your goal."

"If I'd stayed in England another week, I would've made it. Did I get close enough to passing your first test?"

"Sort of. But Charles, you know how these things are." She moved her head down, keeping her eyes up. "There's a search committee, but they already have someone picked for the job."

"Do they really, even with you in charge? And who might that be?"

"Promise you won't tell?"

"I promise."

She picked up her paper and tape measure and left the room. Then she poked her head back into his office and said, "My brother-in-law."

It took him a few seconds to catch on. When he did, they both laughed.

Through the laughter he looked into Steve's eyes. Charles was sure he saw disappointment when she asked, "Do you really want this job?"

"Really, I think I'd be an effective dean." He was hesitant to say the rest because it made him feel less competitive with Ed, but decided to admit it anyway. "And I took a financial beating on this sabbatical and could use the money."

"Well, Sir, prepare your resume and we'll consider you along with the rest of the candidates."

One more applicant was to be interviewed, and Steve was grateful that after the second of two full days, the process would be nearing an end. Charles entered the conference room where professors and administrators gathered to interview applicants. He sat in the usual place, at the head of the oval table flanked by the search committee.

Steve sat directly opposite him and was silent but attentive as the committee members held their pens and forms with their preplanned questions and filled in the spaces underneath. It brought back her interview and all the feelings associated with it.

When the committee seemed to have run out of questions, they deferred to her.

"I have only a few questions." She picked up a note pad, faced Charles, who seemed to be more nervous now than at any other point in the interview. "You're the only candidate from the college. How do you think your colleagues see you?"

He appeared surprised by her question and waited a few seconds to respond. "I think they respect me, believe I have high integrity."

She jotted down respect, integrity. "And your students?"

"They think I'm an effective teacher, dedicated, have high standards, demand excellence from them. Tough." He paused. "I think they initially balk at that fact, but come to appreciate that I have their interests in mind."

She knew that was true. She believed the students thought the same of her. Nevertheless, she wrote dedicated, high standards, and excellence under integrity. "What strengths would you bring to this job?"

Charles took a while before answering. "You know I've been here a long time, really know the place. I think my philosophy of education has been and will continue to be a strength. High expectations from students and faculty, a genuine concern for both. Demanding quality performance on all levels from the security guards through the administration. I'm organized, dedicated." He touched his fingertips to his forehead. "Oh, I mentioned dedicated before. A hard worker. I hope I've already demonstrated this through example."

"How would you describe your management style should you be the one who gets this position?"

He hesitated. "I like to get input from as many people as possible before making decisions that would affect them. I believe I'm open to new ideas as long as they make sense, and can be intellectually, you know, empirically supported. Though I'm not particularly creative myself with respect to the curriculum, I would entertain creative suggestions from colleagues, if those suggestions met the criteria I just described."

"What is your vision for Graham, where would you like to see Graham in the next five, ten years?"

That lock of hair had just freed itself and settled in his part.

"Considering the types of students projected to be entering college in the next decade, it might be wise to establish a transitional college, one that would provide an intensive program to assist students in obtaining the skills they need to deal successfully with a strong academic program." His eyes circled the ceiling. "I'd like to see more non-traditional students here, older students, minorities, we have some already but there are more out there. And a more diverse faculty to reflect the demographics of what's predicted to be a more diverse nation."

"Even if having that diversity would mean hiring people not as qualified as those from a more traditional faculty?"

"If and only if they'd be of the highest quality."

"I see." She placed her notepad on the table, stared at it for a moment, then looked back at Charles. "When choosing between the pragmatic, for example the college's financial survival such as catering to students' whims to keep them here even though what they wanted wouldn't be academically sound, and the moral, what you knew to be the right thing to do, which side would we find you on?"

He looked at her strangely, as if he didn't understand the question, or why she was asking it. He crossed his legs.

"I guess what I'm really asking you, Charles, is if you had to make a decision that would mean the survival of the college but it went against your grain, how would you handle the situation?"

Without hesitating he said, "The college would be worth surviving if and only if it was acting in the best interests of the students. They are our responsibility and the reason we exist. Any decision I made would have students as my main concern or I wouldn't be able to live with myself."

"Thank you for your honesty, Charles. No further questions."

CHAPTER 21

THE LAST SCHEDULED meeting between Paul and Alex had arrived. They had to finish as much as they could before Alex's vacation, a break she was looking forward to the remaining two weeks before the beginning of the fall semester. The first week her family would take that Caribbean cruise they'd been planning. She noted the lack of tropical depressions on the weather map, pleased her family wouldn't run into any hurricanes, which tended to hover around the Caribbean mid-August. And she was no sailor to begin with. The second week she needed to prepare the children for school, and herself for the new academic year.

Today was another one of those days the sun couldn't make up its mind whether or not to remain hiding behind or jump out from the clouds.

She and Paul spent considerable time shifting pages, cutting, Scotch-taping, rewriting sections of the work completed so far.

Paul placed a rubber band around the revised manuscript before sending for Mrs. Knowlton. "Please make me two copies, on one side only."

As soon as Mrs. Knowlton left, he said, "I don't look forward to the first meeting of the academic year. I know it's just a ritual, but everybody's always asking how your summer was, and people expound on it as if it were a question instead of a salutation."

"And they go on and on and on. I can't stand that question, either, I'd prefer a hello, how are you, but how are you could give you the same type of elaborate response as how was your summer."

Paul pulled his chair next to hers. A ray of sun beamed into the office for several seconds, then promptly disappeared. "So now that there are only two weeks left before the beginning of the semester, are you sorry you didn't use your time differently?"

She shook her head. "No way, I think we accomplished a lot, more than we ever could've if the semester was in full swing. What about you?"

"I agree, it was challenging, a unique experience taking me away from the drudgery not to mention tedium of administration, though I must admit I found writing exhausting, much more difficult than I could ever have imagined. I have more respect and sympathy for writers now. When I write my next book review, I'll bring a different perspective to it."

"Never mind book review, what about your next novel?"

"You never give up, do you?" He turned aside, then faced her again. "But before I consider writing another novel, let's finish this one. They've come now to that fork in the road. It's time to go back to the question we've been avoiding from the beginning, the question I asked you when I agreed to write this. How do you think it should end?" A sun ray, following the lead of the first, brightened the room for a few moments before promptly fading away.

"We've skirted around this question ever since we first decided to embark on this project. I've given some consideration to the ending and I think that before we decide, we should come up with some criteria."

"I never thought of criteria, just wanted to go with my gut, but let's give it a shot. Since you've come up with the idea of criteria, you must have already thought of some."

"Actually, the only one I've come up with is whether or not the readers would find the ending credible."

He scratched his chin. "That's a good start."

"I'm curious though, Paul, if you went with your gut, where would you take it from here?"

The sun continued teasing, scooting in and out, alternately brightening, then darkening his office.

Should he or shouldn't he? They'd come this far together, so why not?

"I think he should do what he wanted to do from the first time he saw her, take her in his arms and hold her forever, kiss her to death. Leave his wife, marry his true passion."

The room became quiet, too quiet. They stared at each other. Then Alex looked down at the floor, blinking several times. "You've read enough about her by now to know that if he ever took her in his arms, she'd never be able to leave him."

His stomach left for lower parts. He remained silent a few moments, then he said, "If nothing else, there'd at least be the memory they could always hold on to."

"That sounds like you, your romantic nature. But what does your reason tell you, the cerebral part your dissertation pal, D.H. Lawrence is searching for to find harmony between body and soul."

"Maybe it's beyond the point of reason now, it's___"

Mrs. Knowlton knocked on the ubiquitous part-open door, then entered. She handed him the two photocopied manuscripts. The speed of new technology. He thanked her and gave one copy to Alex.

Mrs. Knowlton left, leaving the door, as always, slightly ajar.

Alex placed her copy of the manuscript on his desk. "You sound like some of the professors of the Sixties, spouting intellectual dishonesty, the ideology guiding the truth instead of the truth, ideology."

"What about emotional dishonesty? Shakespeare said, "To thine own self be true.'"

"That's just the point, Paul, I've been through this a thousand times. Let's thumb through these pages and go back to my original idea, see what readers will find believable." She picked up her copy of the manuscript and turned several pages. Once again the sun poked out of the clouds, this time spending a little more time in the room. "Do you think if she left her family the world would be a better place, as Steve's poster said, because she had lived in it?" She turned a few more pages. "Do you think Steve and Charles would want to be shams, quacks, to their students?"

Paul looked aside. "How about what the readers would like to have happen?"

"And what do you think that is?"

"You know how readers are, that Charles and Steve be together forever."

She hesitated before saying, "The readers wouldn't buy it because it's self-deception. Very utopian, tempting, but as you know, temptation can bring strength or stupidity, and I think Charles and Steve are too strong for that. Besides, do the math, Paul, is it better that two people be miserable or six? Now browse through the manuscript." Before he was able to pick his copy up, she placed her hand over it. "What questions would The Scholars Society come up with? What is the empirical truth about these two people, not other people, but these two?"

"Why do you always have to end up the scientist?"

"Because…because for better or worse, that's what I am. And remember what Steve told The Scholars Society, that scientists must not fool themselves, and each one of us is the easiest person to fool. Now read, Paul." She removed her hand from covering his manuscript and sorted through more pages from hers.

He didn't have to read the manuscript. He already knew it thoroughly, too thoroughly. Nevertheless, as she continued turning pages, he began going through his, even though each page he could spout by heart.

Alex lifted the first few sheets. "Catholic school, that's where it all started."

He stopped turning pages. "Strong foundation in morality, Judeo-Christian morality."

"Strong connection to family, the well-being of children, the havoc, upheaval Steve and Charles would cause. Couldn't rationalize and justify anything without thinking of the consequences."

"Sense of honor, would rather do other things but as he heard in his first confession responsibilities come first...the cult of the self cannot win over the sense of responsibility. The cult of the self debases society as a whole."

Alex put the rest of the manuscript on her lap, then returned it to his desk. She gazed at him. "Unlike Tracy Robbins, Steve and Charles could never live against their value system. They're doomed by, plagued by the curse of conscience."

His eyes deflected her gaze. "Spouses who've done nothing to deserve anything less than fidelity."

"Steve saved Charles' life, Paul. Remember? She's responsible for it forever, she has to be the one in charge. How can it end? What's in their DNA? Only one way. The answer has been crying out throughout this whole endeavor. Could they ignore what effect any other ending would have on so many other people? No. So you see, Paul, they will go on as they did in the text, pretending they don't know how they feel when they're together in a room, don't begin and end the day thinking about each other."

"Not begin and end the day, Alex, think of each other all day long. *You* read the text."

She resumed speaking without seeming to have heard his comment. "Be casual about what they say to each other."

They simultaneously stretched across his desk to gather more pages, and in so doing, his fingers touched hers. He kept them there.

Slowly, very slowly, Alex slipped her fingers away. She stood up, meandered across the room to the wall with his paintings, stopping to examine A Girl Reading a Letter at an Open Window. "What do you think the letter says?"

"It's anyone's guess, what do you think?"

When Alex answered, she spoke into the Vermeer. "It might be about the beginning or the end of a love affair." She examined a few more paintings, then turned around abruptly. "You never did tell me what you looked at to get over writer's block."

"And I'm not going to."

"Some writing partner you are, one day I might catch the block and it might help me."

"I doubt it."

"How would you know unless you tell me?" She again faced the Vermeer and remained silent.

He walked to the door and closed it.

For the first time they were alone.

With her back toward him he finally mustered the courage to say, "Because I don't think that looking at a picture of you, Alex, would help you."

Before she spoke, the second hand on the wall clock made many clicks. Her head remained buried in the painting. "I've been thinking. Maybe it's not such a good idea to try to have this novel published, show it to my agent. Maybe in the future, circumstances might change, Charles. The ending could be different."

He stopped breathing, then took a good helping of air. "Alex, you called me Charles."

"Did I?" She strolled to the Monet before returning to his desk. "But there is another twist the ending could have."

"What...what twist?"

Alex said rather matter-of-factly, "Charles could just tell Steve how he feels about her."

"My God, Alex," he slammed the manuscript closed, "don't you think he's implied it often enough?"

"Yes, but you're forgetting something, something you reminded me about before. She's a scientist. She needs it stated, concrete, not implied." Her eyes were screaming at him when she said slowly and deliberately, "She needs it stated, Paul." Then she softened her look. "Charles."

She quickly moved away from the paintings to the closed door and leaned her back against it.

He stood up briskly, released his chair from it prison behind the desk, and pushed the chair across the room with a force that sent it crashing into the wall. He staggered to the wall opposite the door, pressing his back against the wood paneling propping up the artwork.

The sun flashed in and out, in and out, spurting, finally shouting red, orange, and warmth throughout the entire room.

"Alex...Alex." He had swallowed hard before saying her name, but his voice floundered anyway.

Their eyes were linked as never before.

Tears found the path to his eyes. He was so choked up, he first tried to keep in the tears, but as he let them go, freedom flowed throughout his body. "I love you so much that each second without you, I already know what it's like to suffocate, be buried alive, another shovel of dirt being hurled over my face."

Alex dug her teeth into her lower lip to stop it from trembling, making her words almost inaudible. "Just hearing you say it, just knowing it, can get me through the rest of my life."

In the remaining seconds Paul watched her press her back into the door, while he pressed his against the paneling, feeling the support and imprint of its grain and sturdiness.

Alex's eyes let go of his. Without bothering to blot her eyes, she turned around, opened the door and walked out, leaving her copy of the manuscript on his desk.

The revolving doors to the auditorium lobby were swirling and filling with professors entering for the first faculty meeting of the academic year, which would signal the official start of the fall semester. The usual spread greeted them. Danish, tea, the smell of freshly brewed coffee, and a large display of seasonal fruit—platters of strawberries, grapes, crescent-shaped slices of honey dew and cantaloupe, and small imitation crystal glasses supporting hors d'oeuvre-type toothpicks.

Paul Barone stood at the double-door entrance to the auditorium, chatting with the staff as they entered, offering a smile, handshake, and welcoming comments.

From the corner of his eye he kept watching the remaining faculty gather in front of the snacks and beverages.

It was already a little late, but he decided not to begin the meeting yet.

Where was she? Certainly not stuck in the Caribbean. She should've been home from the cruise almost a week already.

A few stragglers came into the lobby through a side entrance. They, too, filled their paper plates. A breeze from the swinging doors sent a few Graham College-imprinted napkins whirling to the floor.

More of the faculty began to cluster around the auditorium door. He heard snips of their conversations—the Louvre, article submitted for publication, research on chronic welfare recipients.

Then, he caught a glimpse of her, just as she extended her hand to catch the revolving door, her hair a rich henna in the late summer sun.

She passed by the fruit, surveyed it. Instead of taking some, she joined the remaining faculty lined up for his greeting, using the time to chat with some of them. He hoped they weren't asking her how her summer vacation was.

It would be just moments before Alex Vitale would be the next to receive his welcome. His heart was already over-pumping, bouncing around from left to right, in no particular rhythm.

When she finally stood before him, he compressed her hand while shaking it. "Alex, good to see you, you look well-rested." Then he said with a wry smile, "How was your summer vacation?"

She smiled back, just as wryly, compressing his hand in return. "The best summer of my life, and yours?"

"Absolutely, couldn't have been better."

She held on to his hand tightly. "So glad to hear it, having a good summer should lay the foundation for a productive academic year."

"I'm sure it will. I hope you have a successful one."

"You, too."

Alex slid her hand from his, entered the auditorium, and took her seat among the faculty.

Printed in the United States
By Bookmasters